The Day Shirley Temple

Hayley Doyle

Copyright © 2010 Author Name

All rights reserved.

ISBN:1475234600
ISBN-13:9781475234602

***

For my Nan; Magic Mary. You make everything possible.

***

ACKNOWLEDGMENTS

Many thanks to Fay Weldon, Sarah Penny and Celia Brayfield for their support at Brunel University, and Karolina Sutton at Curtis Brown for giving this novel the Curtis Brown Award 2010. Much love and thanks must go to the city of Liverpool where my real memories were made, and my fiction was inspired. Thank you to Kate Smith for letting me finish this novel on the sofa where I started it. The readers; Jean Walters, Angela McLoughlin, and Marea O'Toole, thank you for your honesty, sharp eye, and patience. To the real Nannie, Vera and John... thank you for the fun, the stories and the memories.

And of course, thank you to my childhood idol, Shirley Temple.

*

PROLOGUE

30th May, 1989

The three of them sat in their seats, not moving, barely breathing.

Nannie was by the window with Aunty Vera at her side, clutching her arm. Across the table sat Star, her *My Little Pony* lunch box firm in her grip. Six eyes darted from one person to another, and then looked above, down below, and back to each other.

"Oh, Jesus, Mary," Vera whispered. "What are we doing?"

And then the train let out a gasp of air, and bumped forward.

Bump, bump, bump, became chug, chug, chug, and with every chug they were a split second further away from Liverpool.

Nannie grinned at Vera, but Vera looked over her shoulder. There was a Catholic priest sitting across the aisle, and Vera broke her arms away from Nannie to make a Sign of the Cross. The priest gave a smile, and then winked at Star. It was now Star's turn to grin, which she did to the priest, and then back to Nannie and Aunty Vera.

Vera shrieked with laughter and broke out into song, clapping her hands, "*Well, this is our house, and we're gonna have a do in it…*" and Nannie and Star joined in, laughing, too.

They were on their way to London.

"Let's play 'What have I got, in my hand?'" Star suggested, opening her lunchbox. She couldn't wait a second longer to dive into the ham and piccalilli rolls that Nannie had made.

Nannie lifted her right hand and pretended to catch a fly in the air, locking her fist together. With a tune in her voice, she said, "What have I got…in my hand?"

"Can you eat it?" Star asked.

"No," Nannie replied.

"Can you smell it?" Aunty Vera asked.

Nannie shook her head. No.

"Can you stick it on your head?" Star asked, and they all shrieked again.

"Sorry, Father," Vera bowed her head to the priest.

The game continued until Vera guessed correctly that Nannie had an imaginary sock in her hand. Star offered the priest a bread roll, which he declined, but gave the little girl an Extra Strong Mint. She put it inside her lunchbox for later, and took out her flask of juice. The flask was dark blue with a transfer of Mr. T across it. Christopher McGinty – the boy who lived next-door-but-one – had placed a bet with Star that she couldn't get an aquamarine Crayola crayon up her nose. If he won, he could pull the head off one of her Sindy dolls, but if not, then Star could swap her *My Little Pony* flask for his one of Mr. T. Star won the bet, and although she had a sore nose for a week, it was worth it to see Christopher McGinty with a pink flask at school.

"Why don't you write your letter, Star," Nannie said.

Star pulled a face, scrunching up her nose.

"Go on, Star," Vera joined in. "You said you wanted to."

"But I don't know what to write anymore," Star said, shrugging her little shoulders up and down and up and down. But she took out the writing set that she always kept in the lunchbox - usually to write secret notes during school lunchtimes and pass them around the dinner hall – and Aunty Vera handed her a pen as Star tore off a sheet of paper. The writing set was printed all over with Tinkerbelle patterns and had a floral scent to it.

Star gazed out of the window, watching the train flash through the Runcorn Bridge. She clicked the top of the pen, and began to write;

Dear Shirley Temple,

My name is Star, just like you in the film 'Captain January'. I love all of your films and I watch them every day with Nannie. I know all of your songs and want to be an actress when I grow up. I would like to go to Hollywood and be a film star, but I think I might go to Broadway, too.

Nannie said that you were on the tele last night with Terry Wogan. Me and Nannie and Aunty Vera are all coming to London to see you today in Harrods'. We are going to buy your book. Aunty Vera says that Harrods' is the poshest shop in the whole world. Nannie says it is probably just like Debenhams.

I have never been to London before. And I have never been to America. I am from Liverpool. If you would like to come to Liverpool you can stay at Nannie's house because she has a spare bedroom. Or you can stay at The Adelphi Hotel. Aunty Vera says that The Adelphi Hotel is the poshest hotel in Liverpool.

I would like to ask you, is The Good Ship Lollipop really a plane? I thought it was a ship and Uncle John told me that it is a plane, but he always teases me. I haven't seen the film that The Good Ship Lollipop is in because it has never been on our tele before.

I will give you this letter when I meet you. I am so so so so so excited.

Lots of love from Star Blake. Age 8.

PART ONE

"**Human memory comes in many varieties. Some are disorderly or fuzzy, some selective or short. Mine is long.**"

Shirley Temple Black, Child Star, *1988.*

27th January, 1981

This was not how he had imagined it.

Jimmy Blake emerged from the sliding doors of Fazakerley Hospital and into the bitter January night. His mate Davey should have been there in his taxi, all waiting to take Jimmy down to The King George to wet the baby's head. But nothing had turned out as he had predicted. He should have known better. Nothing in this life could be predicted, could it? Even with Kevin Radcliffe in defence for Everton, a win could never be predicted on a Saturday afternoon. Jimmy had the nurse call him a private taxi home. Davey, the gang, and The King George would have to wait.

Only hours before, Jimmy had run down Flinder Street - just six doors away on the same side – banging on Mary Mack's window. He never used the doorbell. It hadn't worked in over thirty years.

"It's Linda," he said, his heart beating so loud that the whole of Liverpool could probably hear it. "Her waters have broken."

Mary cracked up laughing and tossed Jimmy's hair with her hand. "Well, what are you telling me for, Son? Get her down the 'ossie!" She clicked her finger as a magician would to disappear.

And back Jimmy ran to his own house to find his Linda all calm, cool, and perched on the arm of the couch on the telephone to Davey Cabs. She twirled the green cord around her index finger as she spoke into the handset.

"Davey's picking us up himself," Linda whispered to Jimmy, putting her hand over the mouthpiece. "He said he had a feeling it'd be tonight."

"He's crackers," Jimmy picked up where Mary Mack had left and continued to toss his hair and scratch his head. "He reckons he's a psychic. Charging a quid to read palms down the King's recently, you know. It was only the other day he thought he was an artist and tried flogging his daughter's paint-by-numbers pictures to the local day centre."

Linda shushed her husband. "Thanks Davey, see you in a sec."

Jimmy switched the television on. He pressed each channel button again and again, too impatient to even see what was showing. Linda was laughing, but biting her nails as she kept an eye peeping through the net curtains for their taxi. For such a pretty woman, she always had her fingers in her mouth, chewing away.

"You'd think the baby was coming out of *you*," she said.

Jimmy was punching channel one for the twelfth time. But she winced suddenly, holding her belly with one arm, and still keeping a thumb tightly in between her teeth. Jimmy jumped up from his knees, knocking their wedding photo off the mantelpiece. Leaving it to lie on the carpet, he whipped over to Linda, wanting to cuddle her, soothe her, but afraid of hurting her.

"I don't know what to do, Linda."

"Just sit down, or stand outside."

"I can't leave you, Linda."

"I wish you would. You're getting on my bloody nerves."

"How am I supposed to know what to do, eh?"

"How am I?" Linda winced again. "Ooh, that was a nasty one."

"Christ." Jimmy's hair was in danger of being ripped out.

"Oh, come here, soft lad," Linda said. Jimmy cradled her as she stayed sitting on the arm of the couch. Her head slotted into his skinny shoulder blade and he swayed to and fro. "I'll tell you what you can do."

"Anything, Linda."

"Pick our wedding photo up. You know I hate mess."

Jimmy kissed his wife on the nose just as the honk of Davey's horn woke up Flinder Street, and they left so quickly that Jimmy was afraid that he had forgotten to lock the door. But never mind that, it seemed that Davey had forgotten to take his hand off the horn, and it was like the ships on New Year's Eve had arrived on Jimmy and Linda's doorstep. Faces appeared at the windows, through the net curtains or pulling them high above their heads.

"What the bloody hell's going on?" said a voice from number twenty-four.

"Are you deaf as well as stupid?" cried another voice from the opposite side.

"Sorry, luv," Jimmy said. "It's Linda…"

"Thanks!" Linda punched him.

"She's having the baby!"

Mary Mack came charging out of her house carrying a plastic bag full of ham sandwiches, cold buttered scones and a large flask of tea. She handed them to Jimmy and winked, then kissed her own fingers and placed them hard onto Linda's cheeks. 13

Davey's taxi pulled away – and honked away – as the neighbours waved, cheering them on their way to Fazakerley Hospital.

It was going to be a quick one, according to the midwife. She just glanced at Linda and ordered Jimmy to take a seat in the waiting room. He thought it was ridiculous that a waiting room only consisted of three orange plastic chairs, a coffee machine that said 'out of order' and one great, big, ticking clock. And he was convinced that the clock was running low on batteries; the second hand chugged along much slower than once a second. Another father-to-be passed by and tossed Jimmy a copy of the *Liverpool Echo*.

"You finished with it, mate?" Jimmy asked.

"Nah, I can't read a sentence," the man replied. "Too nervous."

"Too right. I've been in the men's more tonight than during the sixty-six cup final," Jimmy rattled around inside the plastic bag. "Ham butty?"

The man declined. "Couldn't."

"Your first, too?"

"Nope. My fourth. It doesn't get any easier."

A door opened. The ham butty and the *Liverpool Echo* dropped to the floor as a midwife emerged. "Mr Carey?"

"That's me," the man said, and he disappeared, leaving Jimmy alone with the ticking clock.

It was as he was reading over a sentence in the sports section for the sixth time - just trying to make some sense out of it - when Jimmy realised that the radio was playing very quietly in the background. It was the voice of John Lennon, and the song was *Woman*. There was always a Lennon song on these days, thought Jimmy. It had only been a matter of weeks since the poor guy was shot dead in New York. *Imagine* was currently Number One in the charts.

When another door opened, a midwife held it open for Jimmy this time, smiling.

"Congratulations, Mr Blake. It's a little girl."

John Lennon was singing, "*I lo-o-o-ove you-who-who…*" helping the happiest moment of Jimmy's life to take place in slow motion. Linda was lying down, propped up by dozens of blue pillows, and beaming at their baby daughter lying in the little fish tank beside the bed.

"Look at you, soft lad!" Linda let out a little laugh. "Why are you walking in slow motion? You look like you've smoked some dope. Look, there's someone here who wants to meet you, Jim."

He wasn't sure how long he was in the room with his complete family; an hour, a minute, possibly even a second. But it was certainly only a few hours later when he left the hospital, his daughter safe in his arms, but his Linda having to be left behind inside. Jimmy could recall the words; haemorrhage, internal and bleeding. Or was it; internally bleeding and a haemorrhage? These words came before the sentence that took away every nerve in his body, every feeling of life in his blood, to be replaced with what he could only describe as numb. "We're very sorry, but we did all we could."

It had been January 26 as Jimmy and Linda Blake entered Fazakerley Hospital together. By the time it was January 27; Jimmy had gained a child, but lost a wife. The sun was not even winking yet. He kept trying to relive his final moments with Linda again and again in his mind, yet it was already a puzzle with so many missing pieces; pieces he knew that he would never find, no matter how much he stuck his hand down the back of the couch or turned up the carpets. She had been sulking because Jimmy had called his baby a little ball of fluff. "There's your first insult, my love," Linda had

said. And he had said, "But aren't kittens described as balls of fluff?" And Linda had said, "Yes, but she is a baby. Not a cat." He had stroked Linda's forehead and she had slapped his arm away saying that she hated it when he did that; she was embarrassed because it was sweaty. "Do you want to hold her?"
Linda had asked him, and smiled as if to say, "Go on, then." It was as Jimmy cradled his daughter for the first time, that Linda cried out in pain, shaking, and began to slip away from him. From them. "She's just tired, isn't she?" Jimmy had asked the doctors as they rushed into the room. "Isn't she? Isn't she?" But he was the man with the baby, and the doctors were the ones with Linda. He heard, "We're losing her." But he couldn't be *losing* her. It was too soon. They were only just beginning. You can't lose something that hasn't even had a chance to start yet. He was holding half of him, half of her. She had to be here with him, she had to see it through with him. They had far too much living to do, so many memories to create.

But Linda was lost, and so were Jimmy's memories of everything that happened until he found himself waiting for a taxi that was not Davey's. He could not feel the winter chill, did not notice the white breath escape from his lips as he breathed out into the early air. Tears rolled off his face and fell onto his baby girl's cheeks like raindrops, and she opened her eyes to look at her daddy. Jimmy looked back into her dark blue eyes, and then turned his head up to face the sky. Amidst the blackness, one bright star shone, twinkling down onto them in the car park of Fazakerley Hospital.

"Linda?" Jimmy cried out. "Linda?"

He struggled to get the key into the front door at first - so he had shut it behind him as he left –holding the tiny baby in his arms. Her pink blanket was keeping her warm and she had just slept, not murmuring at all, during the taxi ride home. Jimmy had lifted her so that her face was close to his cheek and he could feel her warm, sleepy breath gently blowing on his skin. It was the only part of his body that felt alive. He had picked up an old habit of Mary Mack's – always getting her keys out of her bag ready, sometimes up to four bus stops before the one closest to Flinder Street – and had rooted in his pockets for his own keys before the taxi dropped them off.

Walking through the dark hall and into the lounge was not a problem. Jimmy knew exactly how many steps it took from the front door to the armchair facing the television. He and Linda had only lived in this house for six months, moving in just a few months after their wedding, but the layout was identical to Mary Mack's where he had grown up. Every terraced house on Flinder Street was the same – a narrow hall with the living room on the right and a small parlour behind it, just before the kitchen at the back, with two bedrooms and a bathroom upstairs. But Jimmy couldn't find the light switch and leant against the wall several times, pushing and pressing. The streetlamp shone through the front window quietly illuminating the room as he laid his baby girl onto the couch.

Having freed his arms, he got the light on in no time, and then wished he had never found the switch. As soon as the bulb lit and woke up the living room, Jimmy's eyes fell onto his and Linda's wedding photograph lying on the carpet upside down. He froze, wondering how he would ever be able to pick it up, that being the last thing that Linda had ever told him to do. *"You know I hate mess,"* she had said. To leave it there would be like she was waiting for him to do something for her; maybe she would get annoyed at him and he would hear her nagging him, like how he never wore slippers in the house or forgot to take the used teabags out of the teapot.

The baby let out a little cracked cry, and paused. Then she really started crying.

"Come on, Star," Jimmy said to her. "Let's go to Mary Mack's."

He had not even picked her up when the doorbell rang. Mary Mack had beaten them to it.

"You can't call her Star," Mary said, drawing back all of the curtains to let the morning sun spill into the living room.

"I can and I will." Jimmy was sitting in his armchair. He hadn't slept, just stared at the television test pattern of the little girl standing by the chalkboard all night. The sausage on toast on a tray by his feet had gone cold, untouched. "And I said keep the curtains drawn."

Mary ignored him. Jimmy wanted the room in darkness because it was how Linda had last seen it, just as he had refused to sleep because he did not want to wake up on a day in which he had not seen her.

"But there's no such name as 'Star'," Mary went on.

"Says who?"

"Says me. Can't you call her Sarah?"

"Three of my mates have a kid called Sarah," Jimmy scratched his head. "Or one might be Sara."

"Well what about Elizabeth?"

"After the Queen? Get lost!"

"Barbara?"

"Are you serious?"

"Are *you* serious, Jimmy my lad?" Mary stopped doing whatever she was doing for a second. Since Jimmy had broken down in her arms during the early hours of this morning, she had fed the baby, made extra bottles, put her to sleep, washed out and dried two nappies, cleaned the living room and the kitchen, and made a breakfast. But she stopped and looked right at Jimmy. "You obviously listened to too much music as a teenager."

Jimmy huffed. "There is no such thing as listening to too much music."

The baby started to cry, so Mary snapped back into work-mode, disappearing and reappearing with a hungry newborn and a bottle. She kicked Jimmy with her right foot, forcing him to sit up, not slouch, and without argument, placed the baby into his arms.

"You do it," she said.

His hands were shaking – from the shock, from lack of sleep, from fear – but he held his daughter tight, using every muscle in his body to pull himself together.

"What I am going to do, Mary?"

Mary knelt beside him. "Just put the bottle to her mouth. Go on, she'll do the rest."

"No, Mary. I mean, what am I… How am I…?"

"Go on, Son."

"What if I do everything wrong for her? What if I let her down? What if we're in the park and she runs off, and I lose her? Or if I make her jam butties and she wanted strawberry not raspberry?"

"She'll hate you for all of ten seconds," Mary smiled. "You always fell out with me if your boiled egg wasn't runny."

"No I never!"

"You did. You used to say that it was 'dead unfair' and that I mustn't love you anymore because I gave you moldy old eggs. Then you'd go on and on and on about how if I was your real mother, I would always give you runny eggs."

"Christ, I'm sorry, Mary. I can't even remember."

Mary Mack had taken Jimmy in to live with her when his mother – Mary's dearest and oldest friend - died of pneumonia. It happened only a year after a tragic accident had taken his dad, and Jimmy Blake was just ten years old. Mary Mack had had no children of her own. Jimmy was her family.

Jimmy gave Mary a half-smile, but turned all of his attention to the baby. "And what if she has long brown hair and flicks it out on the shoulders," he said. "And wears that turquoisey-blue-ish colour all the time, and sings The Carpenters' songs when I'm in a good mood and it'll put me in a bloody bad mood? And what if she hates mess? I'm a messy sod at the best of times."

"You mean what if Star is just like Linda?" Mary picked up the cold sausage on toast. "Easy. You'll love her." And she went back into the kitchen, back to work.

Jimmy nodded, and cried. He cried heavy, slow sobs that came from deep inside where the numbness had rested all night and begun to drop away, leaving a dull pain behind.

"Her name can be Rebecca," he whispered. "You know, in case she becomes a doctor or erm, a barrister, or something. But we'll never call her that."

"Well don't think for a second she'll grow up calling me Grandma," Mary shouted from the kitchen. Did that woman have ears in every room, not to mention eyes actually in the back of her head? "Grandmas are old. Grey hair in a bun and varicose veins. If I'm to call that child, Star, then she'll call me, Nannie."

28th April, 1989

It was impossible to keep quiet backstage. The older kids were always shushing the younger ones if they so much as coughed. And it was dusty back there, amongst the cardboard trees and the boxes covered in false poppies. The spray paint used to decorate the backdrop of the Emerald City had already set off about seven asthma attacks and the house had not even landed in Oz yet.

Star felt silly, all dressed up as a munchkin. The red tights and purple smock were not so bad, but it was the headdress with antlers that confused her. Not a single munchkin in the movie had antlers coming out of their head, and to make matters worse, Kelly Keene – a girl in the Top Juniors – had drawn two big red dots onto Star's cheeks with lipstick and made the other Top Junior girls say, "Ahhh."

The girls from Mrs Taylor's class were onstage doing the Tornado Dance. They wore black leotards and darted around with long pieces of silver material, whilst Dorothy stood in the middle twirling around and screaming. But it wasn't *Dorothy*. It was Emma-Jane Duggan, who only got the part because she was Mrs Duggan's daughter. She couldn't even sing out loud and never once attempted to try an American accent. Star had asked Mrs Duggan is she could audition for the part, but was told, no, she was too little, but maybe next year. Star wished that Nannie was the Deputy Head. Then the ruby slippers would definitely be on her feet.

A cymbal crashed. A murmur of laughing simmered over the audience, a little shocked from the noise. Emma-Jane Duggan spoke out, "I don't reckon we're in Liverpool anymore, Toto," to which louder laughs echoed from the parent's watching. Star cringed; saddened by the injustice of it, but this was the munchkins' cue to giggle from the wings. They all giggled longer than they were supposed to, a release from having to stay silent for so long, until it filtered out and just Anthony Tucker was left making a noise which sounded like a pig snort. He would be in so much trouble later.

"Miss?" a voice from the back of all of the munchkins whispered. "Miss?"

A wave of "shshshshsh" travelled over to the voice, and Star had no doubt that the whole audience heard it.

"Miss," the voice said again. "Peter Healey's done a wee."

"No I haven't," Peter Healey said.

"Yeah, you have. It's all over the floor!"

A chorus of "eeuughhhs" and "eeeeeeehs" snapped the children out of stage-fright, causing much commotion. Star sighed. Yes, she was not proud of being a munchkin, but the school play was very important to her and she wanted it to look good, professional. It was so typical of Peter Healey to wee on the floor.

She wasn't surprised that Jimmy hadn't shown up, but it would have done him good to get out of the house. Mary Mack was disappointed. At least Star wouldn't be too bothered; she had told her daddy not to bother coming because if he blinked he would miss her. Besides, she was constantly singing and dancing at home, putting on her own plays, that Jimmy could watch her perform anytime. But Mary had prayed that Jimmy would have just mustered up the energy and come along. Every few minutes, she glanced over to the school hall's entrance in the hope that he had waltzed in late, but all she saw was the headmaster dozing off beside a statue of The Holy Family.

It was a decent little school, St. Stephen's, but it did look overdue for a good coat of paint. The ceiling sometimes flaked onto the heads of the children in assembly, and it would have been nice to listen to a piano that was in tune. Still, the walls were always splattered with creative artwork by the children, large wooden panels that each class would decorate. There was The Last Supper, and one with the heading 'We Love Our Family' with photographs and drawings of some children's parents. Star's class had been responsible for the very colourful interpretation of Jesus feeding the five thousand. Mary had helped Star to make the five fish – using kitchen foil and an old Cornflakes' box – seeing as the child was so enthusiastic about school that she had volunteered to do it for extra homework. When Jimmy was a little lad, he would just rush his sums, not wanting to waste any football time in the street with his mates. And the amount of shattered windows that that boy had been responsible for…

Mary loved watching Star on the stage. She took her along to tap and ballet lessons every Saturday morning at St. Stephen's church hall, and there was a concert performed at the local civic centre not so long ago where Star got to do a small solo. It was a shame that the school only allowed her to be a munchkin, as Mary knew how much she had dreamt about being Dorothy. But it was turning out to be a dismal production. Star's class teacher, Miss Murphy, was sitting alongside Mary, and she had been looking at her watch every thirty seconds. Probably a bit gutted that she would miss *Blockbusters*. She looked the type to be into that, or even a contestant maybe, all young and university-like with baggy clothes and dangly earrings.

Yes, the play was a right state. Yet, it would still be a better environment for Jimmy right now rather than spending his afternoon at home watching the first showing of *Neighbours* and chain smoking roll-ups. Unless he had gone round to The King George for what he claimed to be the meeting place for the 'union'. Mary had not given him a penny this week, making it clear that she would cook Star's dinner and make her a packed lunch every day, but not a snitch of her pension was going to him. And all because she knew where that money would end up. It was bad enough that little Star had a father out of work, never mind a drunken father out of work.

He wasn't a bad daddy to Star, not at all. Perhaps Mary Mack was being harsh on Jimmy. He had always worked, ever since he was fourteen and got a job at the local garage. That was how he had met Linda, when she used to come in and buy a packet of Wrigley's and a Dairy Milk from him every day after school. Linda would always make sure to let him know that the Dairy Milk was for her Granddad, who she popped in to see every evening for half an hour. It took the lad nearly two years to ask her out to the pictures. It took her just over a month to agree to go with him. Oh, how Mary wished that Jimmy was here now, and with Linda, too, together watching their daughter's school play. Who knows, there might have been another little Blake in the Infants and even another in a pram. Knowing how quickly Linda had got pregnant with Star, Mary didn't doubt that the potential for a large Blake family had been right on the cards.

It was a month ago when Jimmy had come over to Mary's house with the news that he had lost his job. Star was there, but upstairs reading aloud to some teddies and the rag-doll that looked like Sheila Gilhooley, the woman from the end house on Flinder Street who cleaned the church in her winter coat and slippers. Star's voice echoed down the stairs and into the parlour.

"But how do you lose a job like that?" Mary had said. "It's supposed to be a job for life."

"You're telling me?" Jimmy said. He had quit the garage after a couple of years to work on Liverpool's docks. "I'm not the only one, but it doesn't make it any easier, Mary. What am I going to do? It's not like I've got much else going for me."

Mary made a fresh pot of tea, promising him that something would turn up. But even she knew that this was a paper thin promise. As thin as the *Liverpool Echo* a day out of date and damp with tea stains smudging the headlines.

"What's the matter?" Star had appeared at the kitchen door.

"Nothing, my luv," Mary said. "Do you want a Jammie Dodger?"

Star shook her head. "Is it that bloody Maggie Thatcher again, daddy?"

Mary dropped the packet of Jammie Dodgers. "Don't use bad words like that."

"Which one's the bad word?" Jimmy huffed. Star had overheard him say the same thing over and over, and although she should not be repeating it, surely she didn't really know what she was talking about. Mary told Jimmy to take Star home, put her to bed and not have any phone conversations that night that "little ears" could listen to. No good could come of that.

And now Jimmy Blake was not at work, and not at his daughter's play. He might be tied up in a union meeting, but whatever he was up to, there was no good to come out of that either.

*

Star was pleased with her performance, right up until Emma-Jane Duggan stood on her toe – by accident, of course – during the 'Follow the Yellow Brick Road' sequence. However, she was still buzzing from the applause, as were all of the munchkins. The make-up girl, Kelly Keene, was doubling up her duties as chaperone, too, and escorted the munchkins out of the wings, through the corridors and back to a classroom where they would have to wait until the finale.

There was something so exciting about being in a classroom without a teacher present. True, Miss Murphy would be on her way to supervise any moment, but the lack of any grown-ups present created a mood in the air that made the children giddy and silly. The girls could not stop laughing, fits and fits of hysterical laughter, which was not helped much by Christopher McGinty grabbing the chalk and drawing a pair of boobs and a large penis onto the blackboard.

"Young man, young man," Star said in an attempted Yorkshire accent, putting her hands on her hips. "That ain't wise, Mr McGinty. That ain't wise."

The laughter rose, but the little girls covered their mouths with their hands, knowing that it was verging on naughty now. Star was doing her Miss Murphy Impression, and Christopher McGinty played along saying, "Sorry Miss," and Star clapped twice, just as their teacher always did to change the subject.

"Children, children," Star went on, "Where is my guitar? It's time for a sing-song." The guitar case was on Miss Murphy's desk, and Star opened it up but leaving the guitar inside for fear of actually breaking it. She strummed the strings and sang aloud, "*Animal crackers in my soup…* Come on children, repeat after me… *Animal crackers in my soup…*"

All who could control their chuckles repeated, or shouted rather, "Animal crackers in my soup!"

"Good children, and again, after me…" Star continued, her Yorkshire drawl becoming more exaggerated. "*Monkeys and rabbits loop the loop…*"

"MONKEYS AND RABBITS LOOP THE LOOP," her classmates yelled.

"*Gosh oh gee but I have fun, swallowing animals one by one.*"

The followers lost the beginning words, this being a song that they had never heard before, but managed a loud, "ONE BY ONE!"

But by this time, Star was away; lost in the moment of being not just Miss Murphy, but being in a musical and singing around a classroom of people all dancing around her. This was a real-life movie. The tables with tubs of pencils in the middle, the book corner, the art tray full of poster paints and Copydex glue; all of this was in black and white, a silver screen. And she just carried on and on singing;

"*In every bowl of soup I see,*

Lions and tigers watching me,

"Ooh, children, ain't this fun, ain't this fun, I feel like Maria from *The Sound of Music*...

I make 'em jump right through a hoop

Those animal crackers in my soup..."

Star stopped when she realised that the entire hubbub had drawn to a halt. She felt her tummy flip over like a pancake but not land smoothly into place, and her whole face filled in from pink to red, matching the lipstick circles on her cheeks, flushing with heat.

"Young lady," Miss Murphy said from behind Star's head. "That ain't wise, Miss Blake. That ain't wise."

Star turned around and whispered, "Oh my goodness."

Caught.

*

The thought had crossed Jimmy's mind to just stay in bed all day. Sleeping killed time and as time went on, something else might happen to overtake the drama of the night before. Serious riots could break out, war even. Not that Jimmy Blake was wishing for war, but if it happened out of his control, then it was a possible answer to avoid the consequences of the fight on the dock road.

He had not stayed in bed all day since Star was a tiny baby and he was struggling to live his life without Linda. That was his grieving time, which he needed, and which Mary Mack had helped him through and finally dragged him out of. Today was the first day in eight years that Jimmy felt like regressing to that again. There were times when he had felt like just sleeping, not facing the day, of course. Time and time and again; Linda's birthday, their wedding anniversary, and after having unpredicted dreams of her being alive and they were teenagers again, dancing together at the social club, or her just being there in the present, un-aged and playing with Star. But he always forced himself up as he did this morning. Only he got as far as his armchair and stayed there, not even bothering to make a slice of toast.

The day dragged. No matter what the television yapped at him about, he couldn't hear it. His hands shook, his stomach churned and his head felt full of a thousand little hammers, battering away at his forehead.

It was a few long hours later when the battering became a noise not inside his head but outside in the real world. It was at his front door.

They were here.

*

"Shall we have bacon ribs for tea or a cooked chicken?" Nannie asked Star.

"Bacon ribs please," Star said, licking her lips. Nannie very rarely asked for her opinion on the choice of what was for dinner. It was a case of eat it or starve. Unlike in Laura Fenton's house. Star went to Laura Fenton's for tea one night after school, and Laura was allowed to make her own food. They had potato alpha-bites and chicken nuggets. Apparently Laura Fenton had chicken nuggets every night of the week and was never told off for not eating vegetables.

"Do you like bacon ribs, my luv?" Ron the butcher asked.

Star nodded. "My favourite."

Ron's shop was opposite St. Stephen's, smack in the middle of Si's newsagents and Denise's hair salon. Si's was empty for most of the day, making all of its money between three thirty and four o'clock selling penny sweets and bubble gum, while Denise who had six children at St. Stephen's – with another on the way – had skin that was almost orange from Rio Sun tanning products.

Ron wrapped up some boiled ham which Nannie had also ordered to make the packed lunches with for the rest of the week. He kept glancing at Star, no doubt at the ridiculous blotches of red that would not come off no matter how much water and paper towels she had scrubbed with.

"What happened to you? Been playing in paint or something? I'd've thought you'd want blue on your face, you being an Evertonian like that dad of yours." His laugh came from the root of his belly, and that was a long way seeing as his belly was huge.

"It was our school play," Star said, lacking all enthusiasm. "Make-up."

"But I thought you wanted to be an actress, Star," Ron said. "Why the tut-tut ting face?"

"It wasn't my best performance. Still, I've got time to improve. Fred Astaire was nearly forty when he made it big, not everyone got the same break as Shirley Temple." Star comforted herself with this.

"Fred Astaire, he was a crackin' dancer," Ron said. "And the other fella, what's his name; you know the one who sings in the rain…"

"Gene Kelly," Star and Nannie said together.

"That was a fantastic picture. I love his mate; you know the one who runs up the wall…"

"Donald O'Connor."

"Hey, you two know your stuff, don't you? Do you like Deanna Durbin? I always had a soft spot for her."

Star scrunched her nose, shaking her head. "Nah. But I do love Judy Garland. Only, Shirley's my favourite. Definitely."

Ron wrapped up the ribs and a quarter of boiled ham. He placed it on top of the counter and unscrewed the jar full of lollipops, offering a freebie to Star. Before she dived in, her eyes rolled up to Nannie who gave a nod, "Go on then."

"Ooh, thank you, Ron," Star smiled.

"Don't tell anyone," Ron pointed his finger at her.

"I won't," Star gave a big wink.

Ron straightened up and lowered his voice. "So Mary, how's Jimmy getting on? Any luck?"

Nannie said no, shrugged and gave a gesture to above.

"Something will come up soon."

"When the halibuts start running," Star said.

Ron and Nannie looked down at Star and her red face, sucking away on the Vimto lollipop. They clearly did not understand.

"Daddy will get a job once the halibuts start running."

"Star," Nannie said. "Little ears should not join in with big ears' talk."

"I know, but it's true. The halibuts will start running soon. And then there'll be lots of jobs for daddy, I just know it."

Nannie put her hand on Star's head, turning her towards the door and guiding her out, thanking and saying goodbye to Ron, who stood there amongst beef, chicken and pork – baffled - yet thinking very hard about fish.

It wasn't far back to Flinder Street. Nannie and Star could walk it in less than twenty minutes, but if it rained they caught the bus. They walked today, a bright May afternoon, with a touch of heat in the air giving a hint that summer would be here soon. The summer uniform was already being worn at St. Stephen's and Star loved it; a green gingham dress with a white belt. It beat the black and red striped tie and grey pinafore any day.

All the way home, Star quizzed Nannie on every single person's performance in the show, keen to hear her opinion. By the time they got round to dissecting the motivation behind the Cowardly Lion, it was clear to Star that Nannie had pretty much snoozed through the show once the munchkins had left the stage. Star decided to practice her tap shuffles along the street – tapping was a much more interesting way of walking – playing a game with herself to avoid the cracks in the pavement whilst doing so.

"Take the lollipop out of your mouth while your dancing, luv," Nannie said. "You'll choke to death if it comes off the stick."

"Don't worry about me; I'm very self-reliant," Star said, out of breath but determined. She always chose a Vimto lollipop from Ron. They seemed to last a lot longer than those sherbet ones which also started to hurt your tongue after a while licking.

They turned into Flinder Street, where Sheila Gilhooley was sitting on her front step, slippers on but winter coat off for once. Her hair was like a mesh of tangled brown wire and she was always delighted to see Nannie, as if she hadn't seen her in over a hundred years.

"Oh, Mary Mack, Mary Mack!" Sheila shouted. "Isn't it gorgeous today? You know, the Callaghan's from number thirty-nine show off about going to the Costa del Sol every year, but who needs that when we can have sunshine on our doorsteps?"

Nannie never stopped walking whenever Sheila Gilhooley cornered her, usually just slowed down to be polite but always carried on, eager to get away. Only the sight of the police car sat outside of Jimmy and Star's house made them both stop still.

"How long's that been there, Sheila?" Nannie asked.

Sheila stood up and covering her brow with her hands to shield the sun, looked down Flinder Street. She screeched. "Oh good Lord! Oh good God, my Lord!" Sheila paced and paced and started to panic. "I never saw…I didn't see…I never saw…Oh good Lord… It was the sun, Mary Mack. I just sort of zoned out in the sun…"

"Never mind, Sheila." Nannie took Star by the hand and headed towards home. Yes, the car was parked outside of Star's house; a real police car, with the blue light flashing around and around. It wasn't unusual for one to be outside of number twelve's late on a Friday night, but not outside her house. Her daddy's house.

Before they reached the gate, Nannie and Star saw the front door open. Two policemen emerged with Star's daddy jammed in between them, his hands behind his back.

"Daddy!" Star screamed, breaking away from Nannie's grip and running towards him. "You leave him alone… You leave him alone! Daddy!"

"Star! Get back here," Nannie called.

But Star just carried on running, until a policewoman got out of the car and caught her, holding her back. Pinned to the spot, Star's legs carried on chasing one paving stone beneath her feet, as she fidgeted, trying with all her might to wriggle free. "You let me go! You let me go!"

"Star, sweetheart," her daddy cried out. "You be a good little girl. Don't cry. You be good for Mary Mack now…"

The tears fell full speed down Star's cheeks, making clear white lines in the red-smudged make-up that had before not budged with water. She cried. Cried and cried, while still trying to fight for her freedom, terrified of where they were taking her daddy. "Oh daddy, daddy! Why are they taking you away from me? What have I done? Oh daddy, daddy!"

Nannie was behind Star with the struggling policewoman and Star collapsed into Nannie's arms, her heart breaking with all of the tears that she was crying. Consoling her, Nannie whispered into her little ears over and over the words from Star's favourite Shirley Temple movie, *A Little Princess*. "Come on, Star, what does Sara Crewe say? Remember, my luv. What does Sara Crewe say? What did Captain Crewe tell his little girl to say?"

Star stood up straight, watching the police car drive away with her daddy in the back seat, his head down and arms behind his back, stuck together with handcuffs. She murmured, "My daddy has to go away, but he'll return most any day. Any moment I may see, my daddy coming back to me."

10th May, 1989

Star threw the bottle top, aiming it onto the paving stone that had a hint of pink to it. Nannie had a tiny front garden, about six paving stones in total filled it, and all grey except for the one that was pink. The lemonade man was due any minute. He always arrived about ten minutes after the ice-cream man, and Nannie had told Star to wait outside so that they didn't miss their chance to get a bottle of dandelion and burdock. By saving the top of the last fizzy pop bottle, fifteen pence was saved off the new bottle.

The bottle top landed on a grey paving stone, about three centimetres from the pink. Star huffed, sliding her feet over with heavy weight to pick it up and try again. She was happy to have a task though. And especially one that allowed her to wait outside on Flinder Street because if the police car came back with her daddy in it, then she would be the first person to welcome him home. It had been over a week since the police had taken him away from her, but Star never stopped believing that one day soon her daddy would return. Plus, she had used up all of Nannie's blank video tapes to record all of his favourite programmes. There was a repeat of an *Auf Wiedersehen, Pet* episode on last night but the tape ran out just five minutes before the end.

"Hiya, Star," Louise Fitzpatrick was at Nannie's gate with Steph Bradley behind her, both with their lilac Raleigh bikes.

Star said hello, but kept her concentration on aiming for the pink.

"We're going to the field," Louise said. "Come. The trees still haven't been cut down yet so we can climb up and through them."

The field was only around the corner, and actually an old playing field belonging to the college built on its grounds. Star had never known the college to be open; the windows had been forever boarded up with wood that had rude words splattered all over them in graffiti paint. There was always broken glass in the car park area, and sometimes children would play at picking up the larger pieces and throwing them, making them smash into millions of little pieces. Star joined in this
game once and cut her right index finger with the first throw. She had never ever seen so much blood in her entire life, yet she was more terrified of telling her daddy and Nannie how she had obtained this injury. It was all well and good dreaming to be an actress, making up scenes and lines. But, Star was abysmal at telling lies.

"I'm waiting for the lemonade man," Star told her friends.

"But the trees might be gone tomorrow," Steph said, chewing the end of her left pigtail.

"They won't. I reckon it's a rumour," Star said, her bottle top landing safely on the pink. "You know, to stop us all climbing them."

Behind the car park was a row of small trees. Star and her buddies had bent and twisted the branches so that once the first tree was climbed, it was easy to claw through all of the trees right until the end one where they had made a trap door out of leaves that they slid through to get back down onto the ground. Christopher McGinty had told them that the trees were being pulled down, and once that happened, the college would be bulldozed into a mountain of bricks, and new houses would be built there. Or a supermarket.

"Why are you being all grumpy, Star?" Louise said, folding her arms. Her tone of voice was not very nice; Louise could get nasty if she wanted to. "You're in a right mood lately. Everyone's noticed."

"Sorry," was all that Star could manage, but the sound of a vehicle turning into Flinder Street caught her attention, giving her a flutter of hope and nearly making her smile.

"Fine." Louise rode off with Steph following her, giving Star a filthy look.

The vehicle was the lemonade man, and as much as Star loved dandelion and burdock, it was worth never having it again if it meant that it would bring her daddy back.

*

It wasn't like Star to not eat her tea. She always left her crusts – despite Mary telling her that crusts made your hair curly – but it was unusual for her to pick at her food and refuse a chocolate mousse for pudding. As the weeks went by, her appetite was slipping away more and more.

But who could blame her? The poor child had had her father snatched out of her life right before her eyes, and Mary was still struggling to tell Star exactly why this had happened.

"Why have they taken him away, Nannie?" Star asked every night as Mary brushed her long, sandy hair before tucking her into bed in the spare bedroom. Really, the spare bedroom was Star's *other* bedroom; it had a rocking horse and a Big Yellow Teapot, the top cupboard of the wardrobe was full of jigsaws and colouring books, and there were many teddies on the bed surrounding the rag doll that looked like Sheila Gilhooley. "Why him? Why him, Nannie?"

"Your daddy got into a little bit of trouble," Mary said.

"What kind of trouble? He never gets into trouble."

"Now Star, you're a very good little girl, but remember when you got into trouble with Miss Murphy for singing to the class when she left the room for two minutes?"

"Yes, but I never meant to get into trouble for that," Star, usually so sure of herself, was aching with confusion. The unanswered questions were written all over her face, almost hiding her freckles.

"And I am positive that your daddy never meant to get into trouble for this."

"But the police took him away, and the police only take bad men away. My daddy's not a bad man. Or a drunk like Mick Tully from number twelve."

Mary knew that Jimmy Blake was not a bad man. He drank a lot recently, but Star was correct; he was no drunk like Mick Tully. Why, oh why did Jimmy have to get involved in the fighting? Maybe he was stitched up or maybe he was the one who crushed the face of a man with his foot, causing this man to die right there out on the dock road. There were many maybes. The only definite was that Jimmy was not going to be coming home for a long, long time.

Messing around with her spaghetti hoops - getting three, four, five onto the fork and then letting them slide off, plopping back into the tomato sauce – rather than putting them in her mouth, Star was asking questions again. Why's and more why's.

"When a grown-up gets into trouble, Star, it becomes very different to what it was like at school, you know; more complicated," Mary told her.

"I never want to grow up." Star said, prodding a soggy crust with her knife.

"Now that is a silly billy thing to say, Star."

"Why?"

"Because can you imagine Shirley saying a thing like that?"

Star paused, allowing herself to have a little think.

"Shirley looks forward to growing up, doesn't she, Star? Why, in a year or two or three - you'll be as happy as can be…"

"*Like a birdie in the tree,*" Star sang, her voice lightening a touch.

"When you grow up - there's a lot you'll want to do…"

"*I will have real dollies too - like the woman in the shoe,*" sitting up straight, Star recited the words of the song, allowing herself a tiny ounce of energy to sing bits, "*I want to be a teacher so the children can say, teacher dear, the gang's all here with apples today… And if you feel that you need some company, you can call me up and I'll come down when I grow up.*"

"Good," Mary said. "Now, eat your dinner."

"Not hungry."

"Shall I make you a fried egg?"

Star stuck out her tongue and faked vomiting. Mary was puzzled. What was wrong with a fried egg? But Star explained that she had recently dreamt about eating a fried egg but the yolk was not yellow, it was blue; bright, thick blue. And hard and crumbly, too, instead of runny. Apparently it tasted disgusting, like eating dirty plastic.

"Jesus," Mary said, "what is it with you Blakes and bloody eggs, eh?"

The evening air outside was hazy and calm. The back kitchen door was left open, blowing the haze into Mary's house. The noises of the neighbourhood children playing on the field echoed into the back yard; dull thuds of footballs being kicked, screeches and shouting. Star just looked out of the parlour window, through the net curtain and onto the empty back yard. A purple rubber bouncy ball that had a little bell in the middle rocked slowly back and forth on the ground. It looked like a toy that a kitten or a puppy would play with and Mary Mack had no idea how long it had been there, jingle-jangling away.

There was a rat-at-tat-tat on the front door; Mary's younger sister Vera was here with her husband, John. Star darted into the hall, life shooting through her at last. The back kitchen door slammed shut from the draft of opening the front door, banging in time with the lively laughter and banter spilling louder and louder into the house. Star was squealing; John had picked her up by her ankles and was bobbing her up and down. Vera danced over to Mary – a box of Jaffa Cakes under her arm and oozing with a strong whiff of Chanel which began to lace the parlour - greeting her sister with a big cuddle.

"Any news?" Vera said into Mary's ear.

"It doesn't look good," Mary replied. "Tea?"

The women went into the kitchen but Star, who had been put the right way up on her feet, followed them before they could have any sort of proper conversation regarding Jimmy's situation. Both Vera and Mary said, "John!" with an air of disappointment in him for not keeping Star away, only it was obvious from the look on his face that John had no idea what he had done wrong.

"What?" Star asked, breaking the moment of silence, but more silence followed, only the slow bubble of the kettle trying to give her an answer.

John picked up Star's left wrist. "What is that?"

Star giggled. "It's a watch, silly."

"That's not a watch! It's a clock on a strap."

"No it's not. It's a watch." Star looked at her watch. Mary and Vera joined her, all three of them studying the bubble gum pink strap and face. She had got it for her eighth birthday from Louise Fitzpatrick and Mary had always thought of it as tacky, more like a fake watch that you get in a plastic box from a fairground vending machine. Still, the watch did work and Star did wear it, probably to stop Louise Fitzpatrick from picking on her. Mary did not like Louise, or her mother who used to be friends with Linda, influencing Linda into wearing those daft platform boots that she only ever managed to waddle in. For Louise's eighth birthday, Mary sent her a birthday card with, 'Dear Lousie,' written inside. Nobody may have noticed, but it made Mary Mack laugh.

John took the kitchen clock off the wall, grabbed a tea-towel printed with a map of the Isle of Man on it and strapped the clock to his wrist. "Look, Star. It's the same as this!"

"No it's not," Star said, frustrated yet pressing her lips together to hold back a smile.

"Why don't we put your watch on the kitchen wall instead?"

"Uncle John, you're daft."

The back kitchen was now full of laughter and silliness; just as it was a few weeks ago. Star ran upstairs as Mary poured the tea and Vera put the Jaffa Cakes onto a little china plate to take into the parlour. Seconds later, Star emerged wearing one of Nannie's old dresses, a long ribbon tied around her waist to keep the skirt from trailing along the floor, and a tiara made from silver sequins. "Let's do a play!" she announced.

"What'll it be today, Star?" Vera asked. "Snow White?"

"No, there's not enough cast members," Star said.

"But I can do seven very different voices," Vera said, sounding a little offended.

"I know, but you have to shuffle around on your knees and that slows the story down. Let's do the story of the princess and the golden ball," Star said, running outside into the back yard, finding a use for the purple ball at last.

"I don't know that one," Vera said.

Mary tutted. "It's the one where the princess kisses a frog."

"I wonder who I'm playing then." John said, croaking.

And so they got to work; moving the furniture around so that Star could dance around with the ball and drop it in the imaginary pond, listening to Star's directions that she whispered out of the corner of her mouth like a bad ventriloquist, creating a play for an audience of teddies and the rag-doll that looked like Sheila Gilhooley.

*

Once the play was over and John had tired the child out with a tickling war, Vera took Star up to bed because it was what they told her was 'grown-up time'. Vera loved to do this, tucking her in and saying her prayers with her, a glimpse of being a mother with her own little girl. How odd that neither she nor her sister had had any children, while their brother Richie had six, all of whom now had children of their own. Vera would have liked her own baby, but it had just never happened. She often wondered if things had turned out differently for her Mary, whether she may have had a large family, for the woman was a born mother. Even when they were little girls on the evacuation during the war, Mary had looked after Vera throughout, always holding her hand, putting her hair in rags, and making sure that her Sunday best never had a tea-stain down the front. Every day, Vera thanked God that Jimmy and Star had become Mary's life, a miracle saving her sister from her lonely fate. Jimmy would be home again soon, surely? He had to.

When Vera joined Mary downstairs, there was a fresh cup of tea waiting for her. John was outside, checking his car for scratches. He did this too many times whenever they came over to Mary's house, him being used to a nice, cosy garage for his beloved Audi rather than kids in the street kicking footballs and riding their bikes. So far, a scratch had never, in fact, surfaced.

"So tell me, Mary," Vera said. "Do you really think that Jimmy did it?"

Mary pursed her lips, taking a deep breath. "A few months ago, maybe even as little as six weeks ago, I would have said 'no'. I would know that no matter what went on in that fight, who said what or who threw the first punch, our Jimmy would never get that violent. He came home from school twice with a broken nose as a kid, all because he couldn't hit back hard enough…"

"Ah, I remember," Vera said. She and John had taken young Jimmy to the hospital in their car to save Mary the trouble of having to get the bus, the lad's blood gushing everywhere. Jimmy had been distraught, and not due to the pain, or the bullying or even the embarrassment of being beaten up by a fat kid from the year below. No. He had been wearing his new Everton shirt, and the royal blue was all covered in the opposition's colour; blood red.

"He could be a little wimp at times, couldn't he?" Mary went on. "But things have changed, haven't they, Vera? Losing his job was one thing, but he lost his mate at Hillsborough soon after, didn't he? Poor Jonesy, God rest his soul."

Vera nodded, making a small Sign of the Cross with her right hand, thinking of Jonesy; Jimmy and Jonesy. Keith Jones and Jimmy Blake had always been the best of mates, despite Keith being a red and Jimmy being a blue; it had caused daily banter, but it didn't matter. They shared a love for *Ben-Hur*, The Clash and cheese toasties with ketchup. Jonesy, an eternal bachelor who had bought a Bianco and lemonade for every girl in Bootle who owned a Maxi dress and false eyelashes was best man at Jimmy and Linda's wedding. Never one to miss a football game – home and away - Jonesy was at Hillsborough and fell victim to the disaster. Jimmy had not experienced a loss in his life since Linda died; not until April 1989 arrived when he lost his job and his best friend within days.

"But it's as if something has triggered Jimmy's brain, you know," Mary said. "His eyes aren't the same as they used to be, you know, they don't look at you. They look through you, like you're a ghost and he's focussing on the wall behind your head. And his breathing, Vera. It's heavy and fast, all the time. He'd be watching the tele and I'd hear it, through his nose in-out-in-out-in-out, and I'd feel like he was going to burst or chuck the video remote across the room."

"Oh, Jesus…"

"So, Vera, you ask me if I think that he was the one that killed that man down on the dock road? I don't know, I honestly don't know, but it is a possibility."

"Oh, Jesus…"

John came back and joined Vera on the couch.

"The car okay?" Mary asked him.

"It is for now, Mary. It is for now."

It annoyed Vera how precious John was about the flippin' Audi, but clasping her cup of tea tight, she let her other hand slip into John's and squeezed, squeezed hard, not caring if their hands became stuck together forever.

*

Star had lay in bed with her eyes shut tight, but her body and brain was wide awake. She had tried saying the rosary; Uncle John had told her that it was the best way to fall asleep because it was so boring, but Aunty Vera had scalded him and told her to count sheep. But that was silly, silly, silly. How could she count sheep if she didn't know how many sheep were there in her head to start with? It made no sense at all. So Star went through every Shirley Temple song that she knew word for word, hoping that she would drop off during one of her least favourite ones. However, half way through 'On the Good Ship Lollipop' she had a sudden urge to get out of bed and make up a tap routine to show her friends in the playground tomorrow.

Light burst into the room just as Star was heel-stepping around her bed, making her nearly jump right out of her night-dress. Nannie was at the door, hands on her hips, and wanting to know why the spare bedroom had suddenly become the London Palladium.

"I'm sorry, Nannie, but I tried the rosary and everything."

"Nobody falls asleep saying the rosary, my luv. Catholics have too much guilt pent up inside them to drop off before the final Our Father."

"Uncle John can."

"Uncle John is a Protestant."

Star's jaw dropped. "Is it against the law that he married Aunty Vera?"

Nannie laughed at her. "No, my luv."

"But how was it allowed?"

"Because they fell in love, Star."

"Oh." Star crawled back into bed. "Haven't you ever fallen in love, Nannie?"

Nannie blew a big raspberry. "Have you?"

"Yes actually," Star said, full of confidence. "I am in love with Simon Monaghan, aren't I?"

"Still?"

When Star made her first Holy Communion last year, having to wear a long, lacy white dress with a veil, it made her feel like a bride. Her whole class had to walk down the church aisle partnered boy-girl, and Simon Monaghan was Star's partner. He had no idea, but when they took that first piece of Communion, as far as Star was concerned she and Simon were married.

"Why haven't you got married?" Star asked. She had asked Nannie this question so many times and always got the raspberry, but found the face that Nannie pulled whilst making the raspberry hilarious. Like a mouldy beetroot.

But Nannie didn't make any funny noises. She sighed, her eyes drooping with the tired spell that Star so wanted – needed – right now. "Goodnight, Star."

What was the matter with Nannie? She was never tired, ever. Nannie always woke up before anyone else and got dressed quicker than it took Star to brush her teeth. Star started to wonder if she had ever even seen Nannie sleep at all! Maybe Nannie had fallen in love and it was a secret. It was a good thing to fall in love, surely, and Nannie deserved good things. And there was plenty of room for a husband; Nannie already had a double bed.

So why didn't she have a husband? He might have died just as her mother did, but Nannie would have told her. There would be photos of him everywhere like there were photos of Linda all over her house, such as a wedding picture or one of a holiday in Benidorm or riding a donkey on Blackpool beach. Maybe Nannie did have a boyfriend, one that she kept a secret. Her daddy used to have a secret girlfriend called Christine, but she had a stupid laugh which sounded like Roland Rat, although she did have pretty permed hair and wore glitter on her eyelids, so it was a shame about the laugh. Although when Christine didn't laugh, she cried. Lots. Star had heard the laughing, seen the crying, and her daddy didn't have a clue. It was her own secret that she knew all about her daddy's secret girlfriend, and especially because of all the crying, Star got a feeling that it was best to leave it that way. Nannie would never cry over a boy, so maybe she didn't have a secret boyfriend. Perhaps Nannie was too old for one.

Or maybe Nannie just didn't like boys. Louise Fitzpatrick hated boys, and because Louise Fitzpatrick hated boys, Steph Bradley hated boys as well. Star didn't understand. Of course, there were some boys that she hated but not *all* of them. And especially not Simon Monaghan - who she might kiss tomorrow if they all played Catch-the-girls-kiss-the-girls - for Star never stuck to the rules if Simon Monaghan was playing.

But Star dragged her mind away from Simon and his nice strawberry blonde hair and his *Thundercats* rucksack, bringing her thoughts back to Nannie again. She was just next door, so tired and in that big bed all by herself. Star threw back her duvet and let her toes touch the carpet very lightly, and taking baby-steps, she tip-toed out of the spare bedroom and across the landing into Nannie's room. The floorboards were very creaky, but Star was good at judging which ones to avoid because she liked to sneak downstairs for a glass of juice every now and then. She imagined one day pinching a custard cream, sneaking it up the stairs and nibbling it under the covers with her Glo Worm switched on, but she was too scared. If Nannie had eyes in the back of her head, she definitely knew how many custard creams were in the tin at bedtime.

Nannie was lying on top of her double bed, still in her clothes.

"Star?" Nannie said, not moving, not even opening her eyes.

Star took one baby-step back. Cree-eeak.

"I know you're there. Come and lie on the bed with me."

Needing no persuasion, Star picked up speed and leapt into Nannie's bed.

"Now will you go to sleep, Star?" Nannie asked slow and croaky, still keeping her eyes tight shut. "I'm exhausted."

Star agreed. The streetlight directly outside of Nannie's bedroom window always gave the room a misty glow. Star could tell that although Nannie's eye's were closed, she wasn't asleep yet either; her eyelids were too scrunched up as if she was trying, praying to get some sleep, and to stop all the thoughts that only juggle around at bedtime juggling around.

Taking in a breath and trying her very best to be gentle, Star sang;

"What makes life the sweetest?

Best-est and complete-est?

Not a big doll house, or a Mickey Mouse,

But the right somebody to love.

Ice cream, cake and candy,

May be fine and dandy,

But if you ask me, they're not one, two, three,

With the right somebody to love.

One you really care for, and is yours to have and keep,

One you say a prayer for,

And you're now I lay me down to sleep.

Though you're not quite seven,

What is most like heaven?

Is the joy that's found with your arms around,

With the right..."

And the next thing Star knew, it was morning.

18th May, 1989

Vera felt a little over-dressed standing in the playground, waiting for Star to come running through the double doors of St. Stephen's. The other mothers were standing around with push-chairs, some still wearing their slippers and with a head of hair that looked like it hadn't seen the shampoo bottle in over a month. What must their husbands think? Vera wondered if John had ever seen her without her lipstick on.

"Fuck!" The word shot across the playground like a faulty firework. "Fuck! FUCK!"

The blood drained from Vera's Estee Lauder face when she realised that the word was being yelled by a child in a buggy. He was no more than two years old.

"Shut the fuck up, Wayne," his mother said, slapping him across the head with the hand that was *not* holding a lit cigarette. "And who do you think you're looking at, lady?"

Vera had been cornered, staring. It was a habit of Vera's – to stare. Mary had told her time and time again that she was snooty, always looking other people up and down with her eyes, judging them. Only Vera wasn't snooty at all, she was just nosy. She smiled at little Wayne's mother, apologising with a jitter, making a signal that she was in a world of her own and looked in the opposite direction with haste. Good Lord, that woman had probably never seen a lipstick in her life. If handed one, Vera bet that she would smoke it.

"Aunty Vera!" Star skipped over, her grey school cardigan falling off her shoulders and her arms weighed down with a multitude of stuff; a pink lunch box, a plastic folder that looked like it contained a book of some sort, a Sainsbury's carrier bag ready to burst and a large piece of black sugar paper. "I love it when you pick me up. Is Uncle John here, too?"

"Yes, my luv, he's in the car with Nannie."

"Yay!" Star dropped the carrier bag on the floor and a small black plimsoll rolled out. "Oops. I can manage, you know. I'm very self-reliant."

"I'm sure you are. Did you have PE today?" Vera asked, picking the bag up.

Star blew out her lips and sighed, her arms fidgeting trying to get her cardigan back on her shoulders. "Yes. Athletics. I hate athletics. Hate it."

"But why? You love dancing."

"That's what the teachers say! But no one understands. Sports and dancing are so not the same. I try and try so hard, Aunty Vera, but I come last in every race. And not just last, but miles behind everyone else. Mr Broadbent – that's our PE teacher – thinks I'm lazy because everyone knows that I go to dancing every week, but I'm not lazy, I just can't run fast. And I know that my legs are short, but that can't be stopping me because Shelley Bartley is the fastest girl in the class and I'm this much taller than her." Star held up her hand, holding her thumb and finger about an inch apart and scrunching one eye closed to concentrate.

"Oh dear," Vera said. "Well, I was rubbish at sports at school, too."

"Great." There was a hint of sarcasm in Star's voice. Wasn't Star too young for sarcasm? What was this school teaching her?

"What's that supposed to mean?"

"Being good at PE means that you're cool. All I can do is the egg and spoon race because I'm good at balancing. Balancing is not cool."

"Cool?" Vera let out a little laugh.

"It's what they say in *Grease*. You know, the Pink Ladies?"

"I didn't know you'd seen *Grease*."

Star stopped being sulky and looked worried. "I watched it at Louise Fitzpatrick's house. Her big sister is obsessed with it. Don't tell Nannie."

"It can be our secret," Vera said. "At least it wasn't *Dirty Dancing*."

Star took the carrier bag back from Vera, walking ahead out of the school gates, arms full to the brim again. "Oh, I've seen that, too."

Vera looked towards St. Stephen's church and made a Sign of the Cross. She noticed Little Wayne's mother catching her do so, and Vera followed Star hurriedly. "I'll never be cool."

*

Uncle John had come to collect Star in his car because they were all going to take Nannie to Fazakerley Hospital for a check-up on her hip. It was a few years ago when Nannie had had to have a plastic hip put in to replace her bad one, and the doctors liked to double check that everything was still fine once in a while. Star didn't mind, in fact, she quite enjoyed a trip to Fazakerley Hospital. The waiting area had different toys to what she had at home and they always stopped off at the Hen and Chickens pub on the way back for some tea because Uncle John liked the mixed grill there so much. There was a special children's menu with food like turkey dinosaurs, chips and beans, and the Hen and Chickens also had a play area with swings made from tyres. However, it had been raining all day, something that Star knew too well because the stupid rain had not stopped Mr Broadbent from making her class race around the muddy school field.

Aunty Vera had offered to go inside with her sister, but Nannie had told her to wait in the car with Uncle John – who was reading his paper – because she didn't want Aunty Vera to faint again. Every time Aunty Vera went inside a hospital she fainted. It was a good thing, really, that it only ever happened in hospitals because of all the doctors and nurses around to help her. If she fainted in her house, she might die because Uncle John was always in the garden mowing the lawn. Star thought that it must be the funny hospital smell that did it and maybe Aunty Vera was allergic to it, just like Christopher McGinty was allergic to soap.

The hip replacement doctors were on the third floor, which was a bit silly really because people with bad hips could not walk up the stairs. What if the lift broke? Star counted seven vending machines on the way through the corridors, but despite really fancying an Aero or a packet of Hula Hoops, she knew that the only time that she was allowed to use a vending machine was at the swimming baths. Snacks now would spoil her tea at the Hen and Chickens. So it was a pretty big shock when Nannie stopped at the seventh one and took her purse out of her handbag.

"What are you doing?" Star asked. "You'll spoil your tea."

Nannie slipped a twenty pence piece into the slot. "I want some fruit pastels."

Star was amazed. "Why?"

"Grown-ups like sweets, too, you know. If you're good, I'll give you one."

"A black one?"

"If you're good."

Star knew that Nannie loved her sweets. A packet of Mint Imperials and a bag of Liquorice Allsorts were the only thing that she ever asked for at Christmas, and they always got more thanks than the slippers from Marks and Spencer or the Nivea hand cream. However, Star couldn't understand how Nannie saved her sweets for so long. One packet of fruit drops lasted a week in Nannie's handbag, whereas Star – or anyone at her school, for sure – would have to eat them all at once. Why save a sweet for later when you could have it now?

There was a lot that she didn't understand, Star thought, as she took a seat next to Nannie in the waiting area on the third floor. Although it was a nice trip out to Fazakerley Hospital, Star knew that she was in the last building that her mother ever went inside; she had heard her daddy say so lots of times. As she watched Nannie sucking a fruit pastel, Star thought about her mummy, imagining what it would be like sitting next to her instead. She knew exactly what she looked like, there were so many photographs of her around their house; on the mantelpiece, scattered on the walls and there were piles of albums on the top of her daddy's wardrobe. Some pictures were in black and white, but the coloured ones showed her mother's brown hair, much darker than Star's, and the colourful clothes she had worn, like turquoise, lilac and baby pink. In every picture, her mother was smiling and just like Star, she had a dimple in her right cheek. There was a lovely one of her parents on their wedding day cutting the cake, and Star would place her finger on her mummy's dimple, pretending she could feel it. She often wondered what her voice sounded like, whether it was gentle like the mothers in Shirley Temple films or shrill like Louise Fitzpatrick's mum when she laughed loudly at Mick Tully's jokes that weren't funny. And if the doctors could fix Nannie's bad hip, and stop all the blood coming out from her daddy's nose when he was a little boy, and take out Simon Monaghan's tonsils without killing him, how did they let her mummy die when she was only going into the hospital to have a baby? To have *her*.

Yes, there were lots of things that Star didn't understand.

"Mrs. Mack?" a nurse called out.

"Here you go," Nannie dropped a black fruit pastel into Star's lap, and it bounced, sugar sprinkling over her green checked school dress.

*

Vera took her place in the passenger seat of John's car. She was fanning her face with a leaflet on Measles, Mumps and Rubella that she had found on the ground in the car park, having folded it back and forth like a concertina.

"Everything alright, dear?" John asked his eyes fixed on the paper.

"Nausea."

"I told you not to go inside…"

"And I didn't. I went for a little walk, just as I promised, but I saw a child on crutches… a child!"

"Bloody hell," John said. "You get worse. How did you manage to live through the war? We couldn't walk down the street without seeing blood all over the bloody place."

Vera fanned faster. "Yes, and I lost four stone during that bloody war. And it wasn't due to sugar rations!"

John took hold of Vera's hand and took the fan from her. He stroked her forehead and she allowed her head to fall back and rest, as John obliged with the fanning for her. Radio Merseyside resonated through the car speakers gently, Perry Como's voice with 'Magic Moments' humming around the interior.

"What else is on your mind?" John asked.

Vera shook her head, pressing her lips together, so perfectly lined with Clinique's disco-pink.

"Come on, dear. What is it?"

"It's just all so unfair, John. I don't understand it. How can horrible things happen to good people all the time and good things happen to nasty people? I mean, I know it's not *real*, but I'm just using this as an example because life must imitate art, or so they say…"

"Dear, just calm down and get on with it."

"Sorry. Well, you know in *Dynasty*?"

"Mmm."

"Well, the characters are pretty nasty and ooh, John, they are so bitchy, yet they have everything that they want. They have perfect clothes, and stylists and hairdressers and as many attractive men as they could wish for – sorry, and so much money that even if one of them goes to jail, they could probably buy themselves out. And I bet they never go to church, those *Dynasty* folk, do they? And then you've got lovely Jimmy and he lost his lovely Linda, and now Star doesn't have her daddy around because of the stupid goings on down on the docks, and our Mary. Oh, John, I just feel it for our Mary." Vera's eyes had been getting wider and wider, but she blinked and the tears rolled down her cheeks. "Oh, shit!" She reached down and grabbed her handbag, whipping out her powder puff and mascara. "Well, haven't you got anything to say? Or are you just going to sit there, John?"

"Dear. I'm afraid you have a soft soul, too soft and sweet for this world. It's just the way it is. Bad things happen to good people, and good things happen to bad people. But bad things happen to bad people and good things also do happen to good people. We just need to recognise them when they come along."

"But Mary, John," Vera sniffled. "I've got you and despite the comments about all of the attractive men on *Dynasty*, I wouldn't change you for any of them. You know, I've never told you but I wouldn't even change you for Michael Landon in *Highway to*

Heaven although I threaten you with it all the time. But our Mary; she's so good. Yeah, she's bossy and the most stubborn woman on this planet, and she got her hair cut too short when she was far too young to lose her youth like that, but she's a good person. When I think of what she's been through in her life, what she's lost, what if she loses Star next?"

John pressed his finger gently to her lips. "It won't happen, dear."

"I don't know, John. I can feel it in my water."

John turned the volume up on the car stereo. "Listen." The Carpenters were inging 'Yesterday Once More' and it reminded Vera of taking Star to Blackpool when she was just a toddler. Even at barely three years old, every time Karen Carpenter sang a 'sha-la-la-lah' or a 'woah-wo-oh' Star would copy and sing along with so much passion.

"Bloody excellent," John had said. "A kid in the Eighties with the musical taste of Shirley bleedin' Temple and Karen bloody Carpenter. Forget cartoons and puppets and pop stars that do that thing where they rip their skirts off. Shirley Temple and the bloody Carpenters. She'll be very popular."

Vera did end up a touch thwarted, because when the song ended, little Star said, "Again, please. Again, please." The first time she asked, Vera was quite happy to rewind the tape and play the song again; it was a joy to listen to the velvet tones of the lovely Karen.

Only the mistake of rewinding it taught little Star that this was possible, and she asked for it again and again and again and again. Vera had been looking forward to hearing the whole album – especially, 'I Know I Need to be in Love', which always made her cry, yet she embraced the release it gave her.

The disenchantment of the trip continued when after about seven 'sha-la-la-lah's' and just as many 'woah-wo-oh's', Star had tired herself right out and fell fast asleep. John had been driving for nearly two hours, and they were just ten minutes from reaching Blackpool. The only reason that they had decided to go had been to show Star the illuminations, so it was dark, not to mention raining. Vera and John joined the traffic queue and viewed the illuminations from the car window, crawling up the road at ten miles an hour.

"Shall we get some chips and curry sauce?" Vera asked when they had almost come to the end of all the lights.

"Nah, it'll stink the car out," John replied. "Anyway, Chan's might still be open if we turn around and head home now."

Star was so deep in her sleep that the toddler was snoring.

Vera laughed, thinking about the whole trip. It was about five years ago now.

"Bleedin' Blackpool bloody illuminations," John muttered, and they both howled with laughter. "Anyway, dear, you wait here. I'm a bit peckish and off to grab something from the vending machine."

"But we're going to the Hen and Chickens," Vera said, annoyed at his childishness.

"I just fancy some fruit pastels or something. Don't worry; I'll share them with you."

"You're just as bad as our Mary."

John leant over and kissed Vera on the cheek, as to not smudge her lipstick.

"John," Vera stopped him just before he got out. "It would be nice to take Star on a little trip again, wouldn't it? You know, get her out of Liverpool. I reckon it'd do the kid a world of good."

"So long as she stays awake."

*

Star was let down by the toy collection. The Fisher Price garage with the multi-storey car park was no longer there, leaving the grey plastic table just covered with a few Sticklebricks and the odd piece of Lego. It was a guilty pleasure of Star's, to play with boys toys. She loved her dolls, loved her storybooks and loved to dress up, but boys toys were a novelty. It was the only reason that she never kicked up a fuss about going round to Christopher McGinty's house for a couple of hours on a Wednesday evening when Jimmy would take Nannie to the bingo. She could put up with the crusty bogies around his nostrils for the sake of a dramatic car chase on the carpet followed by a session on the Spectrum.

A woman emerged from a treatment room pushing a girl in a wheelchair.

"You stay here," the woman said, leaving the girl in the waiting room, and going back in to see the doctor. Star thought what a ridiculous thing that was to say to a girl in a wheelchair. It wasn't as if she could get very far on her own and in a hospital no less.

But the girl looked sad, or maybe she was fed-up, just like Star felt whenever she had had to listen to Emma-Jane Duggan destroy Judy Garland's dignity.

"Hello," Star said, abandoning the Lego.

The girl looked up, but quickly drew her head down again when she saw that only Star was in the room. She was much older, maybe twelve or even thirteen, and she was wearing her own clothes so she mustn't have been to school today. There would have been no time to get changed.

"Hello?" Star tried again.

"Hello." The girl said without even opening her mouth.

Star took a step closer to the girl. "I'm Star."

The girl laughed, but only through her nose. Star was kind of used it; it was either a peculiar type of laugh or some sort of question about how her name could not actually be 'Star'.

"Well, I am and I promise I won't laugh at your name because to be honest, it's quite annoying." Star's hands were on her hips, just the way Nannie did when she intimidated people. It always worked.

"I'm Claire," the girl said. "Is your name really Star?"

"I get sick of people asking me that."

"Why?"

"Do you get sick of people asking you why you're in a wheelchair?"

"Erm. No, actually," Claire looked a little shocked.

"Oh." Star let her arms drop to her sides, her head cocked to the left allowing her pony tail to swing. "Then, why *are* you in a wheelchair?"

"Because my spine's all twisted, like a helter-skelter," Claire said.

"But what about your legs? Are your legs all twisted, too?"

Claire chuckled, shaking her head.

"Then, why can't you walk?"

"I don't know!" Both girls started to laugh out loud until a nurse walked by and said, "Shhh." They continued snickering through their noses, keeping their mouths shut tight to stop any noise coming out, which proved to be very difficult. It was the same whenever Anthony Tucker swore in school and made Miss Murphy's face go so red that it became purple, or that time when Mrs Duggan slipped on an apple core in the playground and landed right on her bottom.

"How old are you, Claire?" Star asked, taking a big breath to calm her silly self down and taking a step closer to the wheelchair.

"I'm a teenager," Claire said, but she sounded sad. Or maybe fed-up again.

"I go to St. Stephen's school. What school do you go to?"

Claire glanced towards the treatment room where she had been just a few minutes earlier. "I don't go to school."

"Did you know that children who are film-stars don't go to school but have private lessons in a trailer?" Star smiled. "I'd love that."

"My mum teaches me from home. And I hate it. It's lonely."

Star had never thought of it like that. She was used to having tons of boys and girls around her, some who she liked a lot, but some who smelt pretty awful. Taking one more baby-step forward, Star's fingertips reached out to touch the arm of Claire's chair. She walked around her new friend in a circle, letting her hand slowly drag behind her, always touching the frame. Claire started to giggle. "Twirl me," she said.

"Twirl you?"

"Hold the handles and run around in a circle," Claire said.

The handles were higher than Star's shoulders, but she grabbed them anyway and started to move around slowly.

"Faster," Claire said. "Go on, faster and faster…"

They spun together around and around, Star joining Claire with her own giggles and they kept going until the nurse told them to hush down again. Although Claire was still smiling, she was breathless, which confused Star since she had been the one doing all the work.

"How come you don't get bored of people asking why you're in a wheelchair?" Star asked.

"Easy," Claire shrugged, "because nobody ever asks."

"Oh my goodness."

"They just stare. Now that *is* boring."

But how could nobody ask? It was the first thing that Star thought of because she had only ever seen old people in wheelchairs in real-life, or people who were very, very sick, maybe with a tube on their face or a blanket over their legs. Claire was pretty and her hair was all blonde and crimped. She wore a denim jacket with bright pink lining, and if only Nannie didn't think that denim was "common", Star would totally choose a jacket like that.

"Can I touch the helter-skelter, please?" Star asked.

For no obvious reason, Claire giggled again and nodded her head, moving slightly forward in her chair. With full concentration on being gentle, Star touched Claire's back and ran her fingertips up and down her spine in the same way that she had touched the wheelchair.

"What does it feel like, Star?"

Star stopped and looked at Claire, with her lovely crimped hair. "It just feels like a regular back to me."

And suddenly the two girls had nothing to say to each other. The silence hovered around the waiting room, desperate for some more giggling and shushing from the nurse.

"I think you can walk," Star said finally.

"What? Don't be soft!"

"I'm not soft. You should try and walk; I bet if you practised and worked hard you could do it…"

"No, Star. I can't. My mum has told me that there is nothing that the doctor's can do…"

"There is no such word as 'can't'."

"Yes there is, Star. *CAN'T*." Claire did one of her giggles. "*CAN'T*."

It was hands-on-the-hips time. "My ballet teacher always says that there is no such word as 'can't' and it makes us be better ballerinas. And there is this boy in our school called Martin Woods, and he is in the top juniors and has to come to my class during reading time. Everyone says it's because he can't read. But do you know what? I heard him reading out loud and clear to Miss Murphy – that's my teacher – and even though everyone says he can't, I know he can. He can read."

Claire lifted her hands from her lap and out to Star, who took them, first the right and then the left. Her fingernails were painted a bright pink to match her jacket lining, just what Aunty Vera liked to do.

"We have to go slowly, Star," Claire said, a little shake in her voice. Her neck grew tall and her body edged forward, although the grip on Star's hands was tight, so tight that it was hard to hold back an "ouch". Claire was ready.

"After three, Claire. One, two…"

"Claire! No!" A woman cried. Claire jolted back and Star leapt against the far wall. "Just what do you think you are playing at?"

Claire's mum was standing with a doctor, her hands gripping a navy blue handbag, the lines deep set in her face crumpling up.

"Sorry it was my fault," Star said, terrified of Claire being told off by such a cross woman. "We were just dancing." Although Claire was fond of the giggling, Star never thought that now would be a time to have an outburst, but she did, telling her mum to leave Star alone.

"Star? Star?!" Claire's mum clomped right over to Star, still up against the wall, exposing so much nostril that Star reckoned that if she tried hard enough, she might see brain. "How old are you?"

"I'm eight. How old are you?"

Claire's giggles rose.

"How dare you!" Claire's mum said. She had breath like tuna. "Are you being impudent?"

Star had no idea what that meant but it did not sound nice at all. "I'm sorry. My daddy always taught me to be polite to old ladies."

A snort came from the direction of Claire and her giggle fit, just as Nannie stepped out of her treatment room, thanking her doctor. Star wished that Mr Broadbent, the PE teacher, was there to witness it because never in her life had she ran as fast as she did over to Nannie, eager to get away from such a cross old woman. As they left the waiting room together, Star looked back at Claire who had sank into her chair and looked sad once again. Only this time it really was sad, not fed-up.

24th May, 1989

Whenever Jimmy lay on his single bed in the cell that he shared with Addo, the Liverpool supporter, he stared at the ceiling, at the three chips of paint shaped like rough circles. They went in a straight diagonal line, just like Orion's Belt. For hours and hours he would lie, just looking, burning holes into the concrete, trying to set fire to the chips and turn them into real stars. It was during this time when he thought of his own star, his daughter and prayed that no harm would ever come to her. And as the night drew on, lights out, it was his time to think about Linda. This was the worst part, causing insomnia, too guilty to allow himself to drift off and dream away from the reality that he had found himself in. Either way, Jimmy was torturing himself. If he wasn't using all of his mind's strength to relive his and Linda's happy memories - like a home video, a little distorted but cringing and smiling all at once – he was imagining how disappointed she would be in him, how she could never forgive him.

Addo lay awake, too. Jimmy knew this because it took at least two hours every night for Addo's snoring to kick in. This was usually the time when Jimmy's bad thoughts would surface, the noise being too much to hold any fondness.

And of all things, being locked up in a cell with a Red, no less. It was just Jimmy Blake's luck. With a Blue, they could have had a decent talk about the game not to mention a joint passion, a love. However, it could be worse. Jimmy respected Addo as a Red. He had a season ticket at Anfield and had gone to the game with his own dad every Saturday afternoon since he could walk. The same as Jonesy.

The fake stars in Jimmy's cell could still be seen, and he had thought about standing on his bed, reaching up and making a further two marks in the yellow-stained paint to represent the small stars symmetrically either side to the middle of the 'Belt'. It had been New Year's Eve a couple of years back, when Jimmy took Star down to Crosby Marina for midnight. It was a clear night, bitter, but clear and the sky over the River Mersey could have been mistaken for the

Planetarium in the museum. Star had been wrapped and layered up by Mary Mack so much that the child looked like a jumble sale with a face.

"Do you think she's playing out tonight, daddy?" Star asked.

"It's New Year's Eve," Jimmy replied. "If I know your mummy, then she'll be out in her best dress and dancing away more than anyone else up there."

Standing by the rails, overlooking the water lapping in and back out again from the sand before them, they both let their heads flop back to examine the night sky.

"Which one is she?"

Jimmy wanted to point to the North Star, glowing from blue to pink and back to blue again.

"That's her, right there!" Star reached out, pointing her little chubby finger up and down the line of Orion's Belt. "She's three stars."

"Why three?"

"When you talk about mummy, you sometimes call her Linda. And then sometimes you say, 'my wife'. She's three people all in one."

"You're a clever girl, Star."

"I'm on the Yellow Reading Books," she said proudly.

Jimmy picked up his daughter, letting her sit on the rail, but holding her tight, close to him. "Star, can you see there are two small stars either side of the middle of mummy?"

Star nodded.

"They are your grandparents. That star is my ma and da," Jimmy pointed to one, then the other, "and the other star is Linda's parents. They're taking care of her."

"But how can two people be one star and mummy is three?"

He'd asked for it. "Because your grandparents have all been dead a long, long time and they wanted to stick together forever."

"Okay, daddy. Can we get a hotdog now?"

God, Jimmy prayed for Star to be alright, to be the same kid as she was the last day that he saw her. Mary always gave him a full report when she came in to visit; how she had learnt to do a time-step in tap dancing, and that she was still hopelessly in love with that Monaghan kid who both Jimmy and Mary thought was a bit wet. They were of the same mind that it was not right to bring Star in to see her daddy yet. Soon, but not just yet.

Across the table, Jimmy could smell Mary's kitchen; the scones, the pastry, even a whiff of the chip pan smelt good. But he had a rule. He would only talk about his daughter or the football results. Sometimes he asked after Vera and John, and if he remembered he would send his love to Sheila Gilhooley just to wind Mary Mack up. He would not break down. Not in front of the woman who had brought him up and loved him like a son… and yet, he had still turned out as rubbish as all of the other lowlifes he was locked up with. And now he worried for Star, that even with all the love in the world, did she need something more to save her from this life?

Now, in his dark cell, his thoughts were about to turn to Linda when Addo snorted in and breathed out his first snore of the night, although by this time it was already early hours into the next day. Jimmy rolled onto one side, facing the wall and its bubbled yellow-stained paint, and tried not to think about the night on the dock road or asking Linda for forgiveness. Instead, as rain began to tap against the thick window behind bars, he thought about Christine.

*

The trees did get chopped down. Christopher McGinty had been right all along. Star was round at his house – mid way through Daley Thompson's Decathlon on the Spectrum, only Star was still waiting for Christopher to get his dirty fingers off the joystick – when Louise Fitzpatrick knocked.

It was Star who answered the door and she was relieved to not get teased again about being Christopher McGinty's secret girlfriend, seeing as Louise had a good posse behind her including

Steph Bradley and Laura Fenton. Star was surprised that nobody was on their bikes, but then she noticed the rain. It was coming down faster than the shower at Aunty Vera and Uncle John's house, making the grey pavement as shiny as a new ten pence piece.

"It's over," Louise moaned. "Our trees are gone."

"Told yer!" Christopher McGinty bellowed into Star's ear, causing her to hear teeny bells ringing in it for hours afterwards.

"There's just a giant puddle…" Steph Bradley piped up.

"The size of Crosby baths…" Laura Fenton added. "So me mother says."

Christopher McGinty gave a hard laugh that was actually more of a spit from the back of his throat. "I don't believe you. How can a puddle be the size of Crosby baths?"

"I just said, didn't I? Me mother told me."

"Still don't believe you. Show us."

The girls marched off, Christopher McGinty running up behind them not even bothering to fetch his coat, with Star following on. They crossed the road and slipped through the alleyway that led to the entry between the back yards of the odd numbered houses on Flinder Street and the even numbers on Ripton Street. A yappy little dog started barking and chased the children, making them scream much louder than necessary. The rain was showing no signs of easing off, the clouds angry and low, heavy above their heads and as the five pairs of feet touched the grassy field they were covered in thick mud immediately. Star looked down at her white Gola trainers with silver and pink ribbons, now black, splashed with thick filth. She imagined that this was what sinking sand must feel like, soft and mushy up to your ankles, but this no longer mattered once she caught sight of their beloved trees, their climbing frames, gone.

Star had never known such quiet on the field, especially with Louise Fitzpatrick *and* Christopher McGinty sharing the same breathing space; it was pretty much a miracle that none of them spoke a word. Star looked at her pals, their mouths all hanging open in silence and then realised that she was doing the same. If Mary Poppins had been there, she would have told them to shut their mouths please because they are not codfish. Closer to the puddle, to the place where their trees had once stood, were a few more children from St. Stephen's. Anthony Tucker was crouched down with Peter Healy making mud pies, their muddy football lolling about on the grass beside them, redundant.

"Aahhhh," Christopher McGinty cried out, echoing around the field. "Where are we going to climb now, eh?"

"I know," Steph said. "We can't exactly go to the Boysy…"

"No way am I going to the Boysy," Laura reinforced, as Louise stood with her arms folded and shaking her head adamantly.

Of course they could not hang outside the Boys' Club, even though girls went along, too. The Boys' Club was the playing territory of St. Gertrude's kids; the rivals of St. Stephens. They didn't have trees to climb but the roof of the Boysy was low and flat, and the older juniors of St. Gertrude's would stand on it for hours every evening throwing twigs at passing cars and having spitting contests. Star had a particular dislike for the St. Gertrude's boys ever since she bumped into a couple outside of Si's newsagents last year. They flicked sweet dolly beads at her legs - pinging the elastic that connected the small, pastel-coloured lumps of sugar together with their teeth, and then spitting the sweet out of their mouths at top speed - and the pain was so sharp, so intense, it was as if she had been shot. But she did not cry – well, not in front of the boys anyway - because it would let the name of St. Stephen's down if she even so much as flinched in the face of the enemy. And the St. Gertrude's girls were weird, too. They never went up onto the roof, choosing instead to sit on the brick wall by the Boysy car park doing nothing at all except chew Hubba Bubba and letting their legs swing.

So no, the Boysy was out of the question. The field – trees or no trees – was where they would still have to play.

"Do you reckon that puddle is as *deep* as Crosby baths?" Steph asked, looking to Laura Fenton who seemed to be the expert on this subject.

"Dunno," Laura squinted, thinking carefully. "Maybe as deep as the baby end, but I don't reckon you could dive into it. I don't remember the slope being that, erm, slopey."

Louise Fitzpatrick was getting restless. She was doing her breathing and scowling trick, the one where she stuck out her bottom lip and let the air escape slowly through her teeth. Star had seen Louise's mother do the same thing when Christopher McGinty put Flora margarine onto her cat's paws. However, the lad did win himself a four-finger KitKat courtesy of Star's daddy for doing so, and all because the cat's name was Ian Rush.

"Aye, Tucker! I dare you to get in the puddle and see how deep it goes," Louise shouted.

Anthony Tucker pulled himself up to standing, his hands black with soil. "I'm not taking a dare off a girl. But I double dare *you*," he said, flicking mud onto Peter Healy's head. Poor Peter Healy. He had no choice but to do the dare this time. It had only been a few weeks since Peter Healy had said 'no' to a Tucker Dare; he had been triple-dared to pull down Laura Fenton's knickers when their class were drawing each other's shadows in chalk on the playground. Peter had "bottled it" – according to Tucker – and had had his beef paste butties nicked and eaten before lunch-time every single school day since. Sometimes, if Tucker was in a good mood, he left the crisps for Peter, but only if they were ready salted.

Louise started the clapping; slow, loud claps, chanting, "Hea-ly, Hea-ly, Hea-ly…" to which the other children joined in. Peter began to remove his trainers and his socks, which seemed pretty pointless as they were drenched in rain and mud anyhow. He edged up to the puddle, nearer and nearer, and with every step he became less steady due to the ground being so soft, encasing his feet with every splodge.

"Go 'ed, Healy!" Louise yelled.

He was just about to step into the water, his right foot dangling in the air and his hands holding his tracksuit bottoms up at the knees, when Tucker picked up the football and threw it, whacking Peter Healy on the back. He lost his balance and toppled into the giant puddle with a belly-flop, the intensity of the splash covering Anthony Tucker from head to toe.

Peter's head emerged from the water, and he stood up. The water was just past his knees, and despite the mud, he looked rather clean. The rain was pelting down, so he was not much wetter than anybody else on the field. He looked at Tucker, and over at the other children, and grinned. "It's boss!" he yelled, splashing around and making no attempt at getting out.

Tucker jumped in next, unable to resist a splashing match. Star felt a harsh brush against her shoulder as Christopher McGinty rushed past to join the boys, but he tripped on his way causing him to slide all the way into the puddle head first.

"I'm not going in!" Laura Fenton said.

"Me neither!" Steph agreed, only Anthony Tucker was already running towards them like a water monster, chasing the girls around the field.

Star panicked. She was the worst runner at her school, and if anybody knew that, Anthony Tucker did. His favourite game was to pick on people and their weaknesses; he was famous for putting worms in other children's packed lunch boxes and once, he even cut his own fingers with scissors just to scare the squeamish by the sight of his blood. Pushing the girls into a giant puddle was as easy as asking for a hamburger in McDonald's. He was going after Louise first, who could run fairly fast and would put up a decent wrestle before landing in the water, so Star had time to start her escape. But she couldn't. Her feet were sinking more and more into the mud, and her fear took over any energy she had to try. She thought about how back in the olden days, in the Deep South, people were baptised in the river. It was true; it must be, for she had seen Shirley Temple do so with lots of black people in the film, *The Little Colonel*. Star had been watching that film lots lately because it featured the famous stair dance with Shirley and Billy 'Bojangles' Robinson, and Star had been trying to learn the dance so that it would make going upstairs to bedtime a little more exciting. Plus, if she watched really closely, she could try to learn Billy's bits and teach them to Uncle John…

Star's thoughts about stair-dancing vanished when she was swept up off her feet and thrown over Anthony Tucker's shoulder. She started screeching and beating him on his back with her fists, but before she knew it, she was flying through the air, landing with a huge splash. Her entire body fell under the water, her head and her pony-tail saturated, as she popped up wiping her eyes. Around her, everybody was now screaming, yet enjoying themselves, getting over-excited by how wet they all were.

"Hallelujah! We're cleansed!" Star said, throwing her arms up high.

"Y'what?" various voices asked her.

"We're cleansed! All of our sins are washed away."

"Even mine?" Anthony Tucker asked.

"Yes, Tucker," Star laughed, bobbing up and down in the water. "We are all cleansed. All of our bad thoughts are set free. Hallelujah! We are all baptised."

"I got baptised when I was a baby in St. Stephen's church," Laura Fenton said.

"So did I," Steph added.

"Oh, never mind," Star said, and she ducked herself under the puddle again. It was a really great idea to hold onto, that all of her bad thoughts could be set free by being 'cleansed'. Her world seemed to be jam-packed full of bad thoughts lately; Nannie's face had gained extra worry lines, more questions about her dead mother kept popping into her head, and if only, if only Mrs Duggan had let her play Dorothy… Her daddy would have definitely made it to see the school production then, and he wouldn't have been at home for the police to come and take him away. Ooh, the water felt nice and warm – though not quite as warm as Crosby baths – and Star shouted one more time. "Hallelujah!"

"She's crackers," Christopher McGinty said.

*

It gave Mary a right fright when she heard the sound of fists banging on her front door. Even the Jehovah's Witnesses knew about her broken doorbell and always rapped on the window, so she was baffled to think who could be calling round to see her. Standing there on her front step were two women each under a black umbrella; one dressed a bit like Star's teacher, Miss Murphy, all baggy skirts and baggy cardigan-like, and the other resembling a smart model from the Grattan catalogue decked out from head to toe in beige and navy blue.

"Mrs. Mack?" the baggy-lady said, holding out her hand. "Pleased to meet you. My name is Jeanette Young and this is…"

"Susan Lloyd," the catalogue-lady copied the action. Mary stared at both right hands hovering under her nose.

Lloyd. *Lloyd*. Linda Lloyd… Linda's maiden name. Mary caught Susan Lloyd's eyes, those familiar green, almond shaped eyes. It was a shame about this woman's nose, humped like a little village bridge, yet her pale skin was soft and clear, just as Linda's had been. That Jeanette Young had continued to speak, mentioning the words 'welfare' and 'social' something or other, but Mary needed no further introduction. This green-eyed Susan woman was Linda's sister.

And Star's only legal guardian.

"May we come in Mrs. Mack?" Jeanette Young asked, already folding down her umbrella and moving forward.

Mary held the door back and allowed the two women to pass her by. The splatter of the rain was loud, like cymbals crashing over and over, and Mary left the door on the latch so that Star could run straight in without having to wait for even a second. It was almost six o'clock, and she was due back from the McGinty's for her tea at any moment. Mrs. McGinty always offered to let Star eat at their house, but after the corned beef hash episode, Star said that she'd rather starve than have to go through that again. Apparently there was more water than potato lumped onto the plate and Star wouldn't even want to send it to the poor children in Africa; it would be an insult.

"Let me put the kettle on," Mary suggested, seeing as the women had already sat on the couch and begun taking off their overcoats.

"Thank you, but we're fine…" Jeanette Young said.

"I'll have tea, please," Susan Lloyd interrupted with a wide-open smile that could compete with the Mersey Tunnel spreading across her face. "Thank you. I'm not sure if you remember me, Mary – it's alright if I call you Mary?"

Mary nodded.

"Lovely. Mary, we met properly at Linda and Jimmy's wedding. But I guess we have met more over the years…"

"I know who you are," Mary cut in. "You're Susan. You look just like her. Older, but the similarities are quite clear. And I've seen you in dozens of photos, from years ago of course, but people don't change that much really, do they?"

Susan laughed in a sweet manner that confused Mary since nothing she had said was at all funny. It was so sweet that she looked like a thirteen year old girl being asked to the school disco by the captain of the football team. What was this woman's game?

"Do you still live in London?" Mary asked. Susan had moved to London around about the same time as Jimmy started to court Linda. All Mary knew was that this older sister had some posh job as a secretary for a law firm, writing in shorthand and typing quicker than even a Scouser could speak. Apparently she married a barrister. Linda was forever going on about how fabulous it must be to live in the capital city and how proud their mum and dad would have been of Susan if they had been alive. Mary thought it must have indeed been bleedin' fabulous seeing as this Susan had hardly shown her face in Liverpool since she moved and that was for her little sister's funeral. And even then she only stuck around for the day.

"No, I live here now. Well, Southport to be precise," Susan replied, her voice sharp and surprised, and with no hint of her original Liverpudlian accent. "You have an exceptional memory, Mary."

"Not really, Susan. I was just exceptionally close to your Linda." Mary turned on the heels of her slippers and headed into the kitchen. It was only as she picked up the kettle to put it under the tap that she noticed her hands trembling. As she flicked the switch on to begin the boil, Mary whipped open the fridge and started to slice up some red Leicester cheese and a few tomatoes for sandwiches. What were they doing here? *What* were they doing and what did they want? Only Mary needn't ask herself these questions. Anyone as soft as the butter she was spreading onto the white sliced bread would know the answer. But how could a woman not bother keeping in touch with her only sister, and then just turn up one day to snoop about her only niece? Mary pressed hard with the butter knife into the sandwiches. They were all done, carefully cut into triangles and placed on a china plate by the time the tea was in the pot. Thank goodness the trembles had stopped.

"Oh really, there was no need," Jeanette Young said as Mary carried in the tray of refreshments.

"It's no trouble," Mary said, calmly taking a seat in the armchair. "There's a pan of homemade chicken soup out there if you fancy a bowl. I'll be heating it up any minute for Star's tea."

Susan coughed, allowing a sharp laugh to escape, and turning it back into a cough. "You actually call the little girl Star? What happened to Rebecca?"

"It's never been Rebecca. On paper, yes. But she is Star."

Then the quizzing took off. Mary felt as though she was on *Mastermind*, the amount of information about one singular subject that she was asked about. Where was the child? When would she be coming back? How often did she get left at the house next-door-but-one? Was she doing well at school? Did the dancing lessons distract her from school work? Was she attending church every week? The child, the child, the child… The child had a name! Mary found herself using Star's name more during this interrogation than she believed she had done in her whole life. Star! Star! Star! And these women were not listening to Mary's answers, oh no. They were listening out for ways in which they *wanted* to hear the answers, how to catch Mary Mack out. They wanted to hear that Rebecca Blake was unhappy, or dysfunctional, or suffering with her reading books and sums. It made no difference to them that Star Blake had just won a Ladybird book of poems for winning a spelling test or that she could sing a song from a musical in front of a hundred people without feeling nervous. Of course, the child had been down lately, she had witnessed her father being robbed from her life, but she had stability, she had love. There was a cardboard box next to the television set full of felt, old wrapping paper, empty margarine tubs and all sorts of bits and pieces, which was Star's special collection labelled 'Things for Making Things'. Mary helped her 'make things' every Sunday morning – cutting and gluing - while they ate omelettes and watched *The Waltons* followed by *Land of the Giants*. Only a few days ago, they made a Polaroid camera from Imperial Leather soap boxes and a punched out packet of Paracetamol; quite a creation. And Star only had two pairs of school shoes – black patent leather ones for the winter and white sandals for the summer – yet there wasn't a single mark on them and Mary had them heeled every other month. This baggy-clothed welfare woman was in the wrong house; it was that Laura Fenton who had to cook her own meals and turn up to school in a pinafore that had never seen the inside of a washing machine. Mary found herself saying these thoughts out loud, but she was met with just the one conclusion. *I am not her legal guardian.*

Jeanette Young took a sandwich, breaking it into two with her fingers. Her nails were stubby and bitten, and Mary hoped it was due to the guilt that she felt at having a job which allowed her to be so judgemental. "Ms. Lloyd is Rebecca's – Star's – only legal guardian, now that her father is in prison…"

"Yes, but he's innocent. The trial will be soon…" Mary tried.

"Mrs. Mack, the child cannot live a stable life waiting for a positive outcome on a murder trial."

Mary wanted to scream, to yell at this woman that she was wrong. Wrong, wrong, wrong. That Jimmy Blake was not a murderer. He was a good man, a good father, and life had just dealt him a nasty deck of cards. For weeks, Mary had heard the whispers, the talk, on the street or down by the shops, even on the bus. She had risen above it, waiting for the truth and concentrating on protecting Star. And this moment right now was the hardest of all, yet Mary did not scream or yell. She took a breath and listened as Jeanette Young continued.

"Ms. Lloyd is not only Star's blood relation…"

"Blood relation?" Mary exclaimed - the words escaping her unplanned - glancing at Susan who was picking breadcrumbs carefully off her pleated beige skirt, letting them fall onto Mary's carpet. "What the hell… she wouldn't give Star a drop of her own blood if the child depended on it. I bet she doesn't even know the date of Star's birthday. When is it Susan? Tell me…"

"Mrs. Mack, calm down," Jeanette popped the piece of sandwich into her mouth, chewing slowly on the right side only. She waited until she had swallowed before she continued. "Ms. Lloyd is under enough pressure as it is."

"Oh really, then she can hardly be capable of looking after an eight year old who is nothing more than a stranger to her, can she?" Mary sat back into her chair. She was going to have to hold back, stop speaking her mind. But what did it matter? These women hadn't listened to a word of sense that she had said so far and Mary was not soft. This act that Susan Lloyd was portraying – the wide smiles, the Miss-Nicey-Nicey - may impress the social workers, but whatever it was that Susan Lloyd wanted here, it was not Star. The woman would look out of place around a child like a pork pie at a Jewish wedding. Women like Susan Lloyd did not have children. They had dinner parties and wore shoulder pads to rival Joan Collins. They went to charity benefits at night but spent the day in a hair salon and getting their nails polished. They took in their dead sister's child when times got tough because it would make them popular within their social circle. No, Mary Mack was not soft.

"Look, I'm sorry. But believe me, this is all nonsense. Star is happy here; she is loved. Everybody loves her. God, I can't go to the butchers without her getting free lollipops or having the old man behind the desk at the post office asks her to show him a shuffle-off-to-buffalo."

"A shuffle what?" Susan asked, taking another sandwich, that wide smile on the verge of making an unwelcome return.

"A shuffle-off-to-buffalo," Mary reiterated. "It's a tap step. Star'll show you when she comes in…"

"That won't be necessary," Jeanette said, and she was just about to slurp her tea when there was movement coming from the hall. A squelching noise followed by some banging, quite possibly a shoe being slapped against the ground over and over again.

"Is that you, Star?" Mary shouted.

"I'll be two ticks, Nannie," Star's voice travelled down the hall. "There's mud on me trainees but I'll sort it. I'm very self-reliant."

Susan blinked slowly. "She's very self-what?"

Mary just held her stare with the legal guardian. "Self reliant. A little quote from *Curly Top*, 1935. Are you not familiar with Shirley Temple?"

"Shirley Temple?" Susan laughed, as if this conversation were absurd. "That annoying, chirpy song-and-dance child with the curly hair? Why on earth would I be familiar with her?" She looked to Jeanette Young, who reacted in an identical manner, snorting.

"What has Shirley Temple got to do with any of this, Mrs Mack?" Jeanette asked.

"Oh, everything, Miss Young," Mary smiled. "Everything."

The carpet was squelching with every movement that Star made until she stopped behind Mary's chair, permitting the two unexpected visitors to drop their perplexed smiles, and become quite simply just perplexed. They glared over Mary's shoulder at the sight of the child, and Mary spun around to see what had caused the ridiculous looks on their faces.

The high pony-tail that usually swung like a pendulum in Star's hair was ragged over to the side of her left ear, allowing water to drip from the tip onto her shoulder. Plastered to her forehead was her fringe, looking like a thick-toothed comb standing above her pale face patched with dirt. What was a lilac t-shirt printed with Forever Friends bears was now purple, soaked and stained with mud. Her pink leggings at least matched the wet muddy top, and Star stood bare foot on the carpet, looking like nothing less than a street urchin.

Even when Jimmy was snatched away by the police, Mary Mack's stomach had not sank as low as it did when Star made her entrance into the room, looking like this. She rarely raised her voice to Star – there was never cause to for she was such a well-behaved little girl – but this would be an opportunity, or a necessity rather in which a good old-fashioned telling off should take place. Even a quick slap on the back of the legs, a marching up the stairs for a hot bath and then straight to bed would be in order for Star today, but none of this was possible with these two wicked witches sitting here, judging.

Star took a deep breath and opened her mouth, words gushing out in time with the rain splashing down the window panes. "Nannie, I'm so sorry, but the trees were all chopped down and everybody was so sad, and then Anthony Tucker pushed everybody in the water but it cleansed us and took away our sins, so really, I'm not dirty. I've just been baptised…"

"Hello, Rebecca," Susan interrupted.

Star froze, a large drop of rain water plopping onto the carpet from the end of her pony-tail. She gazed at the woman who had called her by her real name and started to edge closer to Mary's chair with tiny side-steps.

"Rebecca?" Susan said. "Darling?"

"It's Star," Star whispered.

"Okay, Star. What a pretty, pretty name for such a pretty little girl. You do know that your real name is Rebecca, don't you?" Susan's Mersey Tunnel grin had come back.

Star straightened herself up a little and a flake of mud dropped onto the arm of Mary's chair. "I know. Like Rebecca in *Rebecca of Sunnybrook Farm*, you know the Shirley Temple film. But we're saving Rebecca for when I become a doctor or a lawyer."

Susan clapped her hands as if she felt compelled to tell the world that she believed in fairies. "Oh do you want to be a doctor or a lawyer when you grow up? Aren't you clever?"

"No. I'm going to be a famous actress. I just might be a doctor or a lawyer on the side, you know, as something to fall back on," Star spoke as if Susan were stupid.

It was Jeanette's turn to speak. She was obviously feeling left out. She spoke very slowly, over-using her mouth as if Star was deaf and had to lip-read, and moving her hands around together like she was washing them with imaginary soap. Jeanette introduced Susan, letting Star know that this lady was her mummy's big sister.

"Before your mummy died, she wrote a very special letter called a Will. It is like a wish list of everything that she would want to happen if something bad happened to her and your daddy. Her biggest wish was for any children that she may have to be taken care of by Aunt Susan here."

"Daddy's coming home soon," Star said. "So I think I'll just stay here until he does. Thank you very much Aunt Susan, but I won't be coming with you."

"We've spoken with your Daddy," Jeanette went on. "He wants you to stay with Susan for a while."

Of every event that had happened since the day Jimmy Blake came home from Fazakerley Hospital with Star and no Linda, it was Jeanette Young's last words that Mary disbelieved the most. Star was edging backwards again. The cushioned arm of the chair did not stop her from moving, and she pressed more and more, determined to become a part of the chair, a part of Mary and as far away from Susan as possible. In this instance, the mud and the dirt and the wet clothes were invisible, they didn't matter. Mary locked her arms around her little girl and Star clambered onto her knees, burying her head into Mary's ample breasts and squeezing tighter and tighter. There was no doubt she would be able to feel Mary's heart against her soft, muddy cheek, banging in her chest, but she hoped that Star was not feeling the pain it was causing.

"I'm so sorry, Nannie," Star said, sobbing. "I love you millions."

Jeanette Young didn't even allow time for a change of clothes, but Susan let Star run upstairs to grab the rag-doll that looked like Sheila Gilhooley.

*

It was just before eight o'clock when Vera's phone rang. She knew it would be Mary, she always phoned at eight on the dot after *Coronation Street* had finished so that they could chew the fat about the episode. Only she was a few minutes early, probably because Mary couldn't stand the sight of Bet Lynch's leopard skin any longer.

"You're early, but I was just thinking, why don't the babies in these soaps ever cry?" Vera said into the mouthpiece. "Their parents and their neighbours can yell on the tops of their bleedin' voices, but the babies just stare into space. Not a peep out of them…"

"Vera, stop," Mary said.

Something was wrong. Mary wasn't even watching *Coronation Street*; Vera couldn't hear the television in the background which was most unusual. She was used to having to remind her sister to turn the volume down.

"Vera," Mary said. "She's gone. Star's gone."

29th May, 1989

A cuckoo clock struck seven and started poking in and out of its pink and white wooden house, in and out. Star sat up, and slid back down again, the satin of her pyjamas slipping on the satin sheets. It hadn't been the cuckoo that woke her though; the sun beaming through the skylight on the sloping ceiling had flashed into her new bedroom hours ago. But now it was time to get up, and Star wriggled her toes against the soft duvet. It felt lovely, but she would swap it in a second for the bobbled mattress that her toenails sometimes caught on in Nannie's house. Or her duvet at home that was double sided; one covered with Snow White dancing through the forest swishing her long yellow skirt, and the other patterned with the heads of the seven dwarfs.

Her old bedroom. The old, old one now. Star had never really thought about it while she had still been in Flinder Street because being at Nannie's was practically being at home anyway. But here, in Aunt Susan's house, she thought about her real bedroom all the time… the pale blue shelves filled with books, some that had large words from when she was learning to read, to newer ones that didn't even contain pictures such as *Little Women* and *The Secret Garden*… the Sindy house that was once taller than her but now Star could see over the roof without even having to stand on her tip-toes… and the mirrored wardrobes that not only made the small room look twice as big, but that Star could practice her ballet steps in front of, or see what she looked like when she performed a song.

Would she ever see this room again? Living with Nannie, Star had not worried about this. She had spent that time worrying about her daddy, and now there was more worry added into her life. It was a pain – a pain in her head that didn't exactly hurt like falling and grazing a knee, or getting hit in the face by a football in the playground. It was a squashed pain, as though there was not enough space for all the thoughts that zigzagged about and pushed to the front of her forehead making her frown. Is that why Aunty Vera always had a headache? Because she was a worrier? Star couldn't worry about Aunty Vera right now. There was just no room, and besides, Aunty Vera had Uncle John to take care of her.

And Nannie had nobody. Star simply *had* to go home. This so-called holiday had gone on long enough. She grinned at the thought.

Maybe today would be the day that she could go home.

At the foot of her bed sat a patchwork Humpty Dumpty, a jointed teddy-bear and a few brightly decorated soft elephants, apparently from Aunt Susan's friend in India. Next to the pillows sat the rag-doll that looked like Sheila Gilhooley, its wonky felt lips grinning along with Star.

Looking at the toys, and then across to the dolls dressed in various world costumes standing on the shelves, Star stretched her arms up high and out wide, singing;

"*Good Morning, Good Morning,*

Nature hums when morning comes along,

Day's dawning, stop yawning, and begin to join me in my song..."

Star did a rollover across her large mattress and danced out of bed, skipping around the wicker chair and the white furry sheepskin rug.

"*Early Bird, up at the break of day,*

Early Bird, sing the dark away,

Early birdies always catch a worm or two,

So don't be late, you've got a date, the worm's awaiting you..."

She even had her own mini bathroom connected to her room, and Star ran the cold water, splashing her face and brushing her teeth whilst practising her shuffle-pick-up tap steps. Grabbing the pink towel with butterflies embroidered onto the corners, she dabbed her face dry singing, "*Whistle in the morning...*" and she blew, trying to whistle but made a pathetic raspberry instead. "*Send the worm a warning...*" followed by another failed attempt at a whistle, but Star threw a t-shirt over her head and looked back at the dolls, singing, "*Sleepy head, tumble out of bed. Be a little early bird!*"

It had been five days since she had been taken away from Nannie's house on Flinder Street to the mansion overlooking the sea in a town called Hillside, near Southport. 'A holiday' so Star had been told by Aunt Susan, who seemed very nice but utterly boring. As far as holidays went, this was the most dismal ever. Yes, the playroom could rival the Toys'R'Us in Birkenhead and the sand dunes gave an exotic feel to the place. Yes, the sun had decided to shine in bucket loads since she had arrived here, and yes, Star was even allowed chocolate chip ice cream every night after her tea; only whilst on holiday would *that* be allowed. Yet, the stuff – the real stuff – that comes with a holiday was not featured in the Aunt-Susan-Southport adventure.

Star had been on four holidays in her life, all in Wales. She couldn't remember going to Butlin's in Pwllheli because she had still been in a pram, but the other holidays were all at Pontins, Prestatyn. It was tricky to differentiate each time; they were all pretty identical except Star remembered that Jonesy went with them once, and that Christine lady was there with a bunch of her friends who all had permed hair and wore white high heels even at the fairground. Aunty Vera and Uncle John would arrive at Flinder Street very early in the morning to follow her daddy's car all the way to North Wales. The trip was supposed to take an hour and a half, but it took up to four hours because Uncle John did not like to drive fast, meaning that the car in front would have to pull over and wait for him to catch up more often than anybody cared to enjoy. Nannie always filled about six carrier bags with ham sandwiches, Mars bars and ready salted crisps because she said that, "any other flavour would stink the car out." A paper bag of barley sugars remained on her lap throughout the journey in case anybody felt car sick (Star once threw up all over the back seat, and then a second time into an empty carrier bag) and her daddy played his mixed tapes of Foreigner and The Police. Nannie would complain that it all sounded like a load of whiny noise, but Star's daddy would state that it was, "his holiday, too," and that if he had to spend five days doing the Crocodile March, drinking Slush Puppies, and watching the Blue Coats imitate Abba every night, then he had the right to choose the music for the car.

Pontin's was a little world all of its own, a secret village hidden away from real life. It didn't matter that the chalets were like run-down council flats, or that the pictures of painted ducks or fish on the walls were wonky. During the Crocodile Club disco, some over-excited (and usually over-weight boy) would always find Star's toe to stamp on. Or, no matter how hard Nannie worked at making a crepe paper fancy dress costume for the Wednesday night competition, some other kid in hired superhero attire always won the goody bag over Star. Even the burgers at the diner didn't taste one bit like a burger, and the tomato ketchup must have been vinegar in disguise. Star always took her tap shoes with her and entered the Junior Talent Contest, however she was always the Runner-Up, losing out to older girls singing Madonna songs or one time, it was a small boy wearing his sister's bathing costume, a mopped cap and a pair of Wellington's, swigging an empty can of lager and telling Knock Knock jokes. At least she won a silver plaque and a five pound voucher for the gift shop. And yet, despite all of this, Star's happiest times were from Pontin's. Like when her daddy sang 'Delilah' on the karaoke night and his performance was so intense that his veins were popping out of his temples, or the time when Uncle John put on Aunty Vera's silky nightdress and did the chicken dance, but was pushed out of the door by Aunty Vera who locked him out of the chalet. Being at Pontin's was where Star saw the people she loved the most laughing and being silly.

So this holiday at Aunt Susan's mansion was a right let down. She hadn't heard one single laugh and there were no signs of silliness for a million miles. Plus, there was nobody in that house that she loved. Except the rag-doll that looked like Sheila Gilhooley.

Star had been taken to Hillside by taxi because Aunt Susan didn't drive. Apparently she had a chauffeur like film stars have, but had not wanted him to come to Flinder Street. Maybe she was a bit like Uncle John about her car. The taxi had to stop at a tall gate with gold balls on the top of each spike, until Aunt Susan rolled down the window and keyed some sort of telephone number into a little metal box on the wall. The gate opened all by itself and the taxi drove around a large fountain, stopping at the front door to the biggest house that Star had ever seen in real life. She heard the taxi driver say, "Bloody hell," and give a whistle, shaking his head, and saying to Star, "you must be a little princess to live here."

"No, I don't live here, this is just a holiday," Star said.

Aunt Susan took Star by the hand, which Star did not like. Aunt Susan's hand was too soft and a bit wet. The front door opened without any bell ringing or window rapping and a very clean man in a smart black suit greeted them.

"My word," he said, glancing down at Star who was still dressed in her muddy clothes, clutching the rag-doll that looked like Sheila Gilhooley.

"Are you the king here?" Star asked. "You look like the king."

The clean man chuckled, bending down to Star's eye level. "Ah little miss, if only the rest of the world could see through your eyes."

"Andrews. Get on the phone to George Henry Lee," Aunt Susan said to the clean man as she pushed Star through the front door. "I want you to order a selection of little girl's clothes, some shoes and a bunch of play things…"

"Play things?" the clean man who answered to 'Andrews' asked.

"Yes, Andrews. Play things," Aunt Susan kicked off her high heeled shoes, leaving them in the middle of the huge black and white hall. A table stood in the centre, filled with white carnations. Other than that, there was not a single piece of furniture in sight. "Toys, books, skipping ropes, I don't know. Whatever little girls play with."

"Whatever little girls play with?" Andrews quizzed.

"Are you just going to repeat everything that I say with that gormless look on your face, Andrews?"

"My apologies. I will find the Yellow Pages right away." Andrews watched Aunt Susan turn her back on him and wander off through a set of double doors. He looked back to Star and winked. Star winked back.

"I'm Star."

"So I've heard, little Miss," Andrews gave a little bow. Star copied him.

"Is Andrews your first name?"

"No, little Miss. It is Bertie, Bertie Andrews."

"Nice to meet you, Bertie Andrews." Star held out her hand for him to shake, but instead, Andrews did another little bow. So Star copied him again. "Why does she call you by your surname? The headmaster at my school calls the boys by their surnames, but you're too old to be in school."

"Yes, but that aunt of yours is not much different from a headmaster, little Miss."

"Oh. Well, I won't call you Andrews. I could call you Mr Bertie?"

"A pleasure, little Miss," he bowed again.

"Why are you always bowing?" Star asked, straightening herself up from yet another bow. "This is making my back ache."

"My word!" Mr Bertie chuckled, but a call for "Andrews" disturbed their amusing conversation, and off he scooted to duty.

Star stood in the grand hallway. This was like a movie set. The long staircase had a banister that was tempting to slide down and the only pictures that hung on the walls were of the beach which Star thought was silly seeing as the beach was just outside. Where were all the photographs? Where was all the noise? For such a big house, it was so quiet that Star had begun to wish that she had whispered when Mr Bertie had been talking to her, the echoing and eeriness of the walls listening in to their conversation was odd. She was used to having to fight hard to be heard, what with Nannie always on the phone to Aunty Vera, or Louise Fitzpatrick bossing everyone about in the playground. The urge overcame her and Star allowed her right foot to do a shuffle on the polished floor. The clear cut noise it made was so loud that Star jumped and jolted into a ridged bean-pole, not daring to move until somebody told her to.

It felt like an eternity, just waiting in silence. Star wondered if any of her friends would be able to come and see her, but it was such a long way away from Flinder Street. Steph Bradley's dad owned a van, so perhaps he could drive them all up at the weekend, but Laura Fenton had once brought dog poo from her shoe into

Nannie's house and Star had felt funny about inviting Laura Fenton in anywhere ever since. She hoped that Aunt Susan didn't have a dog. Star was a bit scared of dogs, especially the pit-bull that always sat outside Mick Tully's front step, barking. Maybe if Mick Tully just took it in and fed it once in a while, the ugly dog would not be so vicious. Anyhow, this house did not look like an animal-sort-of house. Come to think of it, Star doubted that it looked like a house for a child, either.

"Ah, good girl," Aunt Susan re-entered through the double doors with a chubby, older lady following her. "Well done for staying there." And Aunt Susan laughed as if she had just told a really funny joke, but she hadn't.

"Where else would I go?" Star asked.

"Erm, yes. Rebecca, this is Mrs O'Connell," Aunt Susan introduced. "She's going to take you upstairs and give you a bath."

Suddenly it sounded as if Star was the dog of the house.

Mrs O'Connell's cheery face with hundreds of little red veins making up two big rosy cheeks dropped upside down. "Me? Bath the little girl?"

"Well I can't do it," Aunt Susan said, as if bathing a muddy child was the equivalent to sticking your arm right down an unflushed toilet to salvage a lost pound coin.

"But, Ms Lloyd," Mrs O'Connell whispered. "I cook, I clean. It's not my job to wash children…"

"It is now."

Star was beginning to wonder how many more strangers were going to stand and look her up and down with an expression of bewilderment on their faces. Yes - she was dirty, yes - she was small, yes – she was a stranger, too, but come on. It was as if no one had ever seen a little girl before.

Mr Bertie appeared with Aunt Susan's jacket and an umbrella.

"Thank you, Andrews. I'll be back by nine. Make sure Rebecca is in bed and asleep by the time I return." And the giant front door slammed. Slam, slam, slam echoed around until the little buzz of silence was all that could be heard.

"Don't worry," Star said to Mr Bertie and Mrs O'Connell. "I'm only here for five days. And then everything will be back to normal. Plus, I'm very self-reliant."

"Five days?" Mrs O'Connell asked. "Who told you that?"

"Aunt Susan."

"My word!" Mr Bertie exclaimed.

"Well, she said I was coming here for a holiday," Star continued. "And every holiday that I have been on lasts for five days. Although, when Louise Fitzpatrick went to Tenerife, she was away for a fortnight – is that two weeks? Anyway, her family are always splashing out on things like holidays and her mum buys them statues over there for cheap called Lladro, I think. Am I here for a fortnight?"

Mrs O'Connell and Mr Bertie both started to move their mouths around, but no words came out unless the odd, "err," and "umm," could be counted.

"Am I here for a fortnight?"

Mrs O'Connell cleared her throat and smiled. She had very small teeth, all the same size like Tic Tacs. "You're going to be here longer than five days, so maybe a fortnight it is, my love."

She was Irish. Star could tell because she had the same accent as Father Mulcahy, St Stephen's Parish Priest. Only Mrs O'Connell seemed gentle whereas Father Mulcahy was a bit nasty; he gave Star ten Hail Marys and ten Our Fathers as penance when she made her First Confession, all for saying sorry that she didn't help Nannie enough with the washing up after tea. To be honest, Star only confessed that because she couldn't think of anything else to confess to, and her penance was harsh. Anthony Tucker bragged that he was only given one Our Father, yet Anthony Tucker was by far the naughtiest boy in the whole school. Perhaps God thought that there was just no saving a boy as naughty as him.

"I might ask Aunt Susan if I can go back after five days," Star said. "I don't need any longer for a holiday. Five days suits me fine."

*

Jimmy hadn't wanted Mary to visit. He couldn't bear to look at her while she pleaded with him to let her keep Star. Instead they spoke over the phone, even though Jimmy could hardly speak after injuring his mouth in a fist fight, another reason why he didn't want Mary's loving face looking at him, disappointed and hurt. It had happened earlier that day in the canteen when a fellow inmate had been tormenting Addo. Jimmy didn't hear the start of it or even know how it began, but somehow got himself riled up and involved. He should have known better since Addo had been getting bullied by this guy from the day he set foot inside four years ago.

But Jimmy was having a bad day. Someone got the brunt of it, and that someone happened to be himself seeing as he ended up losing two teeth and splitting his lip in three places.

"Think of it this way," Jimmy muttered. "She'll be getting treated like a little princess and have all the things that we could never give her."

"No, it's all wrong," Mary shouted. "Susan doesn't know her. She doesn't love her. She'll fake-love her no doubt, she's so sickly bleedin' sweet... And she's divorced. *Divorced*, Jimmy!"

"Her husband had an affair, Mary. With several women. How do you think she ended up so flamin' rich?"

"Jimmy, we're Catholics. Cath-ol-icks!"

"Mary, stop. Star'll have fun. Didn't they tell her it was a holiday?"

"No she won't, Jimmy! She's eight but she's not soft…"

"Exactly, she's eight. And she's far too young to decide where she wants to live. If you ask me, the child is lucky. Lucky, lucky, bloody lucky. She'll have everything she's ever wanted; she can finally go to a decent dancing school where she can be really pushed instead of prancing around to an out-of-tune piano, listening to that chain-smoking teacher coughing her guts up all over the class. She'll be able to have everything that I could never give her."

"What about what I give her, Jim? I don't even have to tell you how much I love her as if she were my own child. You know. You *know*, and yet, you do this to me, to her."

"I'm sorry, but I had to. She needs a better start in life. Look where I've ended up, Mary!"

"And you think this is my fault?"

"God, no. It's just a different world. Ours compared to the likes of Susan's."

"Yeah, bleedin' well different," Mary said through her teeth. "I've heard Star's getting a pony this weekend."

"A friggin' pony?"

"Apparently she was quite content with the duck…"

"A friggin' duck? Where does Susan live? Old MacDonald's bleedin' farm?"

"Jimmy, the pips are going…"

"You see? Animals. It's friggin' insane, but we could never give Star animals," he let out a laugh but started to sob at the same time. The idea of his little Star in some stuck-up, fancy Southport house surrounded by ducks and ponies was indeed insane. It was just not *them*. But it was for the best, surely?

"Let me come and see you…" Mary hurried.

"No, Mary." The phone went dead.

A duck and a pony. A real live duck and a real live pony… Jimmy used to throw in a pound every Friday night for a sweepstake down on the docks, waiting no less than ten years to actually win the fifty quid prize. He scooped up his winnings and headed straight to Woolworths after work to buy a doll for Star, some craze called Rainbow Brite. By the time he got home, Star was fast asleep because she had left school feeling unwell, so he put Rainbow Brite in her big, new, shiny box on the windowsill next to Star's bed. When she woke up the following morning to be greeted by her present, Star was elated. She ran into Jimmy's bedroom, jumping on the bed and smothering her daddy with kisses. That was when he noticed that Star feeling unwell the night before had been the first stages of chicken pox; the spots had consumed her freckles. The poor kid burst out crying when she saw herself, and only then did she start to itch.

"It's conscientious!" Star cried. "It's conscientious!"

"She means contagious," Mary said out of the side of her mouth, as she went off to fetch the camomile lotion to rub onto Star's arms.

"It's alright, sweetheart," Jimmy smiled. "It's not contagious."

"It is! It is!" Tears trickled over the bumpy red spots on Star's cheeks. "Christopher McGinty told me."

Jimmy stroked his little girl's hair, his fingers brushing against the bumps on her scalp.

"It is, you know," Mary said. "Chicken pox is *very* conscientious... but you only get it once. How old were you when you had it, Jim?"

Jimmy pulled his hand from Star's head and rubbed it onto his jeans. He scratched his chin, and then moved down onto his neck and round to his back, using both hands to reach his itches. Come to think of it, he had been a touch itchy all day, putting it down to buying that cheap washing powder from Davey who said that it was Persil without the fancy packaging.

"Jimmy?" Mary dropped the camomile lotion onto the carpet. "Tell me you had chicken pox when you were little, soft lad... before you lived with me... because I don't recall you having..."

He hadn't. Jimmy Blake had survived the chicken pox swarm as a youngster and would have to pay for it as a grown-up. He and Star lay on his bed all weekend with old socks on their hands cello-taped around their wrists by Mary who made it clear that anyone who itched would not get any bread and butter pudding. And all the while, Rainbow Brite lay between them, clear-skinned and an inspiration to how they would look if they didn't scratch.

Until Star got hold of a red felt-tip pen and drew spots on the doll's face, too.

"She felt left out," was Star's excuse.

Within a week, the Pox had all gone from Jimmy and Star, but Rainbow Brite was forever on Star's windowsill – out of the box – and next to the empty jam jar for collecting pennies from the street, with her chicken pox that faded with the sun, but remained on her face nevertheless.

It terrified Jimmy how much he had hurt Mary, but he *had* to be right. There was no way that living on Flinder Street could compare to living in a palace by the sea. Working on the docks didn't pay Jimmy a bad wage – much more than most of his mates - but still, gifts came at birthdays, Christmas and once in a blue moon with the sweepstake. That was all he could manage. Christ he'd love to buy Star an entire flippin' zoo! But a duck and a pony? A duck and a bleedin' pony? That Susan must be swimming in silly money.

He knew she'd made a success of herself, Linda's sister, although Jimmy never really got to know Susan Lloyd. She moved to London when he just started courting Linda and married some hot shot lawyer at the firm she worked for. It was a rarity for Susan to come home, usually just weddings and funerals and never for Christmas. Still, Linda seemed to love Susan dearly and always spoke so highly of her, in a way that they never really *got* each other but understood that they were different. When their mother passed away, and then their father a couple of years later, Linda made her Will. She was pregnant with Star at the time, so to read that she wanted Susan to have custody of her children must have been genuine. Jimmy would still do anything that Linda had wished.

The cell was shrinking by the day, getting smaller and smaller, Jimmy thought, as he sat on the edge of his bed, trying to imagine Star being happy with a woman who he had only known as an estranged figure in his life. Of course, it was impossible that the brick walls were moving around him, choosing to suffocate him and him alone.

It still felt that way, though.

*

It took about three minutes after Mary had hung up for her to move from the arm of the couch – where she always perched whenever she used the phone – to go and find something useful to do. She had paused. Three minutes could have quite easily become three hours, three days even, just staring with fuzzy eyes, motionless, feeling that there was no point to anything anymore. Hearing Jimmy blubbering on about it being a good thing, Star living with that Susan Lloyd, well, it was just too much.

Mary rarely felt down. There was always too much to do to bother being all miserable; packed lunches to be made, shopping to get in, not to mention washing and cleaning, and the likes of Ethel Finnegan from number nine who was housebound and needed someone to drop off a loaf and a pint of milk into her every other day. She had only said goodbye to Jimmy for five minutes before Star was catapulted into their lives, but it was now, just now, that her house felt lonely; lonely for the first time in more than twenty years. There were just not enough things to do to get through the day. It'd be useless making a packed lunch for herself; if Mary went out to lunch it was usually over at Vera's house, and she didn't do that too often since Vera had started making things like curry and chilli. It made the idea of eating unpleasant, all the watery eyes and runny noses, making food a challenge rather than a necessity or a comfort. What the hell was wrong with a baked potato and cheese? It didn't stink the house out for hours either. And there was still a pile of Star's washing to be done, but once Mary did that, what next? Her own washing would take up an hour or two a week, tops. She just wore regular clothes - one outfit a day – not a uniform, a PE kit, a ballet leotard, playing out clothes. One outfit a day. Sometimes even one outfit over two days. Star was going to start making her own way home from school when she was ten, but that was nearly two years away. Mary had thought she had two years to work out what would replace her regular trips to St. Stephen's. Not two minutes.

Betrayal. That's what she felt. Complete and utter betrayal. Jimmy had done this because it had been in Linda's Will, never mind the flippin' money. Mary had loved Linda to pieces, but she had that lad right where she wanted him when she was alive and he was still under the thumb from beyond the grave. But how could Jimmy do this to *her*, after she had devoted her life to him and his daughter? It hadn't been easy, but Jesus, it had been a pleasure. All of it. She had needed them just as much as they needed her, even if it never seemed that way. And what was it all for? Nothing. To be left with nothing, nothing but a twisted feeling in the pit of her stomach.

She would have a glass of lemonade and watch television. The evening was warm and Mary couldn't be bothered to put the kettle on, so she opened the fridge and poured herself a glass of cold yellow lemonade. The clock had just ticked past seven. This was the time when Star would be winding down for the day by watching a video before having to switch it off at seven thirty for Mary to catch *Coronation Street*.

Mary pointed the remote control at the television set, pressing the top right corner button. Again and again. A spitting sound came through the speakers as though the television couldn't be bothered doing anything this evening, either. Spit, spit. Great, thought Mary, just sitting comfortably, all relaxed finally and the bloody batteries go dead. What's the use in a remote control anyway? It makes the laziest past-time man ever invented even lazier. Mary banged the remote control down against the arm of her chair with a heavy hand. Jesus Christ, she could understand that Star had to live with a relative and she could understand Jimmy being locked up if it happened that he was guilty. It didn't make it fair, though. And Mary was never one for reminiscing, so seeing Star's books and her pile of video tapes didn't set off any draining tears. No. What drove her to the slamming of the remote – not to mention the breaking of the vacuum, the dint in the kitchen door from her foot and the smashing of a saucer – was all the 'what could have been' taken away from her. How could this happen again in her lifetime? To have something so dear, so good, that it just be picked up like an empty crisp packet and popped into the bin, getting rid of experiences that could never even be lost because they were never found, never giving the unmade memories a chance to get made?

Enough, enough, enough. The glass half-full with the cold lemonade in Mary's warm hand was beginning to drip a little onto her skirt. She placed it on top of the mantelpiece and forced herself up to turn on the television. Terry Wogan's face appeared on the screen, his own chat show having just started. As Mary settled herself back into her chair, she heard him announce the words that made her shed her first tear since losing Jimmy and then Star.

"Ladies and gentlemen," Terry said. "Please give a warm welcome to the show, Shirley Temple Black."

*

It was sunny down on Ainsdale beach, but so windy that once Star and Aunt Susan arrived back at the house, Mrs O'Connell had to spend over an hour getting the tats out of Star's long hair with a comb. They had to leave their shoes by the front door because of all the sand stuck to the soles, and Star was shocked to find that a whole load of sand poured out of her socks when she took them off, too. How did it manage to get in there?

Star had only ever been to Crosby Marina with her daddy to watch the tide coming in, or once on New Year's Eve to look at the stars and hear the ships horns blow. She had been to the fairground at Southport Pleasureland a few times and had seen the sea from the car window, but playing on a sandy beach was not something that she was used to... if you could call her day with Aunt Susan *playing*.

Poor Aunt Susan. She tried. She tried too much. It made Star cringe, all the clapping and excited little squeaks, 'oohs' and 'ahhs' that Susan made constantly. And when she spoke to Star, she always placed her hands on her knees and bent down to get on a level with her niece. Her speaking voice went all high pitched and she always finished with a smile so wide that she resembled a crocodile.

They had gone to the beach with two bats and a ball. Star thought it best not to mention to Aunt Susan how appalling she was at sports, and especially not how much she also despised it, either. Her aunt was wearing a brand new tracksuit and showed more enthusiasm than Christopher McGinty did the day that he was chosen to be Anthony Tucker's partner-in-crime collecting worms. The ill-fated bat and ball game ended after about four minutes when not only both parties clearly admitted that they could not hit the ball, but the wind was making the whole thing utterly impossible. The ice-cream van was only a short walk away, so they ventured there and sat on a sand dune, Aunt Susan with a Feast and Star with a Fab. Neither said anything, but although summer was approaching, Ainsdale beach was still a bit too nippy to enjoy the cold of an ice lolly.

It was a Monday, and Star had begun to wonder not just how long this holiday was going to go on for, but how much more school she was going to miss. She loved school and was sure that Miss Murphy would not think it wise her being off for this amount of time when she wasn't even sick. She bet that Louise Fitzpatrick was hassling Nannie no end, knocking round and demanding to know where she was, with Steph Bradley and Laura Fenton making up stories that she was seriously ill with a brain tumour or something just like the character of Lucy Robinson in *Neighbours*. And how much more *Neighbours* would Star miss? It was her and her daddy's favourite. Nannie wasn't too keen, preferring the later soaps, but she always let Star watch it as long as she ate every last scrap of her tea and didn't try to imitate the Australian accent. So far, Aunt Susan had not allowed Star to watch any television at all. Not even a video.

Because Star and Aunt Susan very quickly ran out of things to talk about, Star found herself thinking about her friends back at home all afternoon. Usually she thought about her daddy, and more recently Nannie and Aunty Vera and Uncle John. Missing them so much had made her forget about her friends for a little while. But they were there in her mind now, so close that when she heard some shouting and laughing near the shore, her eyes darted across to see if it were them, if they had come to Ainsdale beach to play. Of course, it was just some other boys and girls, much older than Star and wearing uniforms with blazers.

"My word!" Mr Bertie said, walking past Star's bedroom to see Mrs O'Connell yanking the comb from Star's hair.

"Won't you come in, Mr Bertie?" Star asked, mid-'ouch'.

"I'm dreadfully sorry, little Miss, but your aunt has guests this evening and I have to check that the guest rooms are satisfactory."

"Are any of the guests little girls or little boys?"

"Not in age, little Miss. Although they can act like children once your aunt opens up the drinks cabinet."

"Bertie!" Mrs O'Connell shut him up.

"It's alright Mrs O'Connell, I know," Star reassured. "Grown-ups are always silly when they drink alcohol. My Aunty Vera laughs for no reason and then cries for no reason, and Mick Tully from across the street wets his pants."

Mr Bertie scurried off, leaving Mrs O'Connell to untangle the last tat. She kissed Star on the head and left to make her way downstairs to start the cooking for Aunt Susan's dinner party. Star sat on her bed, taking in the enormous amount of empty space in such a large bedroom for one little girl. There were so many toys, too. What a shame that there was nobody to play with. In the corner by the bathroom, they could set up a house because there was an A La Carte Kitchen and a doll's pram, and they could even play with a skipping rope in the middle without breaking anything.

Star walked over to the shelves where there stood a variety of dolls displayed on stands. One wore a long, frilly Spanish dress, another was dressed up like a Dutch girl, and there were two wearing Scottish kilts. They looked quite old with small, pale lips and eyes with missing eyelashes that blinked if you rocked them, and Star guessed that they belonged to Aunt Susan when she was a little girl. The rag-doll that looked like Sheila Gilhooley was sat on the wicker chair, looking at Star with just the same blank expression as the dolls on the shelf. With a sweet, sad voice, she sang to them;

"*Oh me, oh my,*

I'm so sad that I could cry

With a very good reason why
I've no one to be gay with
That's why I wear a frown
No children I can play with
London Bridge is falling down
My fair lady."

Star sighed. She would give anything for her friends to run in with dirt on their shoes and for them all – Star included – to get into trouble. At least she would feel alive, like something, *something*, was happening. She'd even love it if Christopher McGinty came in holding a big spider. And Star hated spiders!

"*I wanna make mud pies*
In fact I'd like to be a mess
I wanna make mud pies
I know that I'd find happiness
If I got jam on my fingers
Chocolate on my face
And molasses all over my dress..."

The dolls were still gazing at Star, lifeless, but there even still.

"*You're the only friends I've ever had*
But one minute you're good
And the very next minute you're bad!
At times I ought to hate you

You make me feel so blue…"

The rag-doll that looked like Sheila Gilhooley's mouth was so wonky that in the correct sort of light, she could seem as though she was smiling. A cloud blew away from shielding the sun outside, and Star's dolly gave a cheeky grin.

"But honest I can't hate you
When you smile at me the way you do
Oh, my goodness!"

*

Mary had been given Susan Lloyd's telephone number, but so far, whenever she had called she had to make do with an impersonal conversation with an Irish lady who always seemed to be far too flustered to deal with phone calls. With one ear listening to Terry Wogan interview the woman who was once the child star, Shirley Temple, and the other glued to her phone, Mary crossed her fingers that Star was already watching this.

"Susan Lloyd."

"Ah, Susan," Mary sighed. "So glad it's you. Listen, can you tell Star to put BBC one on, please?"

"Who is this?" Susan asked.

"It's me, Susan. Mary Mack."

"Oh, Mary," Susan managed a chuckle. "I can't talk right now, I have guests arriving…"

"Is that Nannie on the phone?" Star's voice came across loud and clear in the background.

"Go back upstairs, Rebecca, and put that new dress on… Sorry, Mary. I'm ridiculously behind schedule…"

"Star?" Mary shouted into the phone. "Hello, Star! Yes, it's Nannie. How are you?"

"Nannie! Nannie!" Star shouted.

"Andrews, take that child back upstairs," Susan snapped. "Mary, it's not a good idea you calling like this. She needs to settle here. You must think I am being harsh but in order for Rebecca to move forward she needs to let go of her past. Her future is here, now. Goodbye, Mary."

It was the first time that Mary had heard Star's voice in nearly a week. Her heart felt tight, so tight and full of pressure that it could burst and break at any moment. She only wanted to tell Star that her idol was on television, and that she was not just a little girl in black and white movies, but a real person. A lady. To show her that the magic did not only exist in the old song and dances, but it lives on. And instead, Star was being forced to forget who she was and all the unique qualities that she had, to become a new little girl. Susan's little girl.

Who on this earth prevented a child from speaking to or seeing the people that she loved? True, Mary had kept Star from seeing Jimmy in prison, but that was to protect her, not punish her. Star would see her daddy again when he was better and back living in the real world. The man locked up was not the daddy that she knew and loved. Mary *protected* Star. Susan was hiding her.

Sheila Gilhooley, on hearing the news that Star had been taken away, had called in to see Mary a few days ago. It was a hot day – as Sheila herself even commented, "the sun was cracking the flags," and still, the coat and slippers were firmly on her, as she stood on Mary's front step clutching a piece of paper.

"Oh, Mrs Mack, Mrs Mack," Sheila started. "I won't keep you, God bless you, but I just wanted to give you this." She handed the piece of paper to Mary. It was a crumpled up picture of Saint Jude with a short prayer printed on the back. "Me mother gave it to me the day I started school."

Mary thanked Sheila Gilhooley. Saint Jude was the patron saint of hopeless causes.

*

Star looked at herself in the mirror. She looked pretty alright, just as Mr Bertie and Mrs O'Connell had said, but her face looked downright miserable. There was a girl at St Stephen's in the Juniors whose name was Erica Binns. The lads called her Binman and Star thought that was why she was so sad all the time. Her skin was greyish and the corners of her lips faced down to her chin, and she sat on the wall a lot picking skin from the palms of her hands. Star felt sad. Her reflection reminded her of Erica Binns.

Her outfit was from George Henry Lee, where Star had only ever gone in with Aunty Vera to get free sprays of all the perfumes and then for a look around the toy department, never actually buying anything. The dress had a magenta taffeta skirt and black velvet bodice with sparkles in the material. Her shoes were the ones that she had wanted ever since the best television advert in the whole world had come onto their screens about a year ago; The Princess Magic Step shoes from Clarks. The advert showed a little girl becoming a Princess and escaping an evil witch in a forest with the help of her magic shoes, and they were white with a tiny diamond on the front and a secret key inside the heel. Still, Star felt awful that even by having the Princess shoes, she couldn't find a way to be happy. She wished her daddy could see her, all dressed up like a princess. He'd make her smile by calling her a "sight for sore eyes," and then tickle her tummy saying, "only kiddin' sweetheart." And her daddy would make this whole evening more entertaining, too. He was brilliant at telling jokes; he learned hundreds of them down at the docks, only Star could never remember them. Actually, she didn't get why most of them were funny, but he could make grown-ups cry with laughter. She liked the Paddy and Mick ones, though. Like when Paddy and Mick were walking up the road and Paddy fell down a hole and said, "Mick, call me an ambulance," and Mick said, "You're an ambulance! You're an ambulance!"

Star could hear music coming from downstairs. It was nice music reminding her of the black and white movies that she was so fond of. She imagined Aunt Susan's guests arriving in long, glittery dresses and tuxedos, dancing cheek to cheek around the single table in the centre of the large entrance of the house. She closed her eyes, hearing the saxophone and the violins and imagined her daddy with her, picking her up and twirling her around the room.

"*An ordinary day, becomes a holiday, when I'm with you,*" Star sang and hummed a little. "*I have lots of toys, but I don't wanna play... when I'm with you.*"

She spun around, letting her taffeta skirt flow out into a big puffball.

"*Oh, daddy, how I miss you.*
You're busy all your life,
I long to hug and kiss you,
Marry me and let me be your wife."

A man clearing his throat interrupted Star. "Excuse me, little Miss. Dinner is served."

Star frowned at Mr Bertie.

"Oh dear," he said. "Why do all the ladies pull that face when they see me?"

"I'm sorry, Mr Bertie. I miss my daddy so much. And Nannie and my friends and everyone. I even miss hearing Mick Tully swearing all over the street on a Friday night."

"My word!"

"I just want to go home."

"But perhaps, little Miss, you are home."

Star managed a smile, even the beginning of a laugh. "Oh no, Mr Bertie. This will never be home, silly."

*

"Mary, *Corrie* hasn't even started," Vera said answering the phone.

"Vera," Mary said, her voice sounding shaky. "I need John to pick me up in the morning. Eight o'clock. Don't ask any questions."

"Alright, but can I come?"

"I said no questions. But yes, you can come. Wear something comfy and don't wear your high heels…"

"I've only got high heels."

"Well the lowest high heels, then. And bring your purse."

"Mary what's going on?"

"No more questions, just promise me you'll come."

"I promise."

*

The two words said together to describe what was happening baffled Star. Dinner and Party. The dinner was not a dinner – small bits of food slapped in the centre of a huge white plate – and this was certainly no party. Where were the balloons, the presents, the cheese and pineapple on sticks? There were no glitzy party frocks; the women all wore baggy trouser suits in bright colours such as purple and red with great big matching earrings and the men wore really dull suits that seemed too tight on them. The only time Star got spoken to was when Aunt Susan told her off for yawning at the table, and it was the most lame telling off ever, full of head-nodding and tut-tut-ting. It just made Star want to yawn again to see if she could provoke Aunt Susan to lose her temper. *That* would liven up this 'party'. And to make matters worse, Star had to sit on two copies of the Yellow Pages so that she was level with the other guests, all of whom were at least four times her age, and the taffeta skirt kept making her slip around so much that it was as though she were sitting on a block of ice.

"Aunt Susan?" Star asked just as Mrs O'Connell served the dessert and the guests had stopped chatting about some sort of boring sounding game called Bridge.

Aunt Susan looked up giving her crocodile smile.

"When can I go back to school?"

The ting tings of silver forks against the china all stopped at the same time.

"You're not at school?" a lady with hair cut very short like a man asked.

"I haven't been in ages."

"Tomorrow," Aunt Susan grinned, the grin becoming wider and wider. "Holiday time is over and you're back to school tomorrow…"

"Does that mean I get to go home tomorrow, too?" Star said, the excitement causing her to slip right off her chair and fall onto the floor.

"My word!" Mr Bertie rushed to Star's side, helping her up.

"Terrific tiramisu, Susan," the man with a shiny head and hairy nostrils pointed out.

"Rebecca, it's time for bed," Aunt Susan said, less giggles emerging. "Andrews, take her up, please. And make sure there is a car ready to take her to school in the morning."

"But I'll need to go back to Nannie's first. My uniform and packed lunch box is there. And my reading book."

"Tomorrow will be a special day, Rebecca. You may wear your own clothes. I'll let the school know…"

"But…"

"Goodnight, Rebecca. Say goodnight to our guests."

Star could not believe her luck. She was escaping the dinner party *and* going to school tomorrow. Some of the guests had become slightly giddy since arriving, more and more so as they drank the punch. Star had not touched the punch, but she felt giddier than if she'd emptied the whole drinks cabinet.

"Goodnight, my love, your little Dutch dolly is yawning..." Star sang, Mr Bertie picking her up and carrying her out of the room. But Star continued to sing, waving goodbye with her hand over his shoulder. *"Goodnight, my love, your teddy bear's called it a day!*

"Sleep tight, my love...

Goodnight, my love...

God bless you pleasant dreams, sweeeeeeet-heart!"

She wondered how she would ever fall asleep, her anticipation for the morning to come mixed with the rumble in her tummy from excitement and hunger; a handful of prawns on a bunch of slimy green beans were not exactly filling. But the soft bed encased her, and Star's eyes flickered beneath the moon shining through the skylight. She was no longer Star Blake in a posh house in Southport, but all dressed up like the little Dutch dolly, complete with a white hat that curled up at the ends and wearing a pair of wooden clogs on her feet. Surrounding her were lots and lots of boys and girls, all wearing Dutch costumes too, and wooden clogs that clomped as they walked. As they danced around, they all sang;

"We'll take a trip, wherever we choose,

We'll dance and skip, in our little wooden shoes."

Star stood in the middle of a circle and asked everybody;

"How many miles will you travel with me?

One mile, or two miles, or maybe three?"

And all the boys and girls held hands around her as she disappeared, flying off to a faraway land.

30th May, 1989

"Stop the car, John," Mary said, taking a large blanket out from one of her carrier bags. "Pull over anywhere here."

Vera flicked her head from side to side and over her shoulder to Mary sitting in the back. "You're kiddin' aren't you? We picked you up just to bring you here? Five minutes away?"

They were parked outside St Stephen's school.

"With all those bags you're carrying full of food, I thought we were going for a picnic somewhere," Vera huffed, sounding all disappointed. "John's even decided not to go into work today, haven't you, love?"

"Vera, get in the back with me. John, get your paper out and read. Go!"

Vera began to question why, but Mary cut her off by grabbing her shoulder-pad and dragging her into the back with her. Being so birdlike and tiny, Vera almost flew backwards from the strength of her big sister's pull, but not without yelping a series of "ouches."

"Duck down," Mary commanded, throwing the blanket over both of their heads. "John, don't really *read*, pretend to read but be looking out for Star. The second you see her, tell us."

John let out a big sigh, mumbling something along the lines of "whatever you say, Mary."

"What the hell is going on Mary?" Vera muffled.

"I miss her, Vera. I just need to see her, to tell her something, that's all."

"So why are we hiding?"

Mary had thought this through. It hadn't been difficult seeing as she hadn't slept a wink last night. "I don't want to see anybody. They'll ask about Star, they'll ask about Jimmy. I can't take it all in at the moment, Vera, and I don't want people prying."

Vera touched her sister's hand and squeezed it. Mary felt her first pang of guilt that morning as she knew how much Vera craved her to open up emotionally and she was using it now as part of her grand plan, not genuinely.

Mary kicked the driver's seat in the back with her foot. "You better not be reading the sports, John."

"Or page three. It's a school, John, for God's sake," Vera added.

*

Star knew that she could not arrive outside her school in a big, flashy car. It would be the end of any popularity she had forever. It was acceptable to get dropped off in a nice new car, normal to arrive in a car that could do with a wash, and cool to be allowed to walk to school on your own. A chauffeur was out of bounds. This she explained to Aunt Susan's driver who seemed to understand. He told Star that he used to be a school boy himself, which Star liked. With St Stephen's in view, Star was able to get out of the car just around the corner.

"Don't wait to see me go in though," Star said. "I'm a bit early so I can nip into the newsagents and buy a snack for playtime."

The driver winked and Star returned the gesture.

Aunt Susan had given her three pounds to get a school dinner, which was way too much money. Star had always envied the children who walked alone to school because they always stopped off at Si's and bought sweets before the bell went, and now was her chance to enter into this world.

Her eyes roamed over the selection of chocolate bars and the jars of sweets on shelves behind. There were boxes on the floor full of ten pence packets of crisps and a group of boys from the Juniors hanging around the comics. Star was just tall enough for her eyes to peer over the counter, her body hidden below. She was glad because already she felt strange not having her uniform on, not liking that everybody else looked the same and there she was in a pretty floral dress from George Henry Lee.

"Can I have a Bounty please?" Star asked Si. "And a quarter of cola pips."

"Of course, queen."

This was so much fun, Star thought, buying sweets before school just like the big kids. She couldn't wait to be their age for real. Leaving Si's, she put the paper bag of cola pips into the pocket on her skirt and unwrapped the Bounty, setting off towards school. She knew she better eat the whole Bounty quick because although she was sure that her friends would have missed her and be glad to see her, it wouldn't stop Louise Fitzpatrick from wanting half.

It was when Star passed the church, just feet away from the school gate that she heard her name called, sharp and loud, just once. She turned around, and around, and around until she had done a full circle, but did not spot any of her friends at all.

"Star!"

Again, there it was, coming from just across the road. But nobody in sight except for the really fat lady who always stood near St Stephen's with a large pram stuffed with three babies and a double buggy with twins. There was a tiny girl from the reception class standing by the railings with her mum, crying so much that her nose was running all down the front of her uniform. She had cried like this every morning since last September, and what she hated about St Stephen's so much, Star could not work out. The crying turned into a huge scream, making Star look away with shock. How could so much noise come from a girl so small? But it was then that Star spotted Uncle John's car parked outside the house where an old lady who looked like a ghost just stared out of her bedroom window all day. Two older boys coming in the opposite direction kicked a football into the playground, causing some commotion amongst the mothers who were standing around with pushchairs, and Star ignored this, running straight over to Uncle John.

He looked up from his paper and moved his lips, smiling and waving. He leant over to the passenger door opening it, and Star clambered inside.

"Head between your legs!" A fierce voice whispered from the back seat.

Star twisted around to see a large picnic blanket with moving bumps beneath it. Nannie's head peaked over the top. "Put your head between your legs! Now!"

Doing as she was told, Star bent over in the passenger seat, her head turned towards Uncle John who was shrugging, a face that told her that he was just as confused as she was.

"John. Drive!"

And off they drove, away from the school gates, past the church and onto the main road that led to Liverpool City Centre.

"Lime Street Station, John," Nannie's voice became clear and she unveiled hers and Aunty Vera's head. "We're going to London."

*

When Mary and Vera were little war evacuees, living in a country village just outside of Ormskirk, Vera had stolen dried fruit from the pantry of the cottage that they were staying in so that the snowman in the garden could have a pair of eyes and a decent sized nose. Mrs Kimble had known exactly how much dried fruit was in the pantry that day - every mouthful of food being accounted for during wartime – and Mary had stood up to take the blame. Vera had watched as her big sister got the broom against her backside twice, followed by some slaps to the calves and an early bedtime without supper. When Vera crawled into bed that night beside Mary, teary eyed and guilty, Mary just said, "Don't ever cry. I promised I'd look after you, didn't I?" And that was the end of that.

Only it wasn't.

Vera had never forgotten about that, and it was only now, now when they arrived at Lime Street Station with a child they should certainly not have with them, that she knew the time for giving Mary what she owed was upon her.

The journey to the station had been manic. There were so many voices talking all at the same time that no sense was made of the situation. Mary had plotted to take Star from school because of some crazy idea that she had to meet Shirley Temple in London… Vera couldn't remember what she asked except she knew that it was over a hundred questions in between trying not to pass out with nerves or have a heart attack… Star was asking both women questions which complicated matters more… and John not only kept hitting his steering wheel, but stalled the car. Twice.

John parked outside the Empire Theatre's stage door, opposite a taxi rank. Star had started to cry, frustration written all over her freckles, and Vera caught John's eyes in the rear view mirror. He was begging her to calm down.

"Don't cry, Star," Mary said passing her a clean handkerchief from her coat pocket. "You're not going to school today…"

"But I want to, Nannie. It's my first day back in ages."

Silence filled the car for the first time all morning. Vera had been under the impression that Star was back at school, and from the still reaction from Mary, she had, too.

"Aunt Susan hasn't even got me a uniform, so I had to wear this."

Mary's dropped open mouth mutated into a smile and she snorted, the snort making her laugh. A right cackle of a laugh, and she nudged Vera who had no idea what the laughing matter could be but copied her sister just the same. Star and John were looking from each other to the two women in bafflement.

"I knew that Susan Lloyd was good for something!" Mary laughed.

"She was good for something, she was!" Vera joined in, still unaware.

"I knew she'd come up trumps!"

"Trumps indeed, Mary!"

"Stop it!" Star shouted. "You're embarrassing me."

"Welcome to my world," John grunted.

Like two naughty little girls, Mary and Vera put their hands over their mouths to control their cackles.

Mary took a deep breath and explained. "I brought Star's jacket, but I didn't bring a change of clothes. I forgot! But I don't have to worry because she's in her own clothes. No one will wonder why she's not in school. Oh thank you, Susan Lloyd, for correcting my mistake. And she goes a whole step further, does our Susan, for she kept Star off until today. Today! Today! So, Miss Murphy won't think it odd for Star to be off today because she's been off for ages. Another day will not hurt a bit! Oh I love Susan Lloyd today!"

Vera actually felt worry in the pit of her stomach that her sister had finally lost the plot. And the banana she'd eaten for breakfast was sitting uncomfortably in there, too. Always a mistake to eat a banana with more than one black bruise.

Star was still not impressed. Her glances to John had not seemed to help and now she was pleading to Vera with her big blue eyes. Mary was verging on delirious and needed a moment to calm down, so Vera paused and pieced together the information that she had worked out.

"Shirley Temple was on Terry Wogan's show on the tele last night," Vera began. "Nannie watched it. Shirley's an older lady now…"

"Sixty-one," Star interjected. "Sixty-one last April."

"Oh, okay. Well, she is in London today. She's written a book about her life and is signing the book today in Harrods', the poshest shop in the whole world."

Mary had calmed herself. She leant over to Star who was kneeling up on the passenger seat facing the women. Taking Star's little hand, Mary finished off what Vera had started. "And we're taking you to meet her. To meet Shirley Temple."

Star's mouth dropped and froze so much that if a fly flew in, she probably wouldn't have noticed. And then, she let out a squeal of delight and threw herself into the back of the car, hugging both Mary and Vera.

"Don't think I'm getting in the back, now," John said, shaking his head.

Vera knew that this was all wrong, and not just wrong, but surely it was illegal. Jesus, Mary and Joseph! This was kidnap! But despite how wrong it all was, it couldn't help but seem right. Totally right. With all the wrong that had happened to Mary and Star - and

God bless him, Jimmy - this was not *wrong*. It was taking a little girl to meet her idol. It was love.

"Now, Mary," Vera started. "I know you're going to say no, but I'm coming with you. I'm going to be there for you. You took the blame when I stole the dried fruit and now, whatever happens, I'm going to be there to stand up for you today and besides, nothing much exciting ever happens to me…"

"Excuse me, dear," John reminded her of his presence.

"Sorry, John. I love you. But anyway, I'm not missing out. I may be your little sister, Mary, but I am not missing out…"

"I know," Mary said. "Why do you think I told you to wear something comfy?"

"You knew I'd come all along? Even though we're…" Vera decided to speak through her teeth, *"breaking the law."*

"Why are you breaking the law?" Star asked loudly.

"Out, out, all of us, out!" Mary said. "And John, take the day off. Enjoy the garden."

The three ladies stepped out of the car, and Mary opened up a carrier bag taking out Star's blue raincoat with Minnie Mouse's face printed all over the inside and her *My Little Pony* lunch box. Vera stood beside John and he wound down the window.

"Be careful, dear," he said. "I'll stay home. Call me from a payphone if you need anything."

"Ready for an adventure, Star?" Mary asked. "Vera?"

Vera smiled through chattering teeth.

Star simply smiled, revealing the dimple in her cheek. "Oh, yes. Let's go and search for the Blue Bird."

*

Jimmy's own mam, Lilly, had been told by doctors that she would never be able to have children. As a young girl, she had suffered terrible injuries during the May Blitz in Liverpool, with bits of shrapnel still in her body the day that she died fifteen years later. Young Jimmy was considered a miracle when he was born completely strong and healthy, but he only remembered his mam curled up in her chair covered by a woollen blanket reading magazines, daydreaming about the life that she could have led if she were fit and able. It was the shock of Flinder Street when Jimmy's father, Sid, died first. He was the local window cleaner and fell from the top of his ladder just two streets away, breaking his neck. Sid hadn't realised that the ledge on the top window he was cleaning was loose - an after-effect from the war that had gone unnoticed – and he lost his balance when he leant his hand on it. Or so the coroner had said seeing the splinters and scratches on the palm of Sid's left hand. Jimmy would go and stand outside that house for months after his father's death, just staring at the hanging window-ledge; the owners couldn't be bothered to fix it, yet his own dad had the good grace to get up there and clean it. A wooden chipped-white painted ledge, just jigging to and fro in the wind.

It was this image that was torturing Jimmy today in his cell. Perhaps it was Addo's fault, talking about his own family, how he missed going down to the pub for a pint on a Sunday afternoon with his dad, or hearing his mother laugh, something he feared he would never hear again in her company. At the very least this took his mind away from the guilty feelings he had over Mary.

Mary Mack was his mother. Yes, he had had a mam who was a good woman, but had been scarred and ruined before he was even born. It was Mary who had been the real mother to him. What would he have done if she hadn't took him in, clothed and fed him, sent him to school and given him a family? And still, he had ended up here. A criminal. Even worse, Jimmy's thanks to Mary had been to take the most precious thing in her life away from her; Star. But what could a loving family do anyway without wealth and connections in this world? He knew that he had now chosen wealth over love when it came to Star but, Christ, it was 1989 and if money had always mattered, it mattered more than ever now.

Jimmy knew that Mary had had a husband, but he didn't ever remember him being around. He also knew that nobody, not even Vera, spoke about it. When Linda had died, Jimmy seemed to turn his house into a shrine whereas he had never seen a single photo of Mr Mack. Many times he had wanted to ask Mary, tried even, but he had not been an adult long when his own world was shattered with the death of his wife for him to have the energy to pry any longer.

He suddenly did not know what was worse; the image of his father's death scene, or wondering whether Star being taken from Mary was the worst thing to happen to Mary since Mr Mack's disappearance.

*

Mary hoped to the high Heavens that her nerves on the inside could not be seen on the outside as clear as Vera's. If someone said to Vera, *don't look behind you*, she'd not only look but make a spectacle of herself whilst doing so. Her head was zigzagging all over the place as they waited in line to buy train tickets.

Mary elbowed her skinny ribs, but Vera screeched, "Ow."

"Subtle, Vera, very subtle," Mary gritted her teeth, but Vera elbowed back only it wouldn't hurt Mary and her extra layers of skin. "Just keep still, will you?"

"What if we get caught?" Vera said. "What if we get found and…"

"Ssh." They were next and Mary marched ahead to the desk. "Three to London, please."

The man behind the desk grunted and tapped away at a machine without speaking or even looking up. When the tickets were printed, he pushed them beneath the glass divider, his long fingernails wedged with dirt pressing down onto the paper.

"Jesus!" Mary whispered looking at the total, but Vera had peered over her shoulder and managed a much louder, "Christ almighty!" and made a Sign of the Cross, which Mary hoped would make the Lord himself just this once hear them and help, for there was not nearly enough money in her purse to cover a cost like that.

*

Star kept bobbing up and down on her tip-toes to see what all the kerfuffle was about. It was clear that the tickets were too expensive, but Nannie would not let her see how much. Giving up, she huffed and glanced upwards, her eyes catching a notice on the wall displaying, 'children aged five and under travel for free.'

"Excuse me, Mr?" Star said to the grunting man.

He grunted.

"I was standing way up on my toes. Really, Mr, I'm this tall." Star let her knees bend, a little more and a little more, just enough so that her bottom was not sticking out like an old lady.

"Huh!" The grunt formed a word. "Y'still look old enough t'pay."

Shooting her head up towards Nannie and Aunty Vera, Star noticed that they were still bickering; counting money into each other's hand in between slapping each other's hand, and then taking a moment to moan at Jesus and his family. Poor Jesus. His ears must burn constantly.

Star had been to Lime Street Station a few times because the trains from there went to New Brighton. Her daddy had taken her and Laura Fenton once on a Bank Holiday Monday. They had played crazy golf and eaten sausage, chips and mushy peas sitting on a bench looking over the Mersey towards Liverpool. Daddy had pointed out the Liver Buildings and the cathedrals that were divided by Hope Street, until Laura Fenton complained that she was bored out of her brains and then accidentally on purpose started choking on a sausage. Star remembered watching a man play his guitar just outside the newsagents in Lime Street Station. He had hair like Boy George and was singing 'In My Life' by The Beatles, and her daddy gave her thirty pence to throw into his guitar case.

There was nobody with a guitar outside the newsagents today, though. Instead, an old man sat on the floor wearing a flat cap and making a half-hearted attempt to play a harmonica. Star wandered towards him, stopping when she was about a metre away. Three musical notes echoed around the station and Star did a shuffle step with her right foot; three quick steps, one-two-three. A further set of musical notes followed - four this time – and as they ended, Star danced a little toe-heel, toe-heel. The old man noticed Star this time, opening his mouth to say something, possibly shoo her away but she spoke first.

"Don't stop… Let me dance to your playing."

His face looked weary, mystified as to why Star was asking this.

"Please."

He gave a smile from just one side of his mouth, revealing a very brown, pointed tooth, and pulled the harmonica back up play.

After every short series of musical notes, Star would copy the amount with tap dancing steps. As the rhythm picked up, the unlikely duo began to respond to each other and the music started to overlap the dance. Star was impressed with her Princess Magic Step shoes; usually the sound of tap dancing sounded dull without her tap shoes, but she could hear her steps loud and clear. Dancing away in the middle of the train station, she started to use her arms – up high and out diagonally – incorporating some stamps to try and get the attention of passersby. A lady in a trouser suit and high heels walked past looking very irritated by the dancing, shaking her head and huffing, but a man wearing some overalls and a builder's hat stopped for a moment. He squinted his eyes, focussing on Star as if she were an alien before he too, shook his head and did a huff, moving on. Then there was some sniggering from a gang of boys, teenagers, with shaved heads and pimpled faces.

"Eeeh!" A boy yelled. "What a meff!"

Anthony Tucker called everyone he hated a 'meff' and Star had once used it when she had seen Christopher McGinty's finger pull a revolting string of green from his nose. With one loud stamp, she decided to stop, defeated.

There wasn't a single coin on the ground in sight.

Just as Star was about to rejoin Nannie and Aunty Vera - still fighting a losing battle with each other – all embarrassed, feeling stupid, the old man said, "Hey!"

Lifting up her chin, she saw the old man take off his flat cap and like a Frisbee, sent it flying in the direction of where she was standing. It actually hit Star on the shoulder and dropped to the floor in front of her.

"Hey!" He said again.

"Hey!" Star echoed back.

A strong musical note blasted from the harmonica and the routine picked itself back up.

"Hey!" Star shouted out with a heel roll and a clap of her hands. "Hey!"

People were definitely staring now; the queue by the ticket desk was facing the opposite direction, everybody trying to see where the strange entertainment was coming from. The ladies working in the coffee shop were leaning over the counter to get a good look and Star noticed four... five... six people stop to watch.

"Hey!"

It felt good to shout out, her brain working so hard to remember every tap sequence she had ever learnt at dancing classes or the ones that she had invented in the playground. There was actually a crowd building up; a few men in suits with long black coats and briefcases had bothered to stop with amused grins on their clean-shaven faces, women with prams and toddlers on reigns, and even the boys who had teased her were now clapping along, giving the odd "whoop". Then someone shouted, "yee-hah!" and Nannie was standing at the front of the crowd, leading the claps with Aunty Vera besides her doing a little awkward dance. Star bent her knees and picked up the flat cap, lifting it to her head and then high in the air, repeating this as she kicked her legs. She caught her partner's eye and winked at him. The old man puffed out one last long, loud finishing note and Star ended down on one knee holding the cap out to catch pennies.

And catch them, she did! A handful of silver ten pence pieces fell in, along with some twenties, even a fifty. And another fifty. Someone dropped a pound, and then a further pound, and another pound again. One lady threw a Milky Bar into the hat, saying, "no change, luv." Star could not stop saying, "thank you," curtseying like a yo-yo as the money rained in.

The crowd filtered away, most people having to run to catch their trains. Star sat on the floor beside the old man, thanking him also, and began to count the coins to divide into two.

"*We should be together…*" Star hummed. "*Like the frame and picture….*"

"Like shoes and stockings?" the old man suggested.

"*Like the clocks tick tockings*," Star started to giggle and slid his half of their earnings across to him, to which the old man shook his head and added a, "N-n-n-no!" He mumbled something about having all day to do this, but could he take fifty pence, "For a cup of coffee?"

Star gave him a pound instead. "And a peachy pie! *We should be together you and I.*"

The old man gave Star the pleasure of seeing his full smile, complete with a few more brown spiky teeth and a lot of gum, which startled her a little, giving Nannie and Aunty Vera the cue to drag her away and get the tickets before they missed the train.

Once they arrived on the platform, Nannie stopped still, grabbing Star's hand and the sleeve of Aunty Vera's jacket.

"What is it, Mary?" Aunty Vera asked.

Nannie squeezed Star's hand tighter. "Police."

The large clock behind told them that they had less than one minute to board the train, but two policemen were walking quite casually along the platform, looking sure of where they were going.

A whistle blew once. And for a woman with hip replacements, Star could not believe how fast Nannie dragged her along, so speedy, as they ran to the first carriage and jumped aboard. The door of the train was barely shut when a whistle blew again. But the train did not move.

"Do not look out of the window," Nannie said as the three of them slotted into a cluster of empty seats. "Just look at me. Vera, *at me*."

"Oh, Jesus, Mary," Aunty Vera whispered. "What are we doing?"

And then the train let out a gasp of air, and bumped forward.

Bump, bump, bump, became chug, chug, chug, and with every chug they were a split second further away from Liverpool.

PART TWO

On 30th May, 1989, Student demonstrators at Tiananmen Square in Beijing erected a 33-foot statue they called the "Goddess of Democracy."

Joan of Arc died on this day 558 years ago.

Gerry Marsden featuring The Christians, Holly Johnson and Paul McCartney were Number One in the UK charts with a charity version of 'Ferry Cross the Mersey'. All profits from the single went to those affected by the Hillsborough Disaster.

30th May 1989
9.23am

The train smelled of burning rubber. That made sense to Star, and Nannie confirmed it as 'rubber' after Aunty Vera had mumbled something about the train smelling like burning flesh. It wasn't the most pleasant of smells, but it beat the alley behind Flinder Street, especially after a Friday night. The speed that they were travelling to London was definitely faster than the train that Star would catch with Nannie into Liverpool's city centre whenever they went clothes shopping, or to George Henry Lee to get free sprays of perfume.

"I wonder what John's doing…" Aunty Vera said, tapping her scarlet red finger nails on the table. She looked as though she missed him. They had only been on the train for half an hour - entertaining each other with guessing games and writing Shirley Temple a personal letter - so it was ridiculous to miss Uncle John already, yet Star felt his absence, too. There wasn't a single time when Star had gone somewhere with Aunty Vera and without Uncle John. He always drove. They were never seen apart, just as Kylie was never seen without Jason on the front cover of *Smash Hits!* And along with Nannie, they were like the three bears. Aunty Vera had even said that from time to time, usually as she was leaving after a birthday get-together or on Christmas night when Uncle John complained that saying goodbye took too long. "They should say 'good bye' when they bloody well say 'hello'," he said.

"Why didn't he come with us?" Star asked, peeling a tangerine from her lunch box.

"Because he'd get kicked out of Harrods' for acting the goat," Nannie said.

Yes, Star missed Uncle John on this adventure. He would be tearing up bits of paper and dropping them onto the top of Star's head, pretending he was all innocent.

Once, Uncle John took Star on a little trip, just the two of them. They went all the way to China. They did, they did, they did, Star told herself again and again. They *must* have gone to China because it definitely wasn't a dream, or an imaginary story gone too far. They had walked around a supermarket and all the food had Chinese symbols printed on the packaging. Instead of bumping into someone from school, or the old lady with lilac hair who Nannie always tried to avoid in Farmfoods by holding a multipack of Quentin Crisps in front of her face, the aisles were full of Chinese people speaking in Chinese. How could they not have been in China? Star had the fortune cookie wrapper and paper fortune to prove it, just as Dorothy had the key in *Return to Oz*. If it was a dream like they had made out in the first movie, then how come Dorothy held the key in her hand during her Kansas life? And China existed even more than Oz in Star's opinion because she had met lots of Chinese people, such as Robert Chan who owned the chippy at the bottom of Flinder Street and his wife, Mrs Chan, who always gave smaller portions of chips. Star had still never met anybody from Oz.

But Star could never remember how she got to China. She had asked Uncle John whether she fell asleep in the car. He shrugged, sticking out his bottom lip. It seems unbelievable, but Star remembered walking alongside the Anglican Cathedral, a heavy and bitter wind blowing in her face causing her to keep her eyes closed and hold onto Uncle John's arm.

"You see that cathedral?" he asked.

Star took a quick peep and nodded. "It's not the Catholic one."

"No, but it was designed by the same man who designed the red phone box."

"Wow. Christopher McGinty loves them phone boxes. He calls ChildLine in them all the time and hangs up when they answer."

Was it possible that as they crossed the road at the bottom of the hill, Star had lost her memory and ended up in China for the day?

Her eyes felt sleepy, blinking slower and slower as she watched the Runcorn Bridge getting smaller and smaller.

"What have I got… in my hand?" Nannie sang to get the game going again as she poured Star a little drop of juice from the Mr. T flask into the white plastic cup.

Star jumped. "Can you eat it?" There was no way she was going to lose her memory on the day she would meet Shirley Temple.

9.58am

Crewe. The train had been stopped at the grey and soulless delight that happened to be Crewe Station. Mary glanced out onto the platform and into The Lemon Tree Café, where the tea-drinkers seemed to look as though they were either contemplating death, or dead. And to make matters worse, that awful song popped into her head just as Star belted out right on cue;

"Oh Mr. Porter, what shall I do?

I want to go to Birmingham but you've taken me to Crewe…"

"Star, no!" Mary stopped her.

Vera pursed her lips together, tight like a cat's bum. "I don't know that Shirley one."

"It's not a Shirley one," Mary and Star informed her in unison.

"Katy-Ann Froggatt sang it at our dancing school concert," Star added.

Vera's Clinique lips pulled in tighter. "Froggatt. What a bloody awful name."

Mary huffed. "The name sounds like angel dust compared to the foghorn of a voice that child has."

"Nannie!" Star tutted. "Oh my goodness."

Remembering the cola pips she had bought that morning at Si's, Star took the paper bag out of her dress pocket and started offering the sweets around. Everybody declined except for the priest who took two.

*

Jimmy rolled over to face the wall, thinking again of Christine. It was funny how often he thought about her these days; when they had been together, he had hardly thought about her at all.

They met in town in a bar just off Mathew Street, the kind of place where no one would start off their night, but end it there for multiple night-caps. Small, sweaty and situated at basement level, it was where the hardcore drinkers gathered after being kicked out of the two-storey 'Beatles' themed club above. Where singles went to avoid going home alone. A compilation of the latest chart music played in the background which made a refreshing change from the booming racket of carwash fever and disco tracks that had been echoing around Mathew Street just an hour earlier, each bar trying to out-do the next with their sound system. Jimmy hadn't heard a single Beatles' song all night.

He felt a tap on his shoulder as he sipped his fresh pint at the bar. "Carol Decker or Sinitta?" said a voice in his ringing ear. He turned around to see a girl with the widest smile, accentuated with bright pink lipstick and lots of tight blonde curls. Lots. His initial thought was that a lion had just approached him.

"Come on! Carol Decker or Sinitta?" she moved her mouth to his ear again. "You've got to choose. Which one would you shag?"

"Ay, Chrissy!" a different voice shouted down Jimmy's other ear. "Got another Sinitta here."

Jonesy had given his answer to 'Chrissy's' mate, a long, thin girl with hair in a high ponytail and so much blue eye shadow that she could pass for a victim of assault.

"Well, she likes 'em 'so macho' doesn't she?" Jonesy flexed his wannabe muscles, invisible behind his grey leather jacket.

"Change the record, lad," Chrissy's mate giggled.

"I'll take Carol Decker then," Jimmy said. "No point in arguing with Jonesy here. He may be far from original but he always gets the girls."

A true statement indeed seeing as Jonesy's hand was already exploring the girl's long, thin frame, only judging by the lycra outfit she wore, there was not much left to discover.

Jimmy turned to 'Chrissy' who was laughing as though he had just told the world's funniest joke. She had very straight teeth, which was nice. Taking a tip from Jonesy, she began to let her hands wander over Jimmy's arms, then his back, and his neck. He could smell Bacardi on her breath as she continued to laugh close to his face, a sign that she didn't smoke.

"I'm Christine," she smiled. "Are you gonna buy us a drink?"

"Are you sure you need another?" he regretted that immediately.

Christine pushed herself away. "I'm not drunk, you know. I've been dancing most of the night." No longer smiling, she began to adjust her sparkly top - which was low-cut and revealing round, large breasts - to cover her chest up a little with a look of insecurity passing over her face. She was older than she looked, maybe twenty-five, twenty-six...

"What are you having, queen?" Jimmy asked, feeling bad.

"We're both on the Bacardi and cokes," she said gesturing with her handbag to her mate whose tongue was now firmly down Jonesy's throat.

And as their friends made out to Belinda Carlisle singing about heaven being a place on earth, Jimmy and Christine sat at the bar and talked. It was either that or sit alone, unless Christine had fancied playing the Carol Decker/Sinitta game without her mate, which she clearly didn't. Jimmy found himself being quite open with this girl, easily uncovering the fact that he was a widower who missed his wife every day, and that he had a little girl who was the most unique character he had ever met. Maybe it was because Christine listened, or maybe it was the drink… Or maybe it was because he was just not interested in this woman yet forced into a situation that he felt so comfortable talking to her. She worked full-time in Boots and had wanted to go to university after her A-levels to study English, but couldn't afford it. Apparently she wasn't so bothered anymore because she got good discount on cosmetics.

The four of them caught a taxi back to Jonesy's flat despite Jimmy insisting that he get dropped off home to see Star. Jonesy pointed out that she was at Mary Mack's for the night. Besides, he was dying to show him the Chesterfield sofa his Auntie Bernie had let him have.

"Not one ciggie burn, Jim," Jonesy said with pride.

And that was when Christine grabbed Jimmy's hand. Grabbed it so hard he had no idea how to tell her that she should let go.

10.19am

Twenty minutes later, Vera made the point that the train still hadn't moved forward. Yes, she knew she had made this comment over and over again, but it had now been *twenty* minutes. Twenty would no doubt turn into twenty-five; she felt it in her gut. She knew, just as her gut had told her that the old gentleman with the glass eye who collected the offertory money in church was in love with Mrs Neary, the Eucharistic minister, and how *Brookside* would kill off Damon. Anyway, the burning rubber was making her nauseous.

"Let's get off," she said, standing up. "We'll never get to London at this rate."

"And how the bloody hell are we going to get to London if we get off this bloody train?" Mary asked.

Vera turned to the priest in a bid to apologise on Mary's behalf, when he opened his mouth and said, "I agree with you. This bloody train's going nowhere."

Eternal rain, fog and dark clouds sat like an oversized umbrella over the train stations of the North West, Crewe being no exception. It seemed odd that there was a shop that sold newspapers, magazines and a few Mills and Boon titles, yet everybody waiting was just staring into the drizzle, blending into the miserable weather. A few teenage boys circled about the platform on their BMX bikes and there was one elderly man doing a crossword puzzle, but he was spending more time tutting at the teens rather than giving his brain a workout.

"Remember the days, Mary," Vera said. "The days when folk would dress up smart just to leave the house. Even during the war, I remember the women all dolled up and the gents wearing suits, and a train station like this would be packed full of people in their Sunday best."

"Even on a Tuesday?" Star asked.

"Yes, luv. Even on a Tuesday."

"Like Mary and Laura Ingles in *Little House on the Prairie*. Their ma made them a Sunday best dress in pale blue, but they always wore it for birthday parties, when guests came to visit or when they had important days at school. And no one goes to school on a Sunday." Star started spinning around in circles. "But *Little House on the Prairie* is always on tele on a Sunday! So they *do* wear their Sunday best on a Sunday."

Mary pointed out that they needed a plan and a quick one otherwise they would all start acting as loopy as Star after too many cola pips and be stuck in Crewe forever. There was a lengthy queue at the ticket booth and it wasn't going anywhere fast, so Vera suggested nipping over to the pub to ask the landlord where they could get a coach from.

"I'm not going in a pub," Mary said. "It's not even eleven o'clock yet."

"Why don't you ever go to the pub?" Star asked. "Aunty Vera goes all the time, don't you?"

"Nannie hasn't gone to the pub since…"

"Shut it, Vera."

Vera hadn't meant to say that, not in front of Star. It had been one of the most stressful mornings of her life so far, and initiating getting off the train and coming up with another plan of action was all a bit much for her. It was always Mary with the ideas. Or John. As they stood there on platform two, wondering how to get to London, Vera knew that she and Mary were now thinking the same thing. Mary had never always been alone. And she hadn't always been a tea-total who would only ever go to the social club if it was a birthday, wedding or christening. There was a time when Mary was not just 'Mary Mack', but she was 'Mary and Will'.

"I know what you're thinking," Mary said hardly moving her lips.

"I'm not…it's just…" Vera felt all nervous again. "It's been years since we spoke about it and sometimes I just hope that you're over…"

"Don't."

"What were you thinking, Aunty Vera?" Star's little ears could hear for Great Britain.

Vera pulled herself upright and straightened her jacket. "I was thinking that the world has started to look a lot scruffier since nurses stopped wearing hats."

*

Mary was the disillusioned one. Vera was sentimental and Brian was romantic, so out of the three of them, Mary thought of herself as disillusioned. Unlike her siblings, the random cruelty of life prevented her from being with the one she loved. And to settle for less would have meant compromises being made in order to just tolerate.

It would have been so practical, so right, and so expected of her to marry the first young man who showed interest. A lot of interest. Meeting and courting Ray O'Toole was like buying a packet of fairy cake mix; it was easy to make, looked good and tasted nice. There were no surprises… even the hundreds and thousands to sprinkle over the icing could be found inside the box. You knew exactly what you were going to get. And that suited some people, *most* people it seemed. Ray had one of those jobs in an office where he had ample opportunities for promotion, only Mary never quite knew *what* he did. Of course he had told her, but she just could never seem to take it in. Her friends loathed her attitude; she should be grateful having a man to court her without any dirt in his fingernails from a hard day labouring, they'd say. *And* Ray was good-looking, the kind that all older women made a show of themselves over, saying things such as, "If I was ten years younger, I'd fight you for him," or "Ooh, can I keep him for myself," and they described him as "dishy". He had his own car. He was never late. He would have a packet of wine gums hidden in his jacket pocket for her, and more than once had he shown up on her doorstep with a box of Rowntree's Black Magic. Mary once told Ray that she didn't like dark chocolate and he was so apologetic that anyone would think he had murdered her cat. She had hoped he would get angry or say she was ungrateful; anything to spark a reaction that wasn't just admiration of her. What was he admiring anyway? On the surface they did look like the perfect couple, but beyond that, what was there? An empty space. Confused energy swaying backwards and forwards, desperately seeking passion.

Mary thought about Ray O'Toole every once in a while. She had broken his heart by declining his proposal – an answer she didn't even have to sleep on. A year later, Ray was married to another girl, and the last Mary ever heard was that he, his wife and three small children had gone to live over the water in Bebington. Sometimes she wondered if she would have become that Wirral wife, with a four bedroom house and a garage for the family car. In many ways she was relieved that had Ray finally got what he wanted, releasing the guilt she felt for saying 'no'.

It became more evident that Mary had never loved Ray O'Toole one night at The Parade, a local club in 1949. A haunt well-known for its live music and regular crowd, Mary and her work friends went there every Friday night if there was nothing special planned. Each Thursday at the sausage works factory, the young girls would start to get excited for their weekend, discussing where to go dancing and who they would be dancing with. Mary found this weekly conversation pretty dull, not to mention pointless; the outcome was more often than not, The Parade. Only this particular Friday *was* a special night - it was Brian's birthday and his new wife, Peggy, had invited the whole family over for a party. Vera - just turned eighteen - was rather put out at missing a night at The Parade, but Mary was quite happy with the change. Plus she was eternally grateful to their Brian for getting hitched and moving out; it meant her and Vera finally had their own bedrooms at the Flinder Street family home.

    The last party at Brian and Peggy's had been a great laugh. It was their house-warming and a combination of Peggy's buffet with Brian's drinks cabinet had resulted in a lively knees-up until sunrise. Mary was looking forward to a slice of homemade flan washed down with a gin and tonic, while Vera no doubt was excited about seeing their Brian's mates. After all, she was wearing her royal blue off-the-shoulder dress that made her tiny waist almost disappear, causing Mary to have to change her outfit last minute not wanting to feel like a wallflower next to her little sister. Mary decided on the yellow dress with a low, square neckline and full skirt. If the party was anything like the last one, they might as well go in their best frocks.

    Only, it was nothing like the last one. Not sure whether to describe it as a 'gathering' or a 'children's tea party', Mary was not impressed to find her brother's house swarming with their neighbours' kids high on strawberry jelly and a circle of adults sitting around the parlour drinking tea. There wasn't even any flan; apparently Peggy's pastry had started to give Brian heartburn.

"I got the best birthday pressie from Peg," Brian said to his sisters with a mouthful of banana cake. "She's having our first baby."

Despite their delight for the new addition to the family, Vera made a subtle suggestion to Mary about getting away from Brian's early to join some of their friends down at The Parade. Mary didn't waste a moment in agreeing. It was a relief when the girls made their apologies for leaving to hear Peggy complain about wanting everyone gone within half an hour anyway. She had been hoping for an early night.

The Parade was packed, people already standing outside to catch some fresh air and stop their heads from spinning. It was even time to leave for some; those who had drunk too much too soon. Mary disliked arriving here later than usual, having to walk into a frenzy of booze and noise and therefore play catch up all night, never quite on the same level as everybody else. It was alright for Vera; a sniff of beer and she was on the floor. However, it was good being around a crowd having fun, unlike the yawn of a crew that was at her brother's place.

Just as Mary thought she had lost her tiny sister into the sea of swing dancing, she spotted Vera's arm waving her over to the bar.

"These nice chaps have just bought us a gin and tonic," Vera smiled.

It was always lovely to have a drink bought for you, but Mary knew she'd need more than a few to be flirting with these 'nice chaps'. They looked like another bunch of Ray O'Tooles, a type of man she couldn't seem to get away from. Judging that they worked in an office and laughed at quite boring jokes during their cigarette breaks, it was interesting to find out that one of the chaps made maps for a living.

"Cartographer," Vera repeated him. "Doesn't that sound fabulous, Mary? *I'm a cartographer.*" All of the 'nice chaps' thought this was hilarious and made the unanimous decision that this little lady was "smashing." Within seconds, Vera was whisked onto the dance floor by the map-maker, which would have left Mary to be entertained by his side-kicks if she hadn't spotted some girlfriends at the end of the bar. However, making her way through the tipsy crowd was not easy and she found herself blocked in amongst groups of strangers.

"Hey," said a man's voice, relaxed as if they had just met at a tranquil park.

"Hey to you," Mary replied, obviously transparent to the people pushing and dancing around her. "Well you must be happy; you have a drink in each hand!"

"So I do! Would you like one?"

"I'm alright, ta," Mary lifted up her gin and tonic. "Cheers."

And then it happened. One of those moments that are often talked about but never experienced, that feature in fairy tales or Hollywood pictures and make married couples with nothing left to say to each other want to sneak out of bed and start an affair; a moment in which somebody such as Mary never believed in... Her eyes met the man's with the two drinks and they laughed together as if one of them had told an inappropriate joke yet they both found it funny.

"I'm Will," he said, his eyes widened. They were blue, clear and alive.

"I'm Mary." For once, that was all Mary had to say... and she liked it.

"Well, this was unexpected."

"Yes."

They moved away from the dance floor, standing against a wall covered with old sketches of London, Manchester and Liverpool. Will placed one of his beer bottles onto a table behind them.

"Somebody'll drink that if you don't keep your eye on it," Mary said.

"It's okay, I don't really want it."

"That's a posh accent. You're not from around here are you?"

"No. I'm from Bedfordshire, not far from London. I guess I'm just on a bit of a holiday."

"A holiday in Liverpool? Are you crackers?"

"There's a great atmosphere to the place." Once again, Will opened his eyes a little wider as he stared at her. There was no joke, nothing comedic about this, yet Mary felt like they were both on the brink of wanting to laugh again. "I'm actually here to play rugby."

"Oh," Mary shrugged. "I know absolutely nothing about rugby. Liverpool's more of a footy place… all I know is that the goal posts are dead high in rugby."

"That's a start. I used to play professionally, but broke my arm and I'm just getting back into it." He showed Mary a thick white scar on his left arm which she ran her index finger across. "We're playing Waterloo tomorrow."

"So how long are you here for?"

"Just another day. We head back down south on Sunday."

"That's a shame."

"I know. A real shame."

Everybody was kicked out of The Parade by one o'clock the next morning to get buses, trams and cabs back home to sleep the hectic night off, but neither Will nor Mary wanted to leave. She kissed Vera goodnight, making sure she was heading in the direction of home with friends. Vera winked, but was incapable of making it subtle, her mouth opening and closing as she did so.

"Let's get the tram to the Pier Head," Mary suggested. "I know a lovely spot where we can just sit and talk. Sometimes I go there by myself just to think. It sounds corny but during the Blackout, I remember me mam saying how the Pier Head was as stubborn as a Scouser because it refused to be completely blacked out."

"And why is that?"

"Because the moon always shone onto the Mersey and lit up its surroundings."

Will stared into Mary's eyes again. "You Scousers are stubborn then? Is this something you're telling me in advance… like a warning?"

"Not stubborn. We just won't be told what to do!"

"I'd better remember that then."

Will offered his arm to Mary and she took it, smiling, and then laughing.

"What *are* you laughing at, Mary?" Will asked.

"You! You keep staring at me and… look! You're doing it again!"

"What?!"

"Stop it, Will. God, I feel like we need some violins and a tragedy, you're so bloody romantic the way you look at me."

Will looked amused. "You are lovely."

Mary stopped, and for once, accepted a compliment.

The water did glisten in the moonlight, but only slightly, dappling spots onto a patch of river. Birkenhead could be seen in the distance, a sight that would have been simply black just a few years before. They sat on a bench overlooking the water. Will took a packet of Camels out of his pocket and struck a match as Mary watched the close light gently illuminate his tanned face. His sandy-brown hair was loose and almost messy on the top of his head and he had a small mole on his left cheek.

"Can I mug a smoke?" Mary whispered into his ear. She kept her mouth right there for a moment and the tip of her nose brushed his cheek as she moved a little.

"So, what do you think about?" It was very dark now, except for the moon and a few dim streetlights, but he found her lips with his fingertips and popped a cigarette into her mouth. "When you come here alone. What does Mary think about?"

"Me dad and me nana. They died in the Blitz. Me mam of course; she's dead frail, you know, like a really old woman but she's only in her forties. Never been the same since she lost me dad." Mary curled her legs up onto the bench, draping her yellow skirt over them. "And I think about Vivien Leigh, me favourite actress. Have you seen *Waterloo Bridge*?"

He hadn't.

"It's the saddest film I've ever seen. It made me happy that I wasn't her in it! She was the gear, though." Mary laughed, loud and unafraid. "I think about me job and how I hate me boss, Eddie Cunny - well, his real name's Edward Cunningham - because he's a right sleaze."

"Where do you work?" Will asked her.

"Oh, just a factory out in Litherland."

"Litherland? That doesn't sound like a real place! *Litherland*."

"It's real alright. Especially when Eddie Cunny's on the prowl!"

Will squeezed her hand. He told her about his sister who had married a barrister, the black cat they had that just ran away one day, and how it was kind of embarrassing but he was afraid of heights. At seventeen he had joined the army, but the war was over before he was sent out to fight. Now in his final year of a degree in Finance at Bristol University, he apologised for being a future accountant. "They're a terribly dull breed," he admitted.

It was clear that there would be a kiss from the moment they met, they both knew it, and it was almost as though they were both prolonging it. Not from nerves or uncertainty, but they were making the build up last without saying so. When they did lean in, their lips softly touching each other's, Mary felt emotional, something she was not used to. It was so different to anything she had experienced before. How could she even compare a kiss from Ray O'Toole to Will McElhone? She had never felt so alive, yet saddened all in one moment.

"You've annoyed me," she said.

"Excuse me?"

"You annoyed the hell out of me, actually." Mary stood up and walked towards the river, but her high heeled shoes were making her feet throb and the cobbles on the ground were not helping so she sat back down again. "The hell out of me."

"Would you like to tell me why?"

"You're not from around here."

"So what?" Will seemed unsure, yet endeared by Mary's erratic behaviour.

"You've annoyed me by walking into my life. I am here and you are out there somewhere, and I was fine before you came along, but I feel like I'll never forget you…"

"I know, but that's okay, we'll work something out."

"No. Things like this don't last, Will. They don't work. You will leave and go back to your life in Bedfordshire, or Bristol or wherever it is down south and you'll forget about tonight."

"I disagree," he was smiling with his wide eyes. Mary punched him in the arm, but a pathetic and gentle attempt on purpose. "It doesn't matter where you live or where I live because. this is amazing…amazing that we have met, don't you see that? And we will work this out."

"I don't want to be naïve and believe you. How do I know you're not just playing me?" Mary did not want to be the cynic, but she had never been soft.

"You don't. And how do I know that *you're* not just playing me?"

He kissed her again.

"I'll see you tomorrow, Mary."

It was almost six o'clock when Will McElhone caught a cab back to his hotel and paid for one to take Mary home. He was due to play rugby in just a few hours.

*

Star, like most eight year olds, couldn't resist sneaking off from the boring bickering that adults do - repeating and repeating their arguments and never getting close to it ending – and going to play on the climbing frames and slide outside of the pub. It wasn't as if she was going far, not even across a road. From the swing tyre she could still hear Aunty Vera's high-pitched voice squeal, "Bloody hell, Mary!"

There was another little girl playing there, too, wearing a boy's sweatshirt with the four Teenage Mutant Hero Turtles printed on the front. She was sitting on the roundabout sucking on an ice-pop that had made the corners of her mouth bright blue, the bottom dribbling out onto Donatello's head.

"Hello," Star said climbing onto the roundabout. "Shall I push?"

The little girl stared at Star, expressionless, chewing on the plastic wrapper of the ice-pop.

"Do you want to go on the tyre swings?" Star asked.

"Got one in me garden," was the reply, mouth still firmly stuck to plastic. "And a climbing frame. From Argos."

"Uncle John made me a swing with some wood from his garage. It's on the apple tree in his garden. But there's always bird poo on it. There are more birds in his garden than I've ever seen. Once, he found a pigeon with a broken leg, so he let it live in his bedroom drawer until the leg had mended. It meant Aunty Vera had to sleep in the spare room for a week on the bed with the broken springs, but he saved that pigeon's life. He loves them and feeds them, and they love him. I've even seen some there in the winter when they're supposed to fly away to hot countries."

Once again, Star was answered with a blank stare.

She decided to go and play on the swings alone when she heard, "Shit."

"What?" Star turned around.

The last dregs of the ice-pop were slurped up the plastic and the word was repeated, "Shit."

"Why are you saying the 's' word?"

"You said 'poo'. Bird poo. I say 'shit'. Bird shit."

Star didn't know what to say so she started to pick the peeling paint from the climbing frame and flick it onto the ground.

But the ice-pop girl now clearly felt like talking. "Have you got Reebok trainers?"

Star shook her head.

"L.A. Gear?"

"Nope."

"I have. Both."

"Have you got a Magnadoodle?" Star asked.

"Er, everyone's got a Magnadoodle. And they're shit."

"Well, they're better than an Etch-a-Sketch. It's impossible to draw people on them." But this reply brought back the return of the stare, only the hanging plastic was replaced with a blue tongue.

A "Yooo-hooo!" was heard in the distance and the two little girls looked towards the pub, The Railway, where Aunty Vera was running towards in her lowest-but-still-high heels, clutching her handbag to her chest. Nannie was scurrying behind, saying, "Vera, it's not eleven yet!" But Aunty Vera was already tapping at the window of The Railway.

"They could just use the door," the ice-pop girl said mid-burp. "Me dad's already in there getting some butties made by Marjorie. She lives above the pub."

Star just waited and watched. Nannie and Aunty Vera were sometimes silly like children and it was best not to get involved. They argued for ages about nothing and then laughed about it, and Star never understood any of it. Neither did Uncle John. He would be pushing her round on the roundabout too fast now if he was here. Nannie looked towards the playground and waved at Star before being dragged inside by Aunty Vera, eager to ask the landlord for help getting to London. Or a drink.

"You see that van over there?"

Star looked at the large white van in the car park with the words 'Stan Moving Man' and a cartoon of a smiley man with a brown moustache and a thumb up painted across it.

"That's me dad's," the ice-pop girl said. "Me dad owns his own business. For people moving house. He used to have five vans like that and loads of people working for him, but now he just has one van and he does it all himself. Me mum calls him Superman."

"Are you going to work with him?" Star asked, wondering why this girl wasn't at school. It seemed unlikely she was going to meet Shirley Temple today.

"Yeah. It's Take Your Daughter to Work Day at our school. Why aren't you going to work with your dad?"

Star shrugged. "My school doesn't do that." Thank goodness St. Stephen's didn't. She didn't fancy telling other children and her teachers that she would have to spend the day in jail. Suddenly she felt like crying; her bottom lip was starting to quiver and she had that tickly-jelly feeling in her knees, the one that made her want to be sick.

"Do you want to see inside me dad's van?" the ice-pop girl asked. "We picked up some furniture this morning and are going back for more in a bit. It's dead good. Come and see."

"Okay," Star said, glad to be distracted. "What's your name?"

"Not telling you."

*

Vera knew there was something wrong about having a sherry before eleven in the morning, but it was offered and it would have been rude to decline. Besides, Mary wasn't going to have one and it would have been embarrassing for the kind landlord of The Railway to be turned down by two women. John had told her to always accept an offered drink. It was polite. And saved him a few bob, too.

"So you're saying that there's a local football team leaving for London on a coach in twenty minutes?" Mary asked the landlord of The Railway.

"See, Mary? I told you I felt it in my gu-..."

"Vera! Shush. And the three of us can get on this coach?"

"I don't see why not. Me son's on it, and me old pal, Billy, is driving so I'm sure they can squash up for you ladies," the landlord smiled. "What are you in such a rush for?"

"We're not now," Vera said calmly, despite being told off *again* by her big sister. "We have twenty minutes to relax, which Mary, I think you should."

"I'll get Marjorie to put the kettle on, Mary," the landlord winked.

Now that put a smile on Mary Mack's face.

10.45am

Inside Stan Moving Man's van was like Aladdin's Cave. No wonder the ice-pop girl had wanted to show Star... A four poster bed draped with vibrant, floral curtains was filled with fancy boxes overflowing with trinkets that glistened like jewels, chairs were covered with exquisite embroidery, and large statues of elephants, camels and dragons stood covered in bubble wrap. Star had played in the back of

Steph Bradley's dad's van loads of times, but that van was much smaller than Stan's, and empty except for some extension leads and a few tins of paint. They either played 'school' or 'mums and dads' in the empty space, and in Star's opinion it was a pretty rubbish location for both games.

"Oh my goodness!" Star exclaimed.

"Me dad says all this stuff belongs to them 'cause they used to be egg-pats."

"What's an 'egg-pat'?"

The ice-pop girl shrugged. "Me dad just said that the couple moving house used to be egg-pats. It has something to do with living in foreign countries for ages."

"Are they moving to another foreign country?"

"Yeah. Wales." The ice-pop girl pulled a beautiful bathrobe from a box, printed all over with colourful butterflies, and wrapped it around herself covering up her dirty Turtle's sweatshirt and jeans. "Hey, do you want me to get some cheese and onion crisps from inside? Me dad'll buy them."

Star nodded, but as the ice-pop girl opened the doors of the van she remembered her lunch box. "Wait! I have snacks in my lunch box… I left it by the roundabout."

"I'll grab it for you."

"Thank you. It's got *My Little Pony* on the front."

The ice-pop girl snarled.

"But the flask has Mr. T on it…" Star added quickly, but her new pal had gone.

It was just her and the 'egg-pat' couple's belongings, so she nestled herself into a space on the four poster bed and opened a wooden box. Inside was a large dragon's head, shiny red and sparkling, trimmed with gold and small diamonds. Just like a button needs to be pushed, this dragon's head needed to be worn, and Star slipped it onto her head. There were two holes were the eyes were and also holes in the dragon's nostrils making it easy to breathe; the plastic monster masks that Woolworths sold every Halloween were more suffocating than this dragon's head.

Star was about to get off the bed and mooch around for a mirror to admire her head, when one van door slammed shut. Stuck behind a large box, her head peered over the top to see a man with a big brown moustache and a smiley face. It was Stan Moving Man.

"Sit tight, pumpkin," Stan yelled into the van. "Lie on the bed and be sensible otherwise I'll make you sit up front with me. And take that dragon's head off. It's not yours to play with." And the second door was closed, locked and Star was left alone in complete darkness as she heard an ignition start and the van pulled away.

*

"Dad, we're leaving now," a young man in a navy tracksuit and a woollen hat ran into the pub, waving his arms, keen to get on his way.

Mary was sat on a bar stool next to Vera, with the landlord of The Railway laughing so hard that his face had turned purple. "Say it again, Mary! Say it again."

"If it took two men two days to dig two holes," Mary said. "How long would it take one man to dig half a hole?"

"You can't dig *half* a hole!" Vera piped in, and the three of them howled with laughter.

"That's not funny," the landlord's son commented. "Dad, we have to leave."

"But son, you can't have *half* a hole," the landlord said, wiping tears from his eyes with a handkerchief. "A hole is a hole, no matter what the size!"

"Yeah, still not funny, dad."

It was time to leave. Funny or not, Mary wasn't going to let that coach leave without them. She thanked the landlord of The Railway for his kindness and hospitality, and Vera thanked him for the sherry.

"Listen, you ladies hop aboard the coach and me son'll go and fetch your little girl from the playground," the landlord said looking directly at his son and shooing him away to do as he asked. Mary was relieved as her hip was giving her a bit of grief and Vera would not want to walk across a sand-pit in those ridiculous heels, even if they weren't that high.

"She's about this tall," Mary said putting her hand out on a level with her stomach, "and she's carrying a pink *My Little Pony* lunch box."

*

Jimmy expected that news of his trouble was spreading fast on the outside. It had been almost a year since he had spoken to Christine, yet here she was visiting him. And she looked so pretty, still with a bright smile on her round face, delighted as always to see him. He could just do no wrong in her eyes, her ever forgiving eyes.

"Oh, Jimmy, are you alright? You look alright. They must be feeding you well in here… you look great actually, considering…" Christine stopped. She started to pick off the bright purple nail varnish on her right thumb, something she always used to do whenever her and Jimmy had an argument. It was always over the smallest things, such as why he never asked her to the pub for one of his mate's birthdays, or if he hadn't noticed when she dyed her hair, or when she had cooked extra food for her tea without asking him but he'd already eaten. Then she would cry and cry, telling him that she was sorry for being so needy, so clingy, and that she didn't want to make their relationship all serious either, and that it was all her fault for having a bad day because she had to train some young lad on the tills who said the letter 'f' for 'th'. Once Jimmy had cuddled her and she had calmed down, Christine would re-paint her thumb to match the other nails.

"You didn't have to come, Christine," Jimmy said, imagining the chain of stories channelling around The King George. "You shouldn't have come. You should be living your life, not worrying about a dickhead like me."

"I know. I know, and I hardly think about you anymore. In fact, there were a few months when I didn't think about you at all, not for a second. It's true what they say, 'out of sight, out of mind'… only, God knows who 'they' are. The cliché police!" Christine laughed that same laugh from when she had played the Sinitta/Carol Decker game. The sleeves of her denim jacket were rolled up, her wrists full of colourful bangles, and she wore a thin, baggy summer dress beneath it. Was it possible that she looked younger than Jimmy remembered? He was aware that for a man of thirty years old, he hadn't aged well, the lines on his face getting deeper by the day. Of course, Christine did spoil herself rotten with cosmetics, but she had never looked more fresh, her youthful spirit shining like a ray of sunshine amongst the grey walls and off-white plastic tables. He could practically feel every man's eye in the room on her, like lasers burning through the denim and onto her caramel-tanned skin.

"You're very brown," Jimmy commented, himself thinking of that skin beneath the summer dress. Seeing any woman right now was enough to give him pleasant thoughts, but sitting before him was a pretty one. A very pretty one.

"Me and Kaz have just got back from a week in Benidorm. It's loads cheaper if you go now rather than in July or something because the weather's supposed to be cooler, but we had a heat wave! We just lay in the sun and fried… oh, and had a lot of Sex on the Beach!"

"Y'what?" Jimmy's mouth dropped open.

"Sex on the Beach. Oh, Jimmy I'm sorry, I'm only kidding. It's the name of a cocktail. It's gorgeous."

"Oh, right. Never heard of it."

"It's brilliant, isn't it?" Christine cleared her throat. "*Hey ladies, what you having? - Oo-er, Sex on the Beach, please*! Hours of fun! Hours! It made us laugh every time… and we had a lot!"

"Of Sex on the Beach?"

"Yes!" Christine howled, but Jimmy just looked around the room self-consciously, which didn't take her long to notice. "I'm sorry. Oh God, I'm just a bloody pain, aren't I? Here's me going on and on about holidays and drinking and having a laugh when you're banged up in here. I just didn't think. I'm…"

He wanted to reach out and touch her hand, probably more so than ever. But instead, Jimmy just put his fingers to his lips to hush her. This girl had no need to apologise, especially not to him.

"They'll probably kick me out," she went on. "I'm more trouble than it's worth. Imagine that Jim, I get thrown out of prison when I don't want to, yet everybody else in here would sell their left arm to get the boot. Oh Jesus Christ, I've done it again! I'm sorry, Jimmy." The nail polish on her right thumb had near enough disappeared. "Remember that time when we were in the chippy, and we bumped into Jackie Bunting from the year above me at school? Remember, we'd been to the quiz at the King George and Jonesy had told me that joke about the kid in a wheelchair so I decided to tell Jackie? And she just turned around and said, 'that's not funny, me brother's handicapped.' See? I always do it, don't I? And I should've known about Jackie's brother. Every year, all the handicapped kids were taken for a day out somewhere in Hackney cabs covered with colourful balloons and we used to wave from the school playground. The drivers would beep their horns and all the handicapped kids would hang out of the windows waving back. Jackie Bunting used to say her brother was in one of those taxis but we'd say, 'no he's not', and she'd just walk away in a huff. I never put two and two together…" she trailed off, scraping off the last bit of nail polish with her teeth. Jimmy noticed her lips quivering around her thumb as if she was about to cry.

"What's the matter, Christine?"

"Jonesy. I mentioned Jonesy. I'm sorry, Jimmy."

He had no response. He didn't want to tell her it was okay, that she could mention Jonesy as much as she wanted because he didn't want to hear it or talk about it. It was still only a matter of weeks since the two lads had shared a pint together and argued about football. An entirely different life ago.

"You look beautiful," he managed to tell her.

"Don't. Don't say things like that," a tear rolled down her cheek and splashed onto her hand, still covering her mouth.

"Why? You do though, you look crackin'."

"Jimmy, stop it. You can't say things like that to me."

"For Christ's sake, why?"

"Because you didn't want me. You can't say I'm beautiful and make me think that you really believe that, which will give me hope that deep down you do love me and when all this blows over we can…"

"Blows over? Christine, this isn't all going to just 'blow over'. You know I'm in here for manslaughter… possibly murder if everything goes against me? Which let's face it, I don't think I was born with a lucky horseshoe printed on my back…"

"Stop it! Stop it!" She covered her streaming face with her hands and sobbed.

It was clear that she had not wanted to bring up the reason Jimmy was even in jail, she had just wanted to see him. Could she really be living with the notion that everything was fine, that this was some dramatic phase and they were going to get a Hollywood movie ending out of it? He had no doubt that Star was living in less of a fantasy than Christine.

"Honestly Jim, I was over you. I was. Like I said, I stopped thinking about you and it felt great. I no longer waited for you to call, no longer imagined our life together and maybe moving in with you, us laughing at things like your Del Boy impression... I stopped. And do you know how? Because I finally realised that everything I felt sad about not having, I'd never had in the first place anyway. I missed your calls, but you never ever used to call me, did you? When I asked why you said that you felt embarrassed talking to my mum, I mean, I know she goes on, she's worse than Father McKenna on a Sunday morning, but... You never gave me an inkling that we would live together, I mean, I don't think I ever stayed over at your house once. And you only ever did your Del Boy impression around your mates; it wasn't something *we* joked about. I created this perfect relationship in my head that had never even existed. So I stopped. You know, I used to walk past this dead nice shirt on the model in the window of Burton's by my work and think how much it'd suit you. I'd think, 'if I bought that for Jimmy as a pressie, will he fall in love with me?' I know, it's crackers, isn't it? But I thought it, every day for months. Then one day, I got on the bus to go home and it wasn't until I'd passed the sausage works in Litherland when I remembered that I hadn't stopped to look at the shirt for a moment. I was thinking about something else, God knows what, but I felt free, Jimmy. I felt free…"

"Go and be free, Christine. You owe it to yourself. Be free."

The poor girl hadn't realised what she had declared before him; if she had there was no denying how many apologises Jimmy would now be exposed to. She was *free*. Had she felt so locked up all the time she had loved him? Had that been her sentence, and if so, what crime had she committed to be put through it?

"But seeing you now, Jimmy, seeing you makes me feel like nothing has changed… with me."

"Everything has changed for me. I'm not the same man you knew a year ago, luv. I don't even know where he is, or if he's ever coming back." As much as this visit was painful and frustrating, Jimmy was enjoying Christine, just looking at her and hearing her innocent trip-ups. It would be rather nice to have her come to visit him, entertain him every now and again; tell a few anecdotes, show a bit of flesh. Only he knew he had to let her go and allow her to not hurt anymore.

"Christine, be free."

She nodded and wiped away her navy blue mascara tears with a crumpled old tissue from the bottom of her handbag. "I have to get going anyway. I'm picking up me niece from our Michelle's and taking her to the fifty pence shop in Walton Vale. She lost a tooth yesterday and the 'tooth fairy' put a quid under her pillow last night so she wants to go on a spree. Bless her."

Jimmy thought of Star and how her front baby teeth had all gone now, the big teeth all jagged and niggling into place inside her little gums. She once lost a tooth while at school and had dropped it on the floor during playtime. Although she never found it – and the tears had been epic – Star had been so impressed and amazed by the tooth fairy's ability to know that a tooth had been lost and still leave money without collection. Ironic that the child insisted on spending her small fortune on Pic'n'mix from Woolies.

"Our Michelle had another baby, you know."

"No, I didn't know." He felt his throat tighten; if he swallowed he would start to cry.

"A boy. David."

"Send her my congratulations."

"Bye Jimmy."

"Bye Christine."

*

Vera had never heard anything like it. The wailing coming out of this child's mouth could rival a doodlebug. And who could cry tears that featured dirt accompanied by a river-running nose? This child could. But who in the name of Jesus, Mary and Joseph was this child?

"I want my DAAAA-AAAADDDD!" Anyone would think someone was slaughtering a puppy before her eyes. "Get me my DAAAA-AAAADDDD!"

As if kidnapping one child this morning wasn't good enough, Vera and her big sister had managed to do it again… and lose the original victim along the way. They were quite possibly the worst criminals ever. Billy, the coach driver, was trying ever so hard to calm this child down and find out where her DAAAA-AAAADDD could be, his handkerchief now soaking wet from attempting to mop up her grubby face.

Vera had hopped onto the coach as soon as they had left the pub, and Mary had waited by the door for Star to arrive with the landlord's son. He crossed the road with a child who was most definitely not Star, but carrying Star's *My Little Pony* lunch box. Within seconds, Vera heard the beginnings of the marathon of wailing and joined her sister to have a nose. Only it wasn't just a bit of a nosy nose, it was much worse. They had lost Star.

The next series of events took place over what felt like hours, but was in fact about five minutes. Mary started to run with her dodgy hips all around the playground, under the slide, behind the climbing frame, and then inside the pub, outside the pub, all the while screaming Star's name. She stopped an oversized man with a bald head walking a Yorkshire Terrier asking if he had seen Star, and when he said 'no', Mary attacked him with, "Yeah, well you can't see your own feet so I guess a missing eight year old is off the radar for someone like you." Even the dog stared at Mary in glum silence, innocent and terrified of the aggressive woman she was acting like. The replacement child's wailing emptied the coach of football players who all took the opportunity to have a cigarette. Vera vomited on the pavement. Twice.

"Okay, okay, she's given me an address!" Billy said in his thick, precise Lancashire accent. "Her dad is Stan, that fellow who does removals. Apparently he's on his way to forty-one Wormweld Lane, that's just around the corner."

"It's where w-w-we were before we went to get butties from M-m-marrrrjorie. The stupid woman moving house had no f-f-food left in her cupboards. W-w-worrm-weld Lane."

"Wormweld Lane?" Vera asked. "What a terrible street name. Fancy living there… Worm-weld."

"Vera, you have lived in Spooner's Way for fifteen years," Mary reminded her.

"Mary, you promised me years ago you'd stop making fun of that."

"Vera, do I look like I'm having fun?"

"I want my DAAA-AAADDDD!"

"Ladies," Billy said. "Let's get going."

10.55am

The van had only been moving for a very short time when it came to a halt. But with a big jolt. Star was thrown off the bed and into a pile of exotic cushions, all covered in sequins and trimmed with tassels, however the dragon's head – still firmly on her – proved to be a life saver as next to the cushions stood a huge marble Buddha. *Oh my goodness*, she thought indeed as it was a relief to hear the clink of steel on marble, not her head on marble. She would have been like the boys in St Stephen's; they were always splitting their heads open. Anthony Tucker had four scars on his scalp and his mother allowed him to have a shaved head which Star never understood. Christopher McGinty split his head open in school having a fight with Peter Healy in the hot-dinner queue which knocked over the tray of Panda Pop and some plastic bottles exploded causing him to slip on the fizzy liquid and smack his head against the cutlery trolley. He had to have ten stitches.

The doors of the van swung open, the dull daylight now seeming like the brightest sunshine as Star could just barely make out the outline of Stan and another man and woman. Where was she? And where were Nannie and Aunty Vera? They would be so worried. What if she had lost them forever?

Star stood up, still wearing the dragon's head. Miss Murphy had once said that an ostrich thinks that nobody can see him if he buries his head in the floor because he cannot see them, however Miss Murphy had never said if the ostrich was correct or just silly. By hiding inside of the dragon, Star hoped that she would become invisible until Nannie and Aunty Vera found her.

"AGGGHHHH!" The stranger-woman by the van door screamed. It was clear to Star that she was not invisible, she was now responsible for traumatising a woman who thought she was a dragon. At least she now knew that ostriches were silly.

"Take that off!" Stan shouted at Star.

Slowly, she removed the dragon's head, placing it carefully down onto an exotic cushion. Before her were three complete strangers, and all grown-ups, too. It was different being around strange children because children just played and became friends quickly and enjoyed similar things to other children such as McDonald's Happy Meals. Strange grown-ups meant one thing. Scary. And Star was faced with three of them.

"Who are you?!" Stan asked, no longer looking like the smiley man on the side of his van. "Where's my daughter? Who are you?!"

Star had heard Sheila Gilhooley ask her friends if the cat had got their tongue whenever she asked them if they had had a good day at school, to which they never replied. Star never knew why a cat would want to go and get one of her friend's tongues, and imagined how painful it would be if they did, but she was always relieved that it would never happen to her because she had never run out of words to say before… until now. The cat had got her tongue.

There was a loud rumble outside on the street and the attention of all three strangers switched to see what it was. Star struggled to get across the boxes, her short legs making it difficult for her, but the stranger-man held out his hand and pulled her out of the van. She had no idea why, but the words, "I want my daddy," came out of her mouth as she held on tight to the stranger's hand, jumping down from the van. Stopped in the middle of the street was a coach - just like the one that she had taken to Rhyl last summer with her daddy, Jonesy and some lady with short spiky hair who Jonesy kept tickling all day long – full of men in matching tracksuits looking out of the window. The street was very narrow with semi-detached houses and shared driveways. Steph Bradley lived in a house just like these and her dad had an argument every evening with their next-door neighbours about who should park their car in the drive. Star asked Steph why they didn't just take turns, or play scissors-paper-stone; there was nothing more fair than scissors-paper-stone. A shrug was the best answer Steph Bradley could give.

"Star!" It was Nannie's voice. "Star!" Yes, it was!

The door of the coach had slid open and there was Nannie! Star freed herself from the stranger-man's grip and ran straight to

Nannie. Only she was met by the ice-pop girl with a face so puffy and blotchy that Star thought for a moment she had been in some sort of awful accident.

"Where's my DAAAA-AAAADDD?" the ice-pop girl screamed into Star's face.

"Joy!" Stan cried out. "Joy!"

"Yes, this is certainly joyous," Nannie shouted over to him. "And bloody lucky. There were a few tears but she's fine. Maybe not full of joy, but she's fine."

"No, Joy is her name," Stan corrected Nannie. "Joy, my little love, come here pumpkin."

"Joy?" was the choral response from Nannie, the coach driver and the stranger-people, as Joy ran into her dad's arms. However, it wasn't much of a loving reunion because Joy started banging her fists onto Stan's chest, squealing about being kidnapped and how she thought that she was going to be one of those bodies found face down in a duck-pond, stripped of her clothes and with her eyes torn out of their sockets.

"Let's get her some dandelion and burdock and get on with the packing, eh?" the stranger-lady suggested.

"I HATE dandelion and burdock," cried Joy. "It tastes like our cat's wee."

"How do you know what that tastes like?" Star asked.

"SHUT UP! I bet you haven't even got a cat."

Joy pushed her dad away and stomped off to the back of the van, sulking. Stan thanked Nannie, ruffled his fingers on the top of Star's head, making her fringe all messy and made his excuses to get back to work. It wasn't a pleasant sight to notice that Stan's fingernails were quite long for a man, and thick with black dirt.

"Where's Aunty Vera?" asked Star, combing her hair back into place with her own, careful and clean hands. Nannie bobbed her head to the right, indicating inside the coach where Star saw Aunty Vera sitting with a very pale face and holding an empty plastic bag in front of her.

"Oh my goodness, not again!" Star said, the coach driver helping her up the steps. "She was sick all the way to Pontin's one year and left no barley sugars for anyone else to have…" But she was interrupted by the screeching sound of Joy wanting her dad's attention. Nannie and Star peered around the edge of the coach door to see Joy standing on the pavement with the dragon's head in her hands.

"It's not yours to have, pumpkin," Stan was saying. Joy cried harder and even started to stamp her feet. Star had never seen a child actually stamp their feet like that in real life, only in cartoons. Poor Stan Moving Man was on his knees trying to calm his daughter down who was cradling the dragon's head and sniffling all over it. What was wrong with her? Everything was fine and dandy now, wasn't it? The stranger-man joined them, probably to see if they would ever start to move into their new house, when Stan stood up. "Excuse me pal, but any chance I can give you a few quid for this dragon's head? Joy has taken a shine to it and she's had such a fright today."

The stranger-man stared at Joy who seemed to have no trouble staring back at him, her lips tightening and becoming thinner and thinner.

"How much for the dragon's head?" the stranger-man said turning around to the coach. "What do we reckon?"

"Fifty pounds!" Star yelled.

"Seventy-five," Nannie added.

The stranger-man looked back at Stan, Stan Moving Man who looked like the very sad twin brother to the man on his van. "Alright mate, seventy-five… nah, actually I'll give you it for fifty."

"Fifty?" Stan whimpered.

"D-AAA-AAA-DD!"

Stan put out his hand to the stranger-man. "Deal."

The coach driver started the engine and told Star and Nannie to take their seats, London wasn't going to move any closer to them so they had to be on their way.

"Hey!" the stranger-man ran over to the coach and winked at Star. "Got that dragon's head as a booby prize for the worst fancy dress costume at a party some years back… don't know why I never chucked it."

Star smiled. "Well, in China, Sun Lo says all things have two prices… one for the foolish."

"That's rather wise," the stranger-man said. "Who is this Sun Lo? He sounds like quite the conversationalist."

"I don't know, but he talks a lot." Star gained another wink, followed Nannie onto the coach, and then turned back to ask, "What did you dress up as? To win the dragon's head?"

"Big Bird from Sesame Street."

Star giggled. "Well, goodbye. We're going to look for the blue bird."

11.22am

The lads on the coach were not too rowdy, just a few on the back row calling each other some stupid names, all sorts of different words for their men's parts which they found to be hilarious. To be honest, it was the snoring from those who had dozed off that was bugging Mary, but she was able to put it aside knowing that Star was content. She had taken out her Tinkerbell note paper and leaning on her lunch box, was drawing pictures of what looked like Cinderella before *and* at the ball. Her medieval fashion designs were really something. Vera was on the seat in front of them, having a little snooze herself.

Mary looked across at Star and did something she hadn't done for so long, perhaps years; she imagined what her baby would have looked like. The universe was trying to take Star away from Mary, and this morning, having lost Star for only minutes disguised as a lifetime, she had started to believe that the fight within her was beginning to let go. And now, on the coach, with Star doodling and Vera sleeping, Mary had the opportunity to sit still with her own thoughts. Only, she didn't really view this as an opportunity, more of a loneliness that unlocked the past.

After the night at the Pier Head, Mary spent that entire Saturday thinking about Will, his wide eyes and gentle kisses, the way he just stared "annoying the hell out of her" and still, it didn't feel awkward. Whenever Ray O'Toole so much as looked at her she used to shout at him, telling him to use his time wisely rather than pulling a face like a child who wanted a biscuit but couldn't reach the jar. This was insane! Or was this what a real crush was? It was Vera who got 'crushes', like the crush on Clarke Gable that had been going on for almost seven years, ever since he kissed Vivien Leigh in that burned out field. Oh, how Mary cringed at herself. And this whole Will McElhone situation was far from ideal because he was leaving the next day, back to his very different world involving university antics, ambitious peers and the middle class countryside. This wasn't even an official date; how could he take her out properly tonight when he didn't even know where she lived? Why hadn't she told him? Mary had behaved in her usual flippant manner and just said goodbye to Will as if he should be blessed with the telepathic ability to guess the exact area, street and number she lived at. She snapped out of her trance (that had happened every other five minutes all day) and slipped on her long floral dress with white collar. The thrill of getting ready was dampened by the thought of having to catch the tram into Liverpool alone and wait at a hotel bar in the hope of him arriving on time. How did she know he would even show up? Or that the hotel he had told her was actually the one he was staying at? Still, Mary had no doubt in her mind that she wanted to see him again. She kissed her mam on the cheek before leaving and took a little white flower from the vase in the parlour, placing it to the side of the curls sitting on her shoulders.

They had planned to meet outside the Ranelagh Hotel. Mary did enjoy reading a magazine on the tram - there wasn't much to see these days out of the window - but after reading the same sentence about the temperature of an oven when baking a bun loaf six times, this evening was one to reconnect with the rubble and derelict buildings passed on the way into town. At the Pier Head, Mary looked out to the bench where she and Will had sat until that morning. The Ranelagh was a further three stops away, so she watched passengers come and go, still unable to get past the word 'oven'. One by one, more people climbed on ensuing a busy Saturday night ahead in the city centre, when she recognised Will

McElhone standing in the queue looking the tram up and down and through the windows, only he was wearing spectacles.

Mary stood up. "Excuse me; excuse me, luv…" she spoke politely but pushed past passengers with a little more force than necessary. "Will!"

Will jumped on. "There you are!" he said. "I was worried I'd missed you."

"I don't understand?" Mary felt her heart beating in her throat, if that was at all possible, and became terrified that her neck was blushing.

His arm held hers. "I didn't want you walking into that hotel alone, so I thought I would meet you, and I knew you were – well, I hoped you were – getting the tram through here like we did last night and…"

Mary put her hands to Will's face and kissed him. "Hello." They kissed again. "Thank you, Will. You idiot. You could've just waited outside the hotel!"

"Are you giving me a hard time again?"

The laughing started again, that unknown, silly laughter that should only come from hearing a dirty joke. "I'm sorry, Will."

"I skipped dinner with my team – we won by the way – to wait for you at that tram stop." Will widened his eyes through his glasses, playfully touching the white collar on her dress. Mary knew that today's waiting for him had been worth it. He was just lovely.

They went to the Ranelagh's wine bar, The Agency. It was a quiet, classic place with a piano playing gentle swing songs and fresh forget-me-nots in a small vase on each table. Will mentioned his spectacles more than once, a recent addition to his life and something that he was a little self-conscious about, trying to avoid it as much as possible. Mary thought he looked very sweet, impressed by his modesty. He ordered a bottle of Chianti (something Mary had never had before but found the name amusing) and although they talked, swapping various war stories and comparing the games they played as children, there was a calm air between them. Will found Mary's nail polish pretty. She noticed he had a birth mark just above his right wrist and didn't know why but she liked it.

There was chemistry. Not a crush, a chemistry. Here was a man, a stranger, who this time yesterday Mary hadn't known existed yet she couldn't imagine her life without. Somehow, she felt different and did not want to go back to whoever she used to be. It was the most odd sensation but even her eyes felt different – physically different - to how they were day to day, looking at the usual mundane things, like a light making her feel alive when she saw him. Will said she was, "lovely, so lovely," and normally, Mary would stick her fingers in her mouth pretending to vomit if a man said such things to her. Not with Will, though.

"We'll keep in touch," Will said. "I can come and see you in a couple of months, once I get a break in the semester."

"Yeah, sure. You'll forget about me. I'll be working in the factory, heart shattered and cursing the day Will McElhone bumped into me at The Parade..."

"Annoying the hell out of you...?"

"You sound dead posh when you say that, so regal! Nothing like me!"

"I think we'd go so well together, so well."

"Me, too."

Just a touch tipsy from the wine, they made their way to Will's room. He had been sharing with another player from their team, but as fate would have it this chap had gone home on the train straight after the game to see his wife and new baby rather than live it up in Liverpool for the night. Mary sat next to Will on the bed, sure of herself and happy. Lying down, they kissed, and talked a little more, and kissed, slowly undressing one another.

"I think you'd make a wonderful Mrs. McElhone," Will said, kissing her neck.

"It's a bit of a mouthful," she giggled.

He laughed, leaning on his elbows to look at her. "Are you turning me down?"

"I only said it was a mouthful, not for you to get on your bike!"

"Well, how about I call you Mrs. Mack? Is that short enough for you?"

"Erm. Okay. Mrs Mack sounds just fine."

Early the next morning, Mary stood outside The Agency watching Will McElhone join his team and board the bus back to his real life. It was only once he turned away from her that she allowed herself to cry; thick, warm tears that fell from her eyes, splashing the white collar on her dress. As she looked around the hotel, taking in the old paintings on the wall of ships and the docks, the mismatching chairs and the couple with two small children who were checking in, her eyes felt heavy. They had lost the light and everything was back to normal.

*

Star was getting restless. She had drawn three pictures of a poor girl in rags, three of her evil twin sister who was a princess, and one of the poor girl when she finally becomes a princess. The story was firmly in her mind and when she got back to school, she would write it all down to show Miss Murphy. Nannie was sitting by the window having a little sleep, which didn't surprise Star as there wasn't much to look at. Drizzle and a few cows, more drizzle and loads and loads of fields. Star hadn't seen a house in ages!

Standing in the aisle of the coach, Star looked down to see a line of boys' feet in trainers stretched out. What a shame there wasn't a girl she could play with. Nannie *and* Aunty Vera were sleeping, which was boring, and these boys were so much older than her. Well, the boys on the back row *looked* older, but they were messing about and saying the sort of things that Christopher McGinty always said to get sent to the headmaster's office in a bid to get out of spelling tests. From a seat near the middle, a paper aeroplane made from an empty Monster Munch bag flew through the air and hit Star on the head. Picking it up, she decided to take it back to its owner, but froze on her way feeling incredibly shy. What if all the boys laughed at her? The older boys who hung around outside Chan's chippy were always laughing at girls, especially ones smaller than them and it was really annoying. It would make Star's face go red and cause her to do things like trip up on the pavement even though there was nothing there to trip over. But right next to Star, one of the boys was talking in a strange voice – with a bad attempt at an American accent – and shaking his hands.

"What is he doing?" Star asked the boy on the seat next to him.

"An impression of Rain Man."

"Who's the rain man?"

"Oh, it's a movie. Dustin Hoffman. You're probably too little to have seen it. It's a grown-ups' film."

Star hated people saying she was too little for things. It was like re-living her Dorothy fiasco over and over again. "I've seen lots of grown-ups films."

The boys laughed and the rain man repeated what Star had just said in that strange voice.

"It's true!" Star said. "Lots of black and white films."

"Why would you want to watch a black and white film?" the rain man stopped the strange voice and sounded more like a human being. "There's no colour."

Star shrugged. "They're good. And they're for grown-ups; grown-ups even older than you two."

The boys looked at each other and made a high pitched "ooh" noise.

"Anyway, is this your Monster Munch plane?" Star asked, feeling stupid. Sometimes she just hated boys. "I don't like pickled onion flavour. Roast beef is the best."

"It's mine!" A very tall boy sat near the back got out of his seat and joined Star and her two non-friends. "Thank you, princess." He said crouching down beside her. He had a wide grin and long – for a boy – curly brown hair. "Whatever you do, take no notice of these idiots."

"I won't," Star said with boldness. "I'm very self-reliant."

The 'idiots' laughed at her, but the tall boy punched one in the arm and said, "Shut up. I bet you don't even know what self-reliant means." And they stopped laughing. "So, princess! Apparently I slept through some sort of kidnap/swap/mix-up earlier on, I always snooze the second I sit on a coach… beats talking to idiots like them lot…"

"Eh, piss off mate," the rain man said.

"Not in front of the lady!"

"That's okay," Star said, touching the tall man's arm. "I've heard that word lots. Practically every day."

"What are you going to London for, princess?"

"To meet Shirley Temple."

The idiots remained silent, and the tall boy looked puzzled. "As in the kid on the Good Ship Lollipop?"

"Yes!" Star liked the tall boy. She thought he was simply extravagant. "And did you know that the Good Ship Lollipop isn't even a ship? My Uncle John reckons it's a plane. Only sometimes he tells fibs to wind people up, but I don't think he's lying about that. I'm going to ask Shirley today when I see her, just to be sure."

"That sounds like a plan, princess…"

"…and when I grow up, I'm going to move to Hollywood and be in movies just like her. Maybe even sing on Broadway."

"Why don't you give us a song, princess?"

"Right now?" Star became a little self-conscious again. The 'idiots' had remained silent and she wasn't sure if she felt more comfortable when they were being loud and stupid rather than just gawping at her. But to be a star, a real star, you had to be prepared for every audience, of course Star knew that. There would be times in her future when she may not feel like performing; Shirley had been like that in loads of her movies such as when she played Betsy in *Little Miss Broadway* and she felt sad being taken away from 'Pop' who she loved… except singing really did do the trick in the end because it made her feel better! So this was good practise.

"Alright."

Star stood up straight, holding onto the arm of an aisle seat to steady herself from the bumpy ride. For a moment she was convinced that no sound would come out of her mouth and that she really was too shy to perform in front of this nice tall boy, a pair of idiots, and whoever else decided to listen in. Closing her eyes tight, she imagined herself on the stage at Carnegie Hall, a spotlight on her, an audience so packed that people were even standing at the back, and she was wearing the white gown wore by Sarah in *Labyrinth* and a pair of ruby slippers.

She took a deep breath and sang;

"*On the Good Ship Lollipop,*

It's a nice trip to the candy shop,

Where bon-bons play… on the sunny beach of Peppermint Bay…"

Not only was the tall boy grinning, but the idiots were, too, and Star noticed the rain man was missing a whole tooth which made her chuckle as she continued;

"*Lemonade stands everywhere,*

Crackerjack bands fill the air,

And there you are, happy landing on a chocolate bar..."

Star started to tap her toes to the beat, dancing down the aisle of the coach, careful to keep her hands on the arms of the seats. The boys even joined in, rocking from side to side and clapping their hands.

"*See the sugar bowl do the tootsie roll,*

With the big, bad devil's food cake..."

She shook her finger in the face of the rain man.

"*But if you eat too much, ooh, ooh,*

You'll awake with a tummy ache!

On the Good Ship Lollipop,

It's a night trip into bed you hop..."

Dancing back to the tall boy still crouched down to Star's level, she sat on his knee and sang the last part just to him, using her acting skills to become very sleepy;

"*And dream away, on the Good Ship Lollipop.*"

The applause was wonderful, as noisy as a packed out Vaudevillian theatre, Star was sure. These boys could make a racket with all their cheering and whooping, and she felt very pleased with herself.

"More!" said the rain man.

Star stood up and made her way back to her seat next to Nannie. "I only do encores for cash." And she looked over her shoulder winking at the tall boy, and then picked up a green felt tip pen to start drawing the land where the poor girl and her evil princess twin lived.

*

Vera had woken up when Star had started to sing 'On the Good Ship Lollipop'. She had wondered if she was still dreaming, the pain in her neck from sleeping whilst sitting upright being enough reality to remember she was on a coach with a teenage football team, so why would Star be singing… but when it came to entertaining, there was no stopping this little girl.

When Star was four years old, she had told Vera that she wanted to be in the movies. It was the summer before she started primary school and as Jimmy worked full-time, Vera invited Star to stay at her house for a few days while Mary went to visit friends in the Lake District. John had recently bought a video camcorder; something which had cost a small fortune but had insisted would be an investment because he was sure that people would start asking him to film their weddings, christenings and first Holy Communions. He was prepared to do it, but not for free.

"You hate going to church," Vera had said.

"I'd hate it less if you paid me to go," was his reply.

Vera knew exactly how they would spend their little holiday with Star… they would make a movie. She told Jimmy and Mary to pack all of Star's best dresses and party frocks, to which Jimmy asked, "How many do you think she's got? She's not exactly Joan Collins." Mary seemed to understand her sister's thinking and sent Star along with her leotard, skirt and ballet shoes from the baby ballet class she had newly joined, a taffeta and velvet party dress, a red and blue stripy swimsuit, and a home-made Snow White costume. Vera owned a collection of wigs and hairpieces, various hats and an impressive assortment of jewellery, so the wardrobe department on the 'movie set' was sorted.

On Star's first day, after giving her a nice bowl of vegetable soup and buttered tiger bread, Vera took Star to the spare bedroom to begin her superstar makeover. Taking her set of pastel Estee Lauder eye-shadows she taught Star how to close her eyes without scrunching up her eye-lids.

"Star, you have to pretend you're snooty, like a posh person who couldn't care less about the smelly poor people," she told her whilst giving a personal demonstration herself. "Now think of that and close your eyes. Give me a couldn't-care-less-look."

Star obeyed, copying the pose to perfection. Vera applied blue eye shadow onto her small eyelids, blending it with a little touch of dusty green.

"Now, all movie stars have fantastic cheekbones, so suck in your cheeks like this," Vera showed her, "and let me apply some blusher."

Star's chubby cheeks did not suck inwards very far, so Vera told her to smile a big cheesy grin. Dabbing the brush into her Clinique pot of rouge, Vera said, "Perfect. Now I can polish the rosy apples!"

Movie stars were always seen wearing deep red lipstick but Star had taken a shine to a bright pink colour with a sparkly silver stick that Vera had gotten free having spent more than fifteen pounds in the department store Owen Owens.

"Open!" Vera said, making an 'O' with her own lips for Star to imitate and her lips became a bright shade of pink.

Star chose a wig of black hair, shaped with a fringe and curly down to the shoulders. "This one's like your hair, Aunty Vera." And she was right. Vera had no idea why she had wasted her money on it.

John was 'on-set' downstairs, all ready to roll with a blank VHS tape inside the camcorder. He filmed Star walking down the stairs in her party frock pretending to be a Hollywood actress, stopping on each step and waving to the crowds of fans (which happened to be just Vera dancing all over the hallway behind John and waving her arms about screaming, "Oh isn't she marvellous? Isn't she beautiful?"). Wearing her swimsuit, Star was given a pair of large sunglasses, a floppy straw hat, and insisted on wearing a pair of Vera's white peep-toe high heels to totter around in. The camcorder captured Star sitting on a garden sun lounger holding a glass of Ribena with a red umbrella sticking out of it, reciting a little Mae

West rhyme that Vera had taught her in the car on the way from Flinder Street to Spooner's Way.

"A little bit of powder, a little bit of paint,
You think you're nice, but you ain't, ain't, ain't,
I've got a face like an angel,
And I'm the girl divine,
And I the one they call Mae West,
Come up and see me sometime."

John tutted behind the camcorder. "Vera, she's four."

Vera shushed him.

"Uncle John?" Star asked, fanning herself with the floppy hat, the late August sun being too much for her. "Can you film me getting into your car? Like I'm on my way to the studios?"

Vera smiled, satisfied. Star was loving this star treatment and bless her, it was a far cry from playing chase in Flinder Street. It was good to let her dream, even if she was so very young. With no mother and a life in a small terraced house, just a stone's throw from one of the most notorious areas of Liverpool, what damage would it do to allow her an imagination, an escape?

Once the three of them had sat down to have some cottage pie for their tea, Star got changed into her ballet outfit and asked John to start filming again. Vera looked through her LPs to find a suitable tune for Star to dance to.

"Have you got Ka-ma-ka-ma-karma Chameleon?" Star asked.

Vera shook her head. It wasn't really her taste. "Where've you heard that?"

"On the radio with my daddy. I love Boy George. But why is she called *Boy* and *George* if she's a girl?"

"A-ha! Here we go," Vera said, finding a few Rod Stewart LPs. She adored this man; his gravel voice, his hair, his legs… Any argument with John always ended up with Vera saying that she would leave him in a New York minute for Rod. However, if that ever did happen, Vera would leave Rod for Michael Landon – given the chance - in a split second. As she slipped the record out of the sleeve, her eyes trailing over Rod Stewart's cheeky grin, Vera felt happy that these opportunities to leave John were highly unlikely for she loved him so, so much.

John was forced to stop eating his apple pie to return to his new post. The coffee table was moved to the wall giving Star plenty of space and she performed an energetic improvised dance to 'Baby Jane' full of jumps, balletic twirls and a lot of throwing herself on the floor. John came up with the idea to keep playing Rod Stewart songs until Star tired herself out and fell asleep which - judging by the conviction and energy she was putting into her dancing – should be quite soon. There was a programme on BBC two that evening about antique cars and he told Vera he was not in the mood to miss it. Thankfully his plan worked out because after a moving, floor-exploring dance with an attempt at the splits to 'Sailing', Star threw herself onto the brown leather sofa and went out like a light.

The following day was Snow White Day. After breakfast, Star was taken through the couldn't-care-less-look and polishing-the-rosy-apples routine. Wearing the same wig and her home-made costume by Mary, Star asked Vera for a dishcloth and a duster. Her props.

"Uncle John, film me cleaning up the house and singing."

Star repeated the words 'whistle while you work' over and over again for hours, not knowing the lyrics to the song, but all the while cleaning Vera and John's house from bath tiles to kitchen lino. As she re-arranged ornaments, almost breaking some, Vera tried to help her (and save her belongings) but Star would not allow it because if Vera was to play the dwarves, they didn't do housework and it would be wrong.

When Star was taken back to Flinder Street, Mary had made a pan of Scouse for everybody to eat whilst watching the home movie. Mary was delighted with Star's singing and dancing, although Jimmy didn't seem too impressed with the Mae West part. However, there was a scene that Vera didn't recognise which involved Star in her 'normal' clothes, just some dungarees and a Mickey Mouse t-shirt, sitting on the arm of the leather sofa swinging her legs and reciting 'Humpty Dumpty'. She was acting all giddy, laughing so much that she could hardly get the words out, and she kept sliding off the sofa and falling on the floor only to get back up and do it all over again.

"What's this?" Vera asked, quite appalled.

"Oh we were just messing about," John said. "While you went to Farmfoods to get some frozen veg."

"This is silly," Mary commented.

"Very silly. John, it's childish. Nothing like the rest of the tape." Vera sulked.

John and Jimmy looked at one another and started to laugh.

"What are you laughing at?" Mary asked.

"Yeah, what's so funny?" Vera joined.

Star was watching all of the adults, perplexity written across her chubby face. "Vera," John said. "She's four."

"Thank God she knows the words to Humpty Dumpty!" Jimmy laughed. "She's four."

"It's not funny," Star said, the laughter coming to an immediate stop. "I'm four isn't funny."

"Did you enjoy doing Humpty Dumpty with John, Star?" Jimmy asked.

Star looked as though she was thinking, thinking very hard for a moment. She sighed and said. "Yes. No. Yes. No. I'd just had enough of Snow White for one day."

On the coach, Vera snapped out of her daydream turning behind her to watch Star doodling away with her pens. Was it wrong that Star entertained them so much? Should they all be pushing her to have a more 'normal' childhood, maybe force her to watch more cartoons? But the old movies made her happy. Never had Vera ever seen a child more content than Star when she was watching Shirley Temple, mesmerised and trying to learn every line, every step and every song. She was a child with hopes, ambition and most of all, a dream. In the world they were living in – that Star was living in – that could only be something good.

*

Seeing Christine had upset Jimmy in a way he would have never imagined. When they split up, he had told her that as much as he wanted to, he could never love her in the way she should – and needed – to be loved. He wished he could! Christ, a pretty girl who made him chuckle and would have accepted Star into her life without question? Jimmy hated that he just couldn't find a way to love her. And once she was out of his life, he rarely thought about her. Not once had he pined for her. Until now.

But it wasn't really Christine he was pining for. It was outside. Hearing a word such as 'Majorca', somewhere he'd never been, just made his head want to burst. Sat in a prison cell, he was thinking about somewhere he had never even fancied going to since hearing about what places like that Palma Nova were all about, all clubbing and foam parties and eighteen year olds throwing up during every hour of sunshine to cleanse their stomachs for the night's party again. And seeing Christine, all pert and sweet, in clean, stylish clothes and big hair… he wanted to see more women. More and more. Or just a woman - any woman - smelling all flowery and full of hair lacquer the way they always do.

It was finding out about Christine's sister having another baby that had really touched Jimmy. In the past, he had been used to girls – especially Christine and her mates, or any girls down the King George – talking about babies, who was having one, when they were due, what they'd had, the names, the weight… Never had Jimmy bothered to pay a blind bit of attention. Everyone had babies, what was the need for an energy-ridden and lengthy conversation about it? But someone he knew had had a baby since he had been locked up. Life was going on and moving at the same pace as always on the outside, whereas for Jimmy, life was waiting, stood still. As for when it would pick up any speed again, he didn't know. His daughter was growing up, day by day, hour by hour, minute by minute, and life was happening to her at a pace in which he could only imagine right now. With this knowledge and these thoughts, it was a hell of a lot less painful to imagine a holiday in Palma Nova.

Actually, it was less painful to think about Linda. At least that was someone else life had stopped for.

1.40pm

The coach pulled into a retail car park, complete with a Morrison's supermarket, a B & Q, and a McDonalds. Mary was under the impression that this was a much needed rest stop, however when the football team began to unload their bags, it was clear that this was the final stop.

"This doesn't look like London," Mary said to Billy, the driver. "I wouldn't be surprised if you'd done a big U-turn by accident and dropped us off in Warrington."

Billy laughed. "What do you mean 'this doesn't look like London'?"

"I mean, where's Big Ben? The Houses of Parliament? St. Paul's where the old woman feeds the birds?"

"Ah, you're looking for the picture postcard? The culture? Mary, welcome to a place called Watford."

Mary felt Star take her hand. Looking down, the little girl's face held no expression as she let her eyes wander over the parked cars and abandoned shopping trolleys. Rain splashed onto their heads, thick, heavy drops of water falling from a grey and hazy sky. This was a far cry from meeting a Hollywood icon.

"But how do we get to Harrods' from here?" Vera asked in a hurry to get her polka dot umbrella up.

"Take a train," Billy said. "Shouldn't take long, maybe half an hour or so. Our lads are playing a local team around here later this afternoon. The pitch is just behind B & Q, which to be honest is bloody marvellous for me. I have a thing for DIY stores; could wander round them all day… sandpaper is my favourite. A great little novelty. Whenever the missus gets in a nark with me, I always take myself off to our local B & Q. Other than the couples who walk about arguing over shapes of dado rail, it's a pretty quiet place, tranquil almost…"

"This is fascinating, Billy," Mary said. "But we need to get to Harrods'."

The three ladies thanked him for the lift, to which he expressed his pleasure at being able to assist. Star gave a tall, curly-headed lad a cuddle and a peck on the cheek and Mary noticed the pub landlord's son giving them all an awkward wave, smiling from just one side of his thin mouth. Vera shouted a 'good luck' to the team and did an embarrassing sort of cheerleading dance saying, "Come on you reds!"

"Our kit is yellow," the pub landlord's son said.

It was time to go. Mary huddled herself and Star under Vera's umbrella, ushering them over to Morrison's. "We'll ask customer service or something. They'll tell us the easiest way into London."

"I hope no one followed us," Vera said, quite out of the blue.

"Like who?"

"Oh, I don't know. Like anyone who might think we've stolen Star…"

"Shut it, Vera!" Mary said through her teeth.

"You can't steal me," Star said. "How can you steal me? I'm yours."

Half-way across the car park, Mary stopped still for a moment – as did her heart - grabbing her sister and the little girl and held them tight, the umbrella shielding them from getting soaked. Catching her breath, she squeezed Vera with affection and kissed Star on the head. And just as suddenly, Mary broke away, continuing to get them inside the supermarket.

"Put your hood up, Star," Mary said. "Don't want to get your hair wet, do we?"

The Morrison's store was much bigger than the one near to Vera's house, possibly by four times. The entrance by the newsagents and magazine racks had a huge promotion for Tetley tea-bags and a small podium decorated with an arch of white balloons. A chubby middle-aged man wearing an obvious wig and thick glasses was talking on a microphone pulling in an indifferent, rather unresponsive crowd of shoppers. With a tweed jacket and name badge, this man was no comedian – although he seemed to be making a bad effort at trying – and more than likely the store manager. A huge banner stood high above the balloons printed in a scroll with the words, 'Helping Hand – Giving a little can change a lot'. Star shook her hand free from Mary's and ran to the front of the crowd to watch.

"Just stay right there…" Mary tried to say to her, but she had disappeared amongst mothers and pushchairs. Still, Mary knew that Star was a sensible child; she'd be fine up there on her own. Vera linked her sister's arm and they went in search for the customer service desk in a bid to get some advice on how to get to that book signing, and fast.

*

Star was delighted. Right there, in a supermarket, was a live talent show! There was a funny looking presenter muffling a lot as he spoke into the microphone, tripping up on his words as he read from his red clipboard. He was wearing a Morrison's name badge that said, 'Neil Brown, Store Manager'.

Neil Brown needed serious help from Uncle Gary Sausage, the best Pontins' Bluecoat ever. Star loved Uncle Gary Sausage, a man with long shiny hair in a ponytail who could make a balloon animal at the same time as telling jokes that only the grown-ups laughed at whilst introducing a magic act and winning over an entire audience of children *and* grown-ups to stand up and do the Crocodile

March. Even Uncle John had done the Crocodile March without moaning or pulling his very upside-down smile. The last year that they all went to Pontins', a Bluecoat had told Star on their first day that Uncle Gary Sausage had left, transferred to Blackpool. She can't remember a time when she had sobbed more; even an orange Calypso didn't cheer her up. But Uncle Gary Sausage hadn't transferred to Blackpool at all… the Bluecoat that Star had made an enquiry to wasn't a real Bluecoat, just a holiday camper who had found a famous Pontins' jacket on the floor of the arcade next to the two pence cash waterfall. Seeing Uncle Gary Sausage onstage that night in the Clwyd Bar with his silver sequin bow-tie singing 'Delilah' could only be compared to Maria returning from the abbey singing 'My Favourite Things' in *The Sound of Music*.

An act going by the name of 'Bing Crosby' was introduced by Neil Brown. There were Brownies standing at the foot of the steps onto the stage, and they were holding buckets with a piece of paper cello-taped to the side that read 'Helping Hand – Giving a little can change a lot' in black marker pen. 'Bing Crosby' started to sing without music, whistling here and there during his performance and it was difficult to make out a single word he said. Star was very confused why a man such as this would call himself 'Bing Crosby' if he didn't sound or even look anything like Bing Crosby. He looked more like Ronnie Corbett.

Just as 'Bing' was about to break into another verse of whistling, a loud crash echoed all over Morrison's, the sound repeating over and over. Star thought that somebody had crashed a thousand shopping trolleys into the aisle of baked beans, except everybody in the crowd started cheering and laughing. Neil Brown walked back onto the stage wiping his brow with a tissue, while a Brownie escorted 'Bing' – who carried on whistling – back to the magazine racks. Star noticed that to the left of the stage were the Boy Scouts, and some were holding up metal bin lids on pieces of string while others were banging on the lids with hammers. One Scout was sitting on a chair, slouched and so grumpy he resembled a toad, holding a poster on a wooden pole advertising 'The Gong Show' as Watford's Helping Hand fundraiser.

The next act brought onto the stage was a man with a brown paper bag on his head with two eyes and a mouth ripped out so that he could see and stick his tongue out. He began to wobble about, very similar to the way that Mick Tully behaved in the middle of Flinder Street at night time. Some toddlers on reigns started chuckling at him, but a wave of 'boos' sang across the audience. Star was appalled. Was this the best in entertainment that Watford could offer? A failed Bing Crosby disguise and a man with a paper bag head? The Boy Scouts didn't hesitate to bang their bin lids.

"L-ladies and g-g-gentlemen," Neil Brown said, trying to shout over the crashing. "I'm afraid that's all the acts we have s-ssigned up for today, but if you have enjoyed today's G-Gong Show, please donate some pennies into the buckets. Unless there is anyone in the audience with any hidden t-t-talents? Maybe the next Madonna? Or the Pet Shop Boys?"

Star shot her arm into the air. "Excuse me? I'll have a go."

Neil Brown extended his hand and pulled Star up onto the stage.

"*You'll* have a go?" He asked.

"Well, I will if you don't start banging those bin lids!" Star said.

"What are you going to do?" Neil stuttered. "S-s-sing a nursery rhyme? T-t-tell us a knock-knock joke?"

"No, that's for babies. I'm going to do some impersonations."

Neil Brown wiped his forehead with his sleeve. The crumpled tissue had fallen off the stage and into one of the donation buckets. "Superb. Impersonations of whom? M-Madonna? The Pet Shop B-Boys?"

Star felt that she was going to disappoint Neil Brown as it was clear who his favourites were, but she had to impersonate her favourites. Besides, she imagined herself being a lousy Madonna impersonator; it was just not her *thing*.

"Just a few of my favourites," Star said, taking her place in centre of the stage. She looked out to her audience, such a shame they were all standing and leaning, looking pretty fed-up. If they had red velvet seats to relax in and a tub of vanilla ice-cream they could eat with a tiny wooden spoon, she bet they'd be happier. Standing up straight, legs together and fists clenched, she thought about her idol, Shirley Temple. Star began her impersonation;

"If something may upset you, don't ever let it get you down,
Or wear a frown.
If fortune should forsake you, don't ever let it make you sigh,
Keep shooting high.
Be a crooner, not a groaner, never kick!
Oh here's a spelling lesson that will do the trick..."

Star smiled thinking about her teeth and her eyes, pretending that her face looked just like Shirley Temple's. Sparkle, she thought, sparkle! If her mother were alive, she imagined her saying that to her, just as Shirley's mother said it to her on the set of every movie she made, "Sparkle."

"You've gotta S.M.I.L.E.,
To be H.A.P.P.Y,
Keep it in mind when you're blue,
It's easy to spell and just as easy to do,
You've gotta S.M.I.L.E.,
To be H.A.P.P.Y!"

The crowd around the stage gave Star a little round of applause, along with the odd 'ahh' no doubt because she was a child. Star didn't mind; she'd become used to that. But she wanted a bigger audience than this! A bunch of bored Brownies and Scouts, mums with prams and an old lady with a walking stick? This was Morrison's on a Tuesday afternoon and it was busy. Star needed to grab their attention.

"Ladies and gentlemen!" She shouted. "Just for fun… I'd like to sing the song again the way it would be done by…." And Star ran on the spot, shaking her fists trying to create a drum roll. "Al Jolson!"

The old lady with the walking stick said, "Oooooh!" rather loudly, which made some new arrivals to the store stop their empty trolleys and watch.

"And…" Star looked around for inspiration, but all she could see behind her was the stationary aisle. "And…" She spotted a giant teddy bear on a table full of raffle prizes behind the Boy Scouts. Crouching down to the Scout who looked like a toad, she whispered, "May I borrow the teddy? Just for a minute?" He obliged, his movements slow and toad-like, also.

Star cleared her throat. "And Ginger Rogers and Fred Astaire!"

There was silence from the crowd, waiting to see what she did next. Star noticed Nannie and Aunty Vera, but hoped that they weren't the only ones who knew of Al Jolson because it was not exactly an easy impression to do. All the same, the show must go on and she had announced what she was going to do…

Star dropped down onto one knee, pouting her lips as much as she could and trying to make her eyes as wide as possible. In a slow, deep voice, the sound coming from somewhere near the back of her throat, she swung her arms as she sung;

"*You... got-ta...S.M.I.L.E...Oh my Mammy!*
Like the birdies, pretty birdies up in the trees,
Pretty flowers, April showers, my Mammy!"

Star stood, picturing Al Jolson singing out as she held her head high – lips still pouting – almost bending backwards, and her arms reached out with splayed fingers before she brought them inwards onto her chest;

"*Life is divine... at a quarter to nine!*"

A tingle of laughter crept over her audience and tickled her. There was even some applause, but Star's show wasn't over yet. She signalled for the audience to sing with her hands, rounding them up to join in, but realised that it was highly unlikely for anybody to be familiar with the song, 'S.M.I.L.E.' And then Star remembered that there wasn't just *anybody* in this particular audience... Nannie and Aunty Vera were there and they weren't just familiar with Shirley Temple, no! They were Star's biggest fans. She had barely caught their eye when they both began to sing – completely out of tune to each other – with utter conviction;

"*You gotta S.M.I.L.E...*"

This was Star's cue to pick up the teddy bear. She put one arm around it's waist and held a paw with her free hand, the teddy's face looking into hers. A Fred and Ginger style dance was performed on the small stage accompanied by the singing sisters' duet from the crowd, Star waltzing around, spinning and finishing with a grand courtesy as she envisioned being handed a basket of red roses.

The overall applause was not the best and nobody shouted for an encore, but Star was positive that the crowd had gotten bigger during her performance. Over the noise of babies crying, Boy Scouts sniggering and trolleys clashing, there was definitely the jingle of coins dropping into buckets as Nannie and Aunty Vera held her hands, leading her out of Morrison's.

And it was a relief that one sound Star didn't hear was the banging on the bin lids. She thought that this performance was one to put on her CV… she had survived a gong show.

2.10pm

Feeling that luck was finally going their way, Vera applied a fresh coat of lipstick to celebrate. Not only did the train to London Euston pull into the station at the same time as Mary, Star and herself arrived on the correct platform at Watford Junction - and by chance - but their original day tickets bought at Liverpool Lime Street were valid on this train! Mary didn't have to put up a fight, Star didn't need to busk, and Vera could enjoy a train ride with a settled stomach.

"Nannie, will you plait my hair please?" Star asked. "In skull plaits?"

"Go on then," Mary said, putting a left-behind copy of *The Sun* on the floor of the train between her feet for Star to sit on. "Have you got an extra bobble?"

Star showed Mary her wrist which had a pink elastic band around it, digging into her pale skin. "Always. Just in case."

Vera watched Mary take the pony-tail out of Star's hair, combing through the tats with her fingers. It was Vera who had taught her sister how to plait hair and now she was much better at it because of all the practice she had on Star.

"Can I do one side?" Vera asked, now wishing she had brought a puzzle book.

"No," Star said. "They won't be the same. Nannie does the plaits tighter than you do, Aunty Vera."

"That's because I don't want to hurt your head."

"I don't mind. I like it getting pulled tight. When you do it loose, it tickles."

"Oh." Vera was craving a word-search, feeling a little left out of the Mary and Star duo, but not ungrateful.

A few years back, Vera had been to see that clairvoyant, Kath, who lived in a flat opposite the bombed-out church in

Liverpool – and believed without being a sceptic – but she knew that no matter what was foreseen, the series of events and how they happened in real life was always more than often unexpected. Kath had predicted a long, happy marriage for Vera but never mentioned any children, and had warned her that she must save her money if she wished to travel beyond Europe one day and in truth, Vera had not saved very well hence never getting any further than Dublin on the ferry. She had also said that her sister would have one child, and that child would only have one parent. It was difficult not to believe Kath, for she was nothing like Vera had presumed; no crystals ball, no Indian music playing on a cassette and no headscarf. Kath taught the art foundation course at Liverpool College and used her 'gift' for a bit of extra cash. For a woman of forty-odd, her flat was a touch shabby - a few posters tacked onto the walls of Jimi Hendrix and The Doors, and an overflowing ashtray on a table high pile of romantic fiction, screaming of someone who just hadn't left their own student days behind them yet. *Fawlty Towers* was blurring on the TV, and Kath was just half-way through a microwavable lasagne when Vera called around for her appointment. Yes, there was a black cat who challenged Vera to a stirring contest during the whole reading, but on the whole, Kath was pretty 'normal'.

One child for Mary, *one parent*. However accurate that Kath's prediction was, it was not as simple as that. Was that one child to be Star, who only had Jimmy as a living parent? Or was it not a prediction but a glimpse into the past; the fate that had made Mary who she was, and who she refused to change?

When Vera looked at John, she felt as though she had known him her whole life. Sometimes, to think of days before then seemed like a blur, a watercolour painting that had had water spilt over it. There were some chaps before John, one of whom broke her heart when she found out she was being two-timed with a girl who had been swish enough to go to boarding school. Thank goodness she had cried and whined and moped about for a month afterwards, making every attempt to let go of those painful feelings and unleash them out, away from her… and thank goodness she had met that two-timing rat, otherwise she may never have met John. It was the brother of the rat who introduced them! And the rest, they say, is sweet history.

Although, not for Mary. It never quite worked out like that for her. Vera had a distant memory from the night when Mary had met Will McElhone; they had escaped from the morgue that was their Brian's birthday do. She remembered Mary talking to a fair, handsome guy, all sun-tanned like a sports player out on the field all day. It was unusual because Mary would spend her nights out chatting to all sorts, always polite but never interested for more than five minutes, no one able to capture her for long enough. Whatever this Will chap had said changed her sister forever.

Days went past after their meeting when Vera noticed Mary being much quieter than normal, deep in thought, locked in a world of her own. They would be chatting on the bus to work about the latest films out at the picture house, when Mary would inappropriately ask how long a train or a coach would take to Bristol. She wanted to stay home more, even on a Friday night, as if there was nothing she felt the need to see or experience. Usually bolshie and sometimes intimidating, Mary became so calm after meeting Will, smiling lots and picking fewer fights. Letters would arrive, maybe one a week – sometimes two - and Mary would sit on her bed for hours, scanning the words, running her fingers over the ink marks. She would laugh out loud and quote some of Will's sentences to Vera.

"When are you going to see him?" Vera would ask.

"Soon," Mary replied. "We're setting a date soon… Oh look, Vera, he says its fate that we met that night! Ha, ha, he's even written *'Dear Mrs. Mack'*. I bet he wants to propose. Is that crazy? I think it's crazy. But good-crazy?"

"He should be knocking on your door. Just like Ray O'Toole."

"Ha! You can't compare Will with Ray O'Toole! When I think of Will, I can't speak properly… listen to me… I lose the ability to speak because, erm, I don't know! When I smile, I feel like

I'm smiling from the inside which I've never done before, Vera. He's just, he's just beautiful."

"He's a stranger."

"No, I know him, Vera. I knew him the minute I met him."

"Fair enough, Mrs. Mack."

So her big sister had met 'him', *The One*. Mary was settled, yet alone.

Vera was more than happy to admit that she fell in love too easily. She could put her hand on her heart and say that she loved every man who ever took her out – including the rat – and all in a very different way to how she loved John, but it was still a form of love all the same. So how did it happen just once to Mary? That she was granted only one night?

About two months after Brian's birthday, Vera woke up on a Saturday morning to find Mary's bed all made. Mary used to be the queen of lying-in, always leaving it to the last second before having to drag her body out of bed, so it was a surprise to find her out of the house so early on her one day of rest. Vera wondered if she had gone into town early to get her birthday present… well, that was what Vera hoped. But her gut instinct was telling her something else, and when Mary returned the next day collapsing into their hallway, her skirt drenched in blood, Vera knew her instinct to be true.

*

Nannie could win a medal for plaiting hair so quickly. Star suggested that she go on *You Bet!*, the Saturday night tele show, and prove to Great Britain how fast she was. Nannie told her that she'd think about it, but only if they sacked that Bruce Forsyth.

"The man thinks he's funny, but he's not," Nannie said.

"I like him," Star said. "There's a boy in the top juniors at our school who reckons he knows every football stadium in England just by seeing a photograph of one seat in each stadium. Louise Fitzpatrick says that he's applied to go on *You Bet!*"

"Good luck to him."

"I wish my daddy was here." Star ran her fingertips over the two tight plaits in her hair, enjoying the bumpy feeling.

"What's brought that on?" Nannie asked, looking straight at her.

"Nothing. I always wish he was here. He loves us."

The train slowed down and stopped in the middle of what could only be described as nowhere. There were no fields in sight, no houses, no car parks, not any motorways in the distance; just tall fences with messy bushes surrounding them. Not even a spot of graffiti was in sight. The train manager passed through the carriage shouting out the message that there was a defective train in front of them and until it was moved out of their way, this Watford Junction to London Euston service would be stationary for the time being.

"How long, Nannie?" Star began to panic. Maybe it was just a dream to go and meet Shirley Temple. Not a dream that people talk about when something comes true, like when everybody at St. Stephen's church prayed for little Jennifer Henry to not have Leukaemia anymore and now she doesn't *and* she got to go to Disneyland in America… that is a dream come true. And when Sheila Gilhooley bought a Golden Goal ticket for an Everton match and won a hundred pounds. *That* was 'a dream come true'.

Star coiled her legs up onto the seat covering them with her skirt, closing her eyes and thinking that meeting Shirley was all just… a dream…

2.35pm

Mary could sense Star's disappointment. Her own frustration was coming across - how could she avoid it? – and Star was picking up on it. How hard could it be to get to London? There were plenty of people in Liverpool, businessmen and such, who went to London on the train every other day. Maybe she should have asked for Susan's permission, gone round to her house properly and devised a sensible plan for an official outing. Stranger things have happened; Susan may have listened.

But it was too late to be thinking like that. Star was all bent over on the seat next to Mary, trying to sleep, but he eyes kept opening and darting out of the window in the hope that the train was on the move again.

"Star, why don't you have a little doze?" Mary suggested. Vera stroked the little girl's fringe and Star's eyelids started to blink in slow motion. "Good girl. You've already had a busy day, and everything always looks better after a little doze."

"Yes, Nannie," Star croaked.

Mary took off her jacket and put it over Star, who snuggled deep into it.

"I'm going to let her down, Vera," Mary said quietly. "Jimmy said she was better off with Susan and you know what? He was right. I can't even take her on a trip to London so how could I imagine her having a decent life with me, just me?"

"Mary! Stop this," Vera said, a level of shock in her voice as if Mary had started talking about aliens landing on earth. "You're tired. Why don't *you* have a little doze?"

"No!" Mary shouted, and then remembered where she was. "I'm sorry, Vera. No. I'm not going to sleep, sleep through this stupid game I've been playing any longer. I live a lie, Vera, a lie. Here I am, thinking I'm this grandmother – no, mother - to some child who isn't even mine. I'll go to jail for this, too, no doubt, and what is that going to do to Star? The most innocent, imaginative child that any bloody Scouser could wish to meet and it'll destroy her. I've already seen a change in her, Vera. Yes, she's still singing and dancing in the aisles of supermarkets, thinking she's on the set of some MGM musical, but she's becoming withdrawn. She draws the little girl in rags more than the princess. She asks questions that no eight year old should have to ask... about prison food, and mummies that go to Heaven, and what does 'manslaughter' really mean, and Vera, I just lie. Lie after lie, after lie..."

"You, Mary Mack, are the most wonderful and true mother that Star will ever have. She isn't destroyed, she's lucky. Most kids would kill for a mother half as decent as you," Vera crossed her arms. "And you know it."

Mary did know it, but it didn't change the truth. If she could just get Star to meet Shirley bloody Temple, she would accept the consequences of her actions and do everything in her power to ensure that Star went back to Susan and got the best of everything. Even if it meant her wearing a friggin' blazer, going to some snooty all-girls school and, God forbid, lose her Scouse accent. If it meant she would succeed, find happiness – her own Blue Bird – Mary didn't mind anymore.

The train was still showing no signs of shifting. Outside, an empty Kit-Kat wrapper blew about in the wind and hit the window. An Arsenal scarf was hanging off a branch on a bush beside the train tracks; some little boy somewhere was probably looking for that. How far away were they from London? Could they open the train door and just walk it? Mary threw her head into her hands. Vera didn't utter a word. The longest silence passed between the two sisters; no fighting, no joking, nothing. Mary stood up, turned around and sat down on the empty seat next to Vera.

"I've been living a lie, Vera…"

"No, Mary, you haven't…"

"I have, Vera. It's time I told you… what really happened."

Star was asleep and Vera's eyes told Mary that she knew what she was ready to talk about.

"Vera, the day I lost the baby, I hadn't been up to the Lakes to see mam's friends – which I suspect you always knew – I had been to Bristol." Mary took a deep breath, uneasy about saying his name out loud for the first time in almost forty years. "Will… he wrote me a letter just weeks before I… saying how he was coming to Liverpool. He wanted to know who he should ask for my hand in marriage; I told him, our Brian. We told each other everything in those letters, you know. I even knew that he learned to play the piano wrong; who learns to play the piano wrong?! His teacher was old, pushing ninety, and told him that the easiest way to read the left hand notes was to turn the sheet music upside down and they read the same as the right hand. The poor bugger was only seven. Isn't that ridiculous? Anyway, I got another letter saying that he had to cancel his plans to Liverpool, that it was a busy time with university and rugby and that he was sorry, but he'd be in touch. Vera, it came out of the blue, I swear. You know I'm not soft, that I never buy into that mushy nonsense that, that..."

"That I buy into..." Vera finished.

"Well. You know. There hadn't been a hint of doubt in any of his letters. I have a nose for trouble, Vera, I would have sniffed it. Until this one, of course. Will just went on and on about how much work he had to do, and how it was interfering with training – or the other way round – and 'normal' life was getting in the way of what he wanted to do, and that not coming to see me in Liverpool was out of his control. Not once did he ask about me. Not once. I thought for a moment that somebody else had written the letter, copied his handwriting and sent me this as some sort of cruel prank. In a perfect world I would've just had a bit of a cry, ripped up his letters and forgot about him, well, tried to. But I couldn't..."

"Because you were pregnant." Vera said, helping Mary out.

As Mary nodded a tear streamed down her cheek, and feeling the warm line dropping, her hand shot up and wiped it away, threw it away. "I thought, well, if he isn't coming to Liverpool, I had better go to Bristol. And I was sure, so sure, that when he saw me, everything would be fine, marvellous even. I told myself that he was stressed, I mean, what the hell did I know about university life and the pressures he could be under? Don't get me wrong, I'm sure Will McElhone had no idea how to make a perfect sausage, never mind clock in and out on time, but..." Mary amused herself, letting out a sigh. "I wore the yellow dress, didn't I? The same one I was wearing the night we met. I caught two trains to Bristol - spending more than a week's wages - in that yellow dress. And I know we've spoke about people wearing their best to go on trains, but that yellow dress is taking the piss a little, don't you think?"

Vera smiled, about to laugh, but stopped.

"Oh, Vera, laugh! It's the least you can do. I must have looked like the Easter bloody Bunny amongst all those suits and boots! Ah, I was so excited. There wasn't one minute of that journey when I stopped thinking about Will, his beautiful blue eyes and that little birth mark above his right wrist. But I felt sick, Vera. So bleedin' sick. I hope I'd done a good job of hiding it until then; I didn't want you or mam to worry. You see, *I* wasn't worried. Will was going to marry me, why did I need to worry? But the train was warm and sticky, and so crowded. It smelt of sweat, smoke and popcorn. Sweet popcorn. Don't know why because I never saw anybody eating any."

Mary looked around the still train that they sat on now. It was practically empty compared to those trains to Bristol, yet forty years ago and not one delay.

"I took a taxi to the university. It was the most expensive day of my life, but I didn't care. I couldn't wait to see his face, tell him the news. Only, I made sure I went into the ladies' first. That train ride hadn't left me with the best complexion and despite feeling like I'd spent a week at sea I wanted to look my best.

"There was a large map of the campus and I found Will's dorm easily. When I got to the desk on the ground floor, the guard told me that the students were playing rugby, only not to worry because they were playing at home, on the sports field across the way. I waited until the game ended... over an hour I waited. There was a lady also waiting, for her son, and her name was Sal. I told Sal all about Will, how we'd met and how this was our first meeting in over two months. When the game ended and I went to meet him outside the changing rooms, Sal kissed me on the cheek and wished me luck.

"I knocked on the door of the changing rooms..."

"Mary!" Vera stopped her. "Have you no shame? What the bleedin' hell did you do that for?"

"I don't know. I just did! Some other fella answered and I just said, will you tell Will McElhone that Mrs. Mack is here."

"So he was in there? Will? He was definitely in there?"

Mary looked down into her lap and swallowed. Her breathing felt quite shallow and she had to stop; this was all going a little too fast.

"Oh God, Mary," Vera said. "He wasn't there? Is it true? Is it true what I believed after all these years?"

"What?"

"That he died? That Will was dead?"

Mary sighed and let out a short laugh.

"No, Vera. Will hadn't died. In many ways, I wish he had. It would've closed the book with a definite ending. He said… he said he didn't *know* a 'Mrs. Mack'. Then when he left the changing room, he looked right through me, not even as if I was a stranger, but as if I wasn't even there."

*

Star fidgeted around. The bed she was lying on was hard and awkward, a chill blowing down her ear. She opened one eye and all she could see was dark wooden walls, a broken window and the doll that looked like Sheila Gilhooley thrown onto the floor. She tried to move but couldn't because of the chill, she was too cold.

"Daddy?" She cried. "Where's my daddy?"

She heard somebody shushing her. *Who was it?* It may be that mean old lady who had taken her away from her lovely home, so she hid beneath the thin covers and wished herself back to sleep again, murmuring, "*My daddy has to go away, but he'll return most any day. Any moment I may see, my daddy coming back to me.*"

*

It was mid-afternoon but Jimmy was sleeping. He reached out and wrapped his arm around Linda, who turned to face him and kissed him on the nose. Opening his eyes, he grinned at her, all groggy from passing out. She was wearing one of those giant, baggy t-shirt night gowns with a teddy bear dressed in pyjamas printed on it. It was the least sexy item of clothing she owned, yet it turned him on. It was cute, and easy to remove. He slid his hand up beneath the cotton, feeling her warm, soft skin, hearing her snigger.

"Jimmy, we have to get up," she wriggled away. "We're so lazy!"

"Come here," he said, ignoring her, but she sat up and started to twirl her hair around her index finger. "What's up?" he asked.

"Where's Star, Jimmy?"

"What?"

"Jimmy! I said, where's Star? Where is she?" Linda started to cry, big breathless sobs, holding her chest in pain. "Where is she, Jimmy? Our baby? Where is she?"

Jimmy sat up, eyes awake and looked around.

Addo was sitting on a chair in the corner playing Patience.

Linda was gone.

"I don't know," Jimmy cried. "I don't know."

*

Mary didn't just let Will go. Standing there, as good as a ghost left her shocked and unsure if it was even *him*. She was tired, pregnant, confused... maybe her sight was playing tricks on her. But she recognised his walk, the shape of his head, had glanced at the mole on his left cheek. It *was* him.

"Will?" She shouted, noticing his broad shoulders getting smaller and smaller, the further he walked away from her. There were young men in her way, each one six feet tall, hurrying out of the changing rooms and down the pathway towards their halls. Jumping, still she tried again, "Will?"

The university was surrounding her, thick sandstone walls with giant-sized windows so old that inside looked black. The lawns stretched out around her were scattered with students, reading, playing, socialising. Two boys were wrestling as a group of girls stood and watched, one fixing the cardigan onto her shoulders that had just slipped off in the gentle breeze. This was not Mary's world. Will did not want her here.

"Will?" Mary watched as in the distance, Will McElhone picked up his pace and ran up a set of grey stone steps and inside a building where she was not welcome.

A hollow sensation travelled through her legs and Mary fell to the pebbled floor. She felt the force of somebody help her up, a slim middle-aged man all very smart in a matching light blue three-piece suit, but she pushed him away, defiant that she did not need his help. Off she stumbled, walking slow and careless, not a single brain cell connecting with what she was doing. It was like the first time she had gone to The Parade and drank too much Martini, her vision blurred as she tried to walk in a straight line and stop herself from being sick. She hurt… Only the pain wasn't one deep, sharp pain like a bad graze on the knee or elbow that bled and stung; this pain was short, itchy and everywhere. Mary found herself hurting in parts of her body that she couldn't even point out with her finger. She wanted to tear off her skin in order to feel something more profound, more sure than this incubator of disappointment she was in. Her forehead felt like it had been struck with a slab of lead, and in her mind she couldn't construct a word of sense. Stupid! She had become everything she had ever despised; a stupid, silly, lovesick girl… and look at where it had landed her; stranded in the middle of Bristol, and young but only too aware of the disillusionment that love was. Never, ever would she allow herself to fall under that spell and open up to hurt anymore. Mary knew right there and then that she would find the meaning to her life in something else, something more remarkable…

But the baby? What about her baby? Their baby? Maybe this was the one thing she could hold onto, the one thing that would save her from not believing in love. Mary decided to get home and reset. She would write a letter to Will telling him everything, and once he knew about their baby, she was sure he would be ready to explain himself.

She found herself back at the train station, with no memory of how she got there. As her second train pulled into Liverpool Lime Street, all of the dull, irritated sensations she had been experiencing stopped, and she held her belly in agony.

*

Vera wrapped a blanket around her sister, lying on their hallway floor and groaning in pain. Their mam was asleep on her chair in the parlour and it would have been too distressing to wake her.

"Hold on to me," Vera said gently. "I'll get you to the 'ozzie."

"I've got no money, Vera," Mary cried. "Nothing left."

Vera had enough bus fare for them both. She was terrified, but was determined to keep calm. Under any circumstance, her Mary never made a fuss about anything, not even when the Blitz killed half of their family and their own mother stopped speaking. As a child, Vera screamed with fear most nights for years after that dreadful month of May 1941, and Mary would sing silly, lively songs and tell her the story about the old woman with a hole in her pocket who kept thinking her purse had been stolen. Vera kept tight hold of her sister, letting her rest on her shoulder and keeping her covered with the blanket. Some passengers on the bus asked if everything was alright and Vera would have liked the help, but Mary was strong enough at least to say, "I'm fine, just a silly tummy bug."

By the time they reached Liverpool State Hospital, Mary was losing consciousness. A nurse sat her in a wheelchair and said, "clearly a miscarriage."

Vera started to cry, and wished she could stop and be strong.

"Where is her husband?" the nurse asked, stern and glaring at Vera.

"I – I don't know," she cried.

"Well, stop crying and find out. What's her name?"

She didn't want her sister to be judged, or sent away or be in any trouble at all. Vera had heard about what Edna Murray's mother had done when she got pregnant without being married and she did not want Mary to be punished by a bunch of nuns for being careless.

"What is her name?" the nurse demanded.

The sisters never spoke of what happened after that day, Mary seemed determined to make a fresh start, putting her energy into spending as much time as possible at home with their mam, and running the house sensibly rather than partying the night away with Vera. Mary had made it clear that whatever trauma had hurt her that day was not going to be dragged up and returned to. Vera respected her sister's wishes.

"Young lady, what is your sister's name?"

"Mrs... Mrs. Mack." Vera had said, presuming Will to be the father. "Her name is Mary Mack."

*

Star was finally comfortable... The rain hitting against the windows could no longer be heard and the draft blowing cold air on her ears had faded... A material against her skin was smooth like satin... yet something was heavy on her head, so she reached up and touched it... it was a beautiful diamante tiara sitting on her curled hair... she held a golden sceptre encrusted with diamonds in her other hand... She sat up to find she was sitting on a large thrown... three ladies - all dressed in matching floor-length lilac dresses - were surrounding her, stroking her arms and smoothing down her satin gown... The ladies' faces looked familiar... Sheila Gilhooley, Miss Murphy, and Mrs Neary, the Eucharistic minister... only, Star couldn't be quite sure as they all had long plaited hair down to the ground, when ... Suddenly! Somebody pinched her nose... It was Uncle John... Only, he was dressed up as a Jester...

    A trumpet sounded and an enormous set of wooden doors opened revealing a perfect blue sky with a scattering of small white clouds, the golden sun gleaming into the palace where Star sat... The parade began led by two giant Liver Birds each strolling along with a royal blue ribbon tied around their neck... each person bowed their head to Star as they passed her... there were boys with footballs, who would usually kick the ball into Star's head and laugh... Ron the butcher, carrying a large silver tray full of bacon ribs... and there was Mick Tully, dancing and cradling a bottle of scotch in his arms...

The parade was interrupted by a siren... through the doors and into the palace ran Mr. Bertie wearing his best suit, but all in a fluster... he said;

"Little miss, oh queen, forgive me,
For troubling you with this bid,
But there's a posh old bat outside,
To report a stolen kid!"

Star was still pleased to see Mr. Bertie, so she smiled;

"Tell her she must do one, now,
Calm down, she's just an angry cow."

Mr. Bertie insisted;

"I politely told her, but she won't,
You must see her, if you don't,
She'll lose the plot..."

Uncle John the Jester jumped in;

"*Tell her to sod off...*"

"*She won't sod off...*" Mr. Bertie cried.

"*Then tell her to piss off...*"

"*She won't piss off...*"

The outside blue skies were instantly turned to grey with a loud crash of thunder... the old posh bat ran into the palace, a woman with an uncanny resemblance to Aunt Susan;

"*I won't sod off, I won't piss off,*

I know my rights, I know I've won,

I know exactly what they've done!"

Star didn't trust this woman;

"*They? Who are 'they'?*"

Aunt Susan clicked her fingers and two policemen wearing badges saying, 'The Bizzies' entered through the enormous set of wooden doors... holding two women by the necks of their cardigans... Nannie and Aunty Vera... Star gasped. Aunt Susan narrowed her eyes;

"*I know these women stole my kid,*

They have the cheek to think I'm stupid...

Don't be fooled by sweets and ice cream,

They're a devilish pair, my queen,

There's a law, I understand,

Against kidnap in this land."

Mr. Bertie stepped forward;

"*Little miss, oh queen, this law I have heard,*

To jail they could go, oh no, my word."

But Uncle John the Jester huffed;

"*Ah but queen, I'd bet a few quid,*

These ladies did not steal a kid…"

Aunt Susan rudely cut him off;

"Shut it, lad, I know the law,

What I say I saw, I saw!

What I saw…"

"*She's on a see-saw!*" Uncle John the Jester sang. "*I saw! You saw! He saw! She saw!*"

And Christopher McGinty ran into the palace chasing Louise Fitzpatrick, Steph Bradley and Laura Fenton, screaming, "*On a see-saw, on a see-saw! Eh la, your ma, his ma, her la!*"

Star sensed that the situation was getting out of hand;

"Let's jib this off, stop skitting lad!

Is this the truth or are you mad?"

Uncle John the Jester offered a word;

"The posh old bat won't be amused,

But let's ask the two who've been accused?"

Aunt Susan scoffed;

"I object, that pair will lie,

Next they'll tell you pigs can fly…"

Star held up her sceptre;

"Come ladies, blurt it out,

This is your turn to have your shout…"

One of the 'Bizzies' allowed Nannie to step forward;

"Please my queen, I shall admit,

THE DAY SHE MET SHIRLEY TEMPLE

I took the kid from a right old git,

To make her smile and laugh, not steal -"

Vera butted in;

"That was never part of the deal..."

Nannie continued;

"And the reason was, I shall tell you,

It was to make her dreams come true..."

Uncle John the Jester looked at Star;

"The reason was, they just told you,

Was to make this kid's dreams come true..."

Still, Aunt Susan piped up;

"You see, my queen, they broke the law,

What I say I saw, I saw..."

Christopher McGinty opened his mouth – full of cheesy Wotsits – and was about to start skitting Aunt Susan, but Uncle John the Jester said;

"Please don't start all that again..."

Aunt Susan grinned, her eyes like two tiny pin-holes;

"But they stole a kid, that's plain."

No matter what way she looked at it, Aunt Susan was right. Star pouted sadly;

"It's knocks me sick what I have to do,

I guess I'll have to punish you..."

But just then, an angel appeared in the sky, a pretty lady with dangly earrings and her wings laced with turquoise;

"*Please! Let me geg in!*

I know the situation,

These ladies did not steal my kid,

I gave her to them while I hid..."

Uncle John the Jester looked smug;

"*I told you queen, I'd bet a few quid,*

These ladies did not steal a kid..."

The angel began to disappear – or hide – again, so Star called out;

"*I need to check, just once more,*

They didn't steal this kid, you're sure?"

The angel smiled;

"*Yes, my queen, is right!*

I must fly into the night..."

Star waved to the angel and stood up from her throne;

"*Lad, you're right, I'd bet a few quid,*

These ladies did not steal a kid..."

Mr. Bertie turned to the policemen;

"*Fantastic, the law has been abused,*

And these ladies have been falsely accused..."

Jumping up, Uncle John the Jester bounced over to Aunt Susan;

THE DAY SHE MET SHIRLEY TEMPLE

"These ladies just make dreams come true,

But this posh bat wanted to stop them do..."

Star pointed her sceptre at Aunt Susan;

"You're a meany, meany woman..."

Aunt Susan shrank;

"Oh queen, I am only human..."

Star spoke to her entire kingdom;

"On your bike, and ride it far,

Don't come knockin' on our door again, la!"

The kingdom sang together;

"Is right! On your bike, ride it far,

Don't come knockin' on our door again, la!"

The 'Bizzies' freed Nannie and Aunty Vera, and gladly dragged Aunt Susan out, although she did have a right cob on... Star invited her kingdom to sit around her throne... Nannie and Aunty Vera to her left... Uncle John the Jester taking his pride of place to Star's right... Mr. Bertie beside him... Christopher McGinty and the little girls all sat down cross-legged with their arms folded... and the ladies in lilac returned to stroking Star's arms as she announced;

"Now I'm with me bezzie mates,

And that posh bat is on her skates,

Let's have a few bevvies, I'll get this round,

I think you're all smashing...quite simply sound!"

Everybody in the kingdom cheered, chanting;

"*Star! Star! Star!...*"

3.01pm

"Star!" Mary said, shaking the sleepy child. "Star!"

"Wakey, wakey," Vera said.

Star rubbed her eyes, sitting up. One half of her fringe was sticking up and she had crease marks down the side of her face from lying on Mary's crumpled up scarf.

"What is it?" Star mumbled.

"We're here, Star," Mary said, pointing out of the window to a sign that said, 'London Euston'. "We're in London."

PART THREE

"London is a roost for every bird."
Benjamin Disraeli, British Prime Minister
1804-1881

Euston Station

If Star hadn't known any better, she would have guessed that London was in an entirely different country to England. For starters, it seemed that the population of just about everywhere had decided to get a train to or from the station called Euston. Was it always this busy or was everybody also going to see Shirley Temple? If they were, they were in one goodness gracious rush to get there for Star had not been able to capture an image of one person's face; looking around Euston was like pressing the fast forward button on the remote controls for the video. And although London was the capital of England, why hadn't she heard anybody speak in English since they arrived here almost twenty minutes ago? Even the people working in the station couldn't speak English properly because Nannie had had to ask three different men in blue uniforms for the way to Harrods'. Then, Aunty Vera tried to ask by speaking very slowly like she does when she talks to Mrs Neary, the Eucharistic minister, and still nobody could help. It was so odd because both of them had used the words, 'Harrods', 'Shirley Temple', 'book signing', 'Terry Wogan', and 'Great big posh shop', many times, and the only answer they got was a shrug or the words 'travel card' and 'underground'. There was a huge group of school children – well, teenagers - wearing their own clothes and each with a rucksack almost the size of Star, looking at leaflets and making a racket, only they were talking foreign.

"They must be French kids," Aunty Vera said.

"How do you know?" Star asked.

"All the boys have long hair and wear their jeans far too high above their waist. Blatantly French. Did you know that I was once asked if I was Swedish?"

"Wow. Really?"

"Yes."

"Vera, you look nothing like a Swede," Nannie said. "You've got black hair."

Aunty Vera's face and shoulders dropped. "It was nice to be thought of as exotic. That's all."

Star recognised the newsagent W H Smith and read the word 'London' on the billboards around the station advertising *Phantom of the Opera* and *Cats*. She knew that the Queen of England lived here, and Maggie Thatcher, too, so despite everybody talking different, they hadn't left the country. Maybe the confusing language was why her daddy always said, 'bloody Londoners' anytime he watched the news and somebody was speaking with the caption 'Live from London' written across the tele beneath their head. Star presumed they were speaking English, but if she was honest with herself, she never listened. The news was either boring or scary, just showing lots of pictures of sick black people, especially children, just sitting on the ground looking sad with nothing to do. She really had no idea why her daddy even watched it.

Nannie tried to ask some random Londoners how to get to Harrods' but every single person either looked at her as if she was crazy, or completely ignored her. They were all like hunchbacks and kept their eyes on the grey-marbled ground – still, walking very fast – and it was a miracle they knew where they were going. They must be amazing at guessing games; 'What have I got in my hand?' would become quick fire with London people.

Star had begun to wonder if they had become three ghosts, when finally, one man gave them attention. And he was a really happy man! His hair was cut in a bowl shape but rather than neat like the men in Australian soap operas, it was so long that it covered half of his eyes and all greasy like Laura Fenton's. Nannie reckoned that she could fry an egg on Laura Fenton's head it was that full of grease, although Star imagined it would taste pretty rank.

"Dude!" the man said to Nannie.

"Are you American?" Star asked him.

"No, I'm from Coventry," he replied.

"Oh."

This Dude-man had no hands, or maybe very short arms, or wanted to hide something because the sleeves of his hooded sweatshirt were down to the tie-dyed knees of his baggy jeans; he had bought himself clothes in the completely wrong size.

"We're trying to get to Harrods'," Nannie said. "Can you help us? Nobody seems to speak English around here."

"Bogus."

"Are you *sure* you're not American?" Star asked again.

"Bogus."

Star took this as a 'no' since the Dude-man looked quite sad and shook his head, his whole bowl of hair moving in motion with the shake.

"You dudes need to get on the tube and hop on the Victoria Line down to Piccadilly – er – Circus, I think. Or is it Oxford Circus? No, no, Piccadilly. Duh! I'm thick. Of course it ain't Oxford Circus, it's Piccadilly... yeah, you just need the Piccadilly Line..." he stopped. "Bogus."

Star's eyes shot up to Nannie and Aunty Vera who were concentrating the same way as Peter Healy did in Maths, squinting their eyes with open mouths.

"Dudes, you never been to London before?"

"Bogus," Star said.

"Where you dudes from?"

"Liverpool," Nannie said in her most posh voice.

The Dude-man pretended to be all scared and put his hands up as if he were being held at gun-point. "Ooh, I better watch my wallet!" This he - and he alone - found hilarious judging by the change in Nannie's face, which Star knew all too well, was the 'not impressed' face. It was used at times such as when – and only once, ever - Star had taken money from the twenty pence jar for the ice-cream man without asking, or when Jehovah's Witnesses came to the door.

"Piccadilly Circus, it is then," Nannie snapped taking Star by the hand, Aunty Vera by the arm and ushering them down the stairs beneath a sign of a big red circle with 'Underground' written across it.

Star turned around to wave to the Dude-man, but was distracted from doing any gesture by him pretending to play an invisible guitar, as he shouted, "Excellent!"
Was that some sort of London 'goodbye'? Whatever it was, the Dude-man made a colourful impression in comparison to everything else in London Euston.

At the bottom of the stairs, the line to get Underground tickets was longer than the refunds queue in C&A during the January sales. There were people with suitcases blocking the barriers and – if possible – everybody seemed sadder down here.

"Nannie, do I have to sing for money again?" Star asked as she rubbed her throat; it felt dry.

"No luv," Nannie replied opening her purse. "I made sure we had some slummy for our time in London. But thank goodness you did perform this morning otherwise we'd be out in that drizzle walking to Harrods'."

"Phew!" Star wiped her brow. She had seen that done in the movies only was not quite sure why; there was nothing on her brow that needed to be wiped away.

*

Mary had never felt so far away from home. Actually, she had never *been* this far away from home. When they were evacuated during the war, they had been sent to a village called Mawdsley, which seemed like a million miles away from the burning streets of Liverpool. It was a place where they learnt how to milk a cow and climb a tree without a policeman threatening them to get down, and where they could walk for ages without seeing any houses; not because they had been bombed down, but because there wasn't any houses there to begin with, just fields. Mawdsley, in 1941, was very far away from Liverpool, however when John took Mary and Vera back to visit forty years later, they got there by car in less than an hour.

Only a matter of minutes had passed since they had arrived in London, and standing in the queue for tickets to ride through tunnels below the ground, Mary could not see the attraction. Endless movies were made set in the likes of New York, California and of course, London, and yes, they had been marvellous to watch, but she had never had an urge to go. Her lifestyle was so comfortable at home in Flinder Street. Why people wanted to move away and live in cities that were faster, larger, dirtier than your own home, she would never understand. Leaving home meant things changing, becoming no longer safe. She missed her stained brown teapot and her mug painted with yellow roses that had two chips on the handle.

Lesley Hegarty, from number thirty four down the bottom end of Flinder Street, had a daughter who had moved to London to be a model. It was a couple of years ago, and every Sunday morning after mass, all that could be heard next to the parish notice board was Lesley Hegarty's vowel sounds and 'S' sounds - for the woman only moved the bottom half of her jaw when she spoke causing every consonant to come out as an 'S' – saying, 'Our Siobhan this…' and 'Our Siobhan that…' Apparently, she had appeared in some music video for a male singer who was massive in Holland, but whenever anyone was given the opportunity to ask what her Siobhan was actually doing, Lesley Hegarty's reply was always, "Our Siobhan's living in London, she's going to be a model." *Going to be.* Star was always saying she was *going to be* a famous actress in Hollywood. Whenever Mary heard a syllable pass Lesley Hegarty's wrinkled lips, she worried for Star; Mary hadn't even seen a decent photograph of Siobhan, never mind one in a magazine.

*

Just when Vera thought the nausea had passed for the day, it made a depressing return... halfway down the escalator to the Northern Line. A pang of pain had shot across her forehead as they bought the tickets when Vera realised that that boy who liked the words 'bogus' and 'excellent' had given them wrong directions, but the world had started to spin as she stepped onto the downward moving stairs. It was the heat more than anything, and if there weren't so many people flying down the left hand side of the stairs past her, she would have removed half of her clothes.

"I wish to be in that..." Star was saying pointing at every poster of West End musicals pinned against the metal walls. "And that... and that..."

"You don't want to be in that," Mary said, "It's an advert for insurance."

And halfway down, the escalators stopped still with a jerk. Vera yelped, something she always did whenever Mary or John used to drag her onto the chairlifts in Wales. A metal seat that bobbed across a wire fifty feet high in the air was a death wish; they had survived a world war, the most serious injury being a grazed knee from tripping over a brick that used to be part of Bibby's Chemist, and to die in this manner would be downright disrespectful, yet Vera had unwillingly endured a chairlift ride four times. Now, the fear of dying in a sweaty tunnel on a rickety staircase was upon her.

It seemed the natural thing to wait - hand on rail – for the escalators to be fixed and move again, but nobody in London had this trail of thought. Vera supposed that wasn't the worst thing though, because she hated the idea of having to hold onto the sticky black rubber rail longer than necessary, imagining all the millions of hands that had touched it previously from all corners of the world, not knowing where they had been or if they had washed them after visiting the toilet. Those standing still behind Vera pushed against her causing a domino effect of falling onto Star and Star falling onto Mary. Where was everybody going in such a bloody hurry? Could they not wait for a little technical problem to be solved?

*

Star knew that Aunty Vera wanted to be sick because when she had turned around to see where all the pushing was coming from, the perfectly made-up face behind her was green. Not quite as green as the Wicked Witch of the West, but it was amazing how skin with red blood beneath it could turn such a colour. They had to walk down the escalators, so Star looked to her feet to watch her step…

Only it was impossible! Star found her feet almost stuck to the step because she was terrified of toppling over. The small, thin wooden planks making up each step were becoming more and more blurry the more she looked at them, as if the wooden lines were moving about, like a dancing grid. She was too dizzy to move and people everywhere were pushing and Aunty Vera was surely going to puke in her hair…

Luckily, Nannie handed Aunty Vera the carrier bag containing the last squashed ham and piccalilli roll just in time.

And that's when Star started crying.

*

"Let's move to London," Linda said.

It was New Year's Eve, 1979. Jimmy found Linda sitting on the low brick wall that separated the car park from St. Stephen's social club. Every car's windows were laced with thick frost, yet his girlfriend was wearing just a loose blouse over a denim mini skirt with a thick white leather belt around her small waist. Circling the last drop of sparkling wine at the bottom of her glass, Linda's eyes were gazing into the distance, watching the hot air escape from her mouth and melt into cold.

"Are you crackers?" Jimmy asked.

"It's just another city, Jim. Like Liverpool, only bigger."

"I meant you sitting out here. It's the bleedin' ice age."

Linda turned her head to look at him. Her eyelids were coated with sparkles, a touch of glamour against the iron mesh over the windows and garish yellow posters announcing the line-up of local comedians. "No, you think I'm crackers for wanting to move to London."

"I don't…"

"You do."

"Okay, it is a bit out of the blue, luv…"

"Well, it shouldn't be," she snapped, then took in a breath of the cold air. "I was just talking to Siobhan Hegarty in there; she was behind me in the line for the buffet."

"Christ, is she old enough to be in there?"

"She looks it, actually she looks *too* old, it's kind of sad. Anyway, it occurred to me that the last time I had a conversation with her was a year ago. Last New Year's Eve, here."

"I don't understand. You want to be her mate or something? I thought you weren't fussed on Siobhan Hegarty."

"I'm not, and no, I don't want to be her mate. She's a kid! And she's friggin' full of her herself…"

"So?"

"Jimmy, I asked her how she was, and she told me that she had just had some more professional photographs taken – in Manchester this time – and that she was going to move to London to become a model. She mentioned that her nana was still suffering with her chest, but could still manage getting to Farmfoods and back on the bus on her own. Then she spoke of London again, of a place called Camden where she had a cousin making a fortune selling ornate handmade mirrors on a market stall. Apparently they're going to live together in a flat overlooking the canal…"

"Good luck to her. If it's anything like the canal down by the back wall of the sausage works she'll learn some superb expressions for her privates."

Jimmy hated cracking a decent joke and Linda dismissing it. She just continued swirling the dregs of her wine, searching for an answer of some sorts down there, not with him.

"Linda, luv, why are you so sad? It's New Year's Eve… a party!"

"I'm not sad. That's just it, I'm not sad, and maybe I should be," she seemed to snap out of her trance a little, blinking her eyes and allowing herself to shiver, acknowledging the cold. "A year ago, I spoke to Siobhan Hegarty – in the line for the buffet, would you believe – and guess what she said?"

"Erm, *'I'm gonna be a model'*," Jimmy mocked.

Linda nodded. "Yes! She told me she was going to be a model. And she mentioned her nana's chest. And she told me she was moving to London."

"Isn't that what folks call a déjà vu?"

"Only it wasn't a déjà vu, Jim, it was real. I stood in the same place, picking at the same mushroom vol-au-vents and cheese and pineapple sticks, having the same conversation with the same girl as

I did a year ago. Did you notice that Rita Fitzpatrick's wearing the same dress as last year?"

"I didn't notice, no, Linda," Jimmy took out a packet of Silk Cut from his jeans' pocket and lit a cigarette.

"There's not much to notice… material-wise, I mean!"

"She's looking a bit porky, though, I noticed that."

"Jim, she's only just had a baby. But yeah, she should have had the sense not to squeeze into last year's dazzling delight. But what I'm trying to say is, nothing really happens round here, does it? Our little world is just going round in circles, everybody miserably being happy… only, I'm not miserable, and I think - should I be? Should I be wanting more, you know, seeing what is out there beyond this end of Liverpool? I've got no ambition, Jim. I just left school at sixteen 'cause that's what all me mates did, and I just work in the shoe shop and never think about working anywhere else, and I hang around with all the same people 'cause I like them, I do, I like them. Is it wrong that I'm just happy to keep everything how it is? Why don't I want to move to London and make mirrors?"

Jimmy, who had tried so hard to understand Linda so far, just exhaled his smoke with confusion wrinkling all over his freezing cold face. "Mirrors? You are crackers."

Finally, Linda laughed a little and rested her head on his shoulder, tugging at his arm to go around her delicate shoulders. They sat staring at the parked cars for a short while, the voice of

Blondie echoing from the speakers inside singing 'Heart of Glass'. At one point, Mick Tully toppled out of the club and stood shaking his hips, pointed at Jimmy and Linda who turned around to see what he was doing, and sang, *"As it turns out, I had a heart attack…"*

"It's glass, Mick," Linda shouted over. "A heart of glass."

"Fuck off!" Mick walked back into one closed door, and then safely through the wedged open door.

"Did that happen last year?" Jimmy asked Linda, stubbing his cigarette out on the wall.

"No. Last year he was trying to perfect his Boney M dance. You know the one he does whenever he's being arrested?" Linda stood up to do her own Boney M dance, skipping from side to side and flapping her arms about. "Christ, it's freezing!"

"Glad you noticed," Jimmy smiled at her, holding out his hand to take her back inside, only she walked away towards the street. He wondered if she had had too much to drink, something he could never tell with Linda, her always being the one with the best memory and the least embarrassing moments after a night out. The street was very quiet, nobody wanting to be out driving minutes before midnight. Linda was shifting her feet around on the spot, looking into the clear sky, concentrating as if she were counting the number of stars above her.

"You followed me," she said without looking at him.

"I always do," he said.

"Soft lad. Go inside. I'm fine on me own."

Instead of doing as he was told, Jimmy locked his arms around her, letting her slide back onto his chest. He pecked her cheek repeatedly until Linda started to chuckle, and let his own cheek rest against hers which was surprisingly warm. So she was happy being here, but unhappy because she wanted to be someone who was unhappy? He tried not to think about this, it hurt his head. Sometimes he worried that Linda thought too deeply into things, and maybe she was the kind of person to have ambition and seek greater achievements in life only had no way of knowing how to channel it. There was always a part of her so mysterious, something he could never understand about her, as if at any moment she would just change her mind and leave him. It terrified Jimmy, but intrigued him beyond belief.

"New Year's Eve always makes me nervous," Linda said. "I didn't know anything about New Year's Eve until I was five and me mam let me go to a party with them. She put me in my Christmas Day dress, this little grey thing with a lacy collar and a blue ribbon around the neck, and we went round to Aunty Betty's house in a taxi. We never got taxis! There was a spread on the table, loads of trifle, and a whole bunch of her neighbours who I had never met before. Me and our Susan were the only kids, except for this boy who sat in an armchair all night reading his Dandy annual and refused to look at anybody. Okay, so I was only five, but it seemed to be that everybody there was talking really fast, as if they were over-excited and dashing around the house; even drinks were being spilled on the carpet. I asked me Uncle Harry what was going on and he picked me up and said, 'at midnight tonight, it will be the start of a brand new year, everything will be different and you will even hear all the ships sounding their horns…' and I don't know why Jim, but it scared the shit out of me! For starters, I had never been awake at midnight before and it seemed like a long time to wait, but the idea of everything changing once the clock struck twelve gave me jitters in my tummy. I couldn't even stomach any of Aunty Betty's trifle."

"You've come far in the last fifteen years then, luv. You managed to stomach a fair few of those vol-au-vents before."

"Ssh. What I'm saying is that funny feeling of everything possibly changing always returns every New Year. It's the same feeling I get when I see an old man in a restaurant eating alone."

Bank Holiday Monday, last August, Jimmy and Linda had gone to Blackpool for the day, which was a mistake in itself because it had been so busy they had had to queue for an hour just to get on the Big Dipper. At lunchtime, they decided to splash out and eat at a restaurant attached to a seafront hotel to avoid standing in mile long lines just to get a tray of chips and curry sauce. The plan was working out well until Linda just started to sob! Rarely had Jimmy seen his girlfriend crying, always being the one to hold it together, even at funerals. Yet, there she was in despair and all because there was an old man sitting across the way, alone. This observation sparked a series of irrational questions from her… "Where is his wife?", "Where are his children?", "What happened to his wife?", "Will he ever love again?", "When was the last time someone made him his tea?", "What state is his house in?", "Is he thinking that his wife should be sitting in that empty seat?" Jimmy had made a joke about his wife being a bitch from hell who always attempted to poison his cottage pie and that the old man was actually having a quiet escape, enjoying his own thoughts and the tasty batter on the fish. Only Linda didn't enjoy the joke, just carried on sobbing and wishing that the old man didn't have to eat alone, getting herself all worked up about the fact that what she was witnessing was a product of what happens to everyone in the future. By the end of their meal, Jimmy was broken-hearted about the old man, too; the mood didn't half ruin the taste of his Cumberland sausage.

It was five minutes to midnight. There were no lonely old men around St. Stephen's social club, except for the few who had decided to hide from their wives wanting to drag them onto the dance floor to Gloria Gaynor's 'I Will Survive'. It was fair to say that Jimmy didn't know a single bloke who liked that bloody song, nor a single woman who disliked it.

"Linda, what's wrong? You look like you're going to start crying, luv."

"I don't know… well, I do. I'm afraid of change and everybody around me wanting things to change…"

"Come back inside. Sheila Gilhooley's still trying to do the twist to every song they play and I don't know what's getting in the way of her succeeding; The Clash or the friggin' skirt she's wearing. It's so tight around her calves that she's walking to and from the bar like a bleedin' penguin."

"Do you think London is very different to Liverpool?" Linda asked, not appreciating one of Jimmy's jokes, again.

"It's probably not that different. It still rains all the bloody time whenever I see it on the news. But it's full of foreigners, isn't it?"

"There are foreigners here, too."

"Way more down there though. There are no Scousers in London."

"Except our Susan. And Cilla Black."

"Lovely, let's move then!"

Linda nudged Jimmy's ribs, but this made him hold her tighter. Her hair smelt of honey beneath the instant whiff of smoke. It seemed silly to be worried, having just had confirmation from Linda that she hated change. This news should have been enough to eliminate the constant fear he had that one day she would leave him, find something better than what he could give her, but it didn't. Any moment now, the crowd currently propped up at the bar and step-digging on the dance floor would join them outside, Jonesy holding his portable radio up high trying to get a decent signal for the countdown. Jimmy had had his speech prepared for months, exactly what he wanted to say after Linda would wish him a Happy New Year. It circled about his head one more time;

"Linda, there's a little brown envelope sitting behind the carriage clock on my mantelpiece. It contains exactly one month's wages, and between you and me, I think it's a bit soft leaving it there. So, what do you say I take you shopping – ring shopping – and we blow the lot on the prettiest rock you can find? I'm sick of you being Linda Lloyd, and I want you to be Mrs Blake. I love you, Lin. Marry me."

Jimmy felt a heavy hand smack across the back of his head when he turned around to see Jonesy standing there shaking a can of Carlsberg screaming, "It's the Eighties, mate! It's the fuckin' Eighties!" And he pulled the ring of the can back allowing the lager to explode and spray all over them. Jonesy pulled his mate into him, hugging him tight and fast, letting Jimmy go as quickly as he had been grabbed. Soaked with lager seeping into his new Burton's shirt – a Christmas present from Mary Mack – Jimmy felt the chill of the liquid touch his cold skin. He should have known better than to wear his new clothes tonight because Jonesy had pulled exactly the same stunt last year. Shivering, he looked around trying to find Linda. A circle had gathered in the middle of the street with everybody linking arms and attempting to sing 'Auld Lang Syne', although it was more like a warped version of the 'Okey Kokey'. Slotted in between Siobhan Hegarty and an overweight girl he recognised from school but could never remember her name, was Linda. She had been so right; yes, it was now 1980, but this scene could have easily been 1979 or 1978... nothing around here ever changed. Yet Linda was smiling, that gorgeous smile that put a dimple in her right cheek as she scrunched up her perfect little nose and laughed out loud rather than pretend to know the words of the song.

Jimmy never said his rehearsed speech. The best way to keep hold of his Linda was to keep things exactly the way they were.

Leicester Square

"This is a nuisance," Mary said. "A nuisance."

They had been informed to change at Leicester Square and take the Piccadilly Line to a place called Knightsbridge, only instead of finding their way to whatever the Piccadilly Line was, they had crowd surfed up the staircase of yet another broken escalator with Star's head buried into Mary's stomach complaining that her eyes were "going all dizzy". On seeing a glimpse of daylight near to signs saying 'exit', Vera had made it through the barrier and into the fresh air with a series of speedy moves that could rival Daley Thompson.

Standing near a narrow yet busy, traffic-jammed road outside of Leicester Square tube station, Mary tried to pace around and find a map of the Underground but kept walking into dozy people wearing rucksacks. Vera was coughing, and making a rather dramatic song and dance out of it.

"It's the fumes, Mary," Vera said. "From all the buses."

Really. Anyone'd think Vera had never seen a bleedin' bus never mind taken one every day for the last fifty years.

"Wow, look at the size of those pizzas," Star said pointing to a booth sandwiched into the wall in between a busy coffee shop and an empty coffee shop. Over she ran to the glass cabinet full of cans of coca-cola and huge pizzas sliced into pieces, her fingertips stroking the window as if trying to touch the food. "They look amazing, and so American."

"They look cold and as if they've been sitting there for a fortnight," Mary said.

This is what Star always did when she wanted something. Not the sort of child to demand, Mary had learnt that Star's way of saying, "I want that," was to become attached to something and praise it. She had done exactly that with Loving You Barbie in Baron's. Winnie and Des Baron ran the family-owned newsagent next door to the post office near Flinder Street and had been fortunate enough to expand the shop when the launderette closed down over a decade ago. Their business had stretched into toys, and what was once a room for laundry and suds was Bootle's most magnificent toy chest; an oversized cupboard spilling with dolls, board games, jigsaws and miniature cars. Recently they had started to sell BMX bikes, but this had made the shop even more difficult to manoeuvre around, resulting in the doll's prams having to be hung from the ceiling with string. Baron's had a 'toy bank' where children could have an account to pay their pocket money into until they had enough to buy themselves a toy. Jimmy used to take Star every Saturday afternoon on the way to get cheese and onion pasties for lunch, and Star would give Winnie Baron her fifty pence piece. Only Star was so impatient that she could never save up for longer than a month, resulting in her bedroom being full of felt tip pens, painting-by-numbers, and Playmobile characters without anything to play on. And this had never been a problem for Star until she laid eyes on Loving You Barbie, an enticing doll by name and nature it seemed, casting a love spell over the little girl. Mary had picked up a Liverpool Echo and a quarter of pear drops, heard enough from Winnie about Des's indigestion, and was ready to go and get some chicken drumsticks from Ron's, but Star did not come running when she called. She was found at the back of the toy shop, holding the pink box and staring at the Barbie doll - all dressed in a red top shaped like a heart and a long white shirt scattered in tiny red hearts – and could only be compared to a mother holding her child for the first time.

"She's so beautiful," Star said, mesmerised.

"Come on, Star."

"She has the prettiest eyes in the whole world."

"Well, you can save up for her."

"She's so lonely on the shelf here."

"More reason to save your pennies then, isn't it?"

"She has to stand next to the Transformers section. They're for *boys*." Star narrowed her eyes as she said, 'boys', something she always did whenever she had fallen out with Simon Monaghan.

"Star. Now!" Mary said through her teeth, which always worked when Star was playing up, but instead, the child just brushed her fingers over the transparent plastic, the closest she could get to touching Barbie's face. Star looked up with a face like a street urchin begging for a crumb of bread, but Mary widened her eyes. "Now!"

Star's theatrical sadness did not fade, as she pulled her glance back to Barbie and in the slowest of motion known to man, placed the pink box back onto the shelf in its slot beside a Megatron. Mary took her hand and dragged her out of Baron's, feeling as though she were tearing Heidi away from the Alps.

"Everyone in America eats pizza," Star said. "Jennifer Henry said so when she came back from Disneyland and was cured of Leukaemia."

Vera made a Sign of the Cross, a natural reaction to hearing that child's name.

"That's not American pizza, luv," Mary said pointing to the sloppy slices facing out onto Leicester Square. "It's cold and greasy, nothing like what the Americans eat and you don't want to be disappointed, do you?"

"I guess not," Star let her hand slide off the glass cabinet. "Besides, I'm very self-reliant."

Glad to have Star back on form, Mary now turned her concerns to Vera, who had taken out her handkerchief and placed it over the top of a bollard, and was struggling to perch upon it. If only she would enjoy her food rather than pick at it as though she were searching for a poisonous spider, her backside would not be so bony and she could enjoy so many more places to sit. There was no point in dragging her sister back down into the Underground for she was proving to be more of a liability than a teenager in the King George, so Mary had to go on a mission to find out about a bus that would get them to Knightsbridge.

Only, time was running out. They had already been in London for an hour and Shirley Temple was not going to wait for them. Mary had no idea how long a book signing went on for, or if in fact they had already missed it. The day had flown by, and why was it that when you needed extra time life just moved forward too quickly? And it always ticked by so slowly when waiting for something to happen?

"Nannie, I've got that tickly feeling that I get when we go to Pontin's," Star said putting up the hood on her blue raincoat. Minnie Mouse smiled at Mary from the top of Star's head. "As if there are loads of little men dancing about inside my tummy. And in my knees, too. Is London further away than Prestatyn?"

"Yes, Star, miles further."

"Oh my goodness."

So much further in fact, that Mary felt that they could have been on Mars.

*

Leicester Square was even busier than London Euston, and there were even more gangs of teenagers similar to the French they had seen earlier. Star was somewhere in the middle of feeling starving and sick, eager to get to Harrods' and meet Shirley Temple but also starting to get a bit frightened of seeing her, too. What would she look like? Star had hardly ever seen Shirley Temple in colour.

A park without any swings or slides took over the middle of the square and although Star had felt the odd spot of rain, there were plenty of people lying on the grass as if it were a hot, sunny day. She noticed a small crowd gathered beside a doorway next to a restaurant with lots of tables and chairs outside and people eating spaghetti still wearing their anoraks.

"Maybe Shirley Temple is in there!" Star pointed to the crowd that was full of little girls about the same age as Star, each with an adult. They were dressed in party frocks, which pleased Star as she was so used to seeing little girls her age dressed in shell suits, even for special occasions. When Steph Bradley had a birthday party in McDonalds last year, Star had been the only one wearing a dress, patterned red and blue tartan stitched with fine gold strips, and although she knew she looked nice, she had felt stupid. *And* Laura Fenton was spotted on Easter Sunday in church wearing a purple shell suit with white and black slashes across the middle of the jacket; so much for wearing an Easter bonnet with frills upon it… But now Star felt dressed down. The red flowers sprinkled all over her cream dress and black t-bar school shoes seemed so plain compared to these outfits before her, all shining taffeta and puff ball skirts, patent leather slippers and some little girls even wearing make-up. "Aunty Vera, you need to put some lippy on me."

"Star, that's not Harrods'," Mary said fanning Aunty Vera's face with a leaflet for Starlight Express. "Have you got any juice left in your Mr. T flask?"

Star nodded and passed Nannie her lunchbox, but was more concerned about what was going on with all the little girls rather than Aunty Vera's funny turn; at least her face wasn't green anymore. Edging closer and closer to the crowd, taking baby steps, Star could finally read the poster on a big wooden board stood beside a Japanese couple taking photographs of an Indian family slurping spaghetti. In bold, black letters against an orange background, the words read;

'HAPPY HOUR! SING LIVE ON THE RADIO AND MAKE BRITAIN HAPPY! SPONSORED BY SUNBEAM FM AND BONANZA BUBBLE GUM, NEW BLUEBERRY FLAVOUR!'

Sunbeam FM! Mrs O'Connell listened to Sunbeam FM in Aunt Susan's kitchen, and Mr Bertie loved to stay with her and skive off his duties upstairs because of DJ Spike Smythe who played comedy songs from all over the world, some of them even in different languages. Star had always thought that those songs were silly, not getting why Mr Bertie found them so funny that he made his eyes water, although seeing Mr Bertie laugh in this way always made Star laugh herself. She smiled thinking about the happier moments in that big, boring house, when Mr Bertie would take Star's hands and dance around the kitchen table, Mrs O'Connell flicking them with milk and shouting at them to leave her be… Star had even managed to get Mr Bertie to learn a shuffle hop before Mrs O'Connell could whack their bottoms with a spatula.

The crowd was pushed apart by a young man who stormed out of the doorway heading towards where Star was standing. He was breathing heavily in and out and in and out, with one hand lost inside the large mound of frizzy curls piled on the top of his head. Star had never seen such a pointed chin on a person before, and with the amount of burgundy hair he had in one place, she couldn't help but think that his face was shaped like a strawberry. Perhaps he was a pop star because he was wearing sunglasses and ripped denim, only she had never seen him on the front of *Smash Hits!* or *Fast Forward*. Star was just about to dodge out of the way and avoid being trampled on by a Dr. Martens boot, when the young man was yanked by the shoulder from behind and swivelled around.

"How dare you cut my Tina's song short," a crazed woman yelled into his face. Her cropped hair was bright yellow at the end but jet black at the roots and her face was very sunburnt, making her small round eyes bright and evil. She wore a lot of gold jewellery which jangled as she shook the young man by his shoulders, and her voice sounded just like the ladies from that programme that Nannie enjoyed called *Eastenders*.

"Your Tina's song was long enough," he yelled back at her.

"Thirty seconds? You think it's fair to give a talented child thirty seconds?"

"Talented?" he laughed without laughing, saying, "Ha, ha, ha," slowly. "Yes, Mrs Turner, she is mega talented."

"Why did you call her a baboon injected with helium?"

"Did I say that? Noooo."

"And you told her to stop, it was killing you."

"*You're* killing me!"

"Who the hell do you think you are? The state of you in those glasses, thinking you're all Tom Cruise in *Top Gun*. Who are you anyway? Some tea-boy? What's your name, Edgar, was it?"

"Hector. Hec-Tor. And Mrs Turner, I'm a broadcasting student on work experience…"

"D'ant give a shit!" Mrs Turner pointed a long fingernail into Hector's face and was about to say something when a miniature version of the woman – presumably Tina - revealed herself from behind, reminding Star of the Russian dolls on Aunty Vera's bedroom windowsill. Star had never seen anybody her age with such yellow and black hair before.

"Mum, I'm hungry," Tina whined. "You promised we could go to Wimpy's."

Mrs Turner took her child's hand. "I will make sure you never work in radio, Edgar…"

"It's Hec-Tor…"

"D'ant give a shit!"

Star regretted not dodging earlier because Mrs Turner and her daughter walked purposefully into Hector with full force, knocking him backwards. He tripped over Star and they both fell onto the ground, sunglasses included.

"Woah, I'm so sorry!" Hector said, panic in his voice.

"That's okay," Star said as he helped her to her feet and she brushed a little muck from her hands against her raincoat.

"They're going to get rid of me, I just know it." Hector bent down to retrieve his glasses, and put them back on upside down, adjusted, but took them off again. "Great. They're mega scratched."

"She was stormy weather," Star said, watching Mrs Turner and Tina head towards the Underground station. "Was that little girl's name really Tina Turner?"

Hector looked puzzled, as if he hadn't realised. "Yeah! Oh yeah. I guess that's what they call irony, hey?"

"I don't know, but it sure is funny and peculiar."

"Do you like Tina Turner?"

"I don't like her mother!" Star giggled, and Hector relaxed, joining her. "Actually, there's a lady who lives in my street called Sheila Gilhooley. She loves Tina Turner, but can't sing like her either. I have a doll that looks like her."

"Like Tina Turner?"

"No, like Sheila Gilhooley, silly!"

Star and Hector laughed again.

"What's your name?" Hector asked.

"I'm Star. And you're Hector, aren't you?"

"I am. Yes! Somebody around here remembers my name," he punched the air when he said, 'yes', and Star realised he was younger than she had originally guessed. Sunglasses made young people look older and old people younger. "Star? Is that your real name? That's amazing. I used to work with real stars you know…"

"Like movie stars?"

"Nah, pop stars. Just last week, I was doing work experience for Groovin' FM, Sunbeam's sister station, and guess who I met?"

"Tina Turner?"

He chuckled and touched Star's nose. "No, you little comedian. I met The Bangles *and* Paula Abdul all in one day. It was mega. Jason Donovan's in there today, not that I want to meet him, he's for the girls isn't he, but I'd rather be hanging out with him than with the likes of that Mrs Turner. Look at them… there's hundreds of Mrs Turners all thinking that their kid is the next Madonna."

"What's going on exactly, Hector?" Star said, her nose scrunched up as the sun gently made an appearance through the thick white sky.

"Spike Smythe has to promote that new blueberry flavour bubble gum and he's letting little girls sing live today and calling them Britain's Berry Bubbles… yeah, I mean get real. It's so lame. But they're making me handle the crowds and choose who gets through the doors, while Spike and his producer sit upstairs on wheelie chairs and drink the tea I made them."

Star disagreed with him, embracing the idea of singing live on the radio, but seeing as Hector was having such a bad day – Mrs Turner and Tina being prime evidence – she decided to keep her opinion a secret.

"I mean, I want to be a music journalist. Meeting The Bangles was exo skeleton, but now I'm faced with this. We haven't had a decent kid yet and Spike's team are going to hate me."

"I don't hate you," Star put her hand on his arm.

"Cheers. You're mega, Star. Ha, ha! A Mega-Star! I don't suppose you fancy singing, do you?"

"Well, as a matter of fact, I'd love to. And I have just the song."

"Do you have a parent or guardian with you?"

Star called Nannie, who had now ripped the Starlight Express leaflet into two pieces and was fanning each of Aunty Vera's cheeks. When they heard that not only could Star sing on the radio, but that there was a sofa inside the studio and a cup of tea to be made personally by Hector, the two guardians gave their whole-hearted permission. Star reckoned that unless Aunty Vera had a proper little relax, they would never make it to Harrods' without Nannie wanting to beat her up with the *My Little Pony* lunchbox. According to Hector, Knightsbridge was really close and most buses from a place called Regent Street just past Leicester Square would take them right there. Nannie called him a "good lad", but Aunty Vera told him he was an "angel sent from Heaven". This must have embarrassed Hector because despite the scratches on his sunglasses, he wore them even though they were inside, away from the crowd of mothers and sequins.

Mary couldn't quite believe that she in was a studio, a real studio, with red lights above the doors with the words 'on air' written across them. Vera had perked up, taking a strong liking to this Hector fellow and linking him as they walked along the white carpeted hallway, although she tended to laugh too frequently at anything he said and getting shushed by him.

Spike Smythe, was he very famous? Maybe just in London perhaps. Mary had never heard of him, or Sunbeam FM come to think of it. Then again, she only ever listened to Radio Merseyside on a Sunday morning when Billy Butler hosted 'Hold Your Plums'; the tele was just far too good these days.

"Would you like some bubble gum, Vera?" Hector asked.

"Oh, I'd love some Hector," Vera winked. What had gotten into her? Mary hoped the cup of tea would settle her down because if she carried on being this giddy, she'd choke to death on the blueberry flavouring.

They were told to sit on a white leather sofa which squeaked as their bottoms touched it. Opposite was a large window where they could see Spike Smythe sitting behind a desk, talking into a fluffy grey microphone. A woman in loose black clothes and long, long hair swept over to the side – burgundy, the exact same colour as

Hector's – introduced herself as Trix. By the looks of it, Trix hadn't slept in days and her teeth were stained yellow.

"She'd better sing, Hester," Trix yawned.

"It's Hec-Tor... Hester's a girl's na..."

"Whatever. Hector. The last kid you sent in looked at the microphone and froze," Trix must have been related to royalty with an accent as clipped as this. "When she attempted to sing some nursery rhyme about spinach she'd been going on and on about in the hallway, all that escaped from her mouth was a burp. She made three attempts. Spike said, 'We're not promoting pop!' What a pun!" And Trix let out one long, silent laugh with her mouth wide open and lots of air escaping. "He is *so* in the mix."

"And a burp must have been better than the nasal ear-ache of Tina Turner?" Hector said, laughing along with Trix.

Trix closed her mouth, any hint of amusement gone. "Whatever. Hes, um, Hec, um, whatever. So, Star... is that your real name?"

"Yeah," Star smiled.

"SSSS," Mary pointed out. "Say, 'Ye-SSS. Not yeah." She didn't want this Trix to think that they were common, after all.

"Sorry. Ye-SSS."

Trix did a smaller version of her silent, air-laugh. "Do you get stagefright?"

Star threw her shoulders back. "No, I'm a trooper."

"Do you have adenoids?"

"No, but I'll get some if you want them."

"Awesome. You're next."

As Hector put the kettle on, Trix escorted Star through one door, which opened onto a second door, and into the studio. A set of headphones were placed onto Star's head. She hadn't even begun to sing yet, and Mary was already so proud of Star, smiling confidently and waving at her and Vera through the window.

Spike Smythe spoke live on-air, "Next we have a little lady all the way from Merseyside… what you doing here? Hope you're not going to steal my hub caps!"

"Of course not," Star said, offended, and Mary's pride swelled, although she was pretty sure Star had no idea what hub caps were. Billy Butler was better than this Smythe swine any day. She'd even phone in to Radio Merseyside and tell them so. Star gathered herself. "I'm looking for the Blue Bird."

That shut him up. Without further ado, Spike Smythe – complete with a very puzzled face - said, "Ladies and Gentlemen, presenting Miss Star Blake."

Star took a deep breath and sang;

"What is all this dizzy busy hustling for?
People running helter-skelter on their way,
What is all this hazy crazy bustling for?
No time to notice it's a sunny day,

Why don't you take a vacation?

Looks like you've got to have relaxation,

Aw, come on, forget your troubles for a while

Why don't you try to feel like I do?

If I had one wish to make,

This is the wish I would choose,

I'd want an old straw hat, a suit of overalls and a worn out pair of shoes..."

*

It was impossible to get a decent signal in their cell, yet Addo insisted on making an attempt every day to tune his portable radio into something, anything at all they could listen to. If they were lucky, a small station from North Wales entertained them, playing the latest chart music and running quizzes for mediocre prizes such as a week's supply of Mars Bars or a video of a Touchstone Home Movie. Jimmy particularly enjoyed playing the quiz with himself; the days when he could make it through to the end without a series of hissing and crackling were so far, the 'better' days in prison.

"Sorry mate," Addo said staring at his possession with disappointment. "All I can get is that Spike Smythe and his foreign ditties…"

"Never heard of him," Jimmy said. "But go 'ed, turn it up." Anything was better than the echoes of their existence.

Addo placed his radio onto the floor, pulling up the aerial and shifting it into a position that eliminated any interference, but every time he pulled his hand away, the sound became unclear.

"You just let me roam about,

Laughing at big city blues,

With an old straw hat..." sang the voice from inside the radio.

Jimmy slipped off his bed and fell to his knees, grabbing the aerial with his own hands.

"...a suit of overalls and a worn out pair of shoes..."

He tried to speak, but was glad that no words would escape his lips for he didn't want to miss a moment of hearing the sweet sounds filling his dismal space. Was this a dream? Was he hearing things? Tears filled Jimmy's eyes and his chest tightened, as if his heart was growing too big, not allowing him to breathe.

"What is it, Jim?" Addo asked, only his words seemed too large, too loud for this moment. Jimmy waved his free hand and shook his head, fiercely.

"Howdy Mister Brown!

Ho-hum!

Goin` fishin`? Hope you get a bite! Yes, indeed I do..."

Addo stood up, walking a short away to the door and back.

His footsteps seemed heavy, clumsy and Jimmy let the words drop out of his mouth, "It's Star… It's my little Star."

"Howdy Mister Jones!

Ho-hum!

How`s about a hay ride Saturday night?"

With Jimmy's trembling hand working extra hard at holding the aerial in place, absolute stillness took over their cell as Star finished her song. There was no music to accompany her, just her innocent eight year-old voice resonating around them, substituting the void which had previously been the complete opposite of Star's singing.

"Sing hi-ho the merri-o!

What`ve you got, what`ve you got to lose?

Get an old straw hat

A suit of overalls

And a worn out pair of shoes."

He clapped. Jimmy clapped his hands as if he were giving Pavarotti a standing ovation, and the clear sounds of Spike Smythe became a mixed up muffle. Addo grabbed onto the aerial to salvage the end.

"Thank you Star… a real Star she is, one might say, despite being a Scouser…" Smythe said in a cringey, mock-American accent. "Only joking, princess. Do you want to say hello to anybody before you go, Star?"

"Ye-SSS, please," Star's voice said, so bright and loud that if Jimmy imagined hard enough, she could have been right there in the room with him. "I'd like to say hello to my daddy. Because he's not here."

"Fantabulous, Star… and now for the latest weather update with Sunbeam's own Mindy Mitchell…"

Jimmy waved the radio away with his hand, sitting back against the wall. Addo switched it off, the lack of noise allowing them to recall the melodic tune of the child's song. He was stunned, simply stunned. There was no other word to describe it. Jimmy wondered if wishes did actually come true, for he had wished so hard to just hear his daughter's voice, happy and confident, something that would not be likely if she were brought into this place to visit him. It had been the most incredible moment, to be sitting in the same cell as all day, every day, and hear magic. He wanted to cry, to let the tears resting in his eyes just roll down his cheeks and release the breathlessness inside his chest, but he was afraid that it would become too real, that the moment would then be considered gone. So, he just sat there, his head resting against the painted brick walls, hands touching the cold, hard floor, and hearing the memory of Star's voice without breathing too hard, staying for as long as he could in this reality.

Addo broke the silence. "So your daughter's in London?"

Jimmy blinked; his first step back into the real world. "London?"

"Sunbeam FM comes from London, doesn't it?"

"I don't know. It's not something I'd know… why would I know that?"

"I don't know, do I?"

"I listen to the sports, or whatever shit you can find on that thing, but how would I know that this comes from London? That Star is in London? I mean, why was she even on the radio? What the fuck's going on here, Addo? Did that just happen? Did I hear that? Did you hear that?"

"I did, and you're sure it's your kid, Jim?"

"What do you mean, I am sure? It's my kid, mate. I know my own fuckin' kid." Jimmy stood up and paced the cell as much as he could.

"Keep your voice down, I was just saying. It may not have been her…"

"How many little Scouse girls do you know called 'Star', Addo? For fuck's sake… But hold on. What *is* she doing in London? It's what… Monday, no Tuesday? Why isn't she at school? Why is she in fuckin' London? And who the fuck with?"

"Maybe she won a competition?" Addo tried.

Something wasn't right. Jimmy was most definitely awake; he had heard his daughter singing on the radio, live. So Susan had taken her to the capital for a day out, maybe? But Susan had been very keen to send Star to a private school, a girl's academy somewhere near the golf courses outside of Southport, so she had said. What if Star wasn't even with Susan? London was pretty far away, hundreds of miles from Liverpool and expensive to get to.

Jimmy was a prisoner. But he was still a father. And he would find out exactly where his little girl was, and why.

Trafalgar Square

There were pigeons everywhere. John would have had a field day here, Vera thought, probably found a sick one out of the thousand to nurse. It was a blessing really that he wasn't there with them, pigeon-playing, because it would no doubt put Mary in an even worse mood. She had cheered up; hearing Star sing always made Mary happy, but Vera had made the mistake of reminding them exactly why they were here in London, and the dangers that occurred.

"Jesus, Mary. I hope that Susan didn't hear Star on the radio… she'll know she's not in school."

Yes, Vera had succeeded in ruining her sister's optimism. For the time being.

THE DAY SHE MET SHIRLEY TEMPLE

After Star had sung so spectacularly on live radio, the delightful Hector had escorted them downstairs and past the mob of wannabes, pointing them in the direction to catch the number nine bus. Vera would have preferred to stay inside the cosy studio for the rest of the afternoon, for the pace of London was in her opinion, sheer hell. There was something so calm, so cool, about being in the Sunbeam FM building, knowing that the madness of Leicester Square was just one wall away while she sat on expensive cushions drinking tea from a mug which had been touched with a long line of famous people's lips.

"Did you know that Neil Diamond drank from that mug once," Hec-cute-as-a-button-Tor had told her. "I heard Trix tell the studio manager this morning, and she's a bit of a cow, but mega. As in, she wouldn't lie."

The walk through Leicester Square had been alright, actually. There were no spots of rain anymore, just a light wind and not too many people stopping in their way. Vera just felt a little melancholy thinking back to her moments of slurping with the stars and now having to face the tourist trap once again. At the corner of Trafalgar Square was a stall full of London souvenirs, and on seeing this, Star started to hop about in excitement.

"Oh my goodness, I just remembered the best thing in the world!" Star said, as she unzipped her blue raincoat and started to feel around the pockets of her dress. "Yisssssss!" And she punched the air, something she must have learnt from Hec-cute-as-a-button-Tor, who had done that every other note during Star's performance.

"What is it, luv?" Vera asked.

"Two pounds, and erm, sixty pee," Star said, sounding as if she was the one to have just discovered oil in the Middle East. "I can't believe I forgot. Aunt Susan gave me dinner money this morning, but she gave me way, way, way too much. Mashed potato is only twenty five pee, which is a rip off 'cause it tastes like water and paper. Not very potatoey at all."

"Put it away, Star," Mary said. "Don't flash your cash."

"Can I buy a souvenir, please, Nannie?" Star stroked the tea-towel printed with a cartoon drawing of the Houses of Parliament. "They might have rubbers or pencils that I can add to my stationary collection."

"Hurry up, then. I'm just going to that bus stop to see if the number nine stops there… Vera, keep your eye on Star and join me when she's shopped out."

Vera saluted her sister like the First Mate to his Captain. Mary rolled her eyes. Before there was time to get offended, Star asked Vera to start looking at the prices on the souvenirs. Apparently, less than two pounds would be the best because she would still have sixty pence for emergencies.

"Can I help you?" asked the man behind the stall, only his tone did not suggest wanting to help in the slightest. If he had said, "I *don't* want you to help me," it would have been more fitting.

"I've got two pounds and sixty pee," Star said. "We've come all the way from Liverpool."

"How about a keyring?" Mr Contrary reluctantly held up a miniature replica of Big Ben hanging on a silver ring. "A quid."

Star's nose scrunched. "Nah."

"Magnet for the fridge." Digging into a transparent plastic box with '£1.50' written on it with permanent marker, Mr Contrary showed Star a small photograph of a red phone box.

"No way, we've got them in Liverpool," Star told him.

"Is that so?"

"Ye-SSS. *And*, did you know that the man who designed the red phone box is the same man who designed the Anglican Cathedral? Me Uncle John told me."

Mr Contrary took in this information and folded his arms. "Yeah. Sir Giles Gilbert Scott is the bloke's name. He also designed the Battersea Power Station."

"Oh my goodness. Where's that? In Liverpool, too?"

"No, it's in Battersea."

"Oh, where's that?"

"London."

"Oh."

The amount of information being passed back and forth was starting to give Vera a headache. Why couldn't they have just stayed inside with music, and free chocolate digestives and cute-as-a-button boys? This was turning out to be a right hassle. She was starting to forget why they had even come to London in the first place.

"Here you go," Mr Contrary piped up with. "How about this?"

He handed Star a white pouch with two zipped pockets and a long red strap. The smaller pocket was printed with the word, 'LONDON'.

"A bum-bag!" Star cried. "That's simply 'stravagent."

"Two pound forty-nine."

"Mmm," Star put her index finger to her chin and concentrated carefully, eyes looking up to the white sky. "It's a bit pricey. Leaves me with eleven pee, which
means I could always buy a Chomp and a penny sweet… or some beef Space Raiders and a penny sweet… or even spring onion Space Raiders and a penny sweet, but Nannie says they stink and actually the beef are much tastier…"

Mr Contrary huffed so loud that if any pigs had built houses within the radar of Trafalgar Square, they'd be homeless. Actually, Vera thought this miserable man resembled a pig. A fat one.

Rising onto her tip toes, Star reached across the souvenir stand and handed Mr Contrary her coins, telling him that she'd take the bum-bag. Vera had seen teenagers wearing these pouch-belts all over Liverpool City Centre. In her opinion, why anybody – especially girls – would want to wear something on their waist that made them look fatter rather than thinner was insane. Okay, she could see the point of wearing them on their tummy rather than backside; the contents would be too easily stolen if a bum-bag was worn in its proper place, but what was wrong with the handbag? Maybe young ones these days craved freedom of their arms or something. Again, this baffling brought on more aches in Vera's head.

Mary was waiting at the bus stop just footsteps away from the souvenir stall, looking anxious. Vera wished that she had kept her mouth shut about the possibility of Susan hearing Star sing on Sunbeam FM. She had even thrown an old penny found on the ground beside the souvenir stall into the Trafalgar Square fountains, making that exact wish as she did so.

"Isn't this cool?" Star said to Mary, pointing to below her belly. "I've got a bum-bag, just like the girls in the Top Juniors and that girl who lives next door to Mick Tully who never speaks to anybody but she's fourteen. Can I take it to school? Have you got anything I can put in it?"

Reaching into her coat pocket, Mary pulled out a handkerchief and two old bus tickets. Vera had an Orange Punch lipstick that had almost run out in the zip of her handbag. Star seemed to relish putting all of this rubbish into the main pouch of her bum-bag, the eleven pence change having the smaller pouch all to itself.

"What's the matter, Nannie?" Star asked, taking her *My Little Pony* lunch box from Nannie's carrier bag, opening it up and taking the letter out that she had written on the train. "Do you think we won't meet Shirley Temple?"

"No, luv," Vera said without thinking, "she's worried that your Aunt Susan may have heard you on the radio."

"Vera! Shut up!" Mary said loudly. The only stranger at the bus stop to acknowledge her outburst and step away was a man – no, a woman, no a man – in a beige suit with a silk scarf, painted red nails and far too much rouge on his cheeks. Everybody else waiting was wearing headphones and staring into a trance.

"But…" Star began, trailing off, as she tucked the letter into her bum-bag. Her head was cocked, looking up at Vera and then Mary, and then back to Vera. The little girl clearly had not understood that she was technically kidnapped. "Am I going to have to go back there when we go home?"

"Maybe for a little while," Mary said, looking into the flow of traffic.

"I can promise Aunt Susan never heard me. Honest. I can promise. Mr Bertie and Mrs O'Connell may have heard me, but not Aunt Susan. All she listens to are records of music without any words at all, and only at night time. It's day time now, isn't it? If I promise that she never heard me, can I come back to Flinder Street?"

Mary opened her own handbag and took out a small comb, two Everton mints and both halves of the *Starlight Express* leaflet. "Here you go, Star. Put them in your bum-bag. My bag's getting a bit heavy."

"Okay, Nannie. Thanks."

The number nine bus pulled into the stop and letting other passengers go first, Mary held onto Vera and Star, releasing them once everybody else was on.

"Let's wait here by the stairs," Mary whispered into Vera's ear. "The conductor is down there. We have to hope that we've reached Knightsbridge by the time he gets to us. If not, we hop off. Got it?"

"Got it, Mar."

Vera couldn't believe that within the space of a few hours, they had forgotten about what they had done. True, plenty had gone on today, but how had it just slipped their mind that what they were doing was criminal? If only she could see another penny on the floor, she would make a wish to go back to school and not leave at the age of fourteen, that way she might have earned herself a few more brain cells, or at least some common sense. And why was it only now, into mid-afternoon that the consequences of their actions was beginning to terrify them? She needed to give Mary time to work something out, ease the pressure that she was so visibly starting to feel.

"Look at the size of that tree trunk, Star," Vera said as the bus carried them past a beautiful park, lined with trees on the path running beside it. "Star? Star?"

Staring out of the opposite window, over the sitting passenger's heads, Star was in full concentration mode. "I'm looking out for famous people."

"Like who?"

"Dunno. But famous people live in London, don't they? The cast of *Neighbours* were here last year for the Royal Variety Performance, you know. They came all the way from Australia and my daddy told me that was more than a whole day on an aeroplane. I hope I see some famous people."

"Well, hopefully Shirley Temple!"

Star laughed; laughed big and loud, exactly how she did whenever John tickled her and she could hardly stop to take a breath. "Oh yeah! I'm so silly!"

Vera joined in, but Mary was still quiet, watching the roads as the bus continued along. "Star, remember that tree back there I tried to show you?"

"Ye-e-e…" Star chucked, "SSS."

And Vera thought now was the perfect time to tell Star a little story. Not only would it calm the little girl, but it gave Mary the opportunity to relax within her silence. It surely would not last long. So, Vera told Star about how in the olden days, there was a wedding tradition where the bride would have to hide from her groom before the ceremony. Once he found her, they could marry. One young bride wandered around the green gardens in the grounds of the village church filled with friends and family waiting for her big day to begin, and considered places to hide… Perhaps behind the old stone church, in a nook beside the drain pipe, but that may stain the hem of her white gown… Or she could duck beneath the wall surrounding the vicar's house, only it was very low and no matter how much she crouched, the flowers on top of her head would surely give the game away… And that was when she noticed the great oak tree standing proud, the king of its jungle. Over she scurried to it and hid behind the wide trunk… but, her large bridal skirt was peeping out of the sides and her groom would easily see it… as she manoeuvred around trying to find the most concealing spot, the bride noticed a dark, round hole in the trunk of the tree. Inside, was hollow. Now, this young bride was a slender little thing, with delicate bones and not blessed with height, and climbing through the hole was no difficult task. She stood upright inside the great tree trunk, satisfied that she had found the perfect hiding place.

"I know where the perfect hiding place is for a game of Hido," Star interrupted. "It's tricky, but it's actually behind the person who is 'It'. Rather than go and hide somewhere, you have to follow them everywhere so quietly and carefully, and if they don't know you're there, they'll never find you."

Vera admired this strategy, but was keen to finish her story. She told Star that the time had come for the groom to find his wife-to-be, so he began to search… behind the church, over the stone walls, beneath the tractor, on top of the chicken shed… but she was nowhere to be seen… many times he circled the great oak tree, but never thought to look inside the hole, it wasn't *that* big… but an hour passed, and he called upon his Best Man to help him look… and another hour passed, and another, until the whole church congregation – the vicar and all – became the search party for the missing bride. Some believed that she had gotten cold feet and ran away… few went beyond the green gardens and into the village to ask questions.

"Did the bridesmaids search, too?" Star asked.

"Of course they did. They were very worried."

"I'd like to be a bridesmaid. Louise Fitzpatrick has been a bridesmaid twice, and she hates wearing dresses. Her aunty let her change into cycling shorts and t-shirt for the night-time disco, though."

"How charming," Vera said. "Suddenly, it was dark, the only light being from the moon. The groom had to go home and rest, but he was heartbroken, thinking that the love of his life had left him…"

"But she hadn't, she was inside the tree!"

"Yes, and nobody knew. Nobody at all. Days passed. The days turned into weeks, the weeks into years. The groom had to move on with his life, forget about the bride he had once hoped to marry, which he did. He found a new love and married her…"

"I bet they didn't play Hide and Seek at their wedding."

"I bet they didn't, too. He became a father to three strong and healthy sons. But he never forgot about his first love, the girl who disappeared… Hundreds of years later, a woodcutter came across the great oak tree standing proud, king of its jungle, and decided the time had come to chop it down. As the axe chopped away at the old wood and the tree fell apart onto the green, green grass… the woodcutter gasped at what he found."

Star was silent, her face still and pale.

"Sitting on the mossy ground was a skeleton, in a white wedding dress."

The conductor had almost caught up to them when the bus stopped just past Buckingham Palace.

"Vera, Star," Mary said. "Do one!"

*

Jimmy was surprised to hear Susan's voice answer the telephone. It had seemed that the only logical explanation for Star singing on the radio had been for her aunt to have taken her on a trip to London. He scratched the early stages of a thick beard, but the more he scratched the itchier it became. These itches travelled down his neck and to his torso, making him apprehensive and uncomfortable.

"Susan, it's Jimmy," he said, needing to get to the point. "Where is Star?"

"Jimmy, what's the matter? Why are you calling?" Her voice was shrill, and nothing like her sister's had been. Jimmy wondered if this was a comfort or a shame.

"Susan, please just tell me. Where is my daughter?"

"Rebecca's at school. St. Stephen's. Well, actually she will be back any minute. My driver went to collect her a short while ago…"

"Christ, Susan. She's not there."

"What are you talking about?"

"She's in London."

"What?"

"Susan! I heard her on the radio. She was singing, live from London."

"Don't be ridiculous. Jimmy, you're tired, not thinking straight…"

"Don't patronise me, Susan, I know my own kid. Believe me, Star wasn't at St. Stephen's today. Find out where she is. You promised you would keep her safe…"

And the phone went dead. Time out. Of all the days he had served inside so far, Jimmy had never felt more like a prisoner than he did today.

Hyde Park Corner

The roundabout was the largest and busiest that Star had even seen, and huge black statues and monuments that looked like giant gravestones were scattered all over the area with a white marble archway in the centre. It would take hours to cross the road; that is unless you were killed by a bus or a black cab. Nannie led them down a subway entrance and through a tunnel they went, until they reached a small intersection for two tunnels and no idea of which one to take. The chosen path brought them out onto a subway exit that looked identical to the entrance! There was not a single sign for Knightsbridge to be seen.

"We need a hotel," Nannie said.

"To stay in?" Star asked. When *would* they ever get there?

"No, to ask for directions."

There were plenty of hotels around. Star could tell from the men in smart suits standing on marble steps by glass doorways, carrying suitcases to and from taxis, only they did look a lot like Fred Astaire about to break into a tap routine. How disappointing that they didn't.

"Jesus, they all look a bit flashy," Nannie said. "We might get kicked out."

Aunty Vera had just applied another coat of lipstick and looked offended.

Down a side street, besides a hotel called The Lanesborough, Star spotted a man in a rainbow waistcoat holding a large puppet. He was making his way up some stone steps into a town house with a sign in the window saying, 'Vacancies'. The puppet was some sort of parrot or peacock, with colourful feathers and a head that was poking about, nosing everywhere, as if it were the man's own eyes watching out for anybody following him.

"What's 'vacancies'?" Star asked.

"Empty rooms," Nannie explained, her worried face still firmly in place.

"Why would anybody want to go inside an empty room? What would they sit on?" Star pointed to where the puppet had now gone inside. "Look."

Nannie led the way, Vera following and Star walking with care not to step on the cracks in the pavement. From the outside, this town house really did look like a regular house, but not like the terraced houses in Flinder Street or the semi-detached ones with shared driveways like where Steph Bradley lived. This town house was featured on Christmas cards with a wreath on the black door above the golden knocker and on the front of a Quality Street tin. The only difference being that a sign hung high over the stone steps reading, 'The Variety Guest House.'

Inside smelt of dust and Aunty Vera sneezed in an instant. The red, swirly carpet was thick like a sponge, putting a spring in their step as they treaded across creaky floorboards hidden beneath it. A table by the porch door was filled with brochures advertising West End shows and London attractions. Star picked up some free leaflets for *Phantom of the Opera* and *42nd Street*, and a pamphlet for Madame Tussauds and the Crown Jewels, folded them neatly and tucked them into her bum-bag before joining Nannie. She was stood at the front desk, trying to gather some information about Harrods', only she was having trouble getting any attention because the puppet was talking.

"Hey there, Toots," the puppet said to the lady on reception, and it's beak started to peck at her name badge, saying, 'Francine'. Then, the puppet turned to look down at Star and bit her nose. "And heh-loh little lad-ehh!"

Star jumped back. "Hello. Oh my goodness."

Nannie ignored the feathers and hit her hand on the desk. "Excuse me, Francine, luv. Can you tell me how to get to Harrods'?"

"Just a minute, Kenny," Francine said, speaking in a sing-song accent.

The puppet piped in, getting eye to eye with Nannie. "Ooh. Going to get yourself a bag, are you? A Harrods' bag? Got to buy something first though. Don't break the bank. A chocolate bar should do the trick… And make sure you use the toilet before you go. It's a pound a pop in that place."

"I am not having a conversation with a toy!"

This caused the puppet to release a sigh of agony and nuzzle into the neck of the man in the rainbow waistcoat, whose name must be Kenny. "Uh-oh. You've hurt his feelings," Kenny said. He sounded just like Pat Sharp only looked nothing like him. His hair was short and spiky for starters.

"Aww," Star stroked the feathered creature. "What's his name?"

"Do you want to tell the little girl your name?" Kenny whispered to the puppet, but it should its head sadly. "Ah, come on. Don't be shy. There's nothing to be afraid of, is there?"

"Of course not," Star smiled. As the puppet face revealed itself and was brought down to her level, she watched Kenny's lips as the puppet's beak opened.

"Cosmo."

Wowzer! Kenny's lips didn't move a muscle!

"Do you know Emu?" Star asked.

Kenny's arm dropped and Cosmo hung upside down like a dead bird, swinging alongside Kenny's legs. "Why do all the kids ask me that? Is Emu the only puppet around? Really? Really?!"

"There's Roland Rat," Star said. "He says he's a superstar, but he hasn't been around for a while…"

"Roland bloody Rat! Really? Really?!"

"Okay, Gordon the Gopher. He's so, so cute."

"Gordon the Gopher is not cute. He's manipulative."

"Really?"

"Yes! YES! REALLY!"

Okay, maybe there was something to be afraid of; Kenny's temper. Star turned away and clung onto Nannie's coat. Francine was drawing a map on a piece of white paper with a blue biro, and putting crosses were the guest house was and where Harrods' was. On paper, it was pretty darn close, two, maybe three centimetres apart. They'd be there in no time! Star looked around for Aunty Vera, who was sitting in the small lobby surrounded by four men dressed in matching smart, black suits. They could have been waiters, but there was no restaurant in the guest house that Star could see.

"Star, these gentlemen are a barber shop quartet," Aunty Vera said. "They sing in four part harmony. Isn't that something?"

The men rose and the shortest of the four, complete with a neat black moustache and a slick centre part in his hair, counted them in, "One, two, three, four…"

Slow and sombre, but perfectly in tune, they sang;

"*I love you as I never loved before,*

Since first I met you on the village green…"

The shortest man had a high voice, and he repeated, "*The village green.*"

And on they went;

"*Come to me, or my dream of love is o'er...*"

Star knew this song. This was a classic sung by Al Jolson, and Uncle John's favourite, which he sang in his greenhouse if he didn't feel like yodelling.

"*I love you as I loved you,*" Star sang. "*When you were sweet...*"

"*When you were sweet,*" the four men harmonised.

"*When you were sweet...*"

Altogether, they finished with, "*sixteen.*"

Raucous laughter broke out from the men who clapped and cheered each other and Star, while Aunty Vera wiped a little tear from the corner of her eye.

"Hey, you should move in to this guest house!" the shortest man said, to which his colleagues agreed.

"I'd love to," Star said, "but there's no furniture in the rooms."

The laughing grew louder as did their clapping, but they were interrupted by a group of clowns trudging down the staircase carrying boxes and suitcases. With white painted faces, big smiles and red noses, it was easy to notice how unhappy they were behind the make-up. Star thought that if they took their long, floppy shoes off to walk down the stairs it would have made their job much more effortless.

"So, gents," Aunty Vera said to the barber shop quartet, "what is this place? It's becoming a bit freaky."

"A guest house for performers. We were all part of a charity concert for underprivileged children last night, even Esther Rantzen was there. We're all getting kicked out today, and it's onto Southend-on-Sea for us chaps next, then Brighton at the weekend. This place took care of the corps de ballet from the Ukrainian ballet last week. Who knows who they have coming in after us."

"I bet this is where the *Neighbours* cast stayed," Star said.

With a grin on her face finally, Nannie came to find them, waving Francine's map in the air as if it were a fifty pound note. Kenny and Cosmo were lurking about the reception still, stopping poor Francine from getting her job done.

"I worked with Bernie Clifton once," Kenny was saying. "Actually, he worked with me and Cosmo. He was the support act to us. Morecambe Bay, 1983..."

And Star never heard the rest of Kenny's tale. Nannie and Aunty Vera had hold of her hands and they were already walking in the direction of the poshest shop in the whole world, Harrods'. They would be there in minutes.

*

"Do you want kids?" Jimmy asked Addo, back in the cell.

"I guess so. S'not the kind of thing I ever thought about before I came here. And it's not what I choose to think about now, seems a waste, but I guess so. Yeah. A little lad who I can take to the match with me. Me little mate."

Addo was young, much younger than he looked. His twenty-second birthday had passed just last week. Jimmy had wished him many happy returns which seemed like the most ridiculous thing he had ever said or done. All Addo had said about it was, "A year ago today I got the key of the door. I sure found a way to lock the door and lose the fuckin' key, didn't I?"

Jimmy sat on the edge of his bed and tried to think of something, but his mind was blank. The grief he had felt for Linda had gone, which had been replaced with worry about where his daughter was, but the realisation of knowing that there was nothing he could do about it just left him feeling numb.

"I miss my girlfriend," Addo said. "Her name is Janine."

"I didn't know you had a girlfriend, mate. You never said."

"Yeah. Scared to jinx it. What if she's not my girlfriend anymore? I haven't heard from her since I came here."

"I'm sorry…"

"Nah, it's my own fault, like. She wasn't the one going round fighting with a shit-load of E and cannabis in her pocket, was she?

But still, doesn't mean I don't miss her. I can't think of any other women. I try, like; I imagined what it would be like to be with Banarama - all of them, even the new girl - and yet Janine is the only one I can see in my head. It's funny, 'cause when I was actually with Janine, I thought about Banarama all the time. More than I thought of Janine. I'm so stupid."

Jimmy considered how different his yearning for Linda would be if she was still alive while he was shut away from her in here. What was worse? Knowing that she was out there but he couldn't see her? Or just knowing that she wasn't there at all? He tried to put himself in Addo's situation of pining for the woman he loved, in constant fear that because of his mistakes, she may choose to forget about him and get on with her life without him. This thought actually made Jimmy feel grateful that Linda was gone. At least there was no hope to cling onto, the kind of hope that leads you into an unrealistic ideal which is only met with utter disappointment.

"And you know what else is funny, Jim?"

"What's that mate?"

"The fact that I was in possession of E, yet I was fighting. No one fights on E! I should have popped the pills myself..." Addo sighed. This statement was something he said a lot, at least once a day, as if he were reminding himself of the logic behind the trouble he got into. "But there's no money in taking it, is there?"

"No, mate."

"I was going to marry her, you know. Janine. With the money I was making, I was going to spoil her rotten. You should've seen the houses I've been into belonging to fellas who'd made money dealing. I could've given her everything, took her to Florida… I didn't want to propose with some shitty ring from Argos, did I?"

Linda had got her ring costing one month's wages from Jimmy, but the proposal never did play out the way he had hoped. It was early summer in 1980, an unusually hot day. On his way home from work, rolling up his sleeves and tying his jumper around his waist, he stopped in at Si's to buy an orange ice lolly. As he walked down Flinder Street, sucking the juice dripping from the bottom of the quickly melting ice, he was greeted by Linda sitting on his front step.

"Hiya princess," he said. "Do you fancy going down to Burbo Bank? We could build another rubbish sandcastle and pretend it's our house."

"Maybe, Jim," Linda said, her voice quiet. She was holding a large pebble in her hands, swapping it back and forth.

"I reckon it'll be a laugh, dead busy like 'cause of the smashing weather," he slurped up some juice that was dribbling down his wrist.

"I think we should get married, Jim."

There it was. At first, Jimmy thought he had misheard her, but Linda said it again, "We should get married." And in an instant, he knew that his hopes of proposing to her and saying his little speech were over.

"Okay, well, yeah. I mean, I'd love to marry you Lin, it's all I want."

Still passing the pebble back and forth in her hands, she looked up at him with squinting eyes, Jimmy's body unable to block the strong sun behind him. "Good. Because I'm pregnant."

So, this was not what he expected at all. Kids with Linda, definitely, yes! But he wanted to marry her first, ask *her* to be his wife, and then make the decision that the time was right to have a baby. Not get told by his girlfriend that he was going to be a husband and a dad all in one. Where was the man's choice in all this? Yet, instead of being a man, accepting this information with a mature response, he was overcome with a terrifying sense of paranoia.

"Linda, do you only want to marry me because you're pregnant?"

She stood up, and in such haste that Jimmy was taken aback. The remainder of his ice lolly broke off and smashed onto the ground, turning into liquid.

"Of course not, Jim. But we have to get married! And soon! I can't be unmarried and having everyone pointing at me. What will people think?"

"So, you're only marrying me because of what people will think?"

"No! I love you, soft lad, but don't you see? We don't have a choice."

"Great. You are marrying me because you don't have a choice."

Linda lifted up her arm in frustration and for a second, Jimmy thought she was going to launch the pebble into his head. He turned around and walked up Flinder Street towards the King George. Why did it have to be like this? Why? On the front step of his house… just after an uncomfortable, hot day at work… teatime… needing a wash and a change of clothes to feel at least relaxed, not to mention more attractive, confident… The disappointment he felt filled him with anger, almost hatred, that his idea of proposing had now been confirmed as Jimmy romanticising. So they didn't have a choice? Well, Linda had had a choice in doing this, in asking – or suggesting, rather – that they get married, and in that sense she had taken his choice away from him.

"Actually, I do have a choice," Jimmy said, stopping and walking back towards his house. "What if I choose *not* to marry you?"

"Don't be ridiculous…" Linda almost laughed. "You wouldn't do that to me."

"Really? Wouldn't I? So what you're saying now is, you expected me to just say 'yes'. Why bother even asking me? Why didn't you just handcuff me and march me to the church with a gun to my head?"

"What?!"

"Yeah, yeah. It's not like I actually have a choice, is it, Linda? Is it? I never do have a choice when it comes to you. Because when I wanted to propose to you, you tell me how scared you are of change…"

"I didn't say I was scared of change."

"Yes, you did."

"Oh yeah? When?"

"Doesn't matter when!"

"It does matter when…" Linda broke off. For a second Jimmy thought that she may have remembered what she had said on New Year's Eve. "You were going to propose to me?"

Jimmy said nothing.

"Why didn't you?"

This was not how it was supposed to be.

"Jimmy, why didn't you? I would've said yes."

And he turned around once again, and just went straight to the King George.

Most of the time when Jimmy thought back to his memories of Linda, he laced them with just the good parts, erasing the bad. Sometimes, he invented times that they had shared together, jokes they had laughed at and places they had gone to, which were in truth, just stories he was making up; Jimmy Blake and Linda Lloyd as the two loveable lead characters. It seemed unfair when the reality came charging back into his head at full speed. However, it made it possible to believe that romance was just imaginary, an idea sold to people that gave false hope, and that everybody else's love stories were indeed steeped in disillusionment and just dreams.

He only lasted an hour in the King George before guilt got the better of him. If Linda told Mary Mack what he had said to her, he could expect a school boy telling off at least. Jimmy's heart skipped a beat when he got to Linda's house and saw the outline of her hiding behind the net curtain in the front window. She had been waiting for him. Impulse made him run to the window rather than the door and he held his hand against the glass as she pulled the curtain aside to see him clearly. Her hand matched his, separated by the transparent shield.

"I'm sorry," he mouthed, but she never reacted. He shouted, "I'M SORRY!"

Could it be that Linda had smiled at this? Jimmy couldn't quite judge, but she left the window, running through the living room and through the narrow hallway with the most ridiculous painting of a fish on the wall. A favourite of her mother's and on the wall it would stay.

"Is it the baby?" Linda said, opening the door. "Do you not want to have a baby with me?"

"Of course I want to have a baby with you, Lin… Do you really want to marry me?"

"Of course I want to marry you, soft lad." Linda dropped into his arms and kissed him. "I missed you… just then, when you stormed off. I missed you."

"I missed you, too." As he held her, his hands covering her small back, he realised that for the first time, he was holding his child, too. Although this had not turned out as planned, Jimmy felt so happy that he had Linda forever. There was nothing to worry about anymore; he could never lose her now. Their baby would make sure of that.

"But we must get married soon, Jim. Very soon, before I start showing."

The two pints at the King George had had a relaxing effect, because Linda's words annoyed him, taking the beauty out of the wonderful moment he was experiencing. But, Jimmy kept his mouth shut and just nodded his head. Yes, he'd marry her tonight if it meant never being without her.

"She'll be okay, you know," Addo said.

"Who?"

"Your little girl. She was on a radio show, and that's cool. At least she's somewhere safe."

Again, it was comforting to know for certain he could not see Linda again, because it was *not* knowing where Star was that was tearing Jimmy Blake apart.

Knightsbridge

Mary Mack was delighted that it had started to rain. The thin, pathetic attempt earlier in the day had now become a heavy shower, and it was hoods up and brollies out. Of course, British rain was never particularly enjoyable, but on this occasion it would stop Vera from dawdling, staring into the windows of Knightsbridge's grand selection of stores. At one point, Vera did stop outside a very clinical looking department store called Harvey Nichols, admiring a fur coat at the same time as squealing at the price, but it was a blessing that her shoes were peep-toe, and a dash of water on her feet always sent her running for shelter.

Mary held tight hold of Star's hand pulling her along with a brisk walk, but no running. Her plastic hip had started to ache and she wondered how long it would be until she could sit down. Quite enough time had been wasted. Very soon, they would meet Shirley Temple and on they could venture back home for a decent meal… only that was in fact hours away, so Mary pushed that cosy thought to the back of her mind, just ahead of the fear that lay there of what would really happen once they got back to Liverpool that night.

Just ahead of them, high above their heads was a row of flags representing countries all over the world, hanging from flag poles outside windows on a building large enough to resemble a palace. Below the flags were lots of green canopies, sticking out like umbrellas, with the word 'Harrods' written in gold scroll on each one. They had made it. John Lewis resembled the corner shop compared to this extravagance. Windows upon windows of elaborate displays were passed, everything from a children's nursery inspired by *Peter Pan*, to mannequins of men in tailored suits, to quite provocative ladies lingerie. Mary just wondered where the door to get in was.

Still treading on in an effort to find an entrance, the trio were brought to a halt by an adult disguised in a teddy-bear skin costume. With the amount of waggling this teddy-bear was doing with his big, hairy arms, there was no chance of pushing past, despite how good they had become at doing that given their short time so far in London.

"Yello! Save the children," came from the voice behind the mask. It was possibly the most unenthusiastic teddy-bear Mary had ever had the pleasure of coming across. He made Bungle seem like Father Christmas. "Dig deep in your pockets, ladies. Save the children."

"From what?" Star asked.

"Wha'?" The teddy-bear replied with very little effort.

"What are we saving them from?"

"Oh, erm," and he turned around to wave Little Bo Peep over. Staff in hand and pipe cleaners in her plaited hair, she joined her colleague with an equal bout of his energy. "Wha' we saving the children from?"

Little Bo Peep shrugged. "All kinds. They're sick. In Great Ormond Street Hospital."

Mary attempted to push past. "Sorry, no change."

"Wait!" Star said. She unzipped the front pocket of her bumbag. "Have this."

It was eleven pence, and to be fair, that wasn't going to get Star very far so she might as well earn herself a sticker. Little Bo Peep peeled off a dancing rabbit with the words 'thank you' written in red child's scribble above his head and stuck it to Star's raincoat.

"Will you give it straight to the children from me?" Star asked, fixing her sticker, pressing it down so that it would not fall off.

"Erm, *we* won't," the teddy-bear's voice chuckled, again with as much spirit as a toilet cleaner needing a holiday. "Because we're actors."

"Oh ruin the illusion, why don't you," Mary said.

"You're actors?" Star piped up. At least someone still had some spark left in them today.

"Erm. Yep." Never had there been such a sarcastic teddy-bear.

"It's just I know you're not really a teddy-bear," Star said, even going so far as touching his paw with one hand and Little Bo Peep's skirt with the other, "and I know you're not really Bo Peep. But if you're actors, why don't you want to go to Hollywood? It's where all the movies are made, you know."

"Oh yeah, let's just jump on a plane, shall we, Ted?" Little Bo Peep said, level of enthusiasm going up a notch.

"Nah, Bo Peep, let's swim across the Atlantic," the teddy-bear replied, his voice now more heightened, with – could it be – a note of passion?

"Hmm, let me find a payphone first so I can call my agent and tell them that I won't be at the dance call on Friday for *Cats* because I'll be in Beverley Hills schmoozing with Tom Hanks…"

"Or then again, we could choose to stay right here, Bo Peep, because we love it, don't we? We love dressing up in these sweaty costumes and harassing tourists all day, Bo Peep, don't we?"

"Yes, Ted. It's not just fun standing on our feet all day – in the rain, too, what a bonus - but so stimulating for our minds. As Little Bo Peep, I can really get deep into the character's mind out here on the high street, focussing on what she wants from life and how she must feel being in the city, so far away from her sheep. Yes,

Ted, doing this job, I really feel like I'm making the most of my drama school training…"

"AND the thousands of pounds in fees our parents spent in sending us to drama school are totally paying off with this job, right?"

"Oh, Ted. You have convinced me to stay. I think I'll leave Hollywood for a while; London is just packed with too many opportunities for me to miss. Obviously."

"Yeah, Bo Peep. Of course, if I would've been two inches shorter, I would've been cast in *Crossroads* for two episodes and who knows what that could've led to. But I'm not two inches shorter, am I? That no mark from Huddersfield with no professional experience got the part, didn't he? Good job I'm tall enough for teddy-bear costumes, what do you say, Bo Peep?"

"I hear you, Ted, big time," Little Bo Peep paused, and took a breath.

Mary had had enough of these wannabes and with attitudes like that, it was no wonder they were standing on the street looking like prize idiots. Talented or not, there was no need for that sort of bitterness. Star and Vera were watching these actors vent with an identical look of intrigue mixed with confusion splashed across their faces.

Evident that the two actors had forgotten that they were blocking the way of three innocent, but now harassed tourists, Little

Bo Peep put her hands onto the teddy-bear's arm, nearly taking his fake eye out with her staff, but with sincerity.

"Don't beat yourself up about the *Crossroads* audition, babe. The part was for a freak, and you're better than that."

"Thanks, darlin'. You are so going to get *Cats*, you know. It's your time."

"Thanks, babe. But my throat is really raspy, so I'm going to have to cut down on the cigs this week. Anyway, stop beating yourself up..."

Yes, the harassment had officially stopped. Mary pushed Star and Vera around the sides of the sycophants, contemplating how much damage they had done to Star for wanting a career on the stage.

"Nannie, hold on," Star said, and she wriggled herself free, running back to the actors. "Did you know that Shirley Temple was supposed to be Dorothy in *The Wizard of Oz*, but she lost the part to Judy Garland?"

Little Bo Peep just looked at Star as if she had just spoken in Swahili. Mary could only guess that the teddy-bear was also looking at her, for his head was twisted in her direction.

"I love Shirley Temple, she's like a sister to me," Star went on. "But can you imagine Dorothy being anyone else other than Judy Garland? She *is* Dorothy! So you'll get the right part one day. It's better than getting the wrong part."

As the gobsmacked actors just gazed at the small eight year-old before them, a giant egg in a dickie bow wobbled towards them and ordered them to get back to work. Mary watched the teddy-bear waggle his arms at a new group of shoppers and Little Bo Peep smile through a frown. To be fair, it was a lousy job they were doing.

A doorman dressed from head to toe in green, with black gloves and a black tie, opened a large glass door, and Mary, Vera and Star were let into Harrods.

"Nannie, it's just like we've reached the Emerald City. Only we're supposed to be looking for the blue bird. We're all jumbled up and mixing the films up, aren't we?"

If only life were a film, Mary thought, complete with the happy endings and beautiful music following them around. Star was skipping through the entrance as if she was on the Yellow Brick Road, but she was humming the tune to the Old Kent Road… For Star right now, it was a film, and long may that last, Mary hoped.

*

Star had really believed that they had entered into the Emerald City and was expecting to see the Horse of a Different Colour come striding around the corner, with all of the Harrods staff wearing emerald green clothes, just like the doorman, who looked remarkably like… The Wizard! But, no. Inside was a disappointment. It was just a bigger, busier version of George Henry

Lee, with counters dotted all over the room selling make-up, and ladies in black trouser suits spraying perfume onto little pieces of white card. Aunty Vera had rolled the sleeves of her jacket up and had her wrists out, catching any free squirts she could.

"Jazz?" a young lady said. Aunty Vera stopped and took a piece of card with a men's aftershave called 'Jazz' oozing from it, and then another, and another. Then, she asked the young lady for one more.

"What for?" Nannie asked. "You're handbag will reak of that stuff now."

"It's for John's underwear drawer, Mary. That's all."

The people working in Harrods were much pushier than in George Henry Lee, though; even asking Star if she was interested in buying, "the latest fragrance by…" and a word that sounded French, or Spanish, or Swedish, or something else she didn't understand. Why would a little girl want to buy perfume? Or men's aftershave? That was just silly. In George Henry Lee, sometimes Aunty Vera had to ask three times for a spray because the ladies behind the counter were always having a right old laugh and talking in the same way as the girls in the Top Juniors talk when they huddled together in the playground. In Harrods, there was no gossiping, no giggling, just selling.

"Beauty Queen?" another young lady in a smart black trouser suit said, holding a small glass bottle in her hand. Her name tag said, 'Lindsey'. "It's rare, it's new and it's just for you!"

"Thank you," Star said, showing Lindsey her wrist just as Aunty Vera would do.

"When you grow up, do you want to be a beauty queen?" Lindsey asked.

"Oh no, I want to be an actress."

"Ha! Me too. Big time." Lindsey shot a quick glance over her shoulder as if somebody may have heard her, but there was nobody there.

"So why are you working here?"

"It's what lots of actors do. We don't have much choice."

"Actors work in Harrods? Spraying perfume?"

Lindsey nodded, still smiling. For an actor who wasn't really acting, she was much nicer than the two they had met outside dressed up like characters from a children's television show; but not even a cool show that was on after school before *Neighbours*, more like a show that was on during the daytime for little kids who hadn't started school yet. And Lindsey had a pretty face with smiling eyes and long golden hair. Star imagined she would make an excellent Cinderella. She decided to tell her.

"You're like Cinderella."

Lindsey beamed. "Oh, thank you. I've got an audition for Cinderella, a pantomime in Birmingham next week." Again, she did a quick glance over her shoulder.

"Well, break a leg!" Star said. "Sparkle!"

"Sshh! And thank you," Lindsey gave Star an extra squirt of Beauty Queen on her neck.

It had been valuable so far in coming to London. Star had made the decision that if she was going to be a famous actress, London was definitely not the place to come. It would have to be Hollywood or Broadway, without a doubt.

*

The chaplain, Father Michael, was straight to the point with Jimmy. He didn't sugar-coat the information nor hold anything back, at least that was the impression he gave.

"It is suspected that your daughter has been kidnapped," Father Michael said.

He spoke to Jimmy through the bars of his cell, holding a paper file and reading from the notes written inside. "She was not at school today despite being taken there by a respected employee of Susan Lloyd. The only further information that we have is that it is confirmed that Rebecca Blake was present at the studios of Sunbeam FM in London's Leicester Square this afternoon. Staff at the studio have described her entering and leaving the building with two women in their late fifties, early sixties."

"Well, she's fine then! That's Mary and Vera," Jimmy said. "She's fine! Didn't Susan know? Surely Mary would've told her she was taking Star? And why were they in London anyway? How…?"

"That's all the information we have," Father Michael closed the file. "Police in the West End area of London are aware of the situation and are doing their best to track them down. We will inform you when we know anything further on your daughter's whereabouts."

"But, Father, please…"

Jimmy was ordered to back off as Father Michael walked away.

*

Vera was still in shock that people would eat oysters and drink champagne in the middle of a department store. Okay, she enjoyed a cup of tea and a scone in the canteen of Littlewoods, but who in their right minds would slurp an oyster late afternoon around a crowd of people doing their food shopping? And five pounds for two chocolates in a box. Yes, the temptation was there; the conker-sized truffles were almost glimmering with tastiness, all flakes and crispy sugared, but five pounds? You could get a whole tin of Cadbury's

Roses for less and be just as satisfied. A-ha! This must be how the aristocracy stayed thin! And celebrities, too. Oysters for lunch and a truffle for desert. Yes, that made sense to Vera now.

They had found themselves in Harrods food hall on their search for the book department. Mary couldn't be bothered to ask at the help desk because she had to ask a member of staff how to get to the help desk.

"It can't be that hard to find," Mary had said.

Only standing amongst a counter filled with a hundred different cheeses and biscuits costing the same price as an outfit from C&A, Vera pointed out that unless Shirley Temple was in desperate need to stock up her hotel fridge, she wouldn't be in here.

So, it was back through the cosmetic department and up the escalators. A large statue of an Egyptian Mummy overpowered the moving staircases, and the experience was much more pleasant than earlier on the London Underground. The low lights and shining gold décor was calming, and Vera didn't feel in the slightest bit nauseous as they travelled upwards. Even Mary seemed to be fully enjoying the Egyptian staircase experience, for up and up they went, past the second and third floor.

"Let's get off here," Mary said as they reached the fourth floor. "If she's not here we can work our way downwards."

"Aye, aye, captain," Star said.

It seemed that every child's Christmas and birthday had happened all at once, for they had landed themselves in the toy department. Stacks and stacks of stuffed animals filled the walls and a merry-go-round of toys galore took centre stage of the floor. Miniature helicopters flew just above Vera's head, yet she still ducked, and giant figures and houses made from Lego were scattered about.

"Do you like magic tricks?" an old man said, his beard grey and pointy, so long that it touched the tip of his red tie and he stood behind a table covered with a black cloth. He wore a black cape, and in his stripy waistcoat, Vera noticed a pocket-watch. With a glint of purple to his blue eyes, the old man looked like quite the traditional magician.

"Sorry, but we're looking for Shirley Temple," Mary said. "She's signing her book somewhere around here."

"Not around here, marm," the magician told her. "Downstairs, second floor."

"Thank you! Come on you two…"

"Just one trick, marm!"

"Please Nannie!" Star cried. She already had her hands on a deck of cards, checking inside the empty box with suspicion.

"It won't take a second…" the magician took the cards from Star and spread them out across the table, face down. He told her to choose one card, look at it, but keep it a secret from him. Gathering them back up, he told her to slip her card back into the pack, and gliding his fingers up the sides of it, Star's card rose to the top.

"Yes, that's it!" Star said. "The eight of hearts, yes!"

Vera was not impressed. This wasn't *magic*. This was tapered cards, which wasn't difficult to work out seeing as the box of the pack even read 'Taper Cards'. One end of the card was slim and the other slightly wider, making the selected card easy for the magician to trace.

"Show him your trick, Mary," Vera said.

"Get lost, Vera. We've got to go."

"Go on, Nannie," Star winked at Mary. "It's true magic."

Vera folded her arms, staring at her sister. Go on, go on! The magician put the deck of tapered cards to one side and took a step back from the table, and to Vera's delight, Mary put down her handbag and the carrier bag containing Star's *My Little Pony* lunch box and a bunch of serviettes from the food hall.

"It's best done with four Oxo cubes, but I guess buttons or stones will do," Mary said. "What have you got?"

The magician reached into his back pocket and pulled out a half-eaten packet of Rolos. "Will these do?"

Vera's stomach churned thinking how warm and soft they must be. She preferred to keep Rolos in the fridge so that when she sucked them the chocolate came off in her mouth, leaving a hard toffee to chew on. John loved them this way, too.

"Perfect," Mary said taking two serviettes from her carrier bag and opening them out to make large squares. Four Rolos were laid out onto the table a foot apart making the shape of a square. She rubbed her hands together as Vera stood back a little, allowing any customers around her to see the magic about to unfold before them.

It was a trick that both sisters had learnt while they were on the evacuation. A midget by the name of Albert had taught it to them during the tea-breaks of church choir rehearsals, but Mary had mastered it with such a fine art, that Vera became too worried about giving the game away to keep on performing the trick herself.

Mary waved the serviettes in the air and the small crowd grew larger.

*

When Nannie did this trick, she became Magic Mary. It was none other than *real* magic. Star embraced herself for the show…

Nannie's hands lowered and she took turns to cover each Rolo with a serviette.

"I cover this and I say, and I cover this and I say…" Nannie began. "I cover this and I say, and I cover this and I say…" Leaving the serviettes to cover one Rolo each with two still visible, Nannie picked up an uncovered one and put it behind her back, "I take that one behind my back like a snowball and command it to be there…"

And with a flick of her – now empty – hands, she picked up one serviette to reveal not one, but two Rolos! Back the serviette went to cover the not one, but two Rolos. She repeated the same action with the last visible Rolo, "I take this one behind my back like a snowball and command that to be there…" Once again, the same serviette was raised with empty hands and now there was not one, not two, but three Rolos revealed beneath it! The final part of the magic was upon the crowd as Nannie clapped her hands at the second serviette which was covering the fourth and final Rolo, "Quick Jack, be gone!" And the serviette was pulled away in haste to expose nothing there… Nannie clapped her hands at the serviette hiding not one, not two, but three Rolos, "Be there!" Pulling the serviette away with elegance, yes, there it was… not one, not two, not three, but *four* Rolos, all together.

    The crowd cheered, even the people who had been standing behind Nannie, watching her back. Magic Mary had amazed everyone, and the magician was shouting, "Bravo! Bravo! Again!"

    Nannie wagged her finger in the air. "No, no. A magician never does a trick twice, you should know that." She picked up her bags and led the way to the second floor, Star and Aunty Vera following her with pride.

    "Please teach me the trick, Nannie."

    "I've told you a million times, Star. Not until you're twenty-one."

"Oh my goodness."

As they left the toy department, Star caught sight of a bird in a cage flapping his wings. Not sure whether it was a real bird or a toy, she didn't have time to work it out as the escalators moved down, down, down, until the bird was out of sight. Anyway, real or not, Star couldn't deny the colour of the bird; blue.

*

The book department was on the same floor as the bathroom department. Mary Mack
eyed a set of hand towels that would match her own rose pink bath to perfection, but decided not to look at the price in fear of collapsing. However, it was obvious that the day on the second floor of Harrods had been unusual because in large baskets situated between floral shower caps and china soap dishes were copies of the autobiography by Shirley Temple Black entitled, *Child Star*. Around the perimeter of the room were rows of waist-high red rope, about one metre away from the walls which were laden with carefully folded pastel coloured bath towels. The floor was bustling with people, not shopping for a new sink, no; the customers were standing around with copies of *Child Star* in their hands, reading the opening pages, or flicking through to get to the selection of photographs.

Mary's stomach was churning with anticipation, almost in disbelief that they had finally arrived. For some unknown reason, her hands were shaky, and she felt nervous, unsettled. It was a familiar feeling, but one she had not experienced for a long, long time, not since making the epic journey to Bristol when she was just twenty-three years old. She hated the fact that this memory was still so clear to her as if it had happened only yesterday, that she could still see Will McElhone's face look straight through her as if she were a ghost and he hadn't the power to believe in the supernatural. Running alongside that exact picture in her mind was the other side of Will, feeling self-conscious wearing his new spectacles, his blue eyes sparkling with smiles just for her. For years, years and more years, Mary had told herself that she must never think of him again, because he was not the man she had been introduced to and by learning so early on, it was a blessing. But it had been the regret of feeling so at one with somebody, so complete, that the world had in that instant just clicked into place, when really, it was a lie. Mary had been open, honest, ready to love what was being given to her, and without reason, Will had snatched all of this away from her. Her desire to be a lover, a wife and a mother was shattered in one day, a day never to be forgotten. Was it wrong to take these risks? This was a question Mary had asked herself every day since and the answer she was met with was always a reoccurrence of the pain and hellish disappointment felt from Will McElhone's behaviour. So it was clear; to protect herself from this sorrow, no risks should be run.

Until today.

As the bathroom section ended and the bookstore began, a large sign read;

'This is a book signing. A copy of the book must be purchased to meet the author.'

Mary, Vera and Star stood in front of the sign, each reading the words over and over again. There was no money left in their small London fund to cover the cost of this book, that much was true.

And also, what did it matter? To their left, in a dark corner lit by tall lights seen in photography studios and closed off by more red rope was an empty desk and an empty chair. Shirley Temple Black had been… and gone.

*

Star would not cry, she would not cry. If she did, it would make her eyes go all blurry and that would hinder her and Nannie and Aunty Vera from running down the escalators, dodging the slow, slow, slow moving people everywhere, all with cameras trying to get photographs of the Egyptian Mummy. Anyway, there was no need to cry because Shirley Temple could be just ahead of them… they may have been pushed past her by accident seeing as all three of them were moving so quickly. How was Nannie moving like this with her sore hip? Maybe it was what Mr Broadbent, her PE teacher called adrenaline. When Simon Monaghan got tonsillitis and had been off school sick for a week and two days, his mum allowed him to come back just for Sport's Day and he won first place in the one hundred metre sprint. Mr Broadbent had called him a true athlete who performed on adrenaline. The whole ordeal had made Star a little giggly; she couldn't eat her tea that evening, not even pudding which was arctic roll.

Harrods was busier now than Star had remembered a little earlier on; hoards and hoards of families in all shapes and sizes, small children on reigns and teenagers in gangs all carrying their rucksacks in front of them in their hands. Even by saying, "excuse me," nobody moved, and Star couldn't work out if they just didn't understand English or if they were being rude. It was like pressing rewind on the video player, except it would be silly to walk or run backwards. As they reached the bottom of the escalators it was through the grand hall dripping with lipsticks, eye shadows and face creams that they ran, past all of the ladies in smart black trouser suits with brightly painted faces and huge pearly white smiles. Where they more actresses not acting maybe? And then the lights dimmed as they dashed through floral, sweet, spicy and musky scents, avoiding being sprayed in the eye with, "the latest fragrance by…"

Exits signs were around all corners of the room, but which one to take? It was difficult to remember which one they had come in from because most perfume counters looked identical to the next. Star looked for Lindsey and thought she had spotted her on two occasions, but they were both two different girls who just happened to be the spitting image of her. She hoped that they weren't actresses, too, and auditioning for the part of Cinderella because it would be impossible to choose the best one.

Ahead of them was a lobby area with a help desk, and a large revolving door. Piling into one moving compartment, Star in front of Nannie and Aunty Vera, out of Harrods they shuffled. Luckily, the actors saving children were nowhere to be seen so they could look up and down the crowds without being cornered for money. It was so frustrating being so small, thought Star, when even jumping around like a crazy jack-in-the-box was not making a blind bit of difference in looking for Shirley Temple. And what exactly was she aiming to see? As far as Star was concerned, Shirley Temple was the same height as herself with a mop of curly hair that used to be golden, but she was pretty sure was now dark brown… yet, Shirley Temple was just a little bit younger than Nannie in real life, so of course she couldn't be the same size as Star. This was torture! Whenever she had heard Aunty Vera complain of a headache, she now understood. There was so much mess going on around the front of Star's head, just above her eyes, right on the edge of her forehead, that she feared her head would explode into a million pieces.

"Mary! Mary!" Aunty Vera yelled. "Over there, over there… I can see a limousine…"

Aunty Vera grabbed Nannie's arm and Star's hand, and dragged them to the corner of Harrods, where the flow of shoppers – every single one a grown-up - moving up and down Knightsbridge had stopped to gather and gaze. There wasn't another little girl in sight. Sweeping her up, Nannie and Aunty Vera together held Star up high letting her head rise above those of all the grown-ups.

"Can you see her, Star? Is it her?" Nannie asked from below her. "Is it her?"

Star couldn't tell a lie, but she didn't want to say 'yes', even though it would make Nannie and Aunty Vera so happy. What she did see was the back of a lady with lots and lots of dark brown hair, short, thick and not curly, wearing a royal blue jacket, the same royal blue as the Everton football kit, her daddy's favourite colour. The lady slid into the long, shining car with grace. She certainly could've been a dancer with moves as slick as that.

"Can you see her, Star? Is it Shirley Temple?"

The limousine pulled away, crawling forward down such a narrow street parked with many other black, shiny cars. Slowly, slowly, the car became smaller and smaller as the distance became further from the crowds on the corner of Harrods.

"Oh, Nannie. I don't know."

*

As if Moses had just decided to turn up and part the crowds as he parted the Red Sea, the hundreds of people watching and waving to what could have been a car carrying Shirley Temple Black, just dispersed into various directions. Within seconds, Mary was standing with her sister and Star, the only three to be stationary amidst the shoppers and tourists on Knightsbridge.

What had she expected for Star, really? Never had Mary felt the inclination to go and meet somebody famous before. Even when the music scene in Liverpool created a rock and roll phenomenon in the sixties, she had not acquired a need to be a part of it. Idolising just wasn't part of who Mary Mack was, and today proved exactly why. Putting someone on a pedestal was a recipe for disaster, because what could that someone do other than let down? Shirley Temple Black was no longer an American sweetheart with a mop of curly hair, singing songs on a silver screen and tap dancing with Uncle Billy. She was a woman whose job happened to be having to sign a few hundred autographs this afternoon, all to a bunch of people who she didn't know. If Star had met Shirley Temple Black, the little girl would have been simply another stranger to the woman who was formerly the world's most famous child star. So, why oh why had Mary done this? What had it all been for?

Star was still looking in the direction of where the car had driven off. Moments earlier, there had been people standing in her way, blocking her view, but now the road was spacious and quiet. Mary noticed Star swallow, again and again, something she did to stop herself from crying. Still, Star's face was not sad; it was just blank, expressionless, as if her eyes were fixated on a big black hole.

No. No. No. She could not allow this to affect Star. Yes, life was full of disappointments, that was no big secret, but there must be some surprises out there and how would Star ever find them if she lost hope? It was shameful to lose that hope, as Mary had all those years ago, and become afraid of opening herself up to finding it again, but at least she had made that choice as an adult. She could not – would not – let this happen to Star. The child was eight, for God's sake.

Clearing her throat, and in her best shot at singing in tune, Mary belted out slow and loud;

"*Be optimistic... don't you be a-grumpy...*"

Star didn't move. Vera appeared to try and stop Mary, attempting to hush her, but Mary went on, still slow and with too much emphasis on not feeling self-conscious;

"*When the road gets bumpy, just smile,*

Smile and be happy..."

Vera's lips pouted to make a shushing sound, so Mary shook her head with haste, grabbing her sister's arm. Singing was not their strong point, but if Mary was to lift up Star's spirits, well Vera could bloody well assist her. With how tight she was pinching her skinny arm, Vera had little choice in the matter. Together, with Vera's eyes pinned on Mary's lips to follow along as best as she could, they continued;

"You're troubles can't be as bad as all that,
When you're sad as all that,
No one loves you..."

Star still didn't flinch.

"Come on, Star," Mary said in a much gentler tone than usual, "your turn."

With a little sniff which made her nostrils flare in and out quickly, Star threw her shoulders back, hands by her side, and her bum-bag sticking out on her belly;

"You're troubles can't be..." Star tried, her throat tight, *"as bad as all that..."* and she sniffled again, but began to sob now, *"when, y-y-you're sad as all that, no one lo-..."* But she turned and buried her little face into Vera's side.

Okay, so what did a London crowd care? Would they judge Mary if she made a complete fool out of herself or would they just go on their merry way and ignore her? Either way, it had become past the point of Mary caring, so with full enthusiasm she knew that the time had come to lose all inhibitions. In her very best, very bad voice, she clicked her fingers and added some of the one, the only... swing;

"And a one, a two, a one, two, three, four...

Be optimistic, don't you be a-grumpy,

When the road gets bumpy, just smile..."

And Vera shouted in, perfectly out of key;

"*Smile and be happy...*"

With Star in the middle, the two sisters grabbed her hands and pulled her down Knightsbridge, not walking, not running, but skipping! High, big, long skips, almost pulling Star's arms out of her sockets as they flew her through the air;

"*You're troubles can't be as bad as all that,*

When you're sad as all that,

No one loves you..."

Thank goodness, Star Blake couldn't resist a sing-song, for she joined in to complete the trio as they sang;

"*Be optimistic, don't you be a mourner,*

Brighten up that corner and smile, smile, smile,

Don't wear a long face; it's never in style,

Be optimistic and smile!"

Some did watch, some did ignore, but Mary couldn't give a damn! Even though her skips made her look as if she had a wooden leg, limping with her plastic hip and not able to move in a straight line, but so what? This was hilarious, and their simultaneous laughter confirmed it. They repeated the song, and again, and again, louder each time. A red double-decker route master pulled into a bus stop, and Mary led her two band members onto it, jumping onto the back and all three held onto the stair rail, leaning backwards and continuing to sing out. This was a musical, a Hollywood musical, alive around them and Mary, Vera and Star were the stars! Nobody on the packed out bus rewarded them any attention, looking in the opposite direction with purpose, probably in fear of being roped in.

Only, as Mary turned her head around, she found herself singing directly into a man's face, less than an inch away from it. But this was no ordinary passenger… it was the conductor, who held out his hand and demanded a fare to be paid. Despite the slow flow of traffic, jumping off a moving bus seemed like the most daunting move to attempt, no doubt resulting in broken bones, bruises and embarrassment. Yet, they were still singing, all three of them, singing about optimism and not being grumpy on a bumpy road! The initiative was taken by Vera who, in all confidence, did a scissor-kick off the bus and landed onto the pavement with nothing more than a few wobbles which made her knobbly knees resemble Bambi standing up for the first time… then Star, leapt off and landed, only kept stepping and leaping further and further as if her legs were enchanted with a dancing spell and would not stop… and it was Mary's turn, but how was this viable? The bus wasn't moving at top speed, the other buses, cabs and cars being responsible for that, but it was still *moving* and Mary was getting further and further away from Vera and Star.

"Your fare?" the conductor asked, again. "Times three!"

Mary shrugged her shoulders. "See ya!" she smiled through her terror and soared off the bus, flying through the air until her feet felt the ground, but rather than stopping, she kept running and running because if she stopped she was certain she would tumble over. Yes, it hurt. It bloody hurt, however one foot was going in front of the other which meant that her hip was still intact and no bones were broken.

Star threw her arms around Mary's waist, and Vera wobbled over, killing herself laughing at her own shaking hands, the only words escaping her mouth being variants of all the names that Jesus was called.

The sun had made its way through the heavy clouds and was out to shine in full late afternoon glory. It was only when a thick shadow cast over the three of them, that Mary had noticed the sun's appearance at all. Their space was suddenly dark as the red route master stopped right in front of them, and the bus conductor looked over their heads and waved into the distance.

"These three!" he called out. "These three – fare dodgers!"

It wasn't hard to guess who he was shouting to. As Mary turned around, she was faced with two policemen walking towards her, and after the commotion so far, there was only one word that came into her head to say to Star and Vera…

"RUN!"

Park Lane

Just as cross-country was NOT fun in school, putting on her PE kit with shorts that were tight around the top of her legs and getting on the school coach to go to some remote field where Mr Broadbent yelled at everybody to jog through mud and then suffer a stitch, then out of breath, and then another stitch and needing to spit on the ground lots of times, running around London was becoming equally NOT as fun.

Except for the first time in Star's life, she had something that she must be running from… Okay, when Christopher McGinty decided to chase the girls with worms that he had found in his back yard, hanging from the end of his dirty fingers, well, that was a decent enough reason to be compelled to run as far away from him as possible, but it wasn't *dangerous*. Unless the worms were deadly, and Christopher McGinty sometimes threatened that they were. He also said that his dad had run off with Maggie Thatcher, which was a load of rubbish because his dad worked on the coal mines in Newcastle, and that's miles away from London, so he wasn't always to be trusted with the truth. Plus his mum was half Maggie

Thatcher's age and much prettier, especially when she wore make-up on a Friday night.

Now, it wasn't a playground game, and being caught would not result in '1-2-3-no-breaks-no-escapes' and becoming 'It'. Getting caught right now was serious. Star found her legs moving faster and faster than she ever believed that they could, yet, there was no den, no goal, nowhere to aim for, just a wide street with lanes and lanes of traffic by her side. Opposite was a park with huge trees to hide behind and other children playing who she could camouflage into, only to get there would mean waiting for the pelican crossing to stop the cars whizzing past, and that was just not an option. So, she kept on running… and as predicted, Star began to feel a stitch in her side. It hurt, ouch, ouch, ouch, it really hurt! Unless she found something to duck behind and quick, struggling down an endless line past old buildings and hotels suffering from a sharp, bursting pain would be her destiny. Twisting around to see how far Nannie and Aunty Vera were behind her had not crossed her mind because it would slow her down, something called a 'rookie error' according to the boys in her class. Anthony Tucker said it to Peter Healey all the time. But it had been a while since Star had heard Nannie's voice yelling, "Run, run…" and there were no sounds of footsteps other than her own. Thinking it was safe to make the turn, Star did so, and was faced with nothing; no policemen, no bus conductors, no Nannie or Aunty Vera. Had she really ran so fast ahead that she had lost them all?

Star stopped beside the entrance to a tall, tall, tall hotel, with more men in top hats standing by the front glass doors. She took a breather by leaning against the wall, holding her side, hoping that the stitch would disappear. Her bum-bag had shifted right around her waist and was sitting above her bum… was this where they were supposed to be worn, hence the name? If so, that was silly because how could you reach around and unzip it without looking rude? Sliding it back into place on her tummy, Star's thudding heart sank heavy when she looked up to see one policeman walking towards her. He caught her eye and not knowing how to disguise her fear she opened her mouth in shock and ran inside the hotel's grounds, knowing that she was once again being chased.

A black cab had arrived outside the front glass doors and a couple with a new baby stepped out. The doormen were helping to get the pram out and cooing at the baby, so Star crept past them and into the hotel. She knew it would be another rookie error to stop, but running could not continue in a palace such as this. Marble floors shone through the lobby, so clean that Star could see her own face if she looked down, and crystal chandeliers hung from the ceilings. She now knew exactly how Annie felt when she entered into Daddy Warbucks' mansion for the first time and almost said, "Leaping lizards," however, "Oh my goodness," slipped out instead.

"Hey, you!" said a voice behind her, and Star turned to see the policeman charging through the doors.

The ding of a bell made Star's head dart back forward to see an elevator to her left open its doors with a group of men in long, beige coats holding briefcases empty out of it. Seeing the opportunity, she dashed into the elevator, making it just in time before the sliding doors slammed shut. What floor? What floor? What floor? Thank goodness there was nobody else in the lift, but what floor? What floor? Deciding on 'seven' because one, two, three, four, five, six, seven, all good children go to Heaven, Star watched the numbers going up and up.

But the elevator stopped on two.

The doors opened to reveal the policeman waiting there, a grin on his face and Star expected him to say, "Gotcha!" She remembered that whenever the older boys who hung around outside Chan's chippy would skit Star for being so small, Nannie always said to her, "Good stuff comes in little parcels… poison comes in little packages." With these words ringing through her mind, Star took one look at the policeman and ducked beneath his wide open arms, his attempt at blocking her… And she was running again… of all people that she knew who would have to run so much in one day, she was the last person she ever imagined. Maybe this was good training for the netball team once she turned ten or eleven, something she never contemplated before. It was true that the boys only ever fancied the girls on the netball team, well, the boys worth being fancied by anyway. Simon Monaghan might even start speaking to her...

Seeing a staircase to the side of the elevators, she knew it was the only way, so up she went. Her legs were hot, her knees like jelly and she grabbed onto the rail to keep herself moving so fast, only the policeman was definitely behind her and Star bet that he could run up two stairs at a time. She had no idea why but decided to attempt this move, knowing that her legs were too short to miss a stair in between, and it was the ultimate rookie error because the policeman caught a hold of her right foot. It was a good job that during her tap class a few weeks ago, Star had learnt the Charleston, and keeping her hands tight onto the rail, she shook her right foot forwards and backwards and forwards and backwards until her t-bar shoe came off, leaving the policeman looking like an angry version of Prince Charming, and Star a harassed Cinderella... Lindsey would be jealous... but, now she was free! Free to run again, and off she did, up onto the third and then fourth floor, until she had no more energy to face another stair.

There was a door. And it was open. Voices and clapping could be heard, and many people were sitting on padded lime green chairs with notebooks and pens, some standing and raising their arms to face a small raised stage. Even more chandeliers hung high above, although they were smaller than those in the lobby. Another great place to hide! Just as Star entered into the busy room, her time was up. The policeman, with all of his grown-up strength, put his hands on her shoulders and began to pull her away.

Star couldn't work out what had gotten into her, but once again – although caught and with nowhere to go – she started to fight herself free. Never in her life had she been involved in a fight, no, she was always just the witness to them every day at school and every Friday night on Flinder Street. Her years of being a spectator seemed to prove educational somewhat, for here she was, fists clenched and punching the chest of the policeman whilst twisting and turning trying to break away, and using her left foot – still with shoe intact – she kicked her heel into his shin again and again.

"Let me go! Let me go!" Star started to say, and was about to bite into the policeman's hand despite having a wobbly back tooth, when somebody spoke loud and clear over a microphone, echoing around the room.

"What is it the child wants?" said a woman from behind a long desk.

Every head in the room, whether they were standing or sitting, turned around to look at Star being held by the policeman. There were no little boys or girls, just grown-ups, many of them wearing glasses and peering over the top of them at her. Star gave one shrug and easily broke free of the policeman's grip, for he too must have felt embarrassed at all the eyes staring at him.

"Please," Star found herself walking down the aisle, past rows and rows of padded lime green chairs, shoulders back and pleading for help towards the raised stage where the voice had come from. "Please don't let them take me away."

The woman stood up and leant into the microphone again. "What is it, little girl?" She looked at Star through big brown eyes, with hair to match that was short and set very neat, with so much hairspray that it would be hard for one hair to fall out of place. Her bright floral blouse matched the fresh flowers displayed beside her, and a string of pearls laced her neck. "What's the matter?"

"It's Nannie… and Aunty Vera… they've captured them and I know they think that we've done something wrong, but we haven't… they haven't, all they wanted to do was surprise me…" Star knew she wasn't making any sense, and was overcome with shyness at everybody gazing at her. This wasn't like being on the stage and singing, this was an audience watching her in real life, and that was horrible.

"Can we let the little girl come up here?" the woman asked a security guard to her right, but he slowly shook his head and held out his large hand to say, no. "Fine. Then can we see that her grandmother and aunt are found immediately? Thorough searches to find them before any more policemen drag this poor child away? Look," she pointed at Star's shoulder, "her jacket has even been ripped!" The woman walked past the long desk and down three steps set in the middle of the stage, and Star could see that her skirt was royal blue, the same colour as the Everton football kit. She knelt down next to Star and took hold of her hands. The woman's hands were very soft, and quite cold, but so very soft.

For some reason, the audience with notepads were scribbling away, as if Miss Murphy had just given them ten minutes to write down everything that they had done last weekend. A photographer sprang out before Star and took her picture, which Star knew would be hideous as she was scrunching up her nose again, despite there being no sun in her eyes.

The woman smiled, a stunning, warm smile that made her eyes twinkle, and she ran one of her hands gently over Star's skull plaits, still tight and braided into her head.

"Never change your hair," the woman said. "It's beautiful."

"Thank you," Star said and smiled back to her.

"Oh!" the woman looked surprised, "You have a dimple! Just like me!"

"Yes. Yes I do."

Star felt somebody standing behind her.

"We've found them," the policeman said to the woman, and he held out his hand to Star without being mean, as if he was almost trying to be her friend now. "Please accept my apology for causing a scene during your press conference, Ms Black."

"Not a problem," the woman said, still crouched at a level with Star.

Star hesitated before saying, "What is your name?"

"Shirley. What's yours?"

She mouthed 'Star' for no noise escaped her mouth, and the policeman led her away back down the aisle and towards the large open doors lined with golden trimmings.

"Wait!" Star said, her voice making a welcome return. "Please."

Unzipping her bum-bag, Star fumbled through show leaflets and found the letter she had written on the train with her Tinkerbelle writing set, a little crumpled but it still had the floral scent to it. The envelope just had the words;

'*To Shirley Temple,*

Hollywood,

America'

written across it.

"Erm," Star mustered, struck with no clue of what to call this woman… Shirley? Ms Black? Mrs Temple? Shirley Temple? "This is for you."

"Why, thank you," Shirley Temple Black said. "I'll read it later."

"I mention the Adelphi, which *is* the poshest hotel in Liverpool, but it's not as nice as this one. Just so you know."

Shirley Temple Black gave one nod of her head, her perfect hair not moving, and continued to smile. Star knew it was time to go, and she was in enough trouble as it was, nothing could get any worse… so, she threw her arms around Shirley Temple Black and hugged her, squeezing her eyes tight. Opening them for a second, Star saw the security guard and his mate moving towards her, so she shut her eyes again for one last second.

It was nothing like how she imagined, but Star had met Shirley Temple.

*

Mary would never know how Star felt that day as she and Vera were led away and taken into police custody. How could an eight year old child express her emotions of what had happened? After seeing Jimmy being arrested and how it had broken Star's heart, Mary just hoped that given time, Star would grow up to forget about the last few months of her young life and immerse herself into the new life that awaited her in Hillside, with every luxury she could dream of.

It was possible to look back on hard times with a rose-tinted view. Mary's memories of the war were pleasant, and no doubt Vera's were too. Thinking back to Mawdsley, living on a farm and learning magic tricks in between Christmas carols was what sprung to mind when she envisioned herself as a child. It took deeper thoughts and a longer time to remember the May Blitz, streets caved in rubble and unidentified dead bodies being thrown into the emptied out swimming baths on Balliol Road. The smell of burnt flesh and thick, heavy smoke had been overtaken by those of the farmyard, and although quite a stench that was, it was not a disturbing memory.

And regardless of the fact that Will McElhone had not been the man she had believed him to be, Mary's first thoughts of him always struck back to that first meeting, laughing fondly at her melodic Scouse accent with a beer in each hand.

Sitting in the back of the police car and getting further away from Park Lane and Hyde Park Corner, past an Underground station called Edgeware Road, Mary Mack just prayed that as the days, weeks, months and years passed by, Star would remember simply the sole reason for all this trouble, and that was the moment she met her idol. For Shirley Temple had not disappointed Star; overall, the meeting had proved to be a success, a rarity in the realms of being faced with a wish coming true. Mary pictured Star's face, the last image she saw, and her heart tightened in pain. When the little girl was escorted out of the press conference and into the hotel lobby of the Hilton, seeing the ladies she called 'Nannie' and 'Aunty Vera' handcuffed and guilty of their actions did not frighten her. The reaction was calm and mature, as if she understood, and very unlike how shocked and scared she had been when Jimmy was taken from her.

"Star, I'm sorry," Vera had shouted over as soon as she saw her come through the entrance doors.

"Why?" was all that Star replied.

Mary couldn't apologise. In her own way, she knew that nothing had been done wrong. Star had already been taken from her before, this wasn't something new, and it seemed absurd for herself and Vera to be charged with kidnapping. Mary had practically raised Star Blake; she was *her* child. If she was sorry at all, it was for doing just this all along, being there and loving her, and how could she possibly be sorry for that? It never enters a person's mind to hurt the ones they love, yet when it happens, the inevitable is usually beyond control.

But would it be polite to say sorry? Would it help Star and make her feel better? As Mary contemplated this, the policeman with Star gave her a carrier bag and she took out her *My Little Pony* lunch box, mouthing 'thank you' to him.

"Nannie?" Star said, being led in a different direction, to a different police car than Mary and Vera. "Nannie?" But they just kept pulling her away, and Mary couldn't bear to watch.

Now, whenever she had sat in front of her tele with Star and together they watched an old musical that had been video-taped, Mary always made jokes during the moments when a serious or sad song would be performed, but Star always told her to shush.

"This bit's important," Star would say.

Of course, real life was not a musical and not everybody walked around singing songs to express their heightened emotions.

Except, Star did.

And it was in doing this that she got to say exactly what she wanted – needed – to say to Mary Mack, before she was finally taken away from her.

Just before the police assisted Mary and Vera into the back of their car, a sweet, almost trembling little voice rang through the driveway of the London Hilton on Park Lane, as every policeman stopped what they were doing to just let her sing;

"How can I thank you? How do I start?
The words are somewhere, around my heart,
If I could say in a word or two..."

Star began to sob, but kept on singing;

"How much it means to be loved by you...
Then I could thank you, for all you've done,

She sighed and spoke the words, "But I don't know what to do..."

Mary allowed herself to turn around, keeping strong and showing no emotion, to look at Star. Vera was already facing her, tears streaming down her cheeks, but to Mary's surprise not falling apart. It was just like being in a musical; songs did speak to people. Only this all proved that not every musical has a happy ending, not every character gets to dance their finale on Broadway.

"What can you say when a dream comes true?

How can I ever thank you?"

The song ended. The doors on the cars were slammed. The search for the blue bird was over.

Epilogue

'Jimmy Blake was charged with the murder of Kevin Donahue, a thirty-two year old father of three from Kirkdale, Liverpool. Having been jailed twice previously for assault, an eye-witness came forward to testify that Donahue started the fight that resulted in his death, after a heated argument about the aftermath of the Hillsborough Disaster. Yesterday, the prosecution agreed to accept Blake's plea of guilty to manslaughter, sentenced at Liverpool Crown Court. He will serve a maximum of seven years in prison…'

Mary didn't want to read anymore. She knew the outcome. There were no surprises to be found from reading the Liverpool Echo. Strangely enough though, it felt like the right answer, a fair result if there was anything fair to be gathered from this. Jimmy had had rotten luck, but he should have had the sense to walk away. If he was strong enough physically to do what he did, he could have left the scene to protect himself and his family. There were others involved and charged; it wasn't as if Jimmy was fighting in self-defence. As much as Mary wanted him free, she also believed in justice. It was justice that Susan Lloyd dropped the charges on Mary and Vera, and in that respect, Jimmy Blake had to serve his time.

The house on Flinder Street was so quiet, unusually so. This summer had been the hottest since 1974 according to the News at Ten last night, and Mary wondered why the kids weren't playing out on the street. Too hot, perhaps. There was nothing on the tele, well, nothing worth watching for the next ten minutes. Just that God-awful game show *Going for Gold* with a load of foreigners taking part, or the end of yet another Australian soap opera, some new thing called *Home and Away* which involved too many winey teenagers with attitude problems and was shown not once, but twice daily. What was this country's obsession with down under?

She had had a cup of tea. She had changed the bed sheets. She had washed the egg cup and saucer from her soft boiled egg and toast. She was already holding her handbag and had put on a touch of lipstick, all ready to go, early as always. She just stared at the letter in her lap…

The silence and lack of anything else to do were enough signs to tell Mary that now was the time to open it up. It had arrived in the post forty years ago, just two days after her miscarriage, but she had not been able to face the contents of the letter until now, confirmation there in writing that Will McElhone was not the man she thought he was. The best she could expect was an apology and the hurt she had felt all those years ago would not have gone away from a 'sorry'. Having this letter unopened had given Mary her own sense of closure, and she just didn't want to see the words that would create another downfall. From the moment she had met Will, every minute had dragged on like a year, she so ached to be with him once again. When fate handed her Jimmy, and Linda, and of course, Star, she was glad to find that those minutes began to fly, as did the years.

She noticed her hands – now wrinkled and in the early stages of arthritis - shaking as she began to tear the envelope, remembering how her soft, youthful hands had opened many a letter from this man over a lifetime ago. The letter, written in thick black ink and on heavy, yellowed paper fell into her lap just as a rattling noise coming from the back made her jump and run to the back window. It was just the boys from the estate tying empty coke cans to their most unfortunate mate's shoe laces and chasing him down the entry, the sinful little bullies.

A car horn sounded from outside. Twice.

Vera and John had arrived five minutes earlier than planned. How unlike them! Unless Mary's clock was wrong… but it was never wrong.

"Yoo-hoo!" Vera called from the front door, her kitten heels clobbering down the hallway. "You okay, Mary? It's not like you to not be waiting on the step all ready for us."

Mary stayed standing by the back window as Vera entered the parlour.

"Mary, what is it?"

Vera followed Mary's eyes to the floor where the letter had dropped. It was clear that Vera knew what it was, and did not seem surprised at all that Mary had finally opened it. The trauma of losing Star, yet making one of her dreams come true had changed Mary somehow, softened her and made her talk about the past a little more. She had done so all the way back to Liverpool in the police car with Vera, admitting the hurt and betrayal she had felt that had ruined her hopes of ever loving again.

Taking a step towards the letter, Vera bent down, but looked at Mary for her approval. Mary nodded, saying, "Go on. Read it to me." And she closed her eyes, leaning against the net curtains of the back window and listened to her sister's voice read out loud.

"*My Dearest Mary,*

I don't know how to say this, but you must know the truth. I did see you today in Bristol but could not bear the thought of telling you of my situation to your face in fear that I would see your heart breaking and feel compelled not to do the right thing.

Let me explain. Before I met you, there was a girl who I courted briefly. I had never been in love and thought that the fond feelings I felt towards her was just that. It was only when I met you that I realised I wasn't in love with her, and although nothing was official between this girl and I, the relationship ended when I arrived back from Liverpool. Weeks into our correspondence, I received an unexpected visit from her. She informed me that she was pregnant and the child was mine. I was torn apart because I knew in that instance I could not leave her alone in this dilemma, which meant having no choice but to leave you. I had to do the honourable thing.

Seeing you in Bristol was almost like seeing a ghost. I had to walk away, knowing in that moment that I could never have you, only your presence at the university convinced me that I was in love with you and only you, and despite wanting to be the responsible man, I had to tell the girl of my true feelings. Once I confessed, she too, had a confession. For months she had feared that she was losing me, had felt me pulling further and further away from her and in a bid to keep me, she lied about her pregnancy. I was in shock, of course, having had to come to terms with not only losing you but becoming a father and a husband so suddenly.

I ran after you, Mary. I went to the train station but you had gone. I decided that since our correspondence so far had been so honest and reliable, that I should tell you the truth in writing, rather than be met with you slamming a door in my face if I showed up to see you.

I am so sorry for what happened. I understand if you never want to see me again because I realise that my behaviour yesterday was appalling. If I do not hear back from you, I will accept the consequences of my actions and leave you alone to live your life.

Just know that I will always love you.
   Will."

The quiet that followed Vera's reading aloud was still as baffling to Mary as before. She couldn't even hear the ringing sound of silence in her ears or the ticking of the kitchen clock.

John's car horn snapped the sisters back into this world.

"Jesus, Mary!" Vera whispered. "He loved you. He could still love you!"

"Why the bloody hell are you whispering?" Mary said loudly.

"Dunno!" Vera matched her. "Mary he could *still* love you!"

"Oh give over, soft girl." But her tight grip onto the window sill was all that was preventing Mary from collapsing in shock.

"You must try and contact him!"

"Have you finally lost your friggin' marbles, Vera?"

"Get in touch with that show, you know, Cilla Black... *Surprise, Surpise...*"

"Yes, you have lost your friggin' marbles..."

"No, that show reunites long lost relatives who have changed their names and live in New Zealand and everything... they'll find Will for you..."

"What if he's dead?"

"Mary! Bloody hell!"

"Well, what if he is?"

"You're not dead. We're not dead. Why should he dead?"

"He'll be married…"

"You're not."

Mary didn't reply. A little too much news for a Friday lunchtime. She would come back to this later.

"Vera, we must go. We can't be late for the surprise, can we?"

*

Star had read five chapters of *The Wishing Chair* by Enid Blyton on their way from Hillside to West Kirby, over the water. She had put the book down during the ride through the Mersey Tunnel, and although there was nothing to look at out of the window other than yellow lights and brown walls, it was fun all the same to know that the river was above them.

When they arrived at the harbour, Aunt Susan asked Mrs O'Connell to put some sun screen on Star's shoulders and nose. Apparently they were the most common places that children's skin burnt and it was too hot to wear a cardigan over her new stripy pink and white sundress with Mickey and Minnie printed on the chest. Mr Bertie put some sun screen on his nose, too, but he didn't rub it in properly which made it all white. Everybody laughed at him without stating why, resulting in him simply scratching his head and muttering, "My word."

Aunt Susan's new boat was – according to Star – simply 'stravagent. Named 'Rebecca', it had a beautiful lounge including a television set *and* video player, a kitchen, bedrooms with bunk beds, bathrooms, and even a small playroom with a new Magnadoodle, a doll's house and a desk with paper and Crayola crayons, just like the desks in St Stephen's only it was brand new and had no scratches made with a compass or chewing gum underneath it. She was so glad that she had brought the doll that looked like Sheila Gilhooley with her because the little white rocking chair in the corner was perfect for her to sit on.

"Star," Aunt Susan said, "let's go up onto the deck. I want to show you something."

Mrs O'Connell disappeared into the kitchen and Star followed her Aunt up the stairs leading outdoors, Mr Bertie trailing behind. Star was relieved that she had got herself some sunglasses, shaped like just like stars with a yellow trimming, because it stopped her squinting and scrunching her nose. If only she was allowed to wear them for school and on photographs.

It was peaceful on the deck, the water glistening with the sun around them, and Star wondered if this was what it was like in Spain. With a sigh, she thought about her daddy and how much he would love to be on this boat. He loved everything to do with boats, even the scary stuff which Star didn't understand, such as documentaries about The Titanic which wasn't a very good boat because it sunk and killed so many people, and also the movie *The Poseidon Adventure* which also ended badly and had people dying with their eyes open. Before she saw that movie last Boxing Day, Star didn't know that it was possible to die with your eyes open. It wouldn't be too long before Star could go and visit him, just a few more weeks, and when she did she had a whole routine ready to perform for him to cheer him up. It was a song called 'Polly Wolly Doodle' and Shirley Temple had sung it to her daddy in jail when she played Virgie in *The Littlest Rebel* in 1935. The wooden floors made a shuffle-pick-up sound excellent, even though Star was wearing white sandals, so she had to be careful she didn't trip as she began to rehearse;

> "*Ev'rything went wrong but it turned out right,*
> *Sing Polly-wolly-doodle all the day,*
> *The skies were gray but the future's bright,*
> *Sing Polly-wolly-doodle all the day,*
> *Fare-thee well, Fare-thee well,*
> *Mister gloom be on your way...*"
>
> Star stopped singing because she realised that she was no longer singing solo.

There was one – two – no, actually three voices joining in with her, only one person didn't know the words and sounded like he was yodelling. She looked over to the staircase to see three faces that she hadn't seen all summer, not since the day she met Shirley Temple, who all continued to sing – badly, and out of tune;

"If you think you're gonna worry

You can stop it in a hurry,

Sing Polly-wolly-doodle all the day!"

"Hello Star," Nannie said, standing in the middle of Aunty Vera and Uncle John, her arms open wide and not folded as usual.

Unbeknown as to why she hesitated, Star did not run over to them. Instead she looked to Aunt Susan, afraid in case they were stowaways.

"Every ship needs a captain," Aunt Susan said. "I thought Mary Mack would be the perfect choice..."

"And I'm First Mate," Aunty Vera piped in.

Uncle John pulled out a pair of silver spoons from his trouser pocket and started to play them on his thigh, and Star decided not to hug the boat's new staff – Nannie always hated stuff like that – but instead she grabbed the hands of the two ladies, reuniting the trio that they once were.

And singing along to the beat of Uncle John's spoons, they all sang;

"Come along and follow me,

To the bottom of the sea,

We'll join in the jamboree,

At the cod fish ball!"

Mr Bertie rang a little bell and announced, "Lunch is served."

"Oh I can't have any lunch," Star cried.

"Why ever not, little Miss?"

"Because I haven't had breakfast yet!"

Their laughter echoed all over the River Mersey. Star twirled under Nannie and Aunty Vera's arms, and told them how much of a shame it was that Judy Garland was dead because she was second on her list of famous people to meet. However, thank goodness Kylie and Jason were still alive.

The search for the blue bird never ends…

***

BIBLIOGRAPHY

Temple Black, Shirley. *Child Star*. London: Headline, 1989.

Shirley Temple Quotes, from Flixter, http://www.flixster.com/actor/shirley-temple/shirley-temple-quotes (accessed September 10, 2009).

Captain January, directed by David Butler. (Twentieth Century Fox, 1936).

Heidi, directed by Allan Dwan. (Twentieth Century Fox, 1937).

Poor Little Rich Girl, directed by Irving Cummings. (Twentieth Century Fox, 1936).

The Blue Bird, directed by Walter Lang. (Twentieth Century Fox, 1939).

The Little Princess, directed by Walter Lang. (Twentieth Century Fox, 1938).

The Littlest Colonel, directed by David Butler. (Twentieth Century Fox, 1934).

The Littlest Rebel, directed by David Butler. (Twentieth Century Fox, 1935).

The Wizard of Oz, directed by Victor Fleming. (MGM, 1939).

Animal Crackers in my Soup; lyrics by T. Koehler and I. Caesar, music by R.Henderson

Early Bird; lyrics by S. Mitchell and music by L. Pollack

Goodnight, My Love; lyrics by Mack Gordon and music by Harry Revel

In Our Little Wooden Shoes; lyrics by S. Mitchell and music by L. Pollock

Oh My Goodness; lyrics by Mack Gordon and music by Harry Revel

The Right Somebody to Love; lyrics by J. Yellen and music by L. Pollack

When I Grow Up; lyrics by E. Heyman and music by R. Henderson

When I'm With You; lyrics by Mack Gordon and music by Harry Revel

AUTHOR BIOGRAPHY

Hayley Doyle was born in Liverpool, and graduated with a BA (hon) in Acting from the Liverpool Institute of Performing Arts. She pursued a career in acting, making her West End debut playing Ali in *Mamma Mia!* at the Prince of Wales Theatre, London. During this time, Hayley wrote her first novel *Lazy Days and Lullabies*. After graduating from Brunel University with a Masters in Creative Writing, she re-located to Dubai where she works as a musical theatre and acting instructor for children, writing original plays for her students. Hayley continues to write novels and a collection of her work can be found at www.hayleydoyle.com.